"Buy this book! A truly fantastic summer read!"
                                    —*Gulf Coast Woman*

"A CHARMED PLACE is a great read, filled with extraordinary characters, compelling subplots, long-buried secrets, and a hero who is strong, tender, and irresistible."
                                    —B. Dalton's *Heart to Heart*

"A CHARMED PLACE is a captivating mix of mystery and romance with characters so real they jump off the pages. Stockenberg is adept at capturing family relationships and conveying a real sense of the characters' feelings and motivations. An intriguing and passionate tale which will have readers longing for the next Stockenberg novel."
                                    —Writers Write website

"With each book she writes, [Stockenberg's] style and writing become even more gripping, her characters more complex . . . A CHARMED PLACE has easily earned a place on my keeper shelf. Do yourself a favor—read A CHARMED PLACE."
                                    —One Magical Kiss (Daphne's Dream) website

Dream a Little Dream

"DREAM A LITTLE DREAM is a delightful blend of goosebumps, passion and treachery that combine to make this novel a truly exhilarating read. Ms. Stockenberg delivers once again!"
                                    —*Romantic Times*

"DREAM A LITTLE DREAM is a wonderful modern fairy tale—complete with meddlesome ghosts, an enchanted castle, and a knight in shining armor. DREAM A LITTLE DREAM casts a powerful romantic spell. If you like modern fairy tales, you'll love DREAM A LITTLE DREAM. Run, don't walk to your local bookstore to purchase a copy of this magical romance."
                                    —Kristin Hannah

"This humorous, well-crafted and inventive novel is certain to establish Stockenberg as a major voice in women's fiction."

—*Publishers Weekly*

"Well-developed, likable protagonists; appealing relatives; an intriguing villain; and a ghostly pair of ancient lovers propel the plot of this . . . well-written story with a definite Gothic touch."

—*Library Journal*

"Kudos to Antoinette Stockenberg, who offers her trademark large, solid cast . . . and placed them in a magnificent setting, background to a satisfying, indelible love story. A highly recommended read that paranormal and medieval lovers will treasure."

—*Romance Forever*

"DREAM A LITTLE DREAM is a work of art! With deft strokes of a brush Antoinette Stockenberg layers humor, wit, emotion, intrigue, trepidation and sexual tension in just the right amounts to fill a rich canvas . . . This is writing and storytelling at its best, and as eager as we are to find out 'what happens next!', we savor each sentence."

—*CompuServe Romance Reviews*

"A thoroughly satisfying book. It blends suspense with just the right amount of humor. The characters are finely drawn. I enjoyed reading it and recommend it highly."

—*Under the Covers Book Reviews*

"Stockenberg is able to fully develop the characters and wrap the audience in the spell of the story. It's one of those books that will keep you turning pages well into the night and into the next night as well."

—*Middlesex News*

"Ms. Stockenberg writes with a lively and humorous wit that makes her characters three-dimensional and unforgettable, and had me smiling throughout. It didn't take long for me to become caught in the magic web of the castle and the undercurrent of the mystery."

—*Old Book Barn Gazette*

Beyond Midnight

"Stockenberg's special talent is blending the realistic details of contemporary women's fiction with the spooky elements of paranormal romance. So believable are her characters, so well-drawn her setting, so subtle her introduction of the paranormal twist, that you buy into the experience completely . . . BEYOND MIDNIGHT has a terrific plot, a wicked villain and a sexy hero. But the novel ventures beyond sheer entertainment and it is easy to see why Stockenberg's work has won such acclaim."

—*Milwaukee Journal-Sentinel*

"Full of charm and wit, Stockenberg's latest paranormal romance is truly enthralling."

—*Publishers Weekly*

"Antoinette Stockenberg creates another winner with this fast-paced and lively contemporary romance with a touch of the supernatural. A definite award-winner . . . contemporary romance at its best!"

—*Affaire de Coeur*

"When it comes to unique, eerie and engrossing tales of supernatural suspense, Antoinette Stockenberg is in a league of her own. BEYOND MIDNIGHT is a gripping and chilling page-turner . . . outstanding reading!"

—*Romantic Times*

"Spectacular! A terrific story that had me anxiously turning the well-written pages."

—*The Literary Times*

Beloved

"BELOVED has charm, romance and a delicious hint of the supernatural. If you loved the film *Somewhere in Time*, don't miss this book."

—LaVyrle Spencer

"A delightfully different romance with a ghost story—a great combination that was impossible to put down."

—Johanna Lindsey

"BELOVED is great . . . A lively, engaging, thoroughly enchanting tale. Ms. Stockenberg is a fresh, exciting voice in the romance genre. Her writing is delicious. I savored every morsel of BELOVED."

—Jayne Ann Krentz

"The talented Antoinette Stockenberg continues to demonstrate her talent for delivering unique tales of romance and danger with tantalizing supernatural overtones."

—*Romantic Times*

Emily's Ghost

"A witty, entertaining romantic read that has everything—a lively ghost, an old murder mystery and a charming romance."

—Jayne Ann Krentz

"I loved EMILY'S GHOST. It's an exciting story with a surprise plot twist."

—Jude Devereaux

"Highly original and emotionally rich reading . . . Pure and unadulterated reading pleasure . . . This outstanding contemporary novel is a veritable feast for the senses."

—*Romantic Times*

Keepsake

ANTOINETTE STOCKENBERG

St. Martin's Paperbacks

KEEPSAKE

Copyright © 1999 by Antoinette Stockenberg.

ISBN: 0-312-96975-9

Printed in the United States of America

St. Martin's Paperbacks edition / April 1999

St. Martin's Paperbacks are published by St. Martin's Press, 175 Fifth Avenue, New York, NY 10010.

10 9 8 7 6 5 4 3 2 1

For Christine and Janine

Keepsake

Prologue

The women of Keepsake were afraid.

Young mothers moved cribs into their bedrooms for the night, and grandmothers jammed kitchen chairs against their back doors. Teenage girls agog with terror talked late on the phone with their very best friends, while their older sisters who lived alone made their boyfriends promise to stay over. The news that morning had sent shock waves of anxiety from Elm to upper Main: Alison Bennett's death was no suicide at all, but cold-blooded murder.

If Alison wasn't safe, who was? Her father was strict, her uncle was rich. She was the last girl in Connecticut anyone would have expected to find hanging from a rope above a quarry on a cold October night. That was the consensus as people turned off fewer lights than usual and tried to sleep.

No one wanted to believe that the murderer was one of Keepsake's own—but everyone knew which way the investigation was heading. Only one man in town had been questioned twice by the police about Alison, and that was her uncle's gardener.

As Keepsake tossed and turned, Francis Leary scanned the single shelf in his bedroom in the gardener's cottage at the foot of the Bennett estate, trying to decide which books to pack. It was an impossible dilemma, like choosing which of a litter of kittens not to drown. Tired, confused, overwhelmed by events, the gardener reached for his Gertrude

Jekyll, a signed first edition, and then wondered: Could he fit the Olmsted, too?

His son suffered no such agonies of indecision. With a lightly packed duffel bag slung over his shoulder, Quinn Leary poked his head into his father's room and said, "Dad, let's *go*." He was seventeen and more decisive than his father would ever be.

Francis Leary fully understood his own weaknesses and his son's strengths, but he dreaded the thought of what lay ahead: a stolen truck, a bus ride to nowhere, a life on the run. "Quinn, I know this is my idea, but . . . now I'm not so sure."

His son felt a surge of hope, tempered by exasperation. "You want to stay and take your chances? Fine with me. But the police will be here by morning. You won't have time to change your mind again, Dad. Understand that."

Put that way, the plan to run became more compelling. The gardener took a last look around and said nervously, "Let's go."

They locked up the cottage and waded through a sea of unraked leaves to the pickup truck, registered in the name of Alison's uncle up the hill.

Up the hill, in a bedroom with high ceilings and a marble fireplace, the dead girl's seventeen-year-old cousin and classmate lay awake in her four-poster bed as she listened to the trees bend to the moaning wind. Olivia Bennett was despondent over the loss of her cousin and shocked at the news of her cousin's pregnancy—but Olivia, who lived closer than anyone to the suspect, had no fear of him. Francis Leary had been her parents' gardener for ten years, and Olivia was convinced that she knew him well: Good men didn't kill.

At seven-thirty, Keepsake dragged itself out of bed after a night of no sleep, only to find that the man it feared had fled in the night with his son. Part of Keepsake was relieved; but the other part, the bigger part, spent the next seventeen years sleeping with one eye on the bedroom door.

One

The reindeer were a bigger hit than Santa, no doubt about it. Trekking through falling snow and fading light up the far side of Town Hill, Quinn could see a moblet of small children pressing up against a temporary pen and pitching kernels awkwardly to a pair of tame deer within.

Borrowed from a petting zoo, he figured. Leave it to Keepsake to do Christmas proud. He got a clearer view of the town's copper-roofed gazebo at the top of the hill and saw that Santa, holding court inside, had a fair-sized crowd of his own: The line of kids waiting to read him their lists was impressive for a town so small.

From his vantage on the hill, Quinn studied the intersection—controlled by a traffic light now—that was the center of Keepsake, quintessential New England town. The four corners were anchored by the same historic white-steepled church, granite town hall, one-story library and sturdy brick-front bank as before. Quinn searched for, and found, the little drugstore where he'd hung out during his high school years. It was a CVS now, which meant the soda fountain would be long gone. He could almost taste the strawberry shakes that were the old place's specialty; it hurt to think that they were no more.

He scanned for more landmarks and was jolted by the perky pink-and-white logo of a Dunkin' Donuts. Like the CVS, it was a jarring reminder that time had passed. He was thirty-four now, not seventeen, and on a quest more grim than hopeful. He sighed heavily, then surveyed the crowd gathered to light the town tree.

Plunge right in, or hang around the edges?

Plunge.

The crowd was thickest near the unlit tree. Several hundred citizens were drinking hot chocolate while they waited, as they did every December, for the mayor to plug in the cord and kick off the holiday. The first familiar face Quinn saw belonged to a beefy citizen wearing a jacket in the town's high-school colors. The man had been there awhile: his green cap was white with snow. When he saw Quinn, he did a double take.

"Leary? What the *hell* are you doing here?"

"Coach," Quinn said, greeting him with a wary nod. "It's been a long time." He held out his hand.

Coach Bronsky stared at it as if it were a bloody stump. "You've gotta be kidding," he said with loathing. He swivelled his head left and right. "Where's your old man?"

"Beyond your reach now," Quinn shot back. "He died last month." He had wondered how he'd break that news to Keepsake. Now he knew.

"Dead!" The coach's face congealed into a dark pudding of anger and resentment. "You have a hell of a nerve, in that case. You think you can stroll up here . . . announce that he's kicked the bucket . . . and what? Have us carry you around on our shoulders again? You ran, Leary! You left us in the lurch. Left your team . . . your town . . . everyone. The two of you ran like a couple of scared dogs."

Quinn stood ramrod stiff under the attack, as if he were still a quarterback in the locker room after a so-so half. He didn't have to ask whether Keepsake High had won the state championship that year. The answer was a bitter, resounding no.

Offering no excuses, he said, "I'm not here either to apologize or to explain. I'm sure not here to gloat."

"Oh yeah? Then what *are* you here for?"

Quinn's response was a snort. *To find out who killed Alison. Shouldn't that be obvious?*

"To look up old friends," he said after a deadly pause.

"You won't find any in Keepsake. Get the hell out. Now."

"Thanks for the advice—but I think I'll stick around."

With a snarl the coach said, "Vickers may have other ideas," and brushed past Quinn with the force of a fullback.

Caught off balance by the shove, Quinn staggered, but he managed to say cheerfully, "Sergeant Vickers! He's still around?"

"*Chief* Vickers now, pal." The coach muscled his way into the crowd, undoubtedly to spread the word.

Not exactly the welcome wagon, but it was about what Quinn had expected. He brushed heavy snow from his bound hair and the back of his neck and wished he'd bought a hat. Too many years in La-La Land, he realized. He'd forgotten what a New England winter was like.

The cold wet snow set the mood for his next three encounters, the first of which was with the assistant librarian. When Quinn last saw her, she had been a thirty-year-old single woman who always had enthusiastic words of praise for a quarterback who actually read the novels and not the Cliffs Notes. The lady whom he approached was easily recognized as a grayer version of herself, but any enthusiasm was in short supply.

Quinn gave her a tentative smile anyway. "Hi, Miss Damian. Read any good books lately?" It used to be a standard greeting between them.

The librarian stared over the rim of her uplifted paper cup. Her eyes got wide and she choked on her hot chocolate, then recovered enough to gasp, "It's you! My God, how did you get here?"

"American Airlines and Hertz," he quipped.

Her voice dropped a scandalized octave. "So your father's turned himself in! All these years people have been waiting, and now—"

"They'll have to keep waiting, I'm afraid. My father passed away last month."

She stared at him. Her distress seemed to increase. "Oh,

but . . . but how can we be sure?'' she blurted out. ''He could be a fugitive still!''

Quinn blinked. He hadn't anticipated that one. ''Trust me,'' he said dryly. ''He died in my arms on November twelfth.''

''Yes . . . yes, I'm sure you're right,'' she stammered. Then she threw down her cup and hurried away.

Quinn indulged in a wry smile. Freddy Krueger couldn't have frightened her more.

He reached down to the brown stain on the fresh-fallen snow and picked up the paper cup. Come the January thaw, he wouldn't want litter popping up all over the quaint town green. He was a gardener's son, and he'd been trained well.

He was at a loss during the next encounter. The woman clearly knew him—she was sneaking looks from the edge of the crowd—but he wasn't at all sure about her.

Finally he turned directly to her, a matronly woman whose apple-cheeked face was tightly wreathed in fake fur. ''Myra? Myra Lupidnick?'' he ventured.

''Myra Lancaster now,'' she said, coming forward with a nervous smile to shake his hand. ''I thought it was you. How are you, Quinn?''

''Not bad. It's good to see you, Myra,'' he said with nostalgic affection. ''Really.''

Myra was the first person in Keepsake to befriend Quinn after he and his dad moved into the gardener's cottage on the Bennett estate. Quinn had just turned eight. He had made out with Myra under the bleachers shortly afterward; it was Myra who had taught him how to French kiss. For at least a year after the Frenching episode, he'd convinced himself that he wasn't a virgin anymore.

''You settled in Keepsake, then?'' he asked. She had always gone on about moving up and out of it.

''Sure! I got married—George Lancaster, remember him?''

''Tall guy, red hair?''

''He's a plumber now, and doing really good. We have

four kids. And a four-bedroom house in Greenwood Estates.''

''Hey, that's great,'' he offered gallantly.

She didn't ask Quinn what he had been up to all those years, which was hardly surprising. He could see the struggle in her face as she debated what to say. Suddenly she seemed to give up the effort. She shrugged and murmured, ''Well, I've got to go. The kids'll be wondering where I got lost. I . . . See you,'' she said.

She fled from him as well, with only slightly less panic than Miss Damian, the librarian.

Shit. At the rate he was alienating people, he wouldn't find a friendly ear in the entire town. He had based his whole mission on the belief that after seventeen years, the citizens of Keepsake would have let their guard down about the scandal that had rocked the town like a West Coast earthquake; that they'd be mellowed to the point of apathy. So far, apathy was the only response he *hadn't* got.

He made his way through more of the crowd, searching for people he'd known. Near the cocoa-and-cookies table were stationed half a dozen carollers wearing Victorian capes and top hats. They had been alternating between Santa songs and Christmas hymns and at the moment were belting out a peppy rendition of ''Let It Snow.'' As they sang, Quinn circled behind the listening audience, scanning their faces, looking for anyone who might be sympathetic to his side.

Instead he found the barber. Quinn practically knocked him over as he was making his way toward the gazebo. Tony something? Tony Assorio, that was it. The man looked the same, exactly the same: small, gray, and contained, like one of the bottles of mystery liquid that he kept lined up in front of the mirror on the narrow marble counter in his one-chair shop.

''Mr. Assorio—Quinn Leary,'' he said, shaking his hand. ''You used to cut my hair when I lived in Keepsake.'' Why Quinn expected the barber to remember him as a customer rather than as the son of a fugitive wasn't clear, even to him.

The barber scrutinized him, then said, "I remember. You always did have a good head of hair. Looks like you could use a trimmin' up," he added, eyeing Quinn's ponytail. "Come in tomorrow. Two-thirty. I have an opening."

"Uhh . . . yeah, well—thanks. I may do that."

The barber moved on, greeting people like a Rhode Island politician. Quinn made a mental note to drop in on him the next day. No one had his fingers on the pulse of a town more often than a barber.

Quinn paused where he was, not at all surprised that furtive glances were beginning to be cast his way. He had wanted people to know he was back, and he was succeeding; but he was surprised at how alienated he felt from them all. By the light of the nearby gas lamp, he was able to make out the time: four-seventeen. Soon the tree would be lit and people would begin to disperse. He was, he had to admit, disappointed. He'd hoped to meet a friendly face before then. Any friendly face.

The snow was falling now in big, paper cutouts that lay on his jacket for a mere twinkling before melting into oblivion. Quinn held up a sleeve and marvelled at the sheer magic that was coming and going there. Whether it was the carollers or the children, the deer or the snowflakes—for an instant Quinn was a kid again, in harmony with the universe around him. God, how he'd missed New England.

He felt a tug on his jacket and, still smiling, turned to see a small boy looking up at him.

"Mister? Did your daddy really kill a girl in school?"

Quinn gazed down at the kid. He was six, maybe seven. What kind of parents talked about stuff like that in front of a six-year-old? Jesus.

"My dad didn't hurt anyone, sport," he said as gently as he knew how. "That was just a rumor."

"What's a roomer?"

"It's when someone tells stories that might not be—"

"Andrew!" a woman said shrilly behind the child. "Get over here right now. *Right* now!"

She rushed up to the boy and hauled him off with a brutal yank on his parka. For the first time since he'd stepped into the Currier and Ives scene, Quinn felt some of his resolve falter. If every citizen in Keepsake was going to treat him like a leper . . .

"Quinn, dear! Quinn! Yoo-hoo!"

Surprised at the enthusiasm in the voice, he turned in time to behold a petite, elderly woman angling a four-legged walker before her as she made her way by lamplight across the snow-covered grass. She wore a black wool coat and was muffled under several circuits of a fluffy red scarf; her red knit hat covered all but a few white curls. Only her eyes showed, and that was all he needed to see.

"Mrs. Dewsbury!"

It was his old English teacher, the first and only mentor he'd ever had. He'd had her for homeroom once and for English twice. Quinn had always known he was a natural athlete, but it was Mrs. Dewsbury who had convinced him that he could compete in the classroom as well.

She had to be eighty by now. He didn't like seeing her using a walker; but he liked the fact that she was still out and about.

"Mrs. Dewsbury, it really is you," he said, grinning as he approached her.

She lifted a welcoming arm for his embrace. He hugged her gently and kissed her cheek and said, "You look great. No kidding; you look great."

"Oh, tish! I'm old and decrepit and I've got two new knees that I don't trust a damn. And speaking of bones, I have one to pick with you, young man. Where have you been hiding for the last seventeen years? You might have let me know."

"Right. I'm sorry about that. We, uh, took up residence in California."

She cocked her head thoughtfully and said, "You know,

I'm not surprised. They hired your father, no questions asked out there, am I right?"

"Californians tend to do that," he agreed. "They get lots of practice with illegals."

"Hmph. Well, Frank Leary was a wonderful gardener, and the Bennett estate hasn't looked as good since. Just last fall—*early* fall, mind you!—their latest gardener went and flat-topped every rhododendron he could reach. The things looked grotesque, and after the inevitable winterkill, they looked even worse. Well, never mind. How have you been, dear? How have you *been*?" she demanded, squeezing his forearm through his thin jacket. "Oh, my," she added after she did it. "Do you still play?"

"Football? No, I left that all behind me."

"I always watch for you during the Superbowl."

He laughed and said, "I have a masonry business. I do a lot of stonework. I guess that's what's kept me in shape."

She pulled her scarf away from her face and snugged it under her chin. "And your father I just heard has passed on?"

Quinn nodded. "Last month," he said quietly. "Of a stroke. He didn't linger long . . . two and a half weeks."

"I'm sorry, dear. I know how close you must have been to him."

Somehow Quinn didn't want to talk about it, despite—maybe because of—the sympathy he heard in her voice. He said, "Can I get you something? Hot chocolate?"

"Actually, I've brought my own refreshment." She reached into the leather handbag that was hooked on her walker and came up with a silver hip flask. "Blackberry brandy is what warms me these long, cold nights."

She tipped it in Quinn's direction. Startled, he shook his head. "Thanks, but I'm driving," he said, wondering about her own ability to operate a walker while under the influence. His old teacher and mentor had always been a free spirit. Obviously that hadn't changed. "How did you get here?" he asked. He wouldn't have been surprised if she'd told him on a Harley.

"The senior citizens' van," she said with a sigh of disgust. "I flunked my driver's test last year. Macular degeneration in my left eye. And the right one's fading fast," she added. "I can barely read large-print books with a magnifying glass anymore, but I keep trying." Lifting the flask, she glanced around, then took a single prim sip, screwed the cap back on, and tucked the silver container snugly in her purse. "Well, my dear! How long will you be staying?"

He wished he knew. He had a business to run back in California. "That's up in the air. I've just paid a visit to an uncle in Old Saybrook. He's my father's brother and is ailing himself. While I was in your neck of the woods, I thought I'd drop in just to . . . to . . ."

"To see who got rich, who got fat, and who got out?"

"All those things," he said, smiling. She was making it so easy for him to lie. "And I wanted Keepsake to know that at least one chapter in their history had ended."

"And a sorry chapter it was, condemning your father without a trial! I hope you don't think we were all so foolish," she said, straightening her tiny frame behind the walker.

His response to that was drowned out by the amplified thumps on a microphone being tested for sound. Mrs. Dewsbury explained that the thumper was Keepsake's current mayor, Mike Macoun. Quinn had a vague memory of the man, a restaurateur who was undoubtedly well connected both then and now.

After a pretty little speech in favor of Christmas, the portly mayor took one cord and plugged it into another cord, and the twenty-five-foot balsam fir lit up to happy *ooh*s and *ah*s from the crowd. It was a tree for kids, not grown-ups, all buried in red bows and gaudy colored lights and topped with a giant, lopsided star. There was nothing chic or understated about it, which pleased Quinn. He was tired of the white lights his upscale clients favored.

Someone shot off a cannon and the mayor declared that Keepsake's holiday season had officially begun. Almost immediately, the crowd began thinning. The snow was beginning to pile up, and people were anxious to get on with their chores.

"Where are you staying, Quinn?" the elderly woman asked.

"Let me think, it's newish . . . the Acorn Motel."

"Heavens, don't be silly. You're not staying at any motel. You'll take me home and stay at my house while you're in Keepsake."

He protested, but she wouldn't hear of it, and soon it was settled. He would stay in her overly large and virtually unoccupied Victorian home for the duration, whatever it ended up being. Quinn liked the idea of having daily access to someone who could fill him in on seventeen years of comings and goings in Keepsake. He tried to insist on paying for his stay, but Mrs. Dewsbury wouldn't hear of that, either. They ended with a compromise: he would do a few odd jobs around the house, and they would call it even.

After giving the driver of the senior citizens' van a heads-up, they left Town Hill together to scandalized looks and some sly greetings, although no one approached them to chat. Caught up in conversation with Mrs. Dewsbury, Quinn had little opportunity to look around him, but the one time he did, he saw a man whose face he could hardly forget: his father's employer and the richest man for miles around, Owen Randall Bennett. The textile mill owner was deep in conversation with two other men and didn't notice—or pretended not to notice—Quinn, who instinctively altered course away from him. He wasn't ready to deal with the town's patriarch yet, not by a long shot.

"That way's closer to the car," he said to Mrs. Dewsbury, pointing off in another direction. As they shifted course, he found himself wondering where the rest of the Bennetts were. Owen was around. Was his wife? What about their two kids? Had Princess Olivia married and moved on? And her brother, the Prince? Knowing Rand as well as he did, Quinn guessed that he'd been given an empty title and a corner office by his father.

But it was Rand's twin sister Olivia who came more viv-

idly to mind. Skinny, brainy, infuriatingly competitive—
Quinn and the Princess had butted heads over every academic award the school had offered. He half expected her
to tap him on his shoulder and challenge him then and there
to a spelling bee.

Olivia Bennett. He'd never forgotten her. How could he,
when they'd grown up side by side on the same estate, she
in the big house, he in the cottage?

He drove Mrs. Dewsbury home with extra caution—the
last thing he needed was to smash up a kindly old widow
who'd taken pity on him—and then he hovered solicitously
as she plowed in her fur-topped galoshes behind the walker
through several inches of unshoveled snow on the walk.

Her all-white Queen Anne house was enormous; he was
surprised she still lived in it by herself. But her grandparents
had built it, and four successive generations had lived in it.
It wasn't easy to abandon so much history. The trouble was,
her son was settled in a lucrative career as a financial plan-
ner in Boston, and her divorced and childless daughter lived
out west. Mrs. Dewsbury had dreams—but no real hopes—
that after she was gone, one of them would somehow return
to live in the family homestead.

"In the meantime," she said, handing Quinn her walker
and brushing snow from the banister as she ascended the
ambling, wraparound porch, "my daughter wants me to
move to a retirement community nearer to where she lives.
But I'd be miserable living somewhere else. I wouldn't
know a soul and the food would taste different. No, the only
way I'm leaving this house is feet first."

She pointed to an exterior light fixture hanging by its
tattered fabric cord from the porch ceiling. "One thing you
might do for me, dear, is tuck that thing back into its hole
sometime. I got on a stepladder the other day, but I was still
too short."

Aghast at the thought of her teetering on a ladder in her
new knees and poking at a frayed cord, Quinn assured her
that the job was as good as done.

They went inside to a house that was cavernous and yet

cozy in a varnished, dark-wood way. The ceilings were easily ten feet high, but the arched doorways somehow whittled the rooms back down to size. God knew, there were enough of them: twin parlors, a breakfast room, a music room, a cozy area, a game room, a reading room, a writing room—Quinn got lost just looking for the phone.

But he found it at last, an old black one being used to weigh down a slew of papers and magazines on a cluttered desk in a book-filled nook that smelled of fireplace ashes and potpourri. If rooms had personalities, then this one was smart, interesting, and heedless of other people's opinions. Quinn liked it as much as he liked its owner.

He looked up the number of the Acorn Motel and canceled his reservation there, then meandered back to the kitchen to reminisce with his old teacher over a pot of spiked tea. The second pot was steeping when they heard a sudden, sickening sound of shattering glass from in front of the house.

An accident, was Quinn's first thought; the street was still unplowed. He ran to the front door and flipped on the porch light, which, not surprisingly, didn't work. The wide street was dark, but he could see no cars embraced in a fender-bender on it. All he saw was his rented brown pickup, parked the way he'd left it in front of the house.

Actually, not quite the way he'd left it. The front windshield had been smashed to smithereens.

More surprised than angry, Quinn ran out to the now-deserted street. Hard to believe, but someone must have followed him to Mrs. Dewsbury's house. He peered inside the truck. The front seat was buried under a blanket of broken glass. His camera and suitcase were where he'd left them, but the caller had left a welcoming bouquet: red carnations, strewn all over the broken glass.

Somehow they didn't look right. Quinn reached inside and picked up a couple of them.

What the hell? He fingered the blooms. Wet. He looked at his hand. Red.

A clutch of carnations, dipped in blood.

Two

"*Any sign of* them?" Mrs. Dewsbury called out.

Quinn turned to see his elderly hostess standing in the doorway, her small frame silhouetted in the soft glow of the parlor lamps. "Nah," he said. "They're gone."

He tossed the flowers back on the seat and wiped his fingers on a floor mat, then took a closer look around. He could see evidence in the snow where someone had jumped out of a car, scrambled over to the rental, done the deed, and escaped. The depressions were already filling in with newly fallen snow; no clues there. He scanned the other homes on the street. All were large with lots of windows, but all were dark. No doubt everyone was off doing Christmas errands. Shit.

He went back to the house, brushing the snow from his sweater before he rejoined Mrs. Dewsbury in the more formal of her two parlors. He expected to find a frightened, agitated little old lady. He was wrong. Old and little she might have been, but the lady was clearly pissed.

"I have lived in this house for eighty-one years and I have never—*never*—seen such a thing," she said in a shaking voice. "What will you do? How will you drive?"

Quinn shrugged reassuringly and said, "It's no big deal. I'll have the car towed and rent another if I have to."

"Too bad I sold the Buick to my nephew last year. Really, it's just too *bad*!" Her hands were trembling as she moved from armchair to drum table to davenport to the walker that she'd left in the archway between the two parlors. With white-knuckled fury she reclaimed the walker and began marching out ahead of him.

"We'll just see what Chief Vickers has to say about *this*," she huffed. "Use the phone in the kitchen to call him. It's a speakerphone."

Oh, perfect. "Y'know, Mrs. Dewsbury," Quinn suggested, "Chief Vickers may not be the most sympathetic man in Keepsake."

"Sympathy has nothing to do with this! Someone just broke the *law*, and it's his job to uphold the *law*."

Law, shmaw. Quinn was a lot more worried about staying on in the woman's house and putting her at risk. "Okay, look. I'll call and report this, but under the circumstances I think the best thing would be for me to—"

"Don't even *think* it!" she said in her best schoolmarm's voice. "You're staying here, as we agreed. This mess has gone on seventeen years too long as it is. I blame your father for running away, and I blame this town for hounding him into it. But Frank Leary is dead and gone now. There's no reason why the sins of the father have to be visited on the son."

"There was no sin, Mrs. Dewsbury. My father didn't murder Alison." Quinn had to force himself even to say the words; they caught in his throat like barbed wire. *"He did not murder Alison."*

In her anger the old woman was candid, and in her candor she was brutal. "Some people in Keepsake will never believe he didn't hang her at the quarry, Quinn. Or that he wasn't the one who got her pregnant. I'm sure you know that."

Wincing at the all-too-familiar vision of his classmate twisting from a rope, and unnerved by the ease with which his old teacher alluded to his father as a suspected murderer, Quinn said fiercely, "He was innocent, goddammit!"

Immediately Mrs. Dewsbury's expression softened, and she became everyone's favorite grandmother again. "For what it's worth, I don't believe—I never believed—that your father did it, Quinn. He was far too kind, much too gentle. But he kept to himself, and you know how everyone always thinks that still water runs deep. It was much easier to accuse him than to search for some vagrant—or look closer to home.''

Quinn gave her a sharp look. *Closer to home.* So he wasn't the only one who had glanced in that direction.

She lifted the cordless phone from its base and held it out to him. ''Now, call.''

Olivia Bennett was in her shop, Miracourt, turning a bolt of satin in mistletoe green, when the bells above the door jangled in another cheerful *br-r-ring*. Two snowy children came charging inside, shepherded by Olivia's twin brother and his wife Eileen. The kids should've been droopy after their long day in New York, but they'd reached the stage of unfocused energy that comes from being overtired. Besides, Christmas was coming. Who had time to droop?

''Hey, look who's here,'' Olivia said cheerfully to her niece and nephew. ''Two melting snowmen.''

''*We're* not snowmen,'' said the very literal five-year-old. ''We're just all *covered* with snow.'' The child stomped her boots on the floor, then began brushing the snow from the sleeves of her red woolen coat.

Her mother stopped her. ''Careful, honey, you don't want to ruin Aunt Livvy's fabrics. That's a gorgeous color, Liv,'' she added, pointing to the satin. ''It'd look fabulous on you. You should make something for yourself out of it.''

Olivia laughed out loud at the notion, then tucked a dark curl behind her ear and began feeding the fabric through her Measuregraph. ''Who has time to sew anymore, much less to design?''

Owen Randall Bennett, Jr., her handsome twin brother who was as fair as she was dark, grinned and said, ''Oh, come on, Livvy, we all know you could design a dress in your sleep, weave the fabric before lunch, and sew it together by cocktails.''

''Wow. Am I really that talented?'' she said, giving him a mild look.

Still smiling, Rand said, "No-o; but you *are* an annoying workaholic."

"Oh, dear. I keep forgetting that I have an affliction. How was *The Nutcracker*, Zack?" she asked her nephew.

Zack, who at nine had reached the age of feeling obliged to seem bored about life in general and Nutcrackers in particular, said, "Fine."

His little sister had been turning an endearingly awkward pirouette. Suddenly she stopped and exclaimed, "The Nutcracker was big. He was *huge*."

Zack stuck his ungloved hands in his pockets and shrugged. "Not that huge."

"Yes he was!"

"Wasn't."

"Mom! He was, wasn't he? He *was*," Kristin insisted, dropping into a sudden, pitiable whine.

"Everyone's pooped," Eileen explained as she pulled off her daughter's red-and-white knitted snowflake cap. She ran her hand through the child's blond curls, blonder even than her father's, in an effort to restore some order there. "It's too bad we couldn't catch an earlier train. How did the tree lighting go?"

Liv made an initial snip in the satin, then took up the fabric on each side of the cut, tearing the yardage away from the rest of the bolt. "Don't know," she said as she folded the rich, drapey fabric into a square. "My help's out sick and I've been stuck here since nine. But I assume it went as usual."

She turned to the customer who'd been fingering various bolts of silk bouclé and said, "That was five yards of the floral tapestry, Sue?"

Measure twice, cut once; it was the creed Olivia lived by.

The customer came back to the cutting table, pursed her lips and said, "How much did you say it was a yard?"

"A hundred eighty-nine."

"Hmm. Better make that four-and-a-half yards. I'll make the underside of the cushion out of a plain fabric."

"Are you sure? You won't be able to flip the cushion,

in that case. After all that effort, it'd be a shame—''

"You're right, you're right. Add a yard."

"It's really more cost-effective in the long run."

"Oh! Black thread!" The customer hurried over to the wall display.

"Did Dad drop by after the tree lighting?" Rand asked his sister.

Carefully feeding the heavy fabric through the measuring device, Olivia shook her head and said, "I expect he's off politicking. He's trying to move up the vote on the tax relief proposal; did you know that?"

"Are you kidding?" Rand whispered, amazed. "I'm going to need time to lobby the council for that. What the hell is he thinking?"

Olivia shrugged. "He says he's losing his shirt. Poke your nose in Jasper's. He's probably at the bar with the mayor."

"You bet I will." He gave his wife a quick buss on the cheek and said, "Wait here with the kids, honey. I'll pop in, see if he's there, and then bring the car around for you. Toodle-doo," he said to his daughter, mussing her curls on his way out.

"Daddy, wait," Kristin said in a stage whisper. "Are we going shopping for Mommy's presents now?"

"No, that's tomorrow, remember?"

"Oh, good, 'cuz I don't have my money."

"No problemo."

Rand left, maneuvering his way around an incoming customer laden with boxes and bags bearing the imprints of the town's small but charming shops: the Kitchen Gallery, the Owl and the Pussycat, Cheap Thrills, Best Foot Forward. The lady was not only a shopper, but a local one, and that was the very best kind.

"Hi, I was in here earlier," the woman explained. "I bought a pair of silk tassels? Anyway, somewhere in my wanderings I lost an earring. It's a gold twist, like this one," she said, holding out the mate.

No one had turned in an earring, Liv told her, but she

asked for a phone number, just in case. While she rang up her latest sale, the woman scribbled the information on a Post-it Note.

"Isn't that something, about Quinn Leary?" she remarked as she handed the note over to Olivia. "He was before my time, but—"

Olivia's head came up. "Quinn? What about him?" she asked. She hadn't heard his name mentioned in years. She had a sudden, awful fear that he'd robbed a bank and killed all the customers and had made the six o'clock news.

"He's back, apparently."

"Back," Olivia repeated in a blank tone. "Back where? In jail?"

"Back here! In Keepsake!" The shopper shifted her bags to get more comfortable, thrilled that they hadn't yet heard. "During the tree lighting he was roaming all over Town Hill as if he owned the place. People were shocked," she said with a certain amount of glee. "I wish I'd taken the time to attend, but I wasn't wearing boots."

"But why?"

"Well, they weren't forecasting more than a dusting."

Eileen smiled and said, "I think she means, why would he come back now, after all these years?"

"His father died, they say, so I guess there's nothing to stop him. Not that people didn't try. Someone called the police, but their hands are tied. Quinn Leary's not a fugitive, and his father was never officially arrested, so Quinn never technically aided and abetted a fugitive, so—"

"He's back." Olivia had listened, dumbfounded, to the news. "Good God."

Her reaction took the smug woman down a notch. Nervous now, she whispered, "Do you suppose we'll have to start locking our doors during the day?"

Olivia stared at her. "Why would you do that? Quinn didn't do it. He was at a party with dozens of classmates when it happened. I know; I was there."

"Maybe so, but that kind of thing runs in families."

"What kind of thing?"

"You know—the killer instinct."

"That's ridiculous!"

Eileen jumped in to keep the peace. "Olivia went to high school with Quinn Leary," she explained. "They were on the student council together. They were friends, they—"

"No, we weren't," Olivia cut in. "We were rivals."

"But friendly rivals."

"Hardly. Oh, what does it matter! This is awful!"

"I knew it," the frightened customer said in an undertone. "He *is* dangerous."

Ignoring her, Olivia said to her sister-in-law, "My parents will be outraged. Rand, too. Oh—and my aunt! My *uncle*!"

When they were roommates in college, Olivia had told Eileen the whole shocking story of the fugitive and his son: how the gardener had been seen staring at Liv's cousin Alison on more than one occasion. How the hanging had been staged to look like a suicide, except that the rope had come from the gardener's shed. How the police had been on the brink of arresting Francis Leary when he ran off, accompanied by his son Quinn. And how Olivia's parents—the suspect's employers—had been left to fend off a nosy press and negative publicity.

Olivia had always insisted to Eileen that what little evidence the police had was circumstantial, and that she herself did not believe Francis Leary had murdered her cousin Alison. But then Eileen had begun to date Olivia's brother Rand and discovered that the rest of Olivia's family was convinced that the gardener was guilty.

And now, seventeen years later, Olivia could see that her open-minded sister-in-law was still trying hard to stay that way about the whole affair, but not succeeding. Eileen looked doubtful and troubled as she said to her little girl, "Come over here, Kristin. Let's get your hat on. Daddy's going to be bringing the car by any minute."

An impromptu game of hide-and-seek between Olivia's niece and nephew came to a sudden end when Zack knocked over a bolt of ivory *fleur de soie* onto the parquet floor and into a puddle left by someone's boots. The accident brought an accusing shriek from Kristin, mortifying her older brother and prompting a sharp reprimand from their mother.

"Okay, that's it! Let's go, you two, before you wreck the whole place," she said, picking up the soiled bolt. "Livvy, I'm so sorry. Bill me for this, would you?"

Olivia had two customers waiting with questions and another with a bolt of Ultrasuede in her arms. "Sure, okay," she said, still reeling from the news of Quinn's return.

Eileen apologized again for the silk as she rebuttoned her daughter's coat. A silver Lexus pulled up in front of the shop. Rand leaned on the horn, and his family hurried to the summons.

For the next two hours Olivia did the job of three assistants, which was the number that should've been at her shop in the course of the twelve-hour day. But two were sick and one had asked for the evening off to attend a wedding rehearsal; Olivia couldn't very well flog them into coming in. Still, it *was* the Christmas rush, and they'd put her in a bind.

And now this. Good grief—Quinn Leary. What was he thinking, strolling onto Town Hill in the middle of the tree lighting? It was the most celebrated event in Keepsake, attended by everyone who was anyone. Her father must have seen him. Had they exchanged words? What could you say at a time like that? *Gee, Quinn, the sight of you sure brings back memories of the good old days: reporters peering through our first-floor windows, police rummaging through our garbage cans, neighbors staring over the hedges to see if anyone was coming out in a body bag.*

Olivia's parents had felt utterly betrayed when they learned that their gardener was under suspicion for murder. They'd given Quinn's father a dream job, after all, with a charming cottage for him and his son to live in, good benefits, and frequent raises. Frank Leary himself had once told Olivia that her mother was the best employer he'd ever had.

To be fair, it was also true that the man was a wizard as a groundskeeper: The extensive grounds on the Bennett estate were the envy of the county and had been photographed for *House and Garden* a few months before Frank Leary and his son took off in the night. Naturally the *HG* piece never went to press—one more reason, Olivia supposed, for her father to resent them.

Him.

Damn.

They were going to have to relive the murder all again—the discovery, the shock, the publicity, the depressing realization that Alison would never be a bridesmaid at Olivia's wedding and that Olivia would never be a bridesmaid at her cousin's.

She remembered a Saturday in her junior year when Alison's father was out of town and Olivia's mother had taken Alison and her to New York on a clandestine shopping spree. Olivia had prepared for the day by reading a book on dressing for success, and then had headed straight for the racks of career clothing. Alison, on the other hand, had gravitated toward more feminine, sexier things: V necks that dipped low, and tops with front zippers.

"You'll never get a job wearing something like that," Olivia had chided. She had been young and stupid then; what did she know?

"I don't want a job," Alison had answered. "I want a husband. I want to get out of my house and away from my father. He won't let me go away to a four-year college; I'm going to have to commute to ECCC. No thanks. You pick your clothes, Livvy, and I'll pick mine."

When they found Alison at the quarry she was wearing one of those V-necked sweaters that she so preferred. She had put on weight because of the pregnancy: Her breasts were fuller than ever.

Olivia sighed, then flipped the card that hung by a silken cord in the door window to its CLOSED side. She turned down the lights in the shop and dimmed the recessed halogen lights that hovered over the window display. The holiday window was always her favorite of the year, and this December was no exception. She had draped elegant fabrics—bolts of taffeta, brocade, and tissue in glittering silver and gold—to flow like sparkling streams and tumbling waterfalls into pools of shimmery opulence on the floor of the display window. With the lights dimmed low, the effect was of a winter scene at twilight: pure magic, if only you paused long enough to take it all in.

And she did. Despite the unnerving news about Quinn's return, despite the surge of seventeen-year-old melancholy at thoughts of her murdered cousin, despite her dread that her family was about to be put through the wringer all over again—despite all those things, Olivia found herself responding to the exquisite beauty before her. It appealed to the artistic side of her in a way that gross receipts and profit margins never could.

Once upon a time, she had hoped to design her own fabrics. But somehow the business side of her had taken precedence, and this was where she ended up: buying and selling textiles designed by people other than her. Ah, well. Miracourt was a financial success, and so was the mill-end outlet she'd opened six months ago to handle remnants and misprints she was able to buy dirt-cheap from her father's textile mill. For now, a life in commerce would have to do.

She sighed again, not so cheerful as she had been before, and then she closed up the shop, dreading the slippery drive to her townhouse perched on a steep hill outside of town. She'd been too busy to go car-shopping for that four-wheel drive—or even to have the snow tires put on her minivan— and now she was kicking herself.

I'm either at Miracourt or at Run of the Mill seven days a week. I don't have time to buy a TV dinner, much less an automobile. Rand is right. I'm out of control.

But then, wasn't that what lazy Rand would think?

She sprinted across the snowy street rutted with tire tracks, just two steps ahead of the *sluk-sluk-sluk* of a Jeep Cherokee bearing down on her. After a last look at the softly lit window in all of its holiday charm, she flipped up the hood of her coat and hurried through falling snow to her van.

Three

"*Glad you could* squeeze me in, Tony."

"Ah, don't worry about it," said the barber, shaking out the folds of a white linen smock with a snap, then circling it around Quinn's neck and jamming it inside his collar. "To tell the truth, business ain't been so brisk. I'm losing customers to that . . . that *franchise* down the street. Aagh! Don't get me started. So. How you want it? Short?" he asked hopefully.

"Maybe take an inch off the bottom."

Tony gave Quinn a dry look in the mirror they faced. "And the other twelve?"

"I'll keep a rubber band around it for now."

The gray-haired barber sighed and, with a look of exquisite distaste, rolled down the band from Quinn's ponytail.

"Why you want to look like this?" he couldn't help saying as he took up a comb and a small pair of shears. "You're a good-looking guy. Still in good shape. Why you wanna go around like some hippie?"

"You think this is bad, you should've seen me with the full beard," Quinn said with a smile.

"Aagh."

Quinn didn't bother to explain that the beard and long hair were part of an effort to disguise himself during those first years in hiding. Eventually he had felt secure enough to lose the beard, but the ponytail stayed. He still liked to believe that with his hazel eyes, hawk nose, and ever-present tan, he could dye his sunstreaked hair black and pass for a Native American if he had to.

In the thoughtful pause that hangs between threads of conversation, the barber ran a comb to the bottom of Quinn's hair and began, under Quinn's watchful eye, to cut it back the inch.

"I hear you had a little trouble last night."

Ah. Same old Keepsake. Thank God he hadn't mentioned the bloodied carnations to Vickers.

"Yeah, some jerk bashed in the windshield," he said. "Do you get a lot of that nowadays?"

"Never. Mailboxes, yes. Not windshields. Windshields are in the city."

Quinn grunted, the way men do in barbershops, and then he took a flyer and said, "This guy was driving a pickup."

There was an infinitesimal break in the rhythm between snips. "That so? What color?"

"Couldn't say. I'm figuring a truck by the look of the wide tire tracks."

A much more pronounced gap between snips now. Thinking . . . what?

"Aw, you can't go by tire tracks. That could be anything. SUV, souped-up Camaro, an old clunker Caddy, even. What, uh, did Vickers have to say?"

So he knew that, too. "He didn't offer an opinion," Quinn said. "Just took down the details and warned me to keep my insurance up to date."

"Always good advice."

A dozen snips later, Tony was done. He took a soft bristled brush to the back of Quinn's neck, removed the smock, and after Quinn got out of the chair, spun a push-broom flattened with wear in a quick circuit around the chair's pedestal.

Quinn fished out a ten and a five, then waved away the attempt to make change.

"You're doing all right with that landscaping business, then," Tony said, pocketing the cash.

Quinn had the presence of mind not to show surprise that

the barber knew he had a business. Instead he merely said, "Actually, my father worked the landscaping side of it; I work mostly with stone. You'd be surprised what Californians will pay for an old-looking New England wall."

"I heard millions for the fancier ones," said Tony, fishing for confirmation.

Quinn merely smiled and said, "I'll be selling off the landscaping part."

"Oh?"

"I'm tired of California." Quinn wanted that word out. This was the perfect place to launch the rumor.

"Never been there myself. Took the wife to Vegas once, though."

"How'd you do?"

"Aagh."

Quinn laughed and said, "I've lost my shirt there once or twice myself."

They had something in common, it seemed. The barber warmed to Quinn a little. He cocked his head over his sloping shoulder and said, "So you're thinking of pulling up stakes. Any idea where you'll put 'em back down?"

"I imagine somewhere around here," Quinn said equably. "Know any houses for sale?"

"You're looking for—what? New construction? Because there's a new subdivision going in at the west end that might suit."

Quinn seesawed the palm of his hand in the air. "Something with more character, I think."

Rubbing his cheek thoughtfully with the tips of his fingers, Tony said, "You know what I'd do? I'd go on the Candlelight Tour of upper Main. The houses are open tonight through Tuesday. Check out Hastings House; it's been on the market for a while. The place is maybe older than you're looking for, but it's a local landmark—well, I don't need to tell you that—and it could go cheap. It needs some structural work. Big bucks."

"Thanks for the tip," Quinn said as he shrugged into his

jacket and plucked a brand new ski cap from one of the pockets. "Maybe I'll check it out."

He hiked his knapsack over his shoulder and let himself out of the tiny one-chair shop, stopping to admire the ancient barber pole out front. It was so much a part of the establishment that he'd hardly noticed it on his way inside. The red-and-white-striped icon looked exactly the same as seventeen years earlier, spinning slowly in its glass housing, its motor still whirring along. A barber pole in working order was a rarity; it was probably worth more than the business itself.

Quinn felt yet another twinge of regret. Tony Assorio, no-nonsense barber . . . the shoemaker languishing around the corner . . . the watch repairman, struggling in the shop next to him—all of the shopkeepers were old and gray and all of them were doomed to become mere memories, like the soda fountain that once had served cherry cokes, and the elegant Art Deco theater that someone had hacked into a four-screen multiplex. Throwaway goods and volume discounts, that was the name of the game nowadays. How could the little guy hope to compete?

Maybe Keepsake would be able to hold on to its unique, small-town feel—hadn't Mrs. Dewsbury boasted that they'd recently beat back a Wal-Mart?—but probably it wouldn't. Christ, someone was cramming a subdivision into the west end. Quinn never thought he'd see the day. What next? A theme park?

"Oh, no," said Mrs. Dewsbury later when he mused aloud to her. "We won't get a theme park here. Someone's already beat us to the punch on that one—thank goodness. Can you imagine the traffic?"

Quinn reached down to the top of the ladder for the wire crimper, but, like a surgical nurse in mittens, Mrs. Dewsbury insisted on handing it to him.

"Are you really planning to come back here for good?" she asked as she watched him crimp two wires together in a plastic sleeve.

It was awkward, working with short wires in the small

hole cut into the porch ceiling. And it was finger-freezing cold; he'd hardly had time to adjust to New England's weather. But Quinn's first order of business, cold or no cold, was to get light on the porch. If someone was going to come after him, he was going to have to do it someplace other than at Mrs. Dewsbury's house.

He had to think about how candid he could afford to be with the elderly widow. She was shrewd and she was fearless, but could she hold her tongue?

He decided she could.

"You want the God's honest truth?" he said, gently easing the wires back into the hole ahead of the light fixture. He glanced down at her. She was supporting the back of her neck with gray-mittened hands while she watched him work. Her face had the charming pinkness to it that fair-skinned Yankees, young and old, got when they stood too long on their porches in fifteen-degree temperatures. She looked pleased and satisfied and curious and, yes, she clearly wanted the God's honest truth.

Quinn flattened the collar of the light fixture against the sky-blue tongue-and-groove planks of the porch ceiling. He jammed a fastener into the wood to make it stay, then began screwing it tight. "I have no intention of moving back east," he said simply. "I'm just putting out rumors. I want to see if I can stir things up a little, make people a little nervous."

"Oh. Well . . . pooh, that's disappointing," he heard her say.

"If my father didn't murder Alison," he continued, "then someone else did. I doubt that it was a vagrant. It's too coincidental that some homeless character would have stolen the rope from the potting shed, conveniently implicating a man who happened not to have an alibi for the time of the murder."

He took another screw from his pocket and repeated the routine. "No, I see a deliberate frame-up here. I see someone who knew that my dad always spent Saturday night alone, reading. Someone who knew what he did for a living, and where his tools were stored. Someone local.''

He looked down again. Mrs. Dewsbury was still watching him, still holding the back of her neck with her mittened hands, but her eyes had narrowed in an appraising squint.

"So you think this was all planned beforehand?''

"That's one possibility," he said. "Another is that it was a crime of passion and the murderer was a damned good improviser.''

"It's true, you know. Some people are very good under stress," she said in droll agreement.

After a pause, she said, "Tell me. Don't you think Chief Vickers knows more than he was letting on?''

"About . . . ?''

"The windshield, of course. I've been thinking about it, and you're right. He can't be happy that you're back. It always rankled that your father slipped through his fingers; he told me so himself once. It wouldn't surprise me to learn that the chief had someone smash in your windshield.''

Quinn was thinking more of the bloodied flowers. "I dunno.''

"You need to watch out for him.''

Quinn smiled grimly and said, "Okay, I'll bump Vickers up a few slots on the list of Those Who Wish to See Me Dead. How's that?''

"It's not funny.''

"No, ma'am.''

The last screw slipped through Quinn's numb fingers. He began to climb down the stepladder to retrieve it, but Mrs. Dewsbury insisted on getting it herself. Quinn made himself wait patiently on a rung while she moved the walker to the side, removed a mitten, very slowly got down into a crouch, picked up the screw with an arthritic hand, pulled the walker back to her, and then stood up again.

"Here you are, dear.''

He finished the job and they went inside. One chore down, thirty-seven to go, according to the list that Quinn had put together so far. He had no doubt that the list would get longer before it got shorter. The house was falling apart in a thousand little ways, some of which could lead to disaster. An electrical short and a subsequent fire, a pitch-dark porch and a nimble arsonist. The combinations were endless.

Olivia Bennett had small, slender feet—she was pretty proud of them—but this was ridiculous. There wasn't a foot on the planet that could comfortably fit into the Victorian French-heeled shoe she was trying to wear. The handmade shoe was just one of a vast array of historically accurate reproductions that made up the evening ensemble she had committed to wear in her stint as guide on the Candlelight Tour.

"I feel like Cinderella's evil stepsister," she growled, jamming her foot into the narrow shoe. Which wasn't a shoe anyway—it was an instrument of torture, tight and stiff and with an outrageous tip that surged a good three inches past her big toe.

She threw up her hands in frustration and collapsed back on her white slipcovered tub chair. "I can't do this."

Eileen was standing over her like a maid-in-waiting who wasn't quite sure of her job description. "Maybe you'll get used to them. Try standing up."

"It's this *stupid* corset!" Olivia said suddenly, grabbing at the stiff, steel-boned vise that was responsible for her current Barbie-doll look. "What was I *thinking*?"

"What did you expect? It's French."

"Well, screw the French! I'm not wearing it!" She began tearing at the half-dozen front hooks with a viciousness that she normally reserved for pickle jars.

"Hold it right there, *mademoiselle*. *You're* the one who talked all the guides into wearing period getups."

Olivia sighed and tucked one of the wandering bust enhancers back into place. Her wool drawers itched. Her chemise was too tight. The petticoats were heavy. But Eileen was right—dressing for the period had been her idea.

"Bustle, please," she said grimly.

Eileen let out a little sigh of sympathy.

After some fumbling, they belted the elaborate wire

framework onto Olivia's behind. Feeling like a bronco sad-
dled for the first time, she resisted the urge to try to kick
the thing off and said through gritted teeth, "Okay—the
gown."

Eileen's response was a radiant smile. "This will make
it all worthwhile." She fished the padded hanger out of the
taffeta gown and slipped the dress over Olivia's upraised
arms. Olivia disappeared in a swishy cloud of scarlet iri-
descence, then emerged from a low-cut bodice that was un-
questionably more European than American.

The color scheme was as bold as the plunge of the neck-
line: a swath of bright scarlet draped up toward the out-
landish bustle to reveal a purple skirt beneath, with
silver-gray passementerie looped around the cuffs, the bodice, and the hem. The heavily beaded braid caught and re-
fracted the light from the recessed spotlight above, rimming
Olivia in glittering highlights.

Eileen stepped back with a startled look. "My goodness,
that's daring."

"Oh, I don't know. The only thing daring about this
outfit is the crotchless drawers," Olivia said, squirming in
annoyance. "It's December, for pity's sake. These damn
things give a whole new meaning to the expression 'freezing
your buns off.' "

Laughing, Eileen said, "Well, think about it. How on
earth would anyone go potty, once she was rigged in that
getup?"

"Trust me, I don't intend to find out. Start buttoning;
I've got to be there in half an hour. Thank God women from
that era didn't go in for makeup. I'd be pummeling herbal
extracts into a pot of rouge about now."

"All right, here we go. Suck it in, Miss Bennett."

Several painful moments later, Olivia was tightly skinned
in scarlet. She had achieved the desired hourglass shape at
last. The curves she exhibited, though not her own, were
definitely spectacular.

She said in a breathless gasp, "I think I'm going to pass
out."

"The things we do for love," Eileen said, amused. "Honestly, I wish we'd featured you like that on the flyers we posted around town. The Keepsake Preservation Society would be rolling in dough after this fund-raiser."

"Shoes! What do I do about shoes? Even assuming I could take more pain, I'd fall and break my neck if I went wearing these in the snow." Olivia kicked them off, furious for ever agreeing to be part of the Candlelight Tour. It would have been better to write out a check. She had inventory to stock, she had orders to place—what was she doing pointing out crown moldings and fruitwood étagères to the hoi polloi?

Volunteering seemed like *such* a better idea at the time.

Swishing over to her closet, she yanked open a white louvred door and pointed to the shoerack on the floor. "Take out the black Reeboks for me, would you?"

Eileen was scandalized, but she did as she was commanded, even tying the laces for her immobilized sister-in-law.

"All right, let's see what it all looks like," said Olivia, striding over to the full-length mirror.

"Smaller steps! Smaller steps! Your sneakers show."

They stood together in front of the mirror, these two best friends turned relatives: Eileen, tall and thin and blond and oh-so-Connecticut; and Olivia, shorter, darker, and somehow, despite the elegance of her wardrobe, just a little bit gypsy. Olivia was very conscious of the contrast. She wasn't especially bothered by it—she looked vaguely like her mother, whom she had always considered truly beautiful—but she was definitely aware that she did not have "the look."

She shrugged and said, "I guess I'll do."

"Do? You look fabulous," Eileen insisted. "That creamy skin, those natural curls, those bedroom eyes—what man could resist you?"

"Apparently they make the effort," Olivia said dryly.

"It's your fault. Why do you go everywhere with Eric on your arm?"

"Eric is very presentable."

"Eric is gay!"

"My mother likes Eric."

"What mother wouldn't? But it's keeping you from meeting the man of your dreams."

"I don't dream about men, I dream about fabric." Olivia frowned in the mirror, then grabbed a tube of lipstick from her dresser and ran it lightly across her lips.

"Okay, I'm ready," she declared. "Point me to the drawing room."

Four

Hastings House was built in high Victorian style for a man who, quite simply, loved wood. In 1882, Mr. Latimer Hastings bought a lumberyard just to have first crack at the boards, then spent the next two years in close company with an architect and a construction crew, milling, shaping, and carving those boards for his house on upper Main. The house became an obsession, and more: It became his reason to exist. It wrecked his marriage, it alienated the neighbors, and ultimately it became a bone of contention between his heirs.

It was a nightmare to maintain, with its curved piazza and its multigabled roofline, but it was something, really something, to see. Keepsake was nearly as proud of Hastings House as it was of the Bennett estate, higher up the hill. Most people knew they'd never get the chance to poke their noses in the Bennetts' dining room; but this year they could get a fairly good idea, for a mere four dollars, of how the Bennetts' dinner guests lived.

So they paid and they poked. Despite the biting cold and windy weather, the Candlelight Tour was enjoying an excellent turnout. Keepsake was a historic town with an active Historical Society backed by a mayor who understood the dollar value of tourism. Besides, the cause was worthy: The proceeds of the Candlelight Tour were split between St. Swithin's soup kitchen and free art courses for Keepsake's children.

Olivia felt at home in the heavily carved, overly ornate drawing room of Hastings House; when she was growing up she'd been a guest there many times. Standing straight as a board (she had no choice) near a crackling fire, she greeted each new visitor on the tour as graciously as Mrs. Hastings herself might have done before dumping her husband for another man with a simpler house.

It was fun. Olivia hadn't expected to enjoy playing the part of a Victorian socialite, and yet here she was, flirting and having a great time. *Playing* at flirting, anyway. The pain of being laced into a state of dizziness had ebbed, replaced by the novelty of being the object of men's gapes and women's furtive looks. It was definitely a first for her.

"Either I've just discovered my true calling as an actress, or there's something to this corset business," she said, laughing, after two women she knew well expressed open amazement at the difference in her demeanor.

The women wandered out and another group wandered in: Eric and several of his pals, all of them history and architecture buffs. Olivia knew that one of them was an actor, so she poured it on, hamming it up outrageously until the men moved on, still laughing, to the next room.

And then there was a lull.

Quinn had heard voices in the room ahead of him—several men and a woman—who sounded as if they were having a damn good time. He was jealous; it had been a while since he'd laughed out loud. But by the time he escaped the clutches of the Victorian gentleman whose job it was to explain the Victorian library, the group had left the drawing room, taking their raucous laughter with them.

They left behind them a woman.

Her back was to Quinn, whose first impression was of a mountain of scarlet material bunched on top of a purple skirt. He saw that she wasn't tall, and yet her posture somehow made her seem so. She had dark hair, tied in a knot at the nape of her neck—without much success, Quinn could

see; ringlets seemed to be escaping even as he stood un-
noticed behind her.

She was standing in front of the fire with her hands extended to catch its warmth. He couldn't blame her for feeling cold: Her back and shoulders were as bare as any
red-blooded man could hope for. The sight of her had sent
his genitals lurching beneath his corduroys, and almost immediately he realized why.

She had the most impossibly beautiful figure he'd ever
seen. He had no idea that in an age of protein and aerobics,
women could still look like that: beautiful back and shoulders, tiny, *tiny* waist, flared and intriguing hips. It was an
old-fashioned fantasy, a heart-wrecking dream—and it was
as erotic as all hell. He might have stood gazing at that
hourglass shape forever if she hadn't turned around with a
start.

"Oh, I'm sorry; I didn't hear anyone come—Quinn?"

He blinked. He knew the voice, knew the eyes, he definitely knew the voice . . . He blinked again in disbelief. In
a moment of complete, humiliating weakness his let his gaze
drop down to her cleavage. Was it possible?

"Liv?"

"Who else?" she said, with a wary smile. "You look
the same."

"You don't," he said, stunned.

A couple walked in just then with questions poised: Was
the price firm? Would the owner take financing? Had he had
any offers? Olivia explained with dazzling grace that she
was not the realtor—Jesus, did she *look* like a realtor?—
and then the couple left.

Olivia turned her dark-eyed gaze back to Quinn. "I heard
you were back. Somehow I didn't expect to run into you
here, though."

He took it possibly the wrong way. "Yeah, well, you
know how it is when you throw an open house. Riffraff's
bound to get in."

"Oh no! Is *he* here?" she said, rolling her eyes.

He chuckled. "Okay, I suppose I deserved that."

She shook her head. "You *haven't* changed, have you? I'm . . . I'm sorry about your father," she added. "I know how close you were."

Sympathy from a Bennett? No thanks; it felt too much like pity. "We did all right," he said, "once we got out of Keepsake. We had a good life."

"Yours isn't over."

"His is."

"Yes, but you said . . . Well, I'm glad it worked out. It was an awkward time."

"Awkward?"

"That's the wrong word," she said quickly. "It was . . . horrible, I guess I mean. For everyone."

"So people keep telling me. A girl is killed, my father is blamed, our lives are upended, and what do I hear? I'm the Grinch Who Stole Homecoming."

"Well, in all honesty, we haven't come even *close* to a championship since," she said with a bland look.

He snorted. He remembered that about her now—her ir-reverent sense of humor. She was much less straightlaced than the rest of her clan, and that always had made her an interesting opponent. He jammed his hands in his parka pockets and rocked back on his heels. "So. Which of the Ivy League schools ended up rolling out the thickest red carpet?"

Smiling at the compliment, she said, "I decided to go with Harvard."

He waved a hand airily at her getup. "And this would be—what? A part-time job to pay off your student loans?" he quipped, fighting hard not to resent her. *Harvard.*

He watched her flinch and then recover. "As it turns out, my dad was able to scrape together the tuition. But I did borrow money to get my MBA. Is that any comfort?"

"Not much," he said through a tight smile. "So what *do* you do to pay the mortgage?"

"I own a shop in town, Miracourt . . . on York Street? I sell high-end fabrics—interior, and some apparel."

He nodded. "Oh, well sure, a fabric store. It's logical,

with your father owning a textile mill and all.''

"My father has nothing to with Miracourt!" she said sharply. "It's entirely mine, bought and paid for with my own money."

How wearying, he thought: an heiress who insisted on making her own way. Not him. If someone had been willing to hand him a fortune, he'd have been more than willing to spend it.

In the next breath she confessed, "I do have another, larger store—a mill-end outlet—that my father *is* involved with.''

Even more wearying: an heiress who was conflicted about her family's wealth.

A new batch of visitors, awed and deferential, tiptoed in behind him and began to ask questions in hushed, respectful voices.

It's someone's front room, folks, not the Vatican, Quinn wanted to say, but he, too, was affected by the somber personality of the place, so he took himself over to the balsam Christmas tree that presided over the other end of the room and spent some time inhaling its fragrance while Olivia fielded inquiries.

He overheard all kinds of illuminating tidbits from her about pocket doors, Austrian chandeliers, coffered ceilings, and imported delft tiles, but mostly it was the sound of her voice that kept him rooted to the spot. He loved hearing it, loved the way it spoke in whole sentences free of Valley-speak and New Age clichés. It had an old-fashioned, finishing-school ring to it that blended perfectly with the scarlet gown.

And her laugh! It was the burbling of a brook, flowing and tinkling along its banks but never overrunning them. All in all, he was mesmerized. He felt like some lowborn character—who was it, Heathcliff?—in an English novel. He wasn't sure if he had the era or even the character right, but he damn well had the mood right. He felt . . . unequal, to all this. As if he were there, cap in hand, to announce to madame that her carriage was ready.

And, boy, it pissed him off.

The visitors moved on and he moved back in, reclaiming his right to converse with the Princess. He'd paid his four bucks. He was entitled.

"What about you, Quinn?" she said, turning her attention right back to him. "Where did you end up getting your degree?"

If he'd needed a splash of cold water, that was it. "A degree?" He said wryly, "I decided to pass."

Clearly she didn't get it. "Are you serious? You could've pursued any kind of scholarship you wanted. Academic, athletic . . . *Notre Dame* came looking for you!"

"Did they? Well, they never found me and neither did anyone else. But then, that would be the whole point of living in hiding, wouldn't it?"

Chastised, she lowered her gaze from his and said simply, "Yes."

He felt like a shit, beating her over the head with his unrealized promise. He was doing it because he knew that, more than anyone else, she would feel the waste of it.

Apparently he was right. Her head came back up and she looked him in the eye and said, "You didn't *have* to run, Quinn. You ended up throwing it all away, didn't you? College, a career, inevitable prestige. You could have done anything you wanted to do, been anything you wanted to be."

"Maybe I wanted to be a fugitive," he said coldly.

"But you weren't a fugitive. You were a fugitive's son. That wasn't as glamorous, surely?"

He remembered now that she had a damn sharp tongue. Annoyed, he said, "If I'd been after glamor, I would have gone to L.A."

"What *were* you after? I've always wondered. Fame wasn't enough? You had to turn it on its head and go for infamy, too?"

"What the hell is that to you?" he countered, amazed at her bluntness.

"I'll tell you what it is to me. I grew up with you, Quinn. I thought we were friends."

"Friends? Isn't that pushing it a little?"

"All right," she said, coloring. "Intellectual comrades, then. Call it what you like. I can't tell you how shocked I was to learn—from the police swarming our grounds, no less!—that you had run off. Without saying boo, without a note, without a hint. I was so dismayed . . . so hurt . . ."

"Christ, it's always about you, isn't it?" he said, remembering that as well. "You know what? I was wrong. *You* haven't changed, either. You—"

"Hiii," Olivia said suddenly to a couple entering the room with their teenage son. "Welcome to Hastings House."

Too late. The group knew they'd strolled into a fight, and no bright smile could hide the fact. The parents walked quickly through the room and then out. Their kid took a little longer, slowing down long enough to steal a burning look at Olivia's breasts.

The boy reminded Quinn of himself just minutes earlier. Quinn had acted like a hormonal jerk then, and for all he knew, he was doing it still. It wasn't Olivia's fault that he had cut and run. And it wasn't her fault that she couldn't understand why. Their lives were night-and-day different. No mother, timid father, nomadic lifestyle, never a mattress to call one's own—these were alien concepts to a woman raised in the lap of luxury by a doting mom and a powerful dad.

Let it go, Quinn. Different worlds. Let it go.

"Look . . . what's done is done. Water under the bridge," he said gruffly. "Maybe we . . . well. Good night." He turned to leave.

No, goddammit. He didn't have to run anymore, least of all from her.

He spun on his heel and faced her again. She looked completely bewildered, which gave him back the advantage. With a smile that he knew women considered disarming, he said, "You're not married, are you?"

"No!"

"Why don't we have dinner? You can fill me in on the last half of your life."

"Dinner? _Huh_. Dinner. That would be rather—"

"Quaint?" he suggested, an edge in his voice.

"I was about to say, that would be rather nice," she said, snapping open her fan, "except that I have to be here tomorrow night."

"Ah," he replied, somewhat sheepishly.

She seemed agitated, fanning herself with quick little strokes. Intrigued, he waited to see what she would do next.

"Why don't we have lunch?" she asked with a brittle smile. "I could get away then."

"Fine," he drawled, making a victory fist in his pocket. "We'll do lunch."

He left, taking most of Olivia's wits with him. The encounter with Quinn Leary had left her completely unnerved. Her heart was hammering, her knees were shaking, and inside she was hot, hot, hot—hot enough that she found herself feeling downright grateful for the cold draft that wended its way from the front door and up her gown, fanning those oddly made drawers of hers.

Oh, wow, this is unreal, she told herself. _This is not normal_. No man had ever affected her the way Quinn had just then. Flirting was one thing, banter another, but this was new, this was completely new. . . .

She began to pace the length of the drawing room, trying to work out the tension she felt. In a reverie of wonder, she tapped her closed fan on the palm of her hand and shook her head as she marched up, then down, the parquet floor, ignoring the visitors who wandered through. The tourists assumed she was playing the role of a character from a Victorian novel, but the tourists were wrong.

I don't have time for someone like him. I don't even have the inclination for someone like him. He's too proud, too prickly, too—much too—controversial. What would Mother and Dad say? They'd be appalled to have a Leary rubbed in their noses again.

Seventeen years. Olivia remembered rushing home after the news of Alison's death and finding her mother sitting alone on the sofa and sobbing. Teresa Bennett, being a Bennett, had quickly wiped her eyes as soon as she saw her daughter. But Olivia, who wanted so badly to hold and be held, had blurted out, "She didn't deserve to die; she never hurt anyone," and burst into tears for her cousin, and then she and her mother had hugged and cried some more, but in secret—because wailing was not allowed in the Bennett household.

The sad thing was, by the time of Alison's murder, Owen Bennett had had little contact with Alison's father Rupert. Olivia didn't know why the brothers had drifted so far apart, and she'd never dared ask. Olivia's father had bought out her Uncle Rupert's interest in the mill, that much she knew. But she'd always had the feeling that there was more to the split than a difference in business philosophies.

In any case, the attendance of Owen and his family at Alison's funeral did nothing to breech the growing rift between brothers. After the murder, the rift became as wide as a canyon and stayed that way.

Olivia pushed away all of the memories; all of them were bad. No, Quinn was out of the question. He was too bound up with the worst period of her family's life for Olivia ever to be able to take him seriously. True, there was that box of stuff she'd been keeping all these years. But after she returned it to Quinn, that was it. The town could deal with him any way it liked; it had nothing to do with her.

"Are these parquet squares the kind you buy at Home Depot?"

Olivia turned to the young couple who were linked arm in arm and studying the drawing room floor. "No," she said with a gracious smile, "they're Burma teak, and their value is priceless."

Quinn drove home in a state of near bliss. He'd gone on the Candlelight Tour for no other reason than to keep a high profile, and he'd come away with a date with the Princess.

Socially speaking, of course, he was a frog. He knew it, and it made the promise of taking her out all the more gratifying. Dating Olivia was something he never would have dared try back in high school, which was undoubtedly the reason he had enjoyed trouncing her in the classroom every chance he got. He had enjoyed it even more than trouncing her brother on the field.

But it was all such kid stuff. What a jerk he used to be. He laughed softly to himself as he drove his repaired rental past St. Swithin's Church, past the bank, past Town Hill with its lit-up tree. *Had* he grown up? He hoped so. He hoped that his reason for wanting to be seen in Keepsake with Olivia on his arm was not because she was a royal and he was a commoner, but because she was smart and funny and, okay, knock-down gorgeous.

But he really wasn't sure.

At three in the morning, Father Tom was lying in bed with a brutal case of heartburn. He shouldn't have done it; shouldn't have had the blessed beer with his pepperoni pizza. He had yielded to temptation, and now the devil was claiming his due. The priest shifted onto his side, prompting an ineffectual burp.

It tasted like popcorn. Another temptation yielded to, but who could watch a videotape of *Mystery!* without popcorn? It wouldn't have been right. The priest sighed and sat up, swinging his legs over the side of his bed. The two antacids he'd popped into his mouth before lying down for the night hadn't done a thing; maybe Pepto would help. He reached for his flannel robe and slipped into his sheepskin slippers, then padded sleepily down the hall in search of relief.

I'm getting old. Old and soft and lazy.

What kind of example was he setting for his parish? He, the driving force behind St. Swithin's soup kitchen, now had a pot of his own. He patted his belly in disgust. Tomorrow he would walk a mile before mass, and no dessert. And it'd be a cold day in hell before he'd order green peppers on a pepperoni pizza again.

By the glow of the acrylic angel night-light—a present from his grandniece—Father Tom took the bottle of pink liquid from the medicine cabinet, then filled the dosing cup. He downed it the way he used to do his bourbon when he was a young man, tossing it to the back of his throat and swallowing hard.

He washed out the plastic cup and inverted it over the bottle, then returned it to its shelf. And then, because he was loath to lie right down again, he stood a moment at the window of his bathroom and stared out at the lighted Christmas tree on Town Hill. It gave him pleasure to see it—one of the perks, he liked to tell everyone, of having his living quarters within spitting distance of the hill. In summer there was the bandstand; in spring, the Easter-egg hunt. Everything nice about Keepsake happened right across the road from where he lived and served God. (The good Lord willing, he would live through this heartburn to serve Him still.)

Father Tom was about to return to his bedroom down the hall when something . . . something caught his eye that wasn't quite right. The priest had a keen eye for pattern and symmetry. If the candlesticks on the altar weren't exactly equidistant from one another, he'd rearrange them before he could even think of saying Mass. So he knew: something was out of whack.

He stared at the town tree. Yes, there it was, on the left side. Something long and shadowy and unlike anything else on the beribboned tree. How odd. He'd have to take a closer look in the morning. He began to head back to his bedroom, but then, because he was Father Tom and quietly obsessed with maintaining some sense of order in a disorderly universe, he detoured into the front hall and took out his overcoat from the closet there.

He slipped the coat over his robe, then stepped out of the rectory, catching his breath in the cold night air. His slippers dragged on the rock salt spread over the brick path to his residence; he began to walk on tiptoe, trying to minimize the damage to the deerskin soles. He stepped to the sidewalk . . . then to the curb . . . then to the middle of the empty road.

Salt-melted slush oozed through the seams of his slippers the minute he paused.

No matter. Father Tom was oblivious to the wet and the cold as he stared in shock at the effigy hanging by its neck on a length of rope tied to the Christmas tree. The effigy was the biggest ornament on it: a life-sized figure roughly shaped from a pair of stuffed pantyhose, a wig of blond hair, and a varsity jacket from the high school. The jacket bulged grotesquely at the stomach. Even Father Tom understood that the effigy was meant to depict a pregnant student at Keepsake High. A hanged, pregnant student at Keepsake High.

With a groan of dismay, the priest resisted an overwhelming impulse to cut down the figure and instead ran back to the rectory, where he had to look up the number of the chief of police before punching it in with a shaking hand.

God in heaven. God in heaven. Don't let this be so.

It was the most fervent prayer Father Tom had ever sent skyward, and the one most doomed to go unanswered.

Five

"*The straw in* the pantyhose came from the manger. That's what offended me most."

Returning from yet another trip to the hardware store, Quinn walked in on that bizarre remark, made by a priest he remembered vividly from the old days: Father Thomas Tomczek, one of Quinn's biggest fans and an ex-quarterback himself.

Mrs. Dewsbury had set a plate of defrosted Danish on the kitchen table and was shaking her head in distress as she poured coffee into a delicate china cup resting in a matching china saucer. Hostess and guest both saw Quinn at the same time; neither offered a welcoming smile.

Quinn, who'd been feeling pretty good about the lunch date looming on his horizon, automatically toned down his spirits to match their mood. He stuck out his hand to the priest and introduced himself as if they'd never met.

"Son, I may have got old, but I haven't gone senile—yet," the priest said with a wink at Mrs. Dewsbury. "How've you been?"

"Pretty good, Father," he said, which was the truth. He added, "Am I interrupting something?"

The burly, bald priest fixed his pale green gaze on Quinn. "Not at all. You're the reason I'm here."

Quinn didn't like the sound of that. He nodded and pulled up a chair.

"I was telling Mrs. Dewsbury that we had a bit of excitement on Town Hill,'' the priest began, taking up the dainty cup with a ham-sized grip. He sipped and gave Mrs. Dewsbury a thumbs-up with his other hand, then continued. ''Someone hung an effigy of Alison on the town's Christmas tree in the middle of the night. They used a basketball to suggest . . . well, a pregnancy. It was crudely done, but effective.''

Quinn bit off the curse before it passed his lips and confined himself to saying mildly, ''Shouldn't any effigy have been of me? I thought the figure was always of someone hated and despised.''

Father Tom smiled grimly and said, ''True. But this made the same point in a much more sickening way.''

''This makes me so *angry*,'' said Mrs. Dewsbury, banging the table with her teaspoon to show how much. ''It will ruin the holiday for sure.''

''Who knows about it?'' Quinn asked the priest.

''Probably everyone, by now. I called Chief Vickers— who told me it wasn't the first expression of someone's displeasure that you're back,'' the priest added in his laconic way.

''It probably won't be the last,'' Quinn conceded. Mrs. Dewsbury was right: The whole town would be demoralized by the vicious act. Oddly, Quinn felt both admiration and contempt for the brazen perpetrator.

But mostly contempt. ''It seems to me that whoever did it took a ridiculous risk,'' he told the priest.

Father Tom shrugged. ''Why? There's no real law against it. And say someone did catch him in the act—''

''He'd just be stating what a lot of people are thinking. That they'd like me out of their town.'' Quinn sucked in air and blew it out again in thoughtful silence.

The priest helped himself to a prune Danish. ''If you can believe it, they stole the straw for the effigy's stockings from the crêche we set up in front of the church. There was poor baby Jesus, lying in the hard wood manger with nothing to keep him warm. I like to cried when I saw that.''

That was the thing about Father Tom: Despite his formidable size, he could weep over a statue left in the cold. It was the reason why everyone loved him.

"I'll say one thing," the priest added. "Whoever did it had b—nerves of steel."

"Do you have any idea who could be doing these things, Quinn?" the widow asked, looking more tentative than he'd seen her before. "Any idea at all?"

Quinn said with a tight smile, "I don't want to brag, but I can think of a dozen people who'd be happy to heat up the tar, and another dozen who'd be thrilled to carry the feathers."

Despite his concern, the priest was amused enough to chuckle. Not Mrs. Dewsbury. "Quinn Leary, you're coming with me to my son's house for Christmas. You will celebrate the holiday with us—with people who like and respect you."

Quinn couldn't resist a smile. "They don't even know me."

"It doesn't matter." The widow gave Quinn a look of pure affection, then turned to the priest and said, "Father, this man is an angel from heaven. You have no idea. My son adores me—but my son is in finance; hammers and screwdrivers frighten him. Gerald wants to pay handymen to do the work, but he knows I won't accept that. With Quinn, it's different. He makes it easy for me to take advantage of him."

Touched by her declaration, Quinn nonetheless stuck to his guns. Though he would never admit it to the widow, he had no intention of leaving her beloved house unguarded and vulnerable while she was away.

Sensing an opportunity, Father Tom jumped in with an offer of his own. "You're welcome to join us at the church for Christmas dinner, Quinn. You can mash the potatoes, serve 'em, eat 'em, or all three; we don't stand on ceremony. Everyone with nowhere special to go is invited."

Quinn accepted at once. "I'll not only serve dessert, I'll bring dessert," he added. "How many pies you need?"

"Oh, that's not—six would be fine."

"Done," he said with a smile.

He had the perfect excuse to remain behind on Christmas.

Quinn replaced a worn-out faucet and corroded trap in the first-floor bath in plenty of time to shower, slap on some aftershave, and head out to his rendezvous. It would be his most provocative gesture so far: having an elegant lunch in town with one of its best-known citizens. Whoever hated—or feared—Quinn enough to hang an effigy on the town Christmas tree was bound to go apoplectic over that one. Quinn felt grimly satisfied that all was going according to plan.

More or less.

He kept coming back to Olivia. She hadn't been part of his original plan, which was to flush out whoever had the most to lose from seeing him return to Keepsake. Over the years, and especially during the last few weeks, he had thought about Olivia, naturally, but mostly it had been in terms of nostalgia: she'd been part and parcel of his youthful drive to excel.

But last night? Last night he'd been much more focused on her laugh and her eyes and her . . . well, not her IQ, in any case. And today as he ditched his rental in the town parking lot behind the bank, he didn't care if her last name was Bennett or Sinkelheinkenschtein. He simply wanted to be with her again.

He had it all worked out. They would have lunch at Entre Nous, an intimate bistro that had caught Quinn's eye. It was the kind of place you took a woman like Olivia Bennett. They'd linger over a bottle of wine, laugh about the spelling bees, and with any luck he'd line up another date—this time at night, by God.

Whistling a soft tune, he made his way down wet side-walks and slushy streets until he found her shop. The brick building once had been a single-truck fire station, so it had a funky kind of charm. With its slate roof pitching steeply toward the street and its big front window divided by dozens of small square panes, it looked like something out of a children's fairy tale. Quinn was especially glad to see that they'd kept the original door, carved with the initials K.F.D. in elegant Victorian script.

He pulled open the heavy green door, jangling some bells above it, and stamped his hiking shoes on a mat inside the threshold. There were a couple of customers in the shop, and a fresh young thing cutting material from a bolt of cloth, but . . . no Olivia. It rocked Quinn, the wave of disappointment he felt. Then he spotted her hurrying down a narrow open staircase that ran alongside one wall. She grinned and waved, and like a deep-keeled sailboat that's taken a knockdown, Quinn felt himself righting again. The whole thing couldn't have lasted more than five seconds. He found the intensity of it pretty damn scary.

In the bright sun that poured into Miracourt, Olivia looked night-and-day different than she had in the candlelight of a drawing room—not as overtly seductive, and yet no less appealing. Chalk it up to the fuzzy sweater and flowing skirt she wore, but somehow she seemed more . . . straight up-and-down. More normal, more wholesome, more approachable. Or maybe it was her eyes or the way she smiled. Whatever it was, she looked glad and it made him feel good.

"What do you think?" she asked, turning half way round.

"Very nice indeed," he answered under his breath, and then he realized she meant the shop.

The shop was nice, too. He didn't know much about fabric—zip, to be precise—but he knew enough about rich people's taste to know that the stuff around them appealed to it.

"What does the name mean?" he asked, just to have something to say.

"Miracourt? It's an old-style French bobbin lace—similar to *lille* lace." She batted her eyes and added, "I'm sure that makes it all much clearer to you."

He cocked his head and gave her a penetrating look. "Ohhh, yeah."

One thing Quinn did remember about her: She never lost her cool. And yet here she was, for the second time in twenty-four hours, with heightened color in those nicely shaped cheekbones of hers. Feeling suddenly confident about the prospects for that nighttime date, he murmured, "So—are we all set?"

"Let me get my coat," she said, and off they went.

To the drip-drip-drip of melting snow, they strolled past storefronts decked out for the season, with Olivia grading every window display they stopped to view. "Not enough vertical." "Needs a backdrop." "*Great* use of color."

Window shopping, that's what they were doing. Quinn was utterly charmed by the concept; he'd never done it before. He threw a five-dollar bill into a Salvation Army bucket and thought to himself, *I could get used to this.* He was especially pleased that Olivia was inclined to saunter. That wasn't the drive-ahead girl he remembered at all.

In a merry mood, she reached behind him and gave a little yank on his ponytail. "What's *this* thing all about?" she asked.

And then she slipped her arm through his.

She had Quinn on the ropes. He didn't know which of the hits to respond to first; all he knew was that he never saw them coming. He lied about the ponytail, making something up about a centennial celebration back in California, and as for the arm that was looped through his—he decided simply to savor the heat. So bemused by her was he that he hardly registered the occasional glare aimed his way.

They reached the turnoff for the bistro, but Olivia had other ideas. "That Entre Nous is such a pretentious little place," she said, which naturally made Quinn feel pretentious as well. "Let's grab a couple of deli sandwiches and go back to your car. I have a surprise for you that I think you'll really like."

His disappointment fell away, replaced by curiosity, and he agreed to the terms of her counteroffer. They picked up two monster pastramis on rye and a couple of cartons of milk, then doubled back to the parking lot. He wasn't crazy about driving Olivia around in a lowly pickup truck—hence the choice of a restaurant in town—but she didn't seem to mind.

"Is this the one that got the windshield bashed in?" she asked as she climbed into the passenger seat with their food.

Ah, Keepsake.

"The very same," he said, giving her a bland look. The expression on her face was guileless, but he decided that she was simply a damn good actress. "So. Where to?"

"The gardener's cottage," she answered, breaking into a sudden, broad grin. "I think you know the way."

At first he said nothing. Then, quietly, "You can't be serious."

"Of course I'm serious!" she said, laughing, and then she realized that he had no stomach for going there.

"Quinn, it doesn't look anything like when you and your father lived in it," she said in a more earnest tone. "It's a guest house now. My mother has done it *completely* over. Really, you won't make any associations at all."

Annoyed that she seemed to think he was an emotional wimp, Quinn put the truck in gear and said, "You misunderstand my reluctance. What I mean is, do your parents know you're doing this?"

Even worse. Now it sounded as if he were worried about coming over to play without her parents' permission. Frustrated, he said, "Liv, haven't you noticed? I'm public enemy number one in this town. I'm assuming that your parents are on the long list of people who'd like to see me leave, not the short list of people who're glad to renew an old acquaintance."

"I have no idea how my parents feel," she said, dismissing the subject. "They're not in the habit of saying."

He wasn't surprised; they never *were* in the habit of saying. "You heard about the effigy?"

"Yes, I did. I wasn't going to bring it up."

"Then why did you bring up the windshield?"

"I wanted you to know that I knew. It was less painful to do that with the windshield than with the effigy."

Jesus. Definitely *not* a California girl. Dizzy from breathing the rarefied air of her Yankee scruples, Quinn sighed and said, "All right. We will go to the gar—guest house."

The drive out of town was short; upper Main wasn't that far from the quaint shopping district. The street itself took a sharp turn past a rather grand driveway flanked by two massive granite gateposts—the entrance to the Bennett estate. For reasons he couldn't define, Quinn had so far avoided that end of Main. Hastings House, a block or so down the hill, was the nearest he'd gotten, and even there, Quinn had felt edgy.

Olivia punched in a code and the heavy iron gates that blocked the drive swung slowly open. Quinn drove through them, noting with satisfaction that the landscaping had suffered since his father's tenure. It wasn't so much that the big copper beech was gone—over that, he felt genuine sorrow—as that the grounds simply didn't look loved anymore. Not the way his father had loved them. Francis Leary had been devoted to his job as gardener for the Bennetts; he'd loved every hosta, shrub, and ivy leaf as if it were his own. Like a country doctor, he had felt the need always to be there, which is why he rarely went out on his one day off.

And then came the discovery of Alison in the quarry, and the first round of questions from the police, and the humiliating confrontation between his father and Olivia's father immediately afterward. Quinn could still remember every word of it. There had been no presumption of innocence, no strong expression of support by Owen Bennett; only a cold, seething declaration of shock and anger.

After that came the coup de grâce: Francis Leary was fired. Owen Bennett wanted him and Quinn out of the house within twenty-four hours. Quinn could still see his father standing in the small living room of the cottage with his head bowed, just . . . taking it. Quinn had been so frustrated by his father's meekness that he had charged at Bennett with every intention of knocking him down and killing him, but his father had called him back with a single syllable: "*Son.*"

Such memories consumed Quinn as he parked the truck in front of the cottage that had been built expressly for lucky gardeners to live in. Farther up the winding drive was the main house, blessedly obscured from Quinn's view by a massive bank of rhododendrons. With any luck he'd be able to get in and then out of the cottage without the Bennetts being any the wiser.

Maybe to Olivia the house looked different, but not to Quinn. True, the paint scheme had been changed from a drab gray to a pleasing slate blue with ivory trim and ruby-red shutters. But from the gingerbread gables to the diamond-paned casements, the Hansel and Gretel cottage looked like . . . well, like home. Home before the troubles came and forced them to leave it forever.

"You're very quiet, Quinn, and it's making me nervous," Olivia said as he stared at the impossibly charming house.

Quinn tried to lie himself out of his mood. "I thought I heard a mourning dove calling, and it's way too early in the year—that's all."

Olivia seemed relieved. "Come on in, then. You won't believe what I've got for you." She scrambled out of the front seat and by the time Quinn caught up with her, she had fished a key from her bag and was letting herself in.

She was right: The cottage didn't look or feel or even smell the way he remembered. The plain white walls were gone, and so was the vague but pervasive mustiness. All the dark trim had been painted out, and floral wallpaper made the place look both cozier and yet somehow larger than when he lived there. There was more furniture, much of it rattan and wicker. The lighting was warm and discreet, the refinished floors gleamed like spread honey.

And the smell was downright fragrant: Quinn could swear it was coming from the wallpaper. Whereas before the cottage had had a kind of bland, rental quality to it, now it could probably hold its own in the pages of *House Beautiful*.

Quinn gave the poofy, flouncy fabric over the windows a wary nod and asked, "Your work?"

Olivia laughed and said, "No, my tastes run to simpler treatments than that. But my mother's a big fan of Mario Buatta; she made all her decisions based on his gospel. Lucky for her she comes from a family that can snag deep discounts on fabric."

There were miles of it, florals and stripes and plaids everywhere Quinn looked. To him it was overwhelming, but what did he know? "That easy chair looks familiar," he ventured.

"Well, okay, that *is* from before," Olivia confessed. "It's been slipcovered."

"My dad used to like to read in it," Quinn said quietly. He tried to picture his father sitting in the chintz-covered chair with a book about Frederick Law Olmsted on his lap, but he came up empty. The room belonged to women now.

Quinn turned to Olivia, who was watching him with an intensity that surprised him. Again the color sprang to her cheeks. Again he took heart.

"You're right about this place," he mused. "I feel as if we're standing in some parallel universe. Everything's the same—and yet it's not the same at all." On a whim, he stroked her cheek with the back of his fingers and said softly, "Especially you."

She didn't pull away, but her lashes fluttered down in a gesture that struck him as both shy and seductive at the same time. What was it about her? She was driving him quietly crazy.

She said, "And yet you're just the same as I remember."

Quinn shook his head. "No. Not the same at all. Seventeen years ago, I wouldn't have dared done . . . this," he said, lowering his lips to hers in a kiss. It was lightly given, the kind of kiss a very cool quarterback might give a slightly geeky classmate—but it left Quinn's heart pounding wildly in his chest.

He pulled back, as if he'd got a mild shock, and repeated with wonder, "Not the same at all."

Somehow Olivia didn't seem nearly as self-conscious as he was feeling. Those long, thick eyelashes fluttered back up, revealing eyes that were dark, dancing, forthright. She didn't say a word, only lifted her arms around his neck and pulled him back for another kiss—this one hot, hard, and wet.

Sacked!

But not for long. Still reeling, Quinn felt a rush of testosterone and saw a sudden vision of the end zone in his mind's eye as he caught her in his arms. He was determined to score. His mouth claimed hers with a roughness that was not him, and yet when he felt her gasp, then yield to it, he knew that she was as willing as he was able. He backed her against the sofa and she crumpled into it, lying on her back, legs bent at the knees, her feet on the floor. He fell on top of her as if she were a loose ball that he didn't want anyone else, ever, to possess.

"Liv, Liv, where have you *been*?" he said in a muffled voice as he kissed her throat, nipping, tasting, then soothing with more kisses. He was wild to have her, then, there, anywhere. He gave no more thought to her parents up the hill than he once had to fans in the bleachers; he was focused solely, strictly, and very irrationally, on the soft, sweet-smelling body that was arching restlessly beneath his own. His hand ran up the outside of her leg, but outside of her legs was not where he wanted to be.

Good God, son, what are you doing?

Quinn's head shot up. His father's voice was too loud, too clear, to be ignored. He very nearly said "Dad?" but then he realized it was the house. Chintz or no chintz, the gardener's cottage was so bound up with Francis Leary that part of his soul was still drifting through its rooms.

"Oh, damn," Quinn murmured. He lifted his weight from Olivia and propped himself up on one elbow.

"What?" she said. Her eyes, huge, took on a tragic cast.

"Nothing," he murmured, gently raking her hair away from her face. She was so beautiful, so vulnerable just then.

So utterly seducible. "This is not the best place," he said at last.

"It's fine, sure it is," she argued, still breathless.

He could see streaks of green in her eyes. How had he never noticed before? "You're so beautiful."

She gave him a rueful smile. "I can tell."

"If we were anywhere else . . ." He traced her reddened upper lip with the tip of his finger. "I asked you before if you were married, but . . . are you seeing someone?"

"Seeing someone?" she said, a little blankly. "Do I act as if I am?"

He couldn't believe it. For Olivia Bennett not to be claimed, not to be taken—well, he just couldn't believe his good luck. "Plan to see me, then," he whispered to her. "Often."

She snapped back into focus. "You always were a cocky son of a bitch." The palms of her hands were flat against his chest. She used them to push him away, but not so violently that he had to consider it a rejection. It was more like a gesture of miffedness.

She sat up alongside him and raked her fingers through the curls of her hair—which remained exactly the same as before—and then she straightened her sweater and stood up. "I have absolutely no idea why that happened," she announced.

Oh, yes; definitely miffed. Quinn refrained from reminding her that she was the one who had trumped his kiss with one that had left them both senseless. He said with a shrug, "I assume you have to beat men off with a stick every day."

Her response to that was a wry smile, but he could see that her humor had improved. "C'mon," she told him, taking his hands in hers and pulling him up from the sofa. "I promised you a surprise."

"And, boy, I got one."

"Not that, dope." She began pulling him toward the bedroom, the bedroom that used to be his.

Flirt, imp, *femme fatale*—she was all of those and yet none of those. Completely bemused now, Quinn let her drag him along. One thought, and one thought only, possessed him: *If I can just channel all that energy of hers into sex, somewhere safe . . .*

"Surprise!" she cried, gesturing toward a three-board bench at the foot of the bed.

He stared at the bench in a state of amazement. There, polished to sunshine brightness, was arrayed every trophy and citation he'd ever won. His father had cherished them until their nighttime flight out of Keepsake, and Olivia apparently had appointed herself keeper of the flame. Quinn hadn't thought about the awards in seventeen years. Now, here they all were, lined up like golden ghosts to mock his thwarted ambitions:

STATE ALL-STAR FOOTBALL TEAM
CHAMPION DEBATE TEAM
STATE ALL-STAR FOOTBALL TEAM
FOR HIGHEST ACHIEVEMENT IN MATH
MVP, KEEPSAKE COUGARS
MVP, KEEPSAKE COUGARS
DISTINGUISHED ACHIEVEMENT,
LATIN STUDIES

"Pretty impressive," she said, beaming.

"Uh-huh."

Quinn picked up the biggest trophy, an ungainly, gaudy tribute to his prowess in Latin, of all things. He'd taken the course as an extracurricular activity because he thought it would help him in law school. But that was before he became disillusioned with the concept of due process.

He put the trophy back down and glanced at Olivia, who was standing alongside him with a proud look on her face, her arms folded across her chest in a self-satisfied way that he remembered well.

"So," he said, turning his back on the bench, the bed, and her. "Wanna have those sandwiches now?"

Six

"*Exhume her? Are* you insane?"

Quinn Leary sat in Chief Vickers's office with thighs apart, his fingertips making contact across the divide there. His broad shoulders hulked forward in a relaxed, almost insolent way as he contemplated the dumbfounded police chief. Quinn wasn't exactly enjoying the encounter, but he wasn't exactly in pain.

"It seems like the obvious solution. They say my father murdered Alison because she was carrying his baby and had threatened to tell the Bennetts. I say that's horseshit. A DNA test ought to settle the matter once and for all."

He reached into his pocket and came up with a plastic film canister that he tossed on the police chief's desk. "Here. A snip of my father's hair. I can tell you where to find more," he said dryly, "if you need to verify that it's his. The sooner we resolve this, the better. I plan to stay in Keepsake awhile, and—let's face it—you can't afford too many more episodes like those trashed trophies. Sooner or later, someone is going to get hurt."

Vickers barely glanced at the container. "Who told you about the trophy case? We're not letting that out."

Quinn shrugged. "It's a small town."

Someone had broken into Keepsake High and spray-painted all the football trophies in the trophy case. Worse, they'd smashed in all the team photos, many of them signed. Quinn had heard it from Mrs. Dewsbury, who had heard it from the janitor's sister—but Vickers didn't need to know that.

The chief rocked back in his chair. After a thoughtful pause, he said, "What do you really want, Quinn? Why are you here?"

Quinn nodded at the container sitting on the desk blotter. "I told you: to clear my father's name."

"What difference does it make? He's dead."

"It makes a difference," Quinn said, almost wearily. "You're a son. You're a father. How can you not get it?"

"Suppose we leave my family out of this."

The chief's son Kurt had been one of Quinn's teammates: a fullback with good potential but with a chronic need to walk on the wild side. Quinn had heard (again from Mrs. Dewsbury) that after he and his dad left Keepsake, Kurt Vickers had turned from alcohol to serious drugs—another casualty blamed on Quinn. The list kept getting longer.

Quinn said, "How do I make my request official?"

The chief snorted. "Not by bringing it here. Take it to the D.A. if you feel a burning need."

Quinn stood up and took the plastic container back. "Okay. That's what I'll do."

He was halfway out the door when Vickers said, "Francis Leary did it, Quinn. You just can't bring yourself to believe it, that's all. But the evidence is there. Alison confided to a friend that she thought your father was a hunk. He was seen staring at her just a little too keenly. The rope that hanged her came from his potting shed. Fibers from it were found in his truck. No one could corroborate his alibi for the time of death. And last of all, he ran. Innocent men don't run."

"I repeat: *horseshit*. That's not even decent circumstantial evidence, and you know it."

The two men locked gazes. Pete Vickers, lifelong townie, son of a policeman, father of a drug addict, the only active member of a police detail that would never live down the Keystone Kops reputation that Quinn's father had foisted on them—and Quinn himself, first stirring the pot, now lighting the fire beneath it.

Vickers spoke first. "Go to hell."

Quinn's eyebrows lifted in tacit acknowledgment that he might be headed that way. He sighed and said, "See you around, Chief," and walked past the dispatcher's desk and out to his truck.

"I'll never be able to eat pastrami again," Olivia told Eileen over drinks on Saturday. "It was unbearable, sitting on the front seat of his truck and trying to chew."

"And he didn't take his trophies, after all that?"

"No," said Olivia glumly. "I went back yesterday and boxed them all up again."

She was still traumatized by the disastrous date. What had happened? She'd spent the last day and a half trying to figure it out. This much she knew: She was deeply attracted to Quinn, and he had seemed just as interested in her.

"Almost as interested, anyway," she said. "There was incredible electricity. It started at Hastings House . . . the way he just *looked* at me!"

"The corset," Eileen said as she tore Boston lettuce into a salad bowl.

"That's what I thought, too, at the time. I mean, really, what was not to like? He'd have to have been married, buried, or holy not to react. But the next day—you know what I wear to work—he was just as interested, if not more. Eileen, I'm telling you, something clicked. I don't remember ever enjoying myself as much with a man. Or as briefly, dammit."

"I'm telling you, blame it on the corset."

"No; blame it on kismet." Olivia slid off the island stool in her sister-in-law's designer kitchen and ambled over to the Sub-Zero fridge.

"When we were strolling down Main," she said thoughtfully, "something changed in my life. I've never felt it before. It was like . . . what was it like? Like I was a lock, and someone was turning a key in me." She smiled a faraway smile as she poured more tonic over her gin. She could still feel his arm linked through hers, still see the dimple on the right side of his face when he grinned.

Oddly enough, she couldn't remember much about the episode on the sofa. That part she had pretty much blocked out. "Probably because it was Quinn who called a stop to it," she explained, "and not me."

"Men don't normally do stuff like that."

"Well! Consider where we were."

"True. Can you imagine the look on Rand's face if he'd walked in on you? Or your father?"

Olivia shuddered, then bumped the fridge closed with her rear end. "It could easily have happened. I never thought to lock the front door. Thank God one of us had some sense. But I really believe that Quinn had other reasons for backing off—his father, for one."

"They were that close? Here, do the carrots."

"Very close. Which is surprising, considering that—except for being good-looking—they were nothing alike." Olivia rifled through a drawer and came up with a peeler, then pulled a carrot from the plastic bag waiting on the marble-topped island. "Francis Leary was a very quiet, very timid man. He was always hanging back in the shadows, although I think he never missed a thing. Actually, he—"

She decided not to finish the thought, but Eileen knew her too well. "Problem?"

Olivia focused on her peeling. "I feel guilty admitting it, but . . . Mr. Leary used to make me uncomfortable. I suppose it's because I always feel hopelessly overbearing around shy people like him."

"Overbearing—you?" said Eileen, sprinkling raisins like fairy dust over the salad.

Olivia laughed, then threw a carrot peeling at her. "We can't all be the perfect balance of grace and restraint that you are."

Eileen lifted the peeling from the bib of her apron and dropped it on the others. "Which is why I refuse to get into a food fight with you, missy. I could never win."

They laughed together over the prospect of Eileen—Eileen!—hurling food in her immaculate, ultramodern kitchen, then wandered into a discussion of the pros and cons of marble versus granite counters before coming back, inevitably, to Quinn Leary and why he was in Keepsake.

"He's here because of his father, I'm sure of it," Olivia said. "I think he wants to vindicate him."

"And how would he do that?"

"I haven't a clue."

Eileen had heard about the effigy, of course. "I wonder how many shoes can fall before Quinn decides he's had enough and leaves."

"Don't say that! I . . . I don't want him to," Olivia admitted. "Not yet." She took out eight platters from the birch cabinet. "Where are we eating? Dining or kitchen?"

"Dining, I think; those Chinese-red walls are so appropriate this time of year. We'll dress the table with the white poinsettias. Tell me this: What would you do if Quinn did pull up stakes and leave?"

"Hey! Bite your tongue."

"Interesting." Eileen pulled down the oven door of her Viking range. "You know what?" she said, peering at the thermometer stuck in the leg of lamb. "You sound a little desperate."

"Desperate! *Me*?"

Eileen closed the door, stood up, and looked Olivia in the eye. "It's Saturday night and you're eating dinner with us. You do it often. Does that tell you something?"

"Hey! I've been *busy*. Two stores . . . who's got time for the singles—"

"Hi-dee-ho, ladies." It was Rand, entering the kitchen from the adjacent three-bay garage.

Olivia turned to her sister-in-law. "Not a word," she whispered with a fierce look.

It was an unnecessary warning. Insulted, Eileen pinched her arm lightly as she passed on the way to relieve Rand of his cashmere muffler and suede jacket.

Pecking his wife's cheek, Rand said, "Something smells good."

"Tarragon leg of lamb. Because I love you so madly."

He laughed at that and said, "You know you're the only dish for me."

"You're in a good mood," Olivia said on her way out to the dining room. She was relieved to see it; maybe he was finally done sulking over Quinn's return.

"Am I? Why so many plates?" he asked his twin sister as she passed under his nose.

"Mom and Dad."

"Oh, hell. *Why?*"

"You know why," said Eileen, sounding resigned. "To go over the plans, one more time, for the New Year's gala."

"Oh, great. And while you three women are trying to decide which napkins to use, I'll be stuck with Dad in the den. Just what I need. He's bound to grill me about the tax-break negotiations. Don't I get enough of him at the mill all week? Is it too much to ask to spend the weekend in peace? I need a drink," he said, heading for the wet bar.

"Oh, it won't be as bad as all that," said Eileen in her reassuring way. "You have lots of time before the council votes."

"How do you figure? Dad's on the phone with Mexico every day. I think he's as much as made up his mind to move the mill out of Keepsake. The more the council dithers up here, the more likely it is that Dad's going to make a commitment down there. Then what? I don't want to live in Mexico. Do you?"

Eileen smiled and said reassuringly, "He'd never do that."

But Eileen didn't know Owen Bennett, not the way his daughter and son did. Olivia and Rand exchanged one of their shorthand looks. Olivia said, "He wants to keep the mill up here tax-free. Keepsake doesn't feel it can afford to do that."

"Keepsake can't afford *not* to do that," Eileen pointed

out. "Owen's the biggest employer in town. He's the *only* employer in town."

"Let's not forget the superstores," Rand said with obvious irony as he poured scotch over his ice. "Every day more jobs are moving into the area—so the council keeps reminding me."

"Not jobs that can support a family," his wife retorted. "Your father pays twice the wage that they do."

"Which is, of course, the problem," Olivia said. "He needs to stay competitive or he'll go under. I can sympathize with him," she added grudgingly, even though she didn't approve of her father's hardball tactics.

"He's got to demand less from Keepsake," her brother said before slugging down a good part of his drink. "It's no picnic going out there and trying to make his case."

"Of course not," Olivia said. "You're the bad cop. Dad's the good cop. When he thinks the time is right, he'll cut his demand by half and end up a local hero."

"Which leaves me what? The local villain? Sorry," Rand said bitterly. "Been there. Done that."

It was an unmistakable allusion to the stupid, irrelevant, lost championship that seemed so much on everyone's minds again.

For one brilliant year it had all seemed to be coming together, and Keepsake had come down with a case of football fever the likes of which it had never known before or since. Everyone from the busboys at Jasper's to the nuns at St. Swithin's had joined forces and rallied around the Cougars.

But it all fell apart after Quinn ran away and Rand took over and dropped the ball—many times. The plain truth was, Rand had never been a very good quarterback, and after Quinn, he looked even worse. The season had ended up a disaster. There was no point in trying to deny the fact, so Olivia left the soothing to Eileen while she set the dining room table.

Part of her felt genuinely sorry for Rand. He'd never be able to crawl out from under the burden of the town's long memory, and it didn't help his mood lately that her father really did seem to be making Rand the heavy: variance requests, DEM warnings, OSHA inspections—all of was being dumped on the huge walnut desk in Rand's big office.

Poetic justice? Olivia wanted to think so. She had put herself through a year of graduate school in preparation for a job of real responsibility in the mill, and look what had happened: Rand, who coasted to a bachelor's degree from Yale with gentlemen's C's, was made vice president of mill operations while Olivia, who graduated magna cum laude with an MBA from Harvard, was offered nothing at all.

And why? Because her father was convinced that she was going to fall in love, get married, and start nesting, leaving him in the lurch. Olivia was offended, she was angry, and she let her father know it in a way that left the two of them estranged for almost a year.

Her decision to start up Miracourt right under her father's nose had been made mostly out of spite, although she'd ended up truly loving the shop and was planning to open another branch nearer the city. Recently she and her father were getting along well enough to start up the outlet venture together, but even there . . .

We'll never be close, not really. Not as long as he continues to believe the sun rises and sets on his number-one son.

Olivia sighed as she set out the silverware with scientific precision. She was prepared to work twice as hard as her brother to prove herself—but it would be nice if she could do it without getting an ulcer or giving up men.

Her thoughts rushed back to Quinn and were still lingering there when the doorbell rang: Her parents had arrived.

From upstairs she heard her niece shriek, "Grammy, Grampy!" and then the thunderous race down the steps between her and Zack for the front door.

Olivia popped her head around the corner to greet the arrivals, both of them hard-pressed to take off their coats because their grandchildren were hanging on like lemurs.

Kristin wanted hugs and kisses and Zack wanted his grandfather to play Nintendo.

"Not now, Zack!" said Owen Bennett, shooing him away.

Poor Zack was crushed; his grandfather never missed a chance to take him on in friendly, if fierce, competition.

Olivia glanced at her mother, whose hugs were being handed out with less than her usual abandon. She recognized the signs at once: Teresa Bennett was in tiptoe mode.

Uh-oh. Now what?

"Dad?" she said, giving him a quizzical look.

Behind him her mother shook her head in warning, then said to the children, "Well? Isn't anyone going to show me the latest Beanie Babies?"

Zack and Kristin, easily distracted, dragged her upstairs, leaving Olivia to face down her father's wrath.

"I just got off the phone with Pete Vickers," he growled.

"And?"

"For starters, someone's trashed the trophy case in the high school," he said, brushing past her into the kitchen.

Her father wasn't a big man, but wherever he was, he made the room smaller. Even Rand—taller, more hair, three decades younger—seemed diminished by his presence.

Unlike Rand, who was dressed in Paul Stuart elegance from head to tasseled toe, her father preferred more functional wear: polyester pants that kept a crease, a shirt that didn't look stonewashed after half a dozen launderings, and—his one indulgence—a wool sweater from Scotland that would probably last longer than Dolly and all of her clones combined, or he wouldn't have bought it in the first place.

A snappy dresser he was not. And yet no man that Olivia had ever known radiated more authority than Owen Randall Bennett.

Eileen took one look at her father-in-law, spun on her heel, and headed for the wet bar to fix him a drink.

Rand's face was so carefully devoid of expression that

even Olivia couldn't read it. "Did you say someone trashed the trophy case?" he ventured.

"That's exactly what I said. Goddammit, this has gone far enough! I paid for most of those trophies, one way or another. Uniforms, bus trips, the new bleachers—Keepsake wouldn't even *have* a sports program if it weren't for me. I'll have his ass in a sling for this!"

Olivia blinked. "Whose?"

"Leary's, goddammit! None of the vandalism would've happened if *he* hadn't shown up."

Rand was watching his father warily. Eileen was pretending to be in another county. That left Olivia, who was more than willing to carry the banner onto the field.

"That isn't fair, taking out someone's bigotry on Quinn!" she cried, rising up to her full five feet three inches. "I'm tired of—"

"Tired of *what*?" her father interrupted in a dangerous voice.

"Tired of having to repeat the obvious: Quinn didn't break any laws! He was free to stay or to leave back then, and he's free to stay or to—free to stay now. If he wants."

Her father's eyebrows twitched upward, another dangerous sign. "Since when are you his public defender?"

Since he had me flat on my back and I liked it, she thought about saying. But . . . maybe not just then.

"From all I've heard, the man has been been perfectly friendly to everyone he sees," she said. "Mrs. Dewsbury has told half the town that she worships the ground he walks on. He even makes a point of shopping locally for everything. Ask Mike at the hardware store."

Olivia was getting up a head of steam now, and she couldn't resist taking a potshot at her brother. "And another thing that you probably don't know about Quinn: *He* managed to pick himself up by his bootstraps. *He* owns his own business. *He*—"

"Business? He's a stonemason!"

"He's an artist. An architect in stone. You know how much those people make? And anyway, that's beside the point! The point is, he has integrity and ambition and he's the kind of man you'd appreciate if you weren't blinded by the same *stupid* prejudice as whatever idiot is behind these horrible events!''

''I don't care if he owns a fleet of ships and the stars to steer them by,'' her father said, cutting through the air with the back of his hand. ''I want Leary out of Keepsake!''

Olivia planted a fist on each hip. Her chin came up. ''Just like that; *you* want Leary out of Keepsake. Who're you, the Sultan of Brunei? Quinn can stay if he wants!''

Too far. She watched her father's face turn a ruddy shade of rage. ''Don't even *think* about crossing me on this,'' he said in a low and dangerous tone.

''Of course I will! You're being ridiculous. This is America. This is *New England*. People here have the freedom to—''

''He wants your cousin exhumed, goddammit!''

He might as well have slapped Olivia in the face. She blinked and shuddered from the blow of his words and then stared speechless as Eileen whispered a pained, ''Oh, no,'' and Rand looked stunned.

''You forced me to this, Olivia,'' her father said, obviously furious over his own indiscretion. ''I haven't said anything to your mother and I don't intend to, so—''

''Oh, he can't *do* that,'' said his wife from behind him. ''It's . . . it's . . . oh, it's *wrong*!''

Everyone turned. Teresa Bennett had come in from the hall and was standing there looking deeply scandalized. Her still-unlined face, so like Olivia's in its expressiveness, was ashen and filled with sympathy for Alison, a niece whom she had loved. Her dark eyes were glazed over with tears, her full lips crumpled with grief and horror.

It's like looking at a medieval painting of Mary mourning her son, Olivia thought, touched by the depth of emotion that she saw in her mother's face.

''It's not going to happen,'' Owen said gruffly.

''But what if it does? What if it *does*?''

Olivia's father scowled and said, ''This is why you

shouldn't have been told." Grudgingly, he went over to his wife and put his arm around her. "Come on. Into the den—where you can compose yourself."

Olivia watched in profound distress as her exasperated father shepherded her mother out of the kitchen.

Teresa Bennett was so unlike her husband that Olivia often wondered how they'd lasted thirty-six years together. Her mother was as soft as her father was hard, as emotional as he was rational, as yielding as he was domineering. It was her mother, never her father, that Olivia ran to when she needed hugs and comfort. If Olivia were ever to find herself in trouble, she could count on her father to find the best lawyer in the country to defend her—but it would be her mother who'd be standing on the other side of the bars with a toothbrush, clean pajamas, and Olivia's favorite pillow.

"Perfect," Rand muttered. He turned around and slammed the flat of his hand on the marble-topped island, sending his wife and his sister jumping back. "That son of a bitch! How *dare* he?"

"You heard Dad," Olivia said, wincing. "Nothing will come of it. And besides—"

"Besides, *what*? What can you possibly have to add to this hideous scenario?"

Olivia stared at the fine blond hairs on the back of Rand's manicured hand. In a bare whisper, she said, "What if Francis Leary *is* innocent? At least we would know that."

She raised her head and looked straight into her brother's piercingly blue eyes, startled, as always, that he could be her twin. Surely he was a changeling. Surely her real twin, dark-eyed like her, was being raised by mistake in a Scandinavian household somewhere in Minnesota.

"Listen to me," he said to her in a controlled fury. "Alison is dead. Whether Leary killed her or the milkman did it, Alison will still be dead. How can you think of putting her through the indignity . . . the desecration . . . on the slim chance that you can disprove a dead man's guilt? *She's* the victim here—not Leary. And it makes me sick to think that you can't seem to understand that.''

But you have an agenda, Olivia couldn't help thinking. _You want Quinn to suffer in any way he can. So how can I be convinced by your all-too-emotional argument?_

Olivia wanted so badly to say that out loud, but she was far too aware that if she hadn't shot off her mouth earlier, she wouldn't have provoked her father into telling them about Quinn's intentions. As it was, her mother was now in a state, her brother was aghast, her father was more outraged than ever, and worst of all—Alison.

''I'm sorry,'' Olivia said humbly, recoiling at the inevitable images induced by the thought of exhumation. To disinter a human being . . . it was something you read about in Gothic novels or in newspaper accounts of mass graves; it wasn't something that happened to a member of your family.

Olivia remembered her cousin—gorgeous, dreamy, naive, and yet so obviously secretive and troubled—and tried to fix a positive image in her mind to blot out thoughts of her grave. Her memory obliged with a snapshot of Alison smiling and happy at the animal shelter. Alison loved animals, and before her father made her quit her job as a volunteer at the Keepsake Kat Shelter, she had lived for Tuesdays and Thursdays when she could groom the animals, clean their cages, and change their water.

A smiling, gentle Alison coaxing an abused, hand-shy cat out of its cage—that was what Olivia wanted to remember.

She kept the mental photo propped up against her wineglass all through dinner, which ended up being a grim affair. The adults said little and the children, picking up on it, were almost scarily well behaved. There was no talk at all of the New Year's gala. Olivia's mother kept her red-rimmed eyes aimed at her plate and every now and then let out a sigh. Much to Rand's chagrin, the sporadic discussion that did take place was all about Mexico.

Olivia's parents left directly after dinner, but Olivia couldn't make herself go. Home was alone. Home was dark.

Home was cold. In contrast, the children seemed to explode with pent-up energy the minute their subdued grandparents walked out the door. Hoping somehow to inhale their high spirits, Olivia volunteered to help Kristin with her bath and then to bed.

The bath was a noisy and splashy affair; both aunt and niece ended up getting scolded for making a mess. After that, Olivia kicked off her shoes and sat on top of the pink-quilted bedcovers with Kristin—all clean-smelling and damp and so astonishingly innocent—nestled under her arm. They read together from *The Book of Dinosaurs* while Olivia absently stroked the child's damp hair, until finally, reluctantly, Olivia said, "Time to go to sleep now."

She hugged her niece—clung to her, really—and said, "I just love you so much I could smoosh you."

Kristin's squeaky giggle was light and rippling and so enchanting that it brought tears to Olivia's eyes.

What happens? What happens between her age and ours?

She buttoned a missed button in Kristin's Madeline pajamas and pulled the cover up to her niece's chin. Then she stole one last kiss, one last hug, to last her through the dark, cold night. On a whim, she reached for the Cabbage Patch doll that sat in a child-sized rocking chair and said, "How about if we let her sleep with you tonight?"

"No, I don't like dolls," Kristin said succinctly.

"Oh! I didn't know that." This was new. "Well . . . your mom can save them until you have babies of your own someday who can play with them."

There was no answer. Olivia turned off the bedroom light and was about to close the door when she heard Kristin say, "No babies."

"No babies?"

The child's voice was very firm. "Babies are messy. Too much work. You hafta change their diapers . . . and they're always crying . . . and pooping some more . . . and you can't even hear the TV sometimes. I want to be like you. No babies. I want to be a doctor. I asked my mom how can I not have babies, but she won't tell me.''

Oh boy.

"Well, you won't have to worry about that for a long, long time yet," Olivia said, ducking the hint that had come sailing her way. "You just go to sleep now. Sweet dreams, Kristin. I love you!" she sang out softly.

"I love you, too, Auntie Liv."

Olivia closed the door gently and hightailed it out of the children's wing. No, no, no. Uh-uh. Eileen could handle that one. Wow. Five years old, and she wanted to know about birth control.

I want to be like you. No babies.

Somehow, that stung. Olivia had to wonder whether she gave off such strong vibrations. True, she was obsessed with her business, but that didn't mean she didn't *ever* want children. Necessarily.

Did she? When she came right down to it—did she?

Her mother certainly didn't think so. They'd argued many, many times about the just awful implications of Olivia remaining an old maid. The best furniture would go to the sibling who was married with children, not to the one who lived alone in a townhouse. The folder bulging with recipe clippings would go—naturally—to the daughter-in-law who cooked, not to the daughter who didn't. And as for the estate house at the top of upper Main—that house was meant to stay in the family, which meant that there had to be an actual family in order to stay there. So far, Olivia was a little light on that front.

Because she was nowhere near ready. It would be absurd—immoral—to have children just because her mother's clock was ticking, even *assuming* that Olivia had a sperm donor lined up for herself. Which she did not.

Blame it on the Cabbage Patch doll. Olivia drove home in a mood as dark and brooding as the starless sky that hung overhead.

Seven

On Christmas Eve, Olivia closed Miracourt at noon, gave her employees at Run of the Mill the rest of the day off, and drove her trunkload of trophies, packed as carefully as Dresden china, over to Mrs. Dewsbury's house.

How ironic, she thought. Keepsake's keepsakes were all but ruined, while Quinn's looked good as new. Well, Quinn could do whatever he wanted with his trophies—use them for target practice or eat Cheerios out of them; it made no difference to her. As long as they were out of the cottage and out of her life.

She'd saved those keepsakes for seventeen years. He could have been more grateful. He could have been more pleased. He could have been a lot of things, but mostly he could have *called.* Olivia had just spent five of the most miserable days of her life waiting for the phone to ring.

At first she thought, he doesn't want to seem eager. Then she thought he was visiting his uncle in Old Saybrook. After that she began grasping at straws: He has laryngitis; he's forgotten my name; he's in a coma. But she spotted him, alive and well, driving his rental truck through town that very morning, and that's what had prompted her to close the stores early and load the trunk of her car.

The obvious reason that he might be avoiding her wasn't a reason at all. Olivia had learned from her father that the district attorney, a man indebted to her father for his re-election, had immediately denied Quinn's request to have

Alison's body exhumed, making it a non-issue. Everyone in the family was relieved, especially Olivia. It was *Christmas*, for pity's sake. Did Quinn have no sense of the season at all? He and his father had lived under a cloud for seventeen years. Was it really necessary to go off on a rip right now?

She was wasting her time on him. He wasn't worth defending, and he was an ingrate besides. The hell with him. He was making a shambles of her good will toward men.

Forty-eight, forty-six, forty-four—forty-two Elm. Yes, there it was, a big white house, great bones, needed paint. It looked very much like the home of a pensioned and widowed schoolteacher. Olivia hadn't been down Elm in years; she was surprised to see how tired Mrs. Dewsbury's old house was looking, but she was glad to see an evergreen wreath with a big red bow hanging on the black panelled door. Besides giving the house a much-needed shot of color, it told the world that Mrs. Dewsbury hadn't abandoned *her* Christmas spirit.

Olivia pulled into the drive, genuinely disappointed that Quinn's truck wasn't there. She would have enjoyed seeing the look on his face when she dumped the box in his arms. Unwilling to leave the trophies at risk on the wraparound veranda, she decided to go around to the back and leave them there instead. With an effort, she slid the heavy box out of the back of her minivan and lugged it up the half dozen steps to the small back porch.

She dropped the box with a thud next to the door, then in an attack of conscience, peeled off the green bow that she had mockingly stuck to the cardboard and stuffed it in her coat pocket. Just because Quinn Leary possessed no apparent Christmas spirit, it didn't mean that *she* had to go and get snotty about the season. She was halfway down the steps when she realized that music was coming from inside the house. Nuts. Mrs. Dewsbury must be at home. Olivia couldn't very well skulk away like a Keepsake vandal, so she came back up the steps and knocked dutifully at the back door.

"Door's open!"

He *was* home.

Nuts!

Annoyed that he didn't have the courtesy to come to the door for her, Olivia opened it herself and peeked around it into the kitchen. She was prepared for many things—for embarrassed glances, awkward hellos, muttered excuses— but she wasn't prepared for the sight of Quinn Leary up to his elbows in flour, rolling out pie dough on a pastry board.

"Uhhh . . . hi," she said, wracking her brain for an excuse to be there.

"Hey," he said in greeting. He looked surprised, but hardly sheepish.

Quinn Leary was a stonemason. The realization came home to Olivia, big time, when she took in the heavily muscled arms that were working the rolling pin. Quinn's chest, clad in a navy T-shirt dusted with flour, was definitely the chest of a stonemason. His hands, thickly veined and doughy-fingered, were the hands of a stonemason. Even his waist, tucked all around inside his jeans with a big baker's towel, had the taut circumference of a man who didn't sit around on his duff all day.

So why did he give off the irresistibly warm vibrations of a Julia Child?

"Is . . . is Mrs. Dewsbury around?" Olivia asked stupidly, trying not to gawk.

"Nope. She's gone off to New Hampshire with her son for the holidays. You just missed her."

"Are you—?" Olivia fluttered her wrist at the row of empty pie shells waiting on the counter. "Subcontracting, or something?"

Quinn laughed out loud at that, and all of Olivia's hostile resolve slid away on the sound of his mirth. She was ready to fill the pies, sell the pies, buy the pies, eat the pies— whatever it took to hang around him for just a little bit longer.

"I'm baking these for Father Tom's Christmas dinner at the church tomorrow," he explained, still chuckling at the notion of being mistaken for a professional pie man.

God, his teeth were white. It was so nice to just stare at them. "Can I sit down?" she asked. *To stare at your teeth and everything else?*

"I'm sorry—sure, pull up a chair. My hands—"

"Are all sticky." Olivia wondered what it would be like to lick the raw dough off them and immediately blushed down to her ankles. She cleared her throat and said, "You seem pretty good at that."

"Yeah," said Quinn, rolling out a fat edge to match the rest of the circle. "My dad couldn't stand seeing excess harvest go to waste. He was always bringing produce home from the job and doing something or other with it; I guess I learned by osmosis. I also put up a pretty mean jar of preserves," he added with a grin.

He looked unbearably attractive to her. "A stonemason who bakes," she said a little giddily. "You must have to beat off women with a stick."

Aaackk! Wrap your arms around his knees and cling to him, why don't you?

Mercifully, he pretended not to have heard the fawning remark. "So how come you're looking for Mrs. D.?" he asked as he somehow slipped the circle of dough from the floured board to the pie pan, where it lay draped over the sides like ivory Ultrasuede.

"Who?" she asked.

"Mrs. Dewsbury?"

"What about her?"

He brought those terrifically sexy brows down in a squint of puzzlement and simply waited. Clearly he thought that Olivia had purposely removed one of her oars from the water so that she could row her boat in circles for a while.

"Because—your car was gone!" she blurted out, which made absolutely no sense at all, even to her.

"Yep," he said, expertly fitting the dough to the pan. "I gave up the rental and bought myself a new truck. It'll be delivered this afternoon, with any luck."

That made no sense, either, unless . . .

"It sounds as if you plan to stay awhile."

"Yep." He took up a knife and began cutting away the extra crust.

"And that's because—?"

"Yep."

Shit. Because of what?

He gave her an annihilating look that was clearly intended to put her out of her misery. "Because of you," he said matter-of-factly as he crimped the edge with his thumb and forefingers. "Among other reasons."

Because of you.

Among other reasons.

She kicked away the "other" and clung to the "you." "Then why haven't you called?" she demanded, regaining her footing on the slippery slope of their cryptic conversation.

The heartstopping smile turned serious. "I assume you know how I've been spending my spare time?"

She looked away and said, "Yes. Up to no good."

"Mm. I figured you'd hear, sooner or later." He carried the pie shell over to the side counter and laid it next to four other ones waiting for fillings, then came back to the table and scooped another ball of dough from the huge, very old cracked bowl he was using.

"Did you have to go that route, Quinn?" she almost begged to know.

For an answer, he said, "I guess it won't surprise you to hear that I ran smack into a brick wall at the D.A.'s office."

"Well, what did you expect?" she asked, disappointed that he was disappointed. "The courts don't go to lengths like that to prove someone is innocent, not if he's no longer living. Not if he's not in jail. Why *should* the district attorney do anything?"

"How about because it's the right thing to do?" Quinn suggested, sprinkling flour on the pastry board and slamming the ball of dough just a little too hard onto it.

Olivia didn't know what to say to that, especially since part of her agreed with him. But she wanted him to understand all sides of the scenario, so she said, "The thought of

. . . of doing something like that to Alison hit my parents very hard, Quinn. I can only imagine how my aunt and uncle felt if they heard. I know it's just a scientific procedure—"

"That's all it is," Quinn said flatly.

"—but this is *Alison*," Olivia argued softly. "Someone real. Someone we all knew. The same Alison that you helped out in geometry. The same Alison you played badminton with during our family picnic that time."

"That *one* time."

"But still."

"Obviously I don't see this the way you do, Liv."

She watched in disheartened silence as he worked quickly, almost impatiently, to form the last pie shell. In his haste he tore the circle of dough as he transferred it from the board to the pan. He let out a sound, the barest hint, of exasperation and started over. The second crust went smoothly; she could see that he was focused on the task. It was the Quinn she remembered—cool, deliberate, unflappable. A star at everything he did, even pie crusts.

He broke the awkward silence by saying, "How is it that you don't know how your own aunt and uncle feel?"

"Our families aren't on speaking terms anymore," she said forthrightly. "They were strained even before Alison's death. You didn't know that? I guess we were better at keeping up appearances then. You have to remember, Ricki Lake hadn't been invented yet and people still had a sense of decorum. It was a different age."

"Oh, to have it back again," Quinn said in a wry, musing voice.

"In any case, the rift is an open secret nowadays—and really, what *is* the big deal? Every family has people in it who don't talk to one another," she said, carefully sweeping all the loose flour into a pile with the edge of her hand.

"You don't sound very resigned to it," he said, which she thought was perceptive. He took a pot of filling—pumpkin, by the look of it—from the stove to the counter and began glopping it into the first pie shell.

"To be honest, I don't even know why they're not speak-

ing," Olivia admitted with a sigh. "My parents have always
refused to tell me. It's about money, I'm sure. My father's
brother went through his inheritance in no time; right there
is a cardinal sin."

"Doesn't sound like much of a reason to me," Quinn
said, glancing at her between fillings.

She shrugged, uncomfortable with the notion of talking
about other people's spending habits. She'd been brought
up never to discuss either money or sex, and she was feeling
a vague but very definite unease talking about her aunt and
uncle. Especially her uncle.

"I do see my aunt in church now and then," Olivia said in
her own defense. "I try to get a conversation going, but . . .
she never has much to say."

"You go to church?" Quinn asked her.

"Once in a while. Why? Do I strike you as the heathen
type?"

He smiled. "Maybe a little."

Heathen apparently meant "nymphomaniac" in his
mind. It was the only possible explanation for the look he
was giving her.

Dropping her gaze from his, Olivia splayed her hands
against the edge of the table and self-consciously studied
her neatly trimmed nails. Had she ever had flour under
them? She was fairly sure not. She felt a sudden, very bizarre surge of regret. Flour and church and kids—she didn't
have time for any of them. What a disaster she was as a
woman so far. Her life had been all about the store, the store,
the store. She was like her father, with his obsession with
the mill, the mill, the mill.

Her head shot up. It was true! She was *exactly* like her
father: driven, controlling, and inflexible. It was the most
depressing thought she'd had in a long time.

She stared glumly at Quinn, as at ease in the kitchen as
he was on a gridiron, and wondered how *he* had managed
to turn out so well. "You're amazing," she said, watching
as he slid the three pumpkin pies into Mrs. Dewsbury's
oven. "I wish I had your . . . your range of interests."

Quinn said dryly, "Oh, yeah—I'm a regular Renaissance man." He set the timer and said, "Three down, three to go."

"More pumpkin?"

"Two apples and a mince."

Now that he said so, she did smell other wonderful aromas wafting from the stove. It shocked her, how oblivious she was to everything but his presence.

She made herself look at something besides him. What she saw was wainscoting nubby from a dozen coats of paint and cupboards that couldn't be more plain. A fridge that was old, a stove that was older. Dotted sheer curtains yellowed with age. A countertop buried under clunky mug racks and jugs jammed with utensils that Mrs. Dewsbury couldn't possibly need, gifts from grandkids, perhaps. A kitchen, in short, that was worn and mussy—a little like Mrs. Dewsbury—but a room that resonated with lifetimes of living. It made Olivia feel lonely somehow.

"Is there anything I can do?" she offered. "Peel apples or anything—?"

Very patiently, he said, "They're peeled. They're cooked. They're ready to go."

"Oh! Of course. *That's* what smells so good," she said, completely rattled by now. She had the feeling that he wanted to say something, but that he was holding back out of simple politeness.

Let me finish the damn pies. That's what she decided he wanted to say. Well trained, Olivia stood up; she was determined to exit before she was asked.

"I should be going," she said, pushing her chair in and undraping her coat from the back of it. "It's Christmas Eve and I have a million things to do."

"Yeah, me, too," he muttered, taking a bowl from the fridge.

He didn't sound very happy with her. Was it because she had turned away from the burning look he'd given her? *Had* he given her a burning look? Who knew? When she was around him, her instincts bounced around like bullets in a spaghetti western.

She had her hand on the doorknob and was about to wish him a merry Christmas, but instead she turned and blurted out, "What do you plan to do?"

"After the pies?"

"I mean, now that the D.A. has refused your request to reopen the investigation."

He thumped another wad of dough on the board and said, "I guess I'll have to reopen it on my own."

"Oh, Quinn—is that a good idea? You run the risk of alienating everyone in town."

"Including your parents, of course," he said, giving her a level look.

"Obviously. But that's not why I wish you wouldn't pursue this. The reason is—" She bit her lip, unwilling to trust those haphazard instincts of hers. "It's because . . ."

He was waiting for her answer now. His green eyes were alight with curiosity: What dumb thing was she about to say *this* time?

It made Olivia veer away from the truth—that she thought they really might be able to have something together, if only he treaded gingerly and let people get to know him better.

But there was another truth, and it was nearly as compelling to her as the one she was afraid to say out loud. She looked him straight in the eye and said, "There's something unseemly about hurting innocent people to satisfy your own selfish needs."

That got his attention. He wiped his hands on the dish towel that was jammed in his jeans, then tossed it on the table and walked over to her. Without the towel tucked in his waist, he didn't look so warm and friendly anymore. He looked big and strong and way too threatening.

She winced, afraid that he was going to boot her out of his kitchen. But that, apparently, was not on his mind as he caught her upper arm and brought his face within Tic Tac distance of hers.

"Listen to me, Miss Bennett. There was nothing *seemly* about having to skulk off with my father in the middle of the night. There was nothing *seemly* about changing over to my middle name and putting up with an itchy beard to hide my face. There was nothing *seemly* about running like a bat out of hell from a situation when my father could have—should have—been honored as a hero. There was nothing—"

"What do you mean, 'hero'?"

"Just what I said. It's ironic that he's being blamed for taking a life when the opposite is—aw, hell! Never mind."

He let go of her with something like distaste, which was more shocking to Olivia than his diatribe. She blinked and, after an eternity, remembered to exhale. "I guess you've made your intentions pretty clear," she said in lofty tones. "You're going to press your case for an exhumation."

"Bingo."

"Fine." Her lip began to tremble; she refused to let it. "Then let me wish you a merry Christmas and be on my way."

He gave her a look of cool contempt. There was nothing, absolutely nothing, in it that reminded her of Julia Child.

She turned and pulled the door open so quickly that it bumped her knee. *He's obsessed,* she told herself. *I'm out of here.*

On the porch she tripped over the cardboard box filled with his trophies, which she never did get around to telling him she'd brought. She had started down the steps in a flight to her minivan when she stopped, reached into the pocket of her coat, and pulled out the green bow that she'd stuffed there earlier. She crushed the bow in her hand, then tossed it at the brass football sticking out of the box.

"Merry Christmas, my ass," she muttered, and hurried back to her car.

Eight

Two apples and a mince: burnt to a crisp.

Quinn had checked out Mrs. Dewsbury's backup electric stove in the basement before he used it, and the burners worked fine. But it turned out that the oven was another story. Half an hour after he put the pies in, the piercing shrieks of two new smoke alarms brought him hightailing back from the storage shed where he'd been in the process of installing a motion-detecting spotlight to light up the yard.

By the time he aired out the smoke-filled house, found a supermarket still open, and re-peeled, re-cooked, and re-baked replacements for the three casualties, it was marching up on midnight. Lucky for him that his new Dodge Ram had been delivered as promised earlier in the day; it made his mood a lot less foul.

There weren't many relationships in life more intense than that between a man and a brand-new truck, so Quinn searched for and found an excuse to take his sassy Ram out for another spin: to deliver the pies to Father Tom before Midnight Mass. It wasn't the most logical time to drop them off, but what the hell. It was Christmas Eve, and Quinn had just given himself the only present he was going to get.

He loaded the pies into the sparkling clean tool bins of his shiny blue pickup and then all the way to St. Swithin's had to fight an impulse to drive like a wild and stupid teenager. He liked owning his own vehicle outright. Always had, always would. Leasing left him cold, and renting had caused him physical agony. Yup. Buying a truck on the wrong coast of America was the only reasonable thing to do.

Ah, well. At least he hadn't ordered the plow attachment. Yet.

Quinn intercepted Father Tom as he was about to enter the sacristy to don his vestments for the high Mass. The priest's greeting was distracted: The organist hadn't shown, and he should've been warming up the audience by then.

"I don't really see the parishioners muddling through the hymns _a cappella_, he said wryly to Quinn. "We could use someone to give us the pitch. I don't suppose that you—?"

Quinn crisscrossed his hands in front of him as if poor Father Tom were Count Dracula in a cassock. "Not me, Father," he said in something like terror. "I don't have any musical talent at all."

"Then it's the only talent you don't have," the priest said generously. "Okay . . . you may as well take the pies directly down to the hall. See that exit sign? Take the back steps next to it. You got Saran Wrap?"

"I brought a roll, just in case."

"Good man," said Father Tom, slapping him on the back. They broke up their huddle and the priest went off to nourish men's souls while Quinn made arrangements for their stomachs.

The basement was set up not with the usual long tables but with round tables that seated eight, giving the hall the cozy air of a family restaurant. Red checkered tablecloths and centerpieces of holly and winterberry were a nice touch. The ladies' auxiliary had done a great job. In no way, shape, or form did it look like a soup kitchen.

And really, why should it? People down on their luck or with no place to go should be able to spend Christmas in good company like anyone else. Better, actually: At least no one would be feuding in the halls of St. Swithin's.

Quinn saw the folding buffet table that the priest had told him would be for desserts; it was lined up against the far wall, with cups and saucers arranged on it, along with two stacks of dessert plates way higher than Quinn had pieces of pie for. He hoped that Father Tom wasn't kidding about the brownies and the pressed cookies.

He was impressed to see that they were using real cloth napkins, rolled around what must have been silverware and laid out alongside the plates.

Or not. At first puzzled and then with a quickening sense of dread, Quinn approached the table. What looked from across the hall like large rolled napkins were in reality . . . bleached bones, lined up as neatly as any hostess could wish.

The sight of them in the innocent setting was like being kicked in the stomach, and it left Quinn much more breathless than the smashed-in windshield had done. He dumped the two pies he was holding onto another table and returned to the macabre display. *Bones.* Of what, for God's sake?

A dog, most likely. Someone had dug up the family pet, cleaned off the bones, and laid them here. It was a reasonable presumption, and it left Quinn reeling. Disinterment, that's what this was about. Someone was making a statement about Quinn's latest foray down the halls of justice. And if Quinn hadn't stumbled into the basement hall at that unlikely hour, some white-haired volunteers with kind intentions and weak hearts would have had the shock of their lives when they showed up the next day to help serve. News of the prank would have traveled at warp speed, dinner would have been a disaster, and it would have been Quinn's fault and no one else's.

Damn it to hell!

He worked quickly, clearing the table of everything but the bones and then shrouding them in the cloth that they were laid out on. Quinn's sense of liturgy, never very precise, was turned upside down by the grisly prank. This was the season of birth, not of bones. He stuffed the hapless pet's remains, still in the tablecloth, into a black garbage bag and looped the open end of the bag into a tight knot, and then another.

I'll have to stay here the whole blessed night.

It was going to be pointless to stand guard over the hall—no one would be back, he was sure—but if he went home he knew he wouldn't sleep a wink. He looked around for a nice soft La-Z-Boy, but all he saw were metal folding chairs. So, okay, it was going to be not only pointless but painful to spend the night there.

Quinn slung the garbage bag over his shoulder, feeling more like the Grim Reaper than Santa Claus, and carried it out to his truck. After that, he decided to take a quick walk around the white-steepled church, not so much for the cold night air, which he welcomed, but to see if anyone strange and twisted was lurking in the shrubbery.

Who? That was the question. Obviously it had to be someone who knew that Quinn had gone to the D.A. with a request for exhumation.

Hold it. Back up, Doughboy. It could have been somebody who knew from Chief Vickers that Quinn was *planning* to go to the D.A.

Well, that really narrowed it down.

Whoever did it must also have known that Quinn had volunteered to help out with the church dinner. Could the villain of this disgusting little pageant conceivably be a member of the parish? A deacon, a lady on the auxiliary committee, the freaking organist, even?

Where was the organist, anyway?

Quinn peered behind the flat-topped yews and rummaged through the holly bushes, expecting with every poke to see someone's evil, beady eyes staring back at him. Before long, he realized where the organist was when he was yanked from his spooky reverie by the sonorous notes of the church's old Wurlitzer rising up and through the stained glass windows: "Do You Hear What I Hear?"

The Christmas carol was too appropriate, somehow; it gave him chills. What was he listening for? What was he looking for?

Was someone reminded of his own lost promise in life by Quinn's presence in Keepsake and taking it out on Quinn? Or was someone afraid that Quinn was going to prove Francis Leary's innocence—and in the bargain, prove that person's guilt?

Quinn continued his circuit around the church but paused at the life-sized crêche that was set up facing the busier of the two streets that the church abutted. Although Quinn hadn't practiced his faith for many years, he felt obliged to make sure that no one had stolen the straw from baby Jesus' crib again or committed some other wickedness there.

Things looked okay. Baby Jesus looked snug and warm, and nobody had broken off the nose of one of the three kings or moved the donkey into some scandalous position.

Hey guys. You see anyone suspicious go skulking past?

The swarthy kings were silent, but Quinn had the sense that they knew more than they were letting on. He turned his gaze to the illogically blue eyes of the infant lying in the manger and thought, *I know that* you *know. But you're not gonna say, are you?*

Quinn sighed. He was hoping for an offhand miracle, just like in the movies. He swept his gaze from the kings to Mary to Joseph to Jesus again, but no one moved, no one spoke. The only one puffing white breath into the ice-cold night was Quinn. He was warm, he was alive, and he was utterly alone in the universe.

It was his first Christmas without his father, and it was yet another Christmas without a wife and a family of his own. His isolation threw him into a sudden and profound depression.

"It Came Upon a Midnight Clear . . ."

Again Quinn was struck by the irony of the organist's choice of hymns. He looked up at the sky, awash with stars twinkling cold and remote. It was midnight, and it was clear, but what was it that had come? Who? That's what he wanted so desperately to know.

After a last sweeping glance around the crêche, Quinn decided to head back to the basement hall, to spend the night in dreary vigilance. As he passed the double arched doors of the historic New England church, he heard the strains of a carol that was his father's favorite: "Angels We Have Heard on High."

Quinn stopped where he was at the foot of the steps. He could hear his father asking good-naturedly, "Why are all the best songs always about angels?" He could hear his father's voice, a surprisingly rich baritone, singing the refrain:

"Glo-oh-oh-oh-oh-oh-oh-oh-oh-oh-oh-oh-oh-oh-oh-oh-ria, in excelsis Deo . . ."

And he found himself ascending the steps of St. Swithin's and quietly opening the heavy church door, because inside was where he was sure he'd find his father.

"Son, what does that mean, anyway—*'in excelsis Deo'*?" his father had once asked.

Quinn had answered, "It means 'in exultation of God,' Dad," and had turned the page of his novel, secretly annoyed that his father liked to sing along with his Christmas cassettes. What if someone were passing by the gardener's cottage and happened to hear him?

Quinn paused at the back of the crowded church and then slipped into the last pew. Except for his father's funeral, it was the first time he'd been in a church since he ran from Keepsake. His father used to mourn Quinn's obstinate refusal to go, but what could the man do about it? By then Quinn was eighteen—old enough to drink, vote, and be bitter.

Quinn sighed heavily. He wouldn't stay. What was the point, really? He didn't believe. He would just finish out the one carol . . .

At the main altar, Father Tom looked somehow too big, too real, too ordinary to be conducting Mass. A linebacker, yes. But a priest? Quinn smiled. Father Tom was an excellent priest, but he would've made a damn good father, too. Which, come to think of it, he was. And Quinn's father . . . Francis Leary . . . had been a wonderful father. And Quinn, who was so much less worthy than either of the men, was not a father in any sense of the word.

He felt a lump rise and catch in his throat. His thoughts

became blurred in a glaze of tears as he realized somewhere deep in his soul that Francis Leary—the only father he would ever have—was dead and gone forever.

And he was innocent of the crime. He wasn't a taker of lives, but a saver of them. And somehow Quinn had to let everyone know, and then he himself would no longer be an outcast. He felt his spirit aching to join those of the congregation's, and in the middle of that longing, he felt his soul reach just a little bit higher, a little bit closer to his dad.

It was an amazing moment of transcendence for him, and as the carol ended, followed almost at once by another, more poignant one—"O Little Town of Bethlehem"—he was even more amazed to find his thoughts drifting serenely from his father to Olivia Bennett.

Liv! The brainy kid who'd aced him on a math final in their junior year at Keepsake High, the witch who'd once tricked him into confessing that he didn't have a clue what the capital of Montana was—*she* was there, not in person maybe, because the Bennetts were Episcopalian, but . . . there, nonetheless. Her smile, her dark eyes . . . oh, her voice, he could listen to that voice argue with him all day long and not get tired of it. She was warm and kindhearted and she smelled like an angel and no one looked more beautiful in lavender blue. It scared him, how much Olivia was there . . . and it made him feel profoundly awed.

Because somehow, in that church, in that community, he was able to leave all his bitterness and resentment and self-righteousness at the door and join everyone else, if only briefly, in simple praise of the season.

And for that, he was glad.

Nine

Technically speaking, Olivia didn't belong in her brother's living room. And yet on Christmas morning there she was, dressed in pajamas like everyone else and plopped on the floor near Rand and Eileen's tree, helping their kids read the to-and-from tags on the mountains of gifts stacked under it.

Olivia had been coming over on Christmas Eve and staying the night since Zack was three—ever since she'd seen the videotape of him making a dash for the presents and tripping onto the pile, sending the presents into the tree and the tree into the fireplace, which luckily was still unlit.

"Oh, what I wouldn't give to have been there!" she'd said through tears of laughter as they watched the tape later that day.

"Come over Christmas Eve next time, and stay overnight," Eileen had suggested on the spot.

"You wouldn't mind?"

"Not a bit."

It was a tremendous intrusion. Olivia knew it, and every year on December 24 she'd call her sister-in-law and best friend and say, "Eileen, are you *sure*?" And Eileen would say, "Yes, I'm sure." There might have been a year or two when Eileen wasn't quite as sure as she sounded, but by now it was a tradition. Olivia looked forward to all of it, from the Christmas Eve service at St. Paul's to the waffles her brother made for them on Christmas morning.

This year, shopping for Kristin's gift had been a challenge. The child was at prime doll-bearing age, which should have made it easy—and yet her position on dolls was depressingly clear. Eileen decided to ignore it, choosing instead to blow away her daughter's resistance with a holiday Barbie and a glittering wardrobe to go with it.

Poor Barbie never made it out of the box.

Olivia, taking seriously her niece's remark about wanting to be a doctor (although obviously not a pediatrician), bought her a precision microscope. Kristin was impressed—for five minutes. How long could you stay worked up about a strand of hair magnified two hundred times?

Kristin was much more enthusiastic about the charming Christmas stocking that Zack had purchased from Olivia's shop for her. That was some consolation. But the biggest hits—surprise, surprise—were the Beanie Babies, around which Kristin and Zack immediately began designing elaborate new skits.

"Oh, well. At least they're using their imagination."

"And the toys aren't violent."

"Or sexist."

"So we should be really glad."

But they weren't. Eileen wanted her daughter to fall in love with holiday Barbie, and Olivia wanted to trump Eileen with the student microscope.

As for Rand, he had his own elaborately worked out theory: "Women don't know what the hell they want."

In short, it was a charming, typical Christmas morning. Olivia had all of the pleasure of seeing the holiday through children's eyes and none of the stress of making dinner for her parents later in the day. She had offered, as she did every year, to help in the kitchen, but her sister-in-law was determined, as she was every year, to stage the event herself.

"Damn it, I want *all* the credit," she told Olivia. "This is serious. This involves in-laws."

So while poor Eileen was fretting about turning out an oyster stuffing that was properly moist and getting all those tiny pearl onions cooked and creamed just so, Olivia was back in her townhouse with her shoes kicked off and a cup of tea on her lap, gathering strength for the second phase of Christmas Day.

The odd thing was, she didn't feel drained in the least by the nonstop morning. Just the opposite, in fact: She was feeling restless and almost unbearably edgy. Her cup of Earl Grey tea and plate of Eileen's Christmas cookies simply weren't going to cut it this year. Olivia wanted something else, something more, something new.

She wanted Quinn.

She told herself that she was being perverse. That Quinn came with too much emotional baggage. That he was arrogant, overly principled, and insensitive. That he might even be cruel—how else to explain his willingness to put her family through such agony over Alison?

And yet part of her, the part that mattered, knew that Quinn Leary had more character, more integrity, and a stronger sense of honor than any man she'd ever met. Did honor even matter any more? She didn't know. All she knew was that it was Christmas and she wanted to be with Quinn, if only to see him smile and hear his voice again.

Abandoning her tea and cookies, Olivia changed from her red corduroy jumper into dinner clothes—a winter white sweater and a black skirt that fell softly to mid-calf—and pinned a whimsical cloisonne-and-rhinestone rocking horse pin to the sweater for a touch of color and sparkle. She kept her makeup to a minimum and ran her fingers through the curls of her hair to tame the bounciest ones, then surveyed herself in the full-length mirror that stood in the corner of her cheerful yellow bedroom.

Is this okay for a soup kitchen?

No. She frowned at herself for being frivolous, then took off the pin and slipped it in the pocket of her skirt.

Olivia arrived at St. Swithin's just as the crowd was beginning to show up in force. She was expecting to see a basic turkey dinner being dished out cafeteria-style, but the scene before her was a real community affair, warm and friendly and relaxed. All manner of people were helping themselves to the buffet—from college kids in jeans and sweats to elderly couples in their churchgoing best. Single mothers were there with their freshly scrubbed children, and unattached men who looked, it was true, both jobless and homeless.

But no Quinn. Olivia expected him to be there and was keenly disappointed that he wasn't. Undaunted, she approached the man who was obviously in charge of the event.

"Father Tom? Hi. I don't know if you remember me—"

The priest started when he saw her. "Of course I do. Olivia Bennett, isn't it?" He stuck out his hand and said, "Merry Christmas," though he clearly wondered what she was doing there.

"I was looking for Quinn."

"Dear God, what now?"

"Well, I—excuse me?"

In a low murmur, the priest urged her to give him a moment of her time. They stepped out into the hall, and in a few frightening sentences, he brought Olivia up-to-date on the most recent of the unnerving pranks that were being inflicted on Keepsake.

"Quinn stayed here all night, bless the man's heart," explained Father Tom. "He's gone home to shower, but he should be back anytime. Please," he added, "don't mention the prank to anyone besides your family."

He glanced around him and dropped his voice even lower. "I'm only confiding this bone business to you because you're so directly involved. Quinn told me about his— ill-advised, if you ask me—attempt to have your cousin exhumed for DNA testing."

Olivia could see that the idea was deeply troublesome to the priest, which wasn't surprising. But she could not see the point of keeping anything secret. "It's better that it all gets out, Father, don't you think? That way everyone can be on guard for whoever it is who's doing these horrible things."

"In theory, maybe," Father Tom said wryly, "but do you think that Mr. and Mrs. Snyder in there would go anywhere near the buffet if they knew it had a dog's bones on it a few hours ago? Never mind that we scrubbed everything down with bleach.''

''No, really, Father,'' said Olivia, digging in her heels, ''I think honesty is always the best policy.''

''Ordinarily, yes, but surely this is an exception—''

Catching himself, the priest shook his head and said, ''Will you listen to me? You're right, of course. Tell the truth, Olivia, and let the chips fall where they may.''

He began to walk away, then turned around and added with a poignant look, ''But don't tell the truth until everyone's had pie, okay?''

Smiling, Olivia nodded her assent and gave him a cheery little wave good-bye.

Now what? She couldn't very well go in there and take food out of somebody's mouth. But she couldn't stand in the hall waiting around for Quinn like some groupie, either. She simply could not stay.

But she sure didn't want to go.

What kind of Christmas was *this?*

She ducked into the ladies' bathroom where she spent some time talking to a tube of lipstick, then came out and scanned the diners one last time. Nope. Still not there. Dismayed by how unhappy it made her feel, she turned abruptly to leave.

And ran smack into Quinn, whacking his chest with her shoulder hard enough to send them both off balance.

''Heyyy,'' he said with a grin as he caught her in his arms, instantly turning her knees to pudding. ''I can't believe Bronsky didn't recruit you for the team back when. He missed a bet there.''

''Oh, you *are* here!'' she said breathlessly. Newly showered, his ponytail still damp, the scent of aftershave still fresh on his high-boned cheeks—oh, yes, he was very much there.

''Were you looking for me?'' he asked her with a hopeful, loopy smile.

Olivia didn't disappoint him. ''As a matter of fact, I was.

I wanted—'' What *did* she want? ''To ask you over to Christmas dinner with my family!'' she blurted out.

God in heaven! Where did *that* come from?

A veil drifted down between them. ''Uhhh, gee . . . it's really nice of you to think of me,'' he said. ''But I'm afraid I'll have to pass.''

Praise the Lord.

''Well—what about New Year's Eve, then?'' she followed up brightly.

God in heaven! Where did *that* come from?

Still holding her, still puzzled, still smiling, he said, ''You make it hard for a guy to say no.''

''That's the idea,'' she whispered on a shaky outflow of breath.

''Okay, then,'' he said softly. ''I'd like that. New Year's Eve it is.''

Oh no.

''Great! It'll be fun! My parents throw a really big shindig at the house every year. Just about everyone comes!''

Please don't come. Please, please, please.

''At your parents' house? Ah! Well! Hmm. That'll be a real . . . pleasure. I'm looking forward to seeing them again after all these years.''

Are you serious? They hate you. They'll kill me.

She beamed at him and said, ''And they'll be looking forward to seeing you, too!''

''Good! That's good.''

The conversation had become so surreal that it broke down completely and sat there lost and confused, like a puppy that's wandered too far from home.

Quinn released her at last and nodded sideways toward the gathering inside the church basement. ''Are you—?''

''Oh! No, no. I just came to—to invite you! That's all.''

''Okay. Well, I'll call you soon.''

I might be dead by then, she thought, but she returned his much-too-cheerful smile and said, ''I'll be looking forward to it!''

She fled on pudding knees to her minivan, where she sat

and waited for her heart's thumping to die down. Forgotten entirely was the news about the latest dreadful prank; all Olivia wanted was to make sense of her behavior in that hall. There had to be a reason why she had invited Quinn—the one man in the world who could probably make her mother cry on sight—into her parents' home for the biggest party of their social calendar. Everyone would be there: the mayor, the council, doctors, lawyers, her father's peers in the textile industry.

Is that why she did it? To force Keepsake to deal with Quinn head on, instead of whispering and muttering behind his back? Olivia wanted to think so. She wanted to believe that her reason was as simple and noble as that.

If she had any other motive for asking Quinn, it was buried too deep in her subconscious for her to figure it out just now. She put her van in gear and pulled out of the parking lot. Across town, on another planet far from this one, dinner was about to be served.

Her family was in a wonderful mood.

Owen Bennett had just found out from his son that the town council was willing to negotiate a tax break for the mill. Rand was so proud that he'd been up to the challenge that he walked around practically bursting through his paisley vest. Eileen was thrilled with the sapphire earrings her husband had surprised her with after Olivia left at noon. And Teresa Bennett? She was happy simply because everyone else was happy.

It got better. Olivia's father pronounced himself satisfied with the oyster stuffing, pleased with the gift Olivia had given him, a pair of custom gold cuff links in the shape of a loom, and thrilled that he'd finally—finally!—beaten his grandson at Super Mario three games running.

They sang carols together, hopelessly bungling "The Twelve Days of Christmas," and they enjoyed a fabulous whiskey torte with their decaf espresso in front of a crackling fire while a video of *It's a Wonderful Life* played softly on the large-screen TV in the corner. Everyone was feeling sentimental, Olivia's mother, most of all. All she had to do was glance at the movie, and tears flowed freely.

"It's such a magical film," she murmured, wiping her eyes. "If only people lived that way."

Olivia had been watching her mother with a mixture of affection and apprehension all evening long. She knew that her mother offered the one chance she had of sneaking Quinn under the tent on New Year's Eve. The gala was going to be a masked affair, as usual, which meant that at least half of the guests would be thoroughly disguised. That was one point in Olivia's favor. Another was that her mother had never been able to say no to her; not if Olivia was determined to get a yes out of her.

So it was that right after Clarence was awarded his wings, and Olivia's father and Rand strolled off to the study to enjoy their good news and their Macanudos, and Eileen hauled her two sleepy children and their six new Beanie Babies off to bed, Olivia made her move.

"This has been a wonderful Christmas, Mom, don't you think?" she asked, snuggling close to her mother on the sofa.

Sighing happily, Teresa Bennett said, "They all are."

"But this one was better."

"You're just saying that because your father liked your cuff links so well," her mother said, looping her arm around her daughter.

"He did, didn't he?" Olivia agreed. She laid her cheek on her mother's shoulder. "I hope he wears them on New Year's."

"I'm sure he will. He'll want to show them off."

"Mom?" Olivia murmured. "You haven't asked me who I'm bringing this year."

"I imagine it'll be Eric again," her mother said with a sigh. "He's a *nice* young man," she added, "but when are you going to find someone who'll be able to take you seriously, Livvy? Sometimes I despair that I'll ever see you on the arm of a . . . a—"

"You'll be glad to know that there's been big progress

on that front: I've found myself a heterosexual," Olivia said lightly. "He seems very interested in me and he's definitely good breeding stock—smart, strong, a great-looking guy. I'll bet that sperm banks all over the world send him fan mail."

Her mother yanked at her hair and said, "You don't have to be outrageous. Where did you meet someone like that, anyway, working the hours you do?"

"Actually, I knew him years ago," Olivia said softly. She swallowed hard and added, "Actually, so did you."

The hand that had been teasing her hair in idle affection stopped now, and her mother became very still. Olivia opened her eyes. She couldn't see her mother's face—only her neck with its lined skin, the first telltale sign of advancing age. She thought she could see the pulsing of an artery there. She was certain she could hear her mother's heart, pounding in apprehension.

Teresa Bennett sat her daughter up to face her. Her gaze, darker even than Olivia's, searched her face for some hint that she should laugh at the absurdity of the idea of Quinn Leary popping up at a family gathering.

"You can't be serious."

"Mom, I am. I want to bring him on New Year's. I've already asked him," Olivia confessed.

"_Why_, for God's sake?"

"I don't know, I don't know," she said in a baffled wail. "Something made me do it. I think maybe—it's like the Capra film," she said, seized by an idea.

She jumped up and began pacing in front of the fireplace on the Berber carpet. "Ten minutes ago you were wondering why people aren't like the characters in that movie anymore, and you were right: Look how Keepsake is treating Quinn. But we have a chance—"

She stopped midstride and pointed to her mother. "_You_ have a chance—to change that."

" _Me!_ "

"I know you've never been comfortable in your role as a woman of influence," Olivia said, dropping back down on the pillowed sofa and clutching her mother's hands in hers. "You'd rather be living in a picket-fenced cottage and baby-sitting your grandchildren. But like it or not, you're the wife of the richest man in town. I'm not saying you're Mary Astor; but I *am* saying that if *you* treat Quinn with decency, the rest of Keepsake will follow suit. Most of them, anyway."

Her mother yanked her hands free of Olivia's. "No!" she said sharply. "I can't do that. It wouldn't be right to the family. Think of your Aunt Betty! My God. How can you be so dense?"

"I'm not, I'm not. But, Mom, you know that Frank Leary didn't kill Alison. And even if he did, that's not Quinn's fault. You can't conceivably blame Quinn!"

"Why can't you leave him alone!" her mother said, scrambling to get away from Olivia's grasp. Now it was her turn to pace—less from tension, Olivia thought, than from a desire to be free of her daughter's cajoling influence.

She watched her mother, so self-effacing in quiet beige and a strand of pearls, and wondered for the thousandth time why she didn't stand up for her principles more. Her mother knew that Quinn was being treated unfairly. Why didn't she speak up for him? The emotions were there, the intensity was there, and yet . . .

Olivia understood at last: Everything that Teresa Bennett did was for her family, and only her family. The family came first—her husband and her children and even poor Aunt Betty. Beyond that circle, Olivia's mother rarely ventured.

It was maddening. Teresa Bennett had a true and generous heart and could be the best ally that Quinn could possibly have—except for Olivia herself, of course.

She watched as her mother halted in front of the fire and stared into it. Something about the way she held herself told Olivia that she was beginning to consider and maybe to yield. Eventually she saw her mother's shoulders lift and fall in a silent sigh. Surrender?

Finally her mother turned to her and said in a voice of

obvious mourning, "You have feelings for this man."

"No, of course I don't," Olivia said instantly, and then she remembered her own words, so recently uttered: Honesty is the best policy.

She bowed her head and studied the pearl ring she wore on her left ring finger. Her mother had given it to her on the day she opened Miracourt and had told her, "The world's your oyster now. Congratulations, Livvy. I'm so proud of you."

"Yes, I do have feelings for him," Olivia said at last, twisting the ring around her finger. "There's chemistry between us, Mom, I won't deny it." She looked up and said, "But whether there is or not, I'd still go to bat for Quinn. It's the right thing to do. You *know* that. You're the one who's taught me not to back down from my beliefs."

"And it's a constant balancing act, cheering you on in your independence, yet hoping you won't go too far and do something stupid. You exhaust me," her mother added, and she really did sound tired.

"I know," Olivia admitted with a rueful smile. "Isn't it funny how things work out? Once you were so happy that I was determined to make it on my own," she said, waving the pearl ring in front of her mother to remind her. "And now I don't think a month goes by that you don't say to yourself, 'My poor little girl: one month closer to menopause.' "

"Olivia! How can you say that?"

"Because it's true."

Her mother sighed in tacit acknowledgment. "You're thirty-four, with no children, Livvy. Eileen's a year younger than you and her son is nine years old."

Olivia stood up and whispered in her mother's ear, "Well, hey, there's always Quinn." She stepped back to gauge her mother's reaction and was shocked to see tears spring up in her eyes.

"Please don't joke about that, Olivia. It bothers me in so many different ways."

Too far. She'd gone too far in her teasing again. "I'm

sorry, Mom,'' she said quickly. ''It's just that this whole thing with Quinn has been so *weird*.''

Not for anything would she tell her mother about the bones on the buffet. It would simply cause her more agony—and make Olivia's request that much more likely to be refused.

With a purposely downcast face, Olivia said, ''So how about it, Mom? Are you willing to set a good example for me and for everyone in Keepsake? Are you willing to let me bring a completely innocent man as my date to your party?''

''Will he wear a mask, at least?''

''Absolutely!''

Teresa Bennett tried to smile, but the effort fell flat and her words came out grim: ''Make sure that he does—just in case I lose my nerve when I confront your father.''

Ten

A week later, Quinn walked into Tony Assorio's barbershop without an appointment but with a fair amount of confidence that Tony wouldn't turn him away.

"Take it off, Tony. It's time for it to go."

"No kidding?"

"It's all yours."

"How short you want it?"

"You be the judge."

The barber was thrilled. "You know what? I'm not gonna charge. This one's on me."

Obviously Tony believed that the decline of American civilization had just been halted in its tracks. "You're doing the right thing, kid," he said. "How does it look, a grown man in a ponytail? Daniel Boone—maybe. Or that Fabio. But come on."

He kept up a steady stream of banter as he worked with the scissors, then with the clippers. Quinn watched his sun-streaked hair go up, up, and off until he had the look of a GI at boot camp.

When the barber was done, he whipped off the smock with a flourish. "I wasn't thinking buzz cut when I started," he admitted, "but you know, the look suits you. Yeah. You have the face for it. Strong nose, good eyebrows . . . So? What do you think?"

Quinn grinned and said, "I think I should've waited until August. My head's cold."

"You wear a hat. Big deal."

After some back-and-forthing over whether Quinn would be allowed to pay, Tony accepted the money and said good-naturedly, "You always were a good kid." He seemed to hesitate after that before adding, "Take some advice?"

Instantly attentive, Quinn nodded and said, "From you? Sure."

In a low mutter, the barber said, "Watch your back, kid. You go poking around too much, you're bound to piss off some people. Those kinda people you don't want to piss off. You know what I mean?"

He sounded as if he were talking about the Cosa Nostra. Quinn would have laughed off the caution if it weren't for the fact that he himself had begun to feel a real unease about continuing down the road he was on.

"I don't suppose you feel like naming names?"

The barber shook his head. "I gotta live in this town."

Quinn had no fears for himself, but he was feeling more protective than ever about Mrs. Dewsbury. After installing extra fire alarms, he'd sweet-talked her into letting him have a burglar alarm installed as well. But he continued to be concerned about her, so that morning he told her that he planned to move out of her house to a small apartment he'd found on the edge of town.

Basically he wanted Mrs. Dewsbury to have nothing to do with him; she'd be safer that way. He had expected disappointment, but not tears of disappointment. It shook him. His old teacher had argued for him to stay and had almost succeeded in making him change his mind—until this.

"I appreciate the warning, Tony," Quinn said, shaking the barber's hand.

Tony gave him a tight smile and a parting shot. "Never mind about that DNA business, kid. Let it go."

Quinn had a parting shot of his own. "Frankly? That all depends on Alison's parents."

Quinn had gone into the barbershop with two goals in mind: lose the ponytail and launch a rumor that he planned to continue pressing the district attorney. He had scored on both counts, so why was he feeling so crummy?

He wanted to blame it on the weather. After the bright sun of California, he was having trouble with New England gray. The weather was raw and mean, winter at its worst. The blanket of snow that had seemed so pure and magical on the day he first arrived was now dirty and pockmarked, casting an air of impoverishment on all it touched. Everything that could move seemed sluggish and grudging, from Quinn's shoulders and elbows to the door of his truck. As he drove through streets that seemed no longer quaint but merely old, it was easy to understand how snowbirds had come up with the clever concept of Florida.

Did he want to leave California for good and come back to this?

Yes. Quinn was a son of New England, whether he liked it or not. His character had been formed there. The self-reliance, the sense of reserve, the refusal to promise more than he could deliver—all of those traits marked him as a New Englander. They had served him well during his California exile, but he had always felt like a misfit there. Californians were communal. Friendly. Lavish with their promises to help you with anything. And why not? The weather was bound to cooperate when it came time to deliver. No; Quinn was not, and never would be, a California dreamer.

But there was another reason for his desire to come back, and it was playing havoc with his equal and opposite desire for justice: He wanted to be near Olivia. Near her, with her, on her, under her—his desire for her seemed limitless. And yet the more Quinn pressed the case for his father, the more he knew he would drive a wedge between Olivia and himself.

It was that cruel paradox, and not the cruel weather, that had Quinn feeling so damned bummed out.

Mrs. Dewsbury's hands were too arthritic to tie a knot in Quinn's bow tie for him, but she was able to talk him through the process with good results.

"You look as handsome as can be," she said, tweaking the bow just a bit.

"Even though I'm bald?"

"Even so. Why, you could be on your way to your high-school prom."

"Which, by the way, I never did get to go to," he remarked. As a matter of fact, he felt *exactly* like a high-school senior as he checked himself out in the small, weathered mirror of his room. He ran a hand over the bristled remains of his hair and decided again that he must have been mad, giving old Tony carte blanche.

Mrs. Dewsbury was brushing his tux in a final once-over, although she couldn't possibly see the lint. "Do you have the mask that Livvy dropped off?"

"In my pocket," Quinn said, reaching inside his jacket for it. "I just wish I'd been here when Liv stopped by; I might take some getting used to."

"She was all aglow, my dear, trust me. I don't think a haircut is going to change that."

Looking no more substantial in her yellow cardigan than a goldfinch in April, Mrs. Dewsbury perched her tiny frame on the edge of the chenille spread that covered Quinn's bed. She had dragged the coverlet out of the attic, and she had bought—and hung!—new white curtains in his room as well. The needlepoint rug he was standing on was new, and so was the frilly shade on the lamp. She had gone all out for him. Maybe that's what had prompted the tears when he told her that, for her own good, he was going to have to move out.

Quinn fitted the mask over his eyes. It was a plain black affair, but he felt silly wearing it. Thank God Olivia hadn't dropped off something stuck on a stick. He would have felt like an idiot, brandishing it around as he made small talk.

He felt like an idiot anyway.

"I'm not supposed to wear this thing driving, surely. When *do* I put it on?" he muttered as he yanked it back off. "What the hell was I thinking, telling her yes? What am I supposed to say to all those people? We have nothing in common.''

"Stop it right now!" said Mrs. Dewsbury, as if he'd been caught clowning around during study hall. "You have as much right to be there as anyone else. If you have any doubt, think of that box of trophies downstairs. Every one of them is for merit. You didn't buy them, you *earned* them. You're brilliant, you idiot! When will you get that through your thick skull?''

He laughed out loud at her carrot-and-stick approach to getting him out the door. "Boy, I wish you'd married my father," he said, grinning. "We both could have used you to whip us into shape.''

"Now that's silly," she said, blushing. "Anyway, if you'd ever attended one of these things, you'd know how completely insipid most of the conversation is.''

"Why didn't you say so?" said Quinn, flashing her a rakish grin. "I can do insipid.''

"It's the one thing you *can't* do," she said dryly. "But never mind. You are going to have a wonderful time with your Miss Bennett, and then tomorrow morning you are going to give me a complete account of who was there and, more importantly, who was not." With a doleful sigh, she added, "Lord knows, you won't be around much longer for our little tête-à-têtes.''

"Now don't start," he warned, still smiling, as he slid the mask back in his jacket pocket. "You know I'm moving out for your sake, not mine. Do you think I want someone terrorizing you with the fat end of a Doberman's thigh-bone?''

"Well, pooh, what do I care? As long as it's not still in the Doberman," she said, hauling herself up from the bed.

She whacked him gently across his knuckles and said, "Do you honestly think that someone's going to break in here and burn my house down just to encourage you to leave town? You have too high an opinion of yourself, Quinn Leary," she said, shaking a finger at him. "You always did.''

"I like that! A minute ago, you said I had no confidence."

"Well—never mind. You're a contradiction, that's all," she said, marching past him with a sniff.

Pleased to see that her knees seemed to be working much better nowadays, he said to her retreating figure, "Maybe I should be taking *you* to the ball, Mrs. D. That's a pretty sexy spring you have in your step."

She turned around and gave him an utterly baleful look. "I remember now. You could be *quite* fresh. Will you be back very late?"

"I . . . don't know," he said honestly.

"Will you be back at all?"

"I . . . don't know."

"I suppose I'll have to set that silly alarm, in that case. Well, get moving. It's terrible form to be late on a first date."

Eleven

No bra, sheer stockings, a silver lamé slip dress—it couldn't get more basic than that. It had taken Olivia less than sixty seconds to get dressed, which left her with way too much time to pace the Aubusson rug in her living room as she waited for Quinn to join her in the suicide mission she had planned for them that night.

Her father had no idea that Quinn was going to be one of his guests. At the last minute Olivia's mother had lost her nerve and ditched the assignment. After much agonizing, Olivia had decided simply to wing it. So her father didn't know. So what? He wouldn't make a scene, not with a house full of guests. And if he blew his top after the party, well, it wouldn't be the first time that Olivia had got him to do it.

Currently the plan was for her mother to act surprised when Olivia showed up on the arm of Quinn Leary in the receiving line. It was the only way to spare Teresa Bennett from her husband's inevitable outrage. Olivia and her mother were being completely deceitful, of course, but they were in it too deep to be anything else. Olivia's only concern was that her guileless mother might not be able to pull off the deception.

So much for the honesty-is-the-best-policy route.

Working through her jitters, Olivia fluffed the pillows on her slipcovered sofa and stacked the coffee-table magazines that she had previously fanned, then stacked, then fanned again. She wanted Quinn to be impressed, but she didn't have a clue what impressed a man like him.

If I were Quinn, what would I notice first?

The view, of course. Too bad it was dark.

Her two-bedroom townhouse, one of a dozen on a knoll overlooking the Connecticut River, was pricey for its size. But the mortgage had bought her not only a beautiful view, but such amenities as French doors, a Jenn-Air, a copper hood, and an east-facing kitchen. It was lovely to watch the sun rise over the river as she ate her cereal, and worth every extra nickel. Quinn would think so, too, if . . . if . . .

If.

The chime at the front door sounded as shrill as the steam whistle at the textile mill. Olivia ran to answer it, catching one of her high heels in the fringe of the hall rug and very nearly sending herself sailing through a sidelight. In a fierce effort to compose herself, she took a deep breath and blew it out like a bottlenose dolphin, then put on a smile and swung the door wide.

"Wow."

"Wow."

They stood there, assessing one another in unabashed admiration, until Quinn remembered that he was hiding something behind his back. He whipped out a dozen roses in crinkly cellophane and said, "I sure hope you weren't expecting a wrist corsage."

"Hmm."

"I know; they're not in a box. They're not even fragrant. I'm sorry. It was a last-minute thing."

"No, I mean . . . your *hair*."

"Oh, that. Yeah." He gave her a quirky smile and said, "Aren't you cold, standing there like that?"

Was she? "Oh, I'm sorry. Please. Come in," she said, accepting the roses as if they were gold and frankincense and myrrh.

Looking as grand as her brother ever had in topcoat and tux, Quinn brushed close by her as he passed on his way inside. Olivia's first and only thought was to bolt the door behind them and never let him out again. Ever.

"It's a great haircut," she said, unable not to stare. "You just look so . . . great."

He nodded in embarrassed acknowledgment. His hands were jammed in the pockets of his topcoat, giving him an air so artless that she found it sophisticated.

He said softly, "I can't begin to tell you how beautiful you are."

Her lashes fluttered down. "Thank you. It's the dress."

"That, too." He glanced around, but seemed puzzled why they were still there. "Ready to go?" he asked, gesturing an after-you through his topcoat pockets.

Shy. That's what he seemed. It was their first real date, after all. Olivia found his manner irresistibly intriguing. "We have time," she said, preferring for obvious reasons to arrive with the crush. "Would you like a drink before we leave?"

"Thanks, no," he said with a hapless smile. "I'd better hold on to what's left of my wits."

"Nervous?"

"Uh-huh."

"Me, too." For oh-so-many different reasons.

She looked around them as if she also were seeing everything for the first time. Suddenly, what she saw didn't impress her very much: a small, fireplaced living room that fed into an open foyer that fed into a dining area. Two good pieces of cherry furniture from France. A fairly valuable slant-top desk of yew wood. Top-of-the-line fabric, naturally, on all the upholstered surfaces. And the Aubusson. But that was it, the sum total of her nesting instinct so far. It was nothing compared to the loving care that her mother and her sister-in-law had lavished on their respective homes. Olivia hadn't even got around to doing something about the bare walls and windows yet. Except in the bedroom, of course.

"I don't spend much time at home," she said, feeling obliged to confess to that sin. "I've never even used the fancy exhaust hood in the kitchen. I mostly eat cereal."

"You're not domestic. Okay," he said, giving her a puzzled look. "Duly noted."

How mortifying; she sounded as if she were auditioning

for the part of his wife. "I don't know why I'm—we're—so nervous," she said. "We were a lot more relaxed around one another when we were growing up."

He smiled. "You weren't as pretty then."

"And you weren't as debonair. I need a drink," she said, hoping that wine would calm her heart. "Why don't you take off your coat?"

She went into the kitchen and took a bottle of merlot from a cupboard, then handed it to Quinn to open while she slid out a stemmed glass for herself—and then one for him—from a wooden rack above the counter.

Should she warn Quinn that there might be a ruckus in the receiving line? She didn't see how she could. She held out both glasses; dutifully, he filled them.

So there they stood in their fancy duds, searching for something to toast. He touched his glass to hers. "Here's to the modern woman," he said with a look that Olivia somehow took as mocking.

"Because I don't cook? I can cook," she said, bristling. "Anyone can cook. All you have to do is follow a recipe."

Please, please, don't open the fridge. There was nothing there except a carton of skim milk, some yogurt, and some cigar-looking things that used to be bananas. She had put them in the fridge after the fruit flies showed up, thinking—ha-ha—that she'd use them to make some kind of tea bread for her mother for Christmas.

Ha-ha.

"I guess you're right," she said, sipping to his toast after all. "I'm a pathetically modern woman."

He leaned back against the kitchen counter and gave her a thoughtful look. "What did it say under your yearbook mug shot? I was never mailed a copy, needless to say."

"Oh! Would you like to s—?"

Dumb; why remind him of a year he'd never get back? "Y'know, I think it's buried somewhere in a closet," she amended. "Maybe another time. Anyway, as I recall, it said, 'Olivia Bennett—she hasn't got time for the pain.' "

"Carly Simon."

"Mm-hmm," she said, sipping her wine. "I suppose it was as accurate as any of those predictions are. They're a little like horoscopes, aren't they? You see what you want to see in them."

"Liv, I have a confession to make," he said out of the blue. "All those years that I spent in California . . . well, I thought of you more than once. A lot more than once."

Her heart was on the launching pad, ready for liftoff, when he added, "and every damn thought of you was more bitter than the one before it."

"Oh."

He set the wineglass down on her Corian counter and walked up to the bank of windows in the breakfast area, the windows that had a view of a swift-running river he could not see. For a long moment he was lost in his own private reverie, this buzz-cut, cummerbunded stonemason who'd just confessed to harboring bitter thoughts of her.

Olivia waited, baffled, to hear more.

Soon enough, it came rolling out. "I resented you because you had everything I ever wanted in life: stability, a proper family, the admiration and respect of everyone around you.

"Oddly enough," he added with a shrug, "I never resented your brother. I knew I was smarter than Rand, and better on the field. But you! You had everything I had—ambition, brains, discipline—and wealth and status besides. That gave you an unbeatable edge. God, how I hated that. Hated you. Thought I hated you, anyway," he said with a pained glance in her direction.

He turned back to the river that he didn't know was there. "But guess what? It turns out that I was wrong," he said softly. "It turns out that I've been confusing hate with something else. So maybe I'm not so smart, after all."

He got lost in such profound silence that Olivia, type A that she was, felt the need to prompt him. "Something else?"

"Yeah."

He sounded so resigned, so melancholy. But not very specific.

"Something else?"

"Mmm." Turning from the window, hands still in his pockets, he said, "But honest to God, I'm not sure what."

He came back toward her and when he got close he stopped, half-circling her face with his fingertips. "Look at you," he said in a voice of wonder. "There's not a man alive who could resist you. But there are other beautiful women in the world—a lot of them in California—and I've never felt this way about any of them."

He laughed at himself and said, "God, I sound like an arrogant bastard. Am I out of line, telling you this?"

"I'll let you know," she said, hardly daring to breathe. Beautiful? *She* wasn't beautiful.

"Liv, we're not lovers, so how can this be—?" He made a comical face, lifting his eyebrows and compressing his lips. "Something else?"

"Yeah. That. I spent seventeen years resenting you, and now suddenly it's . . . something else."

Olivia understood completely; she was feeling it herself. She studied his face and marveled that she knew it so well: the hazel eyes, narrowed in self-defense from the sun even when the sun wasn't shining; the eyebrows that were pulled together in determination more often than not; the squared chin with its hint of a cleft; the nose with its bridge more Roman than Celtic; the wide grin with a tiny, endearing overlap in the two front teeth. She knew his face almost as well as she knew her own.

"We grew up together," she said, trying to explain away the comforting sense of familiarity. "That should count for something."

Quinn's response to that was a chuckle. "We grew up together, it's true. But you were a major pain in the butt."

"That's what I thought about you!"

"I never could stand your self-assurance. You were way too cocky for a girl."

"Isn't that funny? I used to think you were rude, refusing to let a girl win."

"I know. You expected me to give up my seat to you, so to speak. And yet *you* always went for the jugular."

"And you always went for the knees."

He nodded in fond recollection. "You remember the day the door of your locker was siliconed shut and you couldn't get at the take-home final you were supposed to hand in? I did that."

"I was sure you did. That's why I stole your term paper from study hall a week later."

"*You* did that?"

"Uh-huh. And then I gave it to Tim Kroft. He got an A."

"You little devil!" Quinn said with a surprised laugh. "If I had known that, I wouldn't have stuck up for you when Jimmy O'Malley wrote that limerick about you and posted it all over school."

"I remember that. You ripped them all down and then you gave Jimmy a black eye. That was really nice of you, Quinn," she said with a sigh, and she meant it. The limerick had been insulting and obscene and she had been completely devastated by it.

She looked up and said, "I was so grateful. I never forgot what you did. I think that's why after you and your father disappeared, I sneaked into the cottage to save your trophies before the police could confiscate them. My parents still don't know that I was hiding them all this time."

"It amazes me that you did that. And even though I reacted like a jerk when I found it out, I have to say, it was a terrific gesture. I should have thanked you properly at the time."

She took a sip of her wine. "Properly?"

Please, please, please.

Quinn smiled, then lifted the glass from her hand, setting it carefully on the counter beside them. He slid his hands behind her head, twining them in the curls of her hair.

"Yeah. Properly," he whispered, bending his face to hers for the kiss. It was tenderly given, a light and yet lingering token that had as much respect in it as it had affection.

She closed her eyes, the better to savor the brush of his mouth against hers, and felt the shiver of his breath as he said, "I want you to know . . . that sometime soon . . . I plan to make love to you, Olivia Bennett."

"Now who's cocky?" she whispered, but the shivers that rippled over her were her own.

Ignoring her challenge, he began to drop feathery kisses on her cheek, her chin, the arc of her throat. She leaned her head back like a cat to savor the strokes and felt his voice rumbling on the surface of her skin as he tested her with tiny, provocative nips and murmured, "I want you to know . . . that I'm not in this . . . for the thrill of it all."

"Oh, gosh, I am," she whispered through a pleasurable haze.

His chuckle echoed close to the beat of her pulse, quickening it. He sounded so sure of himself. "Livvy . . . Liv," he said on a sigh, "you do things to me . . ."

"I can . . . tell," she said as he pressed close to her, signaling unmistakably his arousal.

He brought his mouth back to hers for another kiss, night-and-day different from the first. This one was an expression of raw hunger—rough, ready, a sharp and painful reminder that he meant what he said. Caught off guard by it, Liv made a sound in her throat of surprise and then of surrender as she yielded to the force of it.

His hand caught and cupped her breast through the thin fabric of her dress, sending a surge of desire rocketing through her. He pulled the sparkly string-strap away from her shoulder and ran his tongue in the hollow there, driving her deeper into the ground.

"Christ, how I want you!" he muttered, coming back to cover her mouth greedily with his. He had her pinned against the counter; her hands gripped the smooth Corian in her effort to steady herself against him. His kiss was dark, delicious, an invitation to a steamy netherworld that she rarely had time to visit.

"I'm sorry . . . I'm sorry . . . this isn't what I'd planned," he said hoarsely, but he didn't sound sorry at all.

"I'm sorry, too," she whispered, which also was not true. "The . . . oh, God, the—"

She brought her hands up around his neck and cupped the back of his closely shorn head, pulling him closer, returning his kisses, feeding the fire. It was her one, last, willful indulgence before she broke away and finished her sentence by gasping, "The *timing*. It's awful."

His look seemed blurred and undirected for a second, but he snapped back into focus quickly enough. "The gala?"

She nodded glumly.

He scowled and shook his head, like a boy being offered bad medicine. "I say we stay here instead," he said, bringing his mouth closer to hers again.

"No, wait, stop," she said, laying her fingers against his lips. His face was inches from hers. She stared fiercely into his green eyes, battling the promise of pleasure she found there. She was only a slinky dress and a pair of pantyhose away from saying yes. It would be so easy, so decadent, to hole up with him in her townhouse making love instead of getting on with her campaign to rehabilitate him with the good citizens of Keepsake.

But she had a civic duty.

"We *have* to go, Quinn. They're expecting me. They might think something—"

"Happened to you? Because you were alone with the gardener's son?"

She grimaced and said, "Oh, come on, Quinn. You know that's not what they'd think."

He shrugged. "It was worth a shot." And then he grinned that heart-melting, endearing grin of his and took a big step back from her. "Madame," he said with a deep bow and a graceful flourish of both hands, "your chariot awaits."

She gave him a wary look. "You didn't hire a limo or anything, did you?"

"Are you kidding?" he said as they headed for their coats. "Who's got that kind of dough? High-school seniors, maybe; not grown-ups."

His quip stopped Olivia in her tracks. She turned to him and said softly, "We really are grown-ups now, aren't we?

Where did it go, our youth? It ended so abruptly.''

''No kidding.''

''Oh, definitely for you, but even for me. I worked like a slave through college . . . then graduate school . . . then the shop . . . another shop . . . and where have I gotten? Practically nowhere.''

''Aren't you being a little hard on yourself?'' asked Quinn as he donned his topcoat.

''No. I should be running a company.''

''A textile mill, perchance?'' Quinn ventured shrewdly. ''Why aren't you?''

''My father had other plans, all of them spelled 'Rand.' Don't get me started on that one,'' Olivia said flatly. She reached into the back of her closet and took out a floor-length black velvet cape lined in scarlet. It was a ridiculous extravagance she'd bought years ago and had worn only once, but as she slipped it over her shoulders, she knew that on this night, at this gala, with this man, the velvet cape was finally going to fulfill its destiny.

She fastened the ebony-encrusted button and, feeling wildly romantic, turned around in a small circle for him to survey. ''Well? What do you think?''

He gave her a look that warmed her down to her silk-covered toes. ''I think I'm a damned lucky bastard,'' he said, coming up to her and kissing her softly.

''Hold that thought,'' she said with a sly smile, ''for just a few more hours.''

Quinn didn't have a limo and driver waiting for her, but he did have a rented Mercedes. Olivia scolded him for throwing his money around, but secretly she was pleased that he was treating her like a homecoming queen. Yes, their prom days were definitely behind them, and that was too bad. But somehow Olivia couldn't help thinking that the best was yet to come.

Twelve

Quinn was curious to know why, exactly, Olivia *wasn't* working for her father at the mill. It seemed to him that Owen Bennett was wasting the best resource he had.

"Thanks for the vote of confidence," she said as they drove along the river before taking the turn into town. She explained how disappointed she had been when her father hadn't offered her a job.

"I was furious that my father was willing to hand over responsibility to my brother and not to me. Sometimes I think he just wants Rand where he can keep an eye on him—remember when Rand had that summer job at a camp in Maine, and my dad had to go up there to bail him out of jail?"

"When he was arrested for going on that joyride with those guys who stole a car up there? Yeah, I remember. Rand bragged about it to the whole team when he got back."

"Well, I can still hear my dad yelling that Rand was never going to leave Connecticut again, not if my dad had anything to say about it. Which of course he did—and still does.

"Anyway, out of either stubbornness or stupidity, I decided to stick around and beat my father at his own game. I was determined to be a success right under his nose. I don't know what I thought I was going to do. Start a rival textile mill?"

She let out a rueful laugh and continued. "I came up with the idea of Miracourt: high-end fabrics for decorating and for apparel. The store's a success, but I'm not close enough to the city to really take off. So I've begun to import decorator items for the home, mostly from France, and I'm going to branch out into mail order. And in the meantime, I threw in with my father to open Run of the Mill—because outlet stores are where it's at nowadays, I guess."

"You don't sound thrilled."

"I don't like the outlet," she admitted frankly. "It's in a crumbling warehouse with bad lighting and no windows. I get depressed when I go there, but my father is convinced that when the surroundings are dreary, people feel they get more value."

"He's probably right."

"I know that. He reminds me every chance he gets."

Her answer was decidedly tense. Presumably it had something to do with the fact that they were discussing her relationship with her father, which had been problematic for as long as Quinn could remember.

He recalled an April afternoon in seventh grade when Olivia had stopped to talk to him while he and his own father were raking the grounds of the estate. Owen Bennett happened to drive by. He called from the car for his daughter to come back to the house. She refused. He told her again. She refused again. Quinn wondered then—as he wondered still—if Olivia simply regarded him as a handy stick to poke in her father's eye.

He figured he'd soon find out. He drove the Mercedes through the open iron gates and past the cottage he had once called home and headed for the grand house on the hill, obscured from view by carefully placed evergreens growing among the century-old specimen trees that lent the scene such dignity.

"Funny," Quinn mused aloud. "This hill seemed so much steeper when I was a kid."

"Yes. That's how it always is."

He glanced at Olivia and saw that she was as tight as an

overwound clock. "You're not dragging me here over your father's objections, by any chance?" he asked, suddenly suspicious.

"No way," she answered tersely.

He eased into the last turn of the winding driveway, aware of light ahead. His first glimpse of the manor and its immediate grounds was through the grand sweep of branches on a copper beech. Quinn became aware first of brilliance, and then of magic: every tree and shrub between them and the house was strung with tiny white lights. The effect was spectacular, something out of the robber-baron age and wholly befitting a turn-of-the-century mansion like the Bennett house.

Quinn remembered the old days when his father used to climb an extension ladder to decorate two evergreens, one on each side of the portico, with big colored lights. But this! It must have taken a crew of men and a hydraulic lift to get it done. It was beautiful, all right, but it was completely over the top, like something out of Disney World.

"I miss the colored lights," he found himself muttering.

"Hmm? Oh. Those. Yes. They were nice."

She was still somewhere else. He didn't like it. "I'll drop you off and park the—"

"No, they have a valet for that," she said. "Just pull up to the house."

Of course, a valet. He should have known. Thank God for the Mercedes. "Well, this should be fun," he managed to say in a voice not completely grim. He rolled to a stop under the portico of the brightly lit house.

"Quinn! I have a confession to make!" Olivia blurted out as the valet opened her door for her. Scrambling out of the seat, she said in a single breath: "My father doesn't know you're coming or Rand but my mother does but she's not telling so just play along!"

Before he could say, "With what?" the valet was slamming her door in his face. Feeling as if he'd been zapped with a stun gun, Quinn sat where he was.

Now she tells me? Now she freaking tells me?

He snapped back to reality when he noticed the impatient valet, a kid who by the looks of him was a tackle on Keepsake's current team, waiting for him to surrender the wheel. Quinn got out and handed over the Mercedes to him, not without trepidation, and then turned to face the woman he had considered a friend and hoped to have as a lover.

"You evil little witch—this is a setup!" he said, seething.

"It's not! Oh, Quinn, it's not!" she said with an imploring look. "I was going to tell him, really I was, but—oh, what's the difference! Let's just go in and get it over with, can't we, please? All right?"

"No, it's *not* all right, goddammit," he said in a low growl. He tried to grab her arm to lead her out from under the portico, but he couldn't find it in the folds of the goddamned cape. "I'm not going where I'm not invited—not in there! Town Hill is one thing, but—" He swore under his breath and said, "Hell, I'm outta here."

He turned to go, but she caught his sleeve. "Quinn! You're not going to run *again*!"

Bull's-eye. She got him where he lived. He turned back around and blasted her a look filled with pure felony.

How could someone so smart be so incredibly dumb? Was she trying to provoke her father into all-out war? Jesus! Quinn was going to have to count on the Bennetts' good breeding; he sure couldn't count on hers.

"All right," he said. "We go in; we go out. Five minutes, and then I take you home and you'll be free to come back and party on with your peers or sprawl around and watch Guy Lombardo on TV. Just as long as I'm out of it."

Looking chastened and as near to meek as she got, Olivia allowed him to grab a fistful of velvet and haul her up to the double doors, thrown open to a steady flow of incoming guests. Quinn couldn't tell whether she was more afraid of him or of her father at that moment. What the hell had she been thinking, browbeating her mother into going along and then blithely omitting to tell her father? He found himself actually feeling sorry for the Bennetts—something strange and new.

The lofty entrance hall was a cavernous affair floored in marble. Quinn had been in it only a few times before in his life, none of them social. He remembered the most memorable time: Olivia had fallen out of a tree and got knocked unconscious, and he had carried her home in his arms and handed her over, still groggy, to her shocked and hysterical mother.

Ten years old, and in his arms. He should've quit while he was ahead.

"Is this the point when we put on the masks?" he said dryly.

"Oh! I forgot."

She reached inside her silver-beaded bag and took out a narrow slip of silver that wouldn't hide her face at all. Quinn couldn't help feeling that the mask she'd given him to wear made him a lot more incognito. Was that by design? He took the thing out of his inside pocket and slipped it over his eyes.

Hell. It made him feel more like a gate-crasher than ever. Annoyed, he pushed it up to the top of his brow and let it sit there.

Olivia said faintly, "Whatever."

The hall was a noisy, busy place. The line of masked merrymakers waiting to be received by the host and hostess seemed to be moving slowly, possibly because of the trays of hors d'oeuvres and champagne being foisted on them as they greeted one another in shrill, expectant voices. From somewhere inside, Quinn heard an orchestra launch into a swinging rendition of "In the Mood." Suddenly he got why they called it a gala: the atmosphere really was gay.

Except for him and Olivia. His pride was smarting big time; he couldn't stand the thought of being rubbed in her father's nose like month-old bologna. The last time the two were face-to-face was in the gardener's cottage and Quinn had tried to knock him down. Would Owen Bennett remember?

Quinn gave their coats to a hatcheck girl who was set up for the event in a small reception room off the hall. Then, still operating in a chill of silence, he and Olivia took their place in the line of guests.

"How many people are your parents expecting tonight?" he asked, struggling with the small-talk thing.

Olivia shrugged a shoulder—the shoulder he had kissed in hungry abandon half an hour earlier—and said, "Three or four hundred."

"Are you kidding?" he said to her under his breath. "There aren't that many people in Keepsake who can stay up until midnight."

"My father has a lot of different connections," she said without enthusiasm.

"So it would seem."

That was it for his store of party chat. God, how he wanted out of there.

A couple swooped down on them, kissing air all around and waiting gleefully for introductions. Olivia obliged them. The woman, tall, blond, and languid, said, "Quinn Leary—I have heard so *much* about you."

"I wish I could say the same," he said with a smile that was as bland as hers was sly.

The couple moved on, to be replaced by another one equally curious and insinuating. And another. And another. Pretty soon he felt like Errol Flynn, backing up the winding stairs and holding the evil king's forces at bay with only his trusty sword.

And meanwhile they were moving up the receiving line. Before he knew it, he was hearing the dread words, "Mother, you remember Quinn Leary."

He smiled grimly and held out his hand. A woman of sixty, with fearful eyes in an attractive face that reminded him only marginally of Olivia, said faintly, "Of course I do," and laid her hand limply in his.

He remembered a line from *My Fair Lady*, a movie his father had enjoyed. "How kind of you to let me come," he said, even though he knew she hadn't let him come and was feeling anything but kind.

"And, Dad . . . Quinn," murmured Olivia, who seemed to have run out of steam just when her train had the summit in sight.

Back, back she rolled, under the outraged glare of her father, who had obviously been unaware of their presence until then. This wasn't some annoyed father telling his seventh-grader to get along home. This was a man at the top of his game, ready to do whatever it took to have his will enforced.

And he left Quinn cold. "Sir," he said, sticking out his hand. Let the man take it, or not. Quinn didn't really give a damn.

Owen Randall Bennett Senior chose not.

Fine. Quinn turned to Olivia, who looked utterly miserable. In one of those blinding flashes he got occasionally, he realized that she had brought him there not to make her father's life hell but simply to put Quinn back in touch with Keepsake. She was crazy, she was nuts, but her heart was so much in the right place that Quinn found himself wanting to give her old man the same black eye he'd given to Jimmy O'Malley.

He went one better. "Call me crazy," he said, slipping his arm lightly around Olivia's waist, "but I feel like dancin'. Will you excuse us, sir?"

He ushered her past her stupefied father to the sounds of the Stones' driving classic, "Satisfaction." Perfect.

"Did I just get you disinherited?" he asked Olivia as they headed for the ballroom.

Her voice and smile were resigned as she said, "It wouldn't be the first time. I've been in and out of his will so often that his attorneys call me Rainmaker."

"Joke?"

"I got it straight from their secretary; she works at Miracourt on weekends."

"Oh, hey . . . I'm sorry, Liv. Jesus. I didn't think people

actually did stuff like that. Not outside of mystery novels, anyway.''

''Oh, I don't care anymore,'' she said, waving politely to someone going the other way. ''The older he gets, the worse he gets. He tries to control everything and everyone. Rand is completely under his thumb, and so is my mother. I guess I'm the only holdout and it makes him crazy. I can understand why my mother has to put up with him, but I don't understand why Rand doesn't just strike out on his own. He hates working for my father.''

They entered a forty-foot-long room paneled in wood carved in delicate garlands. The room had been designed for dances, but contrary to Quinn's boast to Owen Bennett, he had no desire to dance. For one thing, he didn't know how.

In any case, neither of them felt like rocking to the beat, so they simply stood on the sidelines, watching sexily clad women gyrate with their dates from the pages of *GQ*.

''You know what I think Rand should be doing?'' she asked, standing on tiptoe and leaning into Quinn's ear to be heard over the noise of the band. ''He should be working with kids—teaching, or maybe even coaching. Of course, there's no money in that. Or status. My brother would rather be vice president of something he hates than be poorly paid doing something he loves.''

Why the hell were they talking about Rand? He wasn't even there. ''Got him all figured out, have you?'' Quinn asked, without really caring.

''Of course I've got him figured out. He's my brother and I know what's best for him,'' she insisted. ''You remember how he was: very emotional. He has that hot temper—but on the other hand, he can be very devoted. He relates to kids on their level, and they love that. And he gets to be the center of their attention, which *he* loves.''

''I remember the temper,'' Quinn said, nodding. The day after an injured Rand Bennett found out that Quinn was replacing him as quarterback of the Keepsake Cougars, he went ballistic. Quinn could picture him still, hobbling around the locker room on crutches, ranting and raving about his injury. At the time, Quinn had actually felt guilty for being chosen as his replacement.

No more.

The band slid into a slow number, "Unforgettable," and suddenly Quinn remembered why he'd agreed to come: to be with Olivia. It was true that he wouldn't be outstrutting Mick Jagger or Michael Jackson at the fast stuff anytime soon, but he damn well knew how to hold a woman in his arms and move her slowly to his will.

"C'mon," he said, suddenly tired of her father, her brother, her mother, and every other Bennett on the planet. "Let's dance."

He took Olivia by the hand and led her onto what was now a crowded floor, and he drew her into his arms. Under the cover of a press of couples, he nuzzled her hair and inhaled deeply the sheer, intoxicating scent of her. Her body felt lithe and free and unbelievably well fitted to his, so much so that he knew it when her breasts lifted and fell in a sigh.

She snuggled her head on his shoulder, and he became aware that he'd never felt more content in his life. There was just something about her; it was like coming home. Home at last. He wanted only to hold her, to protect her, to have her forever in his embrace.

He closed his eyes, lost completely in the essence of her. If he were dragged from the Bennetts' house by thugs just then and shipped off to live alone on a rock in the ocean for the rest of his life, it almost wouldn't matter. He knew that he would always, always have that dance.

Live a moment completely and you possess it forever. It was such a simple formula. How had he not thought of it before?

Liv . . . sweet Liv, he thought, kissing the top of her hair. *I'm falling so much in love with you.*

She lifted her face to his. "What did you say?"

He shook his head, not trusting himself to do justice to his feelings. They ran more deeply than words.

She snuggled her cheek back on his shoulder and they

drifted together on the magic carpet of the melody, and when the song ended, they floated down to the dance floor on the sound of their own sighs. Before Quinn could escape with Olivia from the next dance—a driving, pulsing, shake-your-booty number—he felt someone whack him soundly on the back in jovial greeting.

"Quinn Leary, for chrissake! Quinn!" he shouted over the music. "How ya doin'?"

He turned to face Mike Redding, the most irrepressible of his old teammates. More brawn than brain, but with enough personality and charm that no one seemed to mind much, Mike was the kind of guy who used to make the workouts fun and the losses easier to bear. He was just an all-around, uncomplicated, regular . . . guy.

"Hey, Mike," Quinn said loudly over the music as he shook his hand. "Howzit goin'?"

"Never better. I'm a sportswear manufacturer. High-tech stuff—hot-hot-hot. We can't make enough of it. Geez, I'm glad you came," he said, hugging Olivia with one arm as he latched onto Quinn with the other. "I heard you were back, but I didn't expect to see you *here*, for chrissake. This is great!" he said, whacking Quinn on the back again.

"You gotta come over to Buffitt's house tomorrow—not you, Livvy, of course. A bunch of us guys meet every New Year's Day to watch the bowl games. Buffitt lives in a pig-pen and doesn't care when we spill beer on the rug and knock over popcorn. It's great. No wives to hassle you with coasters, no kids running in front of the tube in the middle of a touchdown play.

"*Ouch!*" he yelped, and turned to a blond woman half his size who had a thumb and forefinger hooked firmly into the back of his arm. "This is my wife, Mitzi."

Mitzi let go of him long enough to shake Quinn's hand. "Pleased to meet you," she said, "and don't you believe him. He doesn't open the door of the rec room during a game unless one of us is showin' blood or guts."

"The first kickoff's at noon. Everyone pitches in twenty

bucks and Buffitt takes care of provisioning. So what do you say?''

Quinn had hoped to spend the day with Olivia, but she was looking way too thrilled that someone was taking pity on him. Come to think of it, she might have set up the whole invitation. But . . . no. She seemed too surprised and too damn pleased about it.

"Sure," he said. "It sounds good."

Another whack on the back and off Mike went with Mitzi, who glanced back at Quinn once or twice from curiosity on their way out of the ballroom.

"Happy now?" he asked Olivia.

"Yes, I am," she answered, preening. "This makes everything worthwhile."

Quinn had to admit, it felt good to be regarded as something more than municipal sewage for once. The plain fact was, he'd lived in half a dozen different cities and towns in his life, and Keepsake was the only place that he had ever considered home. He'd spent the biggest—and the happiest—chunk of his life there, and old memories died hard. It felt good to be back among people his own age with whom he shared a history.

Good enough that he almost forgot why he'd come back to Keepsake in the first place.

Thirteen

Quinn Leary had endured some fairly awful New Year's Eve celebrations in the past seventeen years, but the most dreaded one of all was turning out to be pretty good.

As it turned out, Mike Redding wasn't the only one from Quinn's past who wanted to renew old acquaintance. Over the next hour, a variety of people took the trouble to come over and say hello, and after a while, Quinn detected a pattern: all of them seemed happy with their lot in life. Teacher, nurse, musician, newly adoptive parents . . .

"Obviously they're the kind who look forward, not backward," Quinn told Olivia during a quiet moment alone. They were sitting at a linen-topped table, sampling a plate of sophisticated nibbles that must have cost Owen Bennett a mill worker's annual wage.

Olivia bit into a double-stuffed mushroom and let out a moan of ecstasy that to Quinn's way of thinking was a complete waste of perfectly good passion. "Do you think the reverse is true?" she asked him as she wiped her fingertips on a tiny silver napkin. "Do you think the unhappy ones somehow blame and resent you?"

Quinn shrugged. "Coach Bronsky just walked in and he's spotted me. Check him out—what do you think?"

Olivia glanced up at the coach. "Ouch. He does seem to be sending savage looks our way. Now *there's* someone who should be wearing a mask." She added, "I wonder if he's been drinking."

"Does he have a problem that way?"

"Oh, yes. For years now. It started the year of the murder. He made a fool of himself on local TV after an especially disastrous game, and it's been downhill since. Most of the time he manages to stay sober on the job, but he has a real attitude problem. I have no idea why he's still coaching at the high school. He must know people in high places."

"Speaking of people in high places—here comes your father."

"Oh, no!" cried Olivia, cringing. "Here! Eat one of these! Look impressed! No! Look casual!"

Laughing, Quinn accepted the truffled lobster and then laid it back down on the plate. Sooner or later, this moment had to come. Quinn knew that Owen Bennett was well within his rights to ask him to leave. But the new Quinn, the mellow Quinn, was hoping that he'd be allowed to stay.

Bennett looked—for Owen Bennett—almost pleasant as he came up to their table. "I trust you two are having a good time?" he asked with a fixed smile.

"Very much so," said Quinn, and he, at least, wasn't being wildly ironic.

"Good. Olivia, I wonder if you'd excuse Quinn for a moment? I have something I'd like to discuss with him."

"Oh, Dad, please, don't. Really. Don't. It's my fault—"

"Now, now, you'll have him back in no time. Quinn? Would you do me the honor? I have an excellent collection of antique half hulls in my study," he added, which was relevant to absolutely nothing.

"My pleasure," said Quinn, standing up. He turned to Olivia and said, "Better not go near the shrimp; I remember you broke out in hives at the sophomore dance."

They'd been taking turns pulling out memories, like two kids showing off their baseball cards at camp. The hives reminiscence was new, and Olivia just about clapped her hands with joy at having that memory jogged. Anyone else might have remembered the event with a certain amount of embarrassment. Not Olivia.

Quinn gave her a quick, doting grin and then fell in with Bennett, who, between nods and smiles to his guests, chatted casually about the drive he was spearheading for a new Olympic-sized swimming pool at the high school.

The town of Keepsake, including the high school, belonged to Owen Bennett. That was the message implicit between the lines. Keepsake—and everyone in it—was his. He gave Quinn a sideways look as they walked. Did Quinn understand?

Quinn returned the look. *Yeah, yeah, got it—you're the Big Kahuna.*

Too bad Olivia refused to make it unanimous.

The library was at the end of a roped-off, sentried hall, as far from the merriment as one could get. Bennett took a key from his pocket and slipped it into the keyhole of the massive, paneled door, made from exotic woods that would never again grow on the planet earth.

If Keepsake was Owen Bennett's world, then the library was his sanctum. Everything in it radiated power and prestige: the leatherbound books—all first editions, Quinn had no doubt; the antique spinning globe, roughly the size of a Volkswagen Beetle; framed, fawning thank-you citations tucked like second thoughts on the bookshelves; a fabulous model of a four-masted schooner in its own glass case; and, of course, the ships' hulls. They lined all four walls, a fleet of mastless yachts that weren't going anywhere—except maybe into a list of assets to be probated some day after Bennett sailed off into the Great Beyond.

Geez, Quinn thought, looking around. *If I were his kid and he told me to salute, I'd be damn well tempted to snap my heels and say, "Yessir."* He had to give Olivia credit. It couldn't be easy, resisting the threat of having all those ships' hulls yanked out from under her.

Behind him, he heard a key turn. Owen Bennett was making certain they wouldn't be disturbed. He said to Quinn, "My daughter caught me off guard tonight—she's good at that. It never occurred to me to forbid her from inviting you here. My mistake."

Quinn smiled. "She's a little dickens, all right."

"She's always been a handful," her father agreed with a sigh. He walked over to the leather-topped desk that dominated the middle of the room. "Let's get down to business, shall we?" he asked. He pulled out a side drawer and took out a small white envelope. A small, white, bulging envelope.

"As I say, Quinn, I was caught off guard. I've had to scrape this together from petty cash tonight, but I can no doubt put my hands on more," Bennett said dryly. "Lest you think that those are all twenties in there—they're not." He tossed the envelope on the desk blotter and fanned some of the money out of it. Hundreds, as far as the eye could see, with some McKinleys added for dazzle.

"Door prize?" asked Quinn.

"You've kept your sense of humor. Excellent. I hate to see a grown man whine."

"Au contraire," Quinn said, rocking on the heels of his patent-leather shoes. "Lately it's been nothing but blue skies for me."

Bennett's face, itself a mask of civility, twitched into a sudden scowl. He wasn't a big guy, and that was unfortunate. Quinn was so used to facing a formation of tank-sized brutes on the football field that he found it hard to take a single, smallish, sixty-five-year-old man very seriously, patriarch or no.

Except for the money. The money, Quinn took very seriously indeed. If Owen Bennett could come up with that many thousands just to get Quinn to stop buzzing around him and his family, think what he'd be willing to pay if the stakes were *really* high.

"This money is to buy you a ticket back to California," Bennett said, twitching his lips into a thin smile. "I'll triple the amount if you make it one-way."

"Gee, I dunno," said Quinn with a bland look. "The airlines really penalize for that."

"How much do you want, you son of a bitch?"

The explosion into profanity was just a colorful expression, Quinn knew, but it sent a sharp surge of resentment through him. Who the hell did Bennett think he was talking to?

"Sir," Quinn said, leaning on the desk with the flat of his hands. "I don't think we're communicating real well here. That's my fault, I'm sure. You're a Yale grad, I have a GED. But let me just take another shot at this."

He picked up the envelope and tossed it nearer to Bennett's side of the desk. "I don't want your money. I don't need it, and I don't want it. All I want is to prove my dad's innocence. Now, that strikes me as a mission that any father can endorse. I understand your concern about having Alison exhumed. I understand it. But with the trail to the real murderer paved over and cold, I don't see any other way to exonerate Francis Leary. Can't you comprehend that?"

He stared hard into Owen Bennett's blue eyes, trying to find some hint of who the man was. It was like trying to see water through the ice pack at the North Pole.

Quinn was surprised by Bennett's next remark. "Whoever murdered Alison didn't necessarily get her pregnant. Have you thought of that?"

"I have."

"And?"

"You have to start somewhere."

There was a long, deadly pause. Quinn had the sense that Bennett had played a wild card and was regretting it.

"You're doing this out of respect for your father," Bennett said, taking another tack. "All right. But has it occurred to you that Alison had a father as well? Don't the living deserve some consideration?"

"Your brother Rupert, you mean. In your opposition to the idea of DNA testing, are you speaking for him?"

Quinn knew that he wasn't; the brothers weren't speaking, period.

"Don't underestimate a father's love for his child," Bennett said gruffly, looking away. "Let it go, Quinn," he said, turning back to face him. "I'm telling you, let it go."

Something in his answer touched Quinn. For the first time in seventeen years, he actually felt an inkling of generosity toward the man.

"Look," he said quietly, "I'll go see Alison's parents. I'll explain what I'm doing, why I'm doing it. If they have a problem with it, I'm sure they'll let me know. But I won't see an attorney about pursuing this until I've talked to your brother and his wife. You have my word on that."

It was half a loaf. Bennett, who could buy any bakery he chose, didn't look impressed. Quinn shrugged. It was the best he could do.

"Where does my daughter fit in?"

Quinn shrugged again, but this time he was faking the nonchalance, and he had the flushed cheeks to prove it. "That depends on her," he said.

"Touch her, Quinn, I'll make your life hell."

Lucifer himself couldn't have said it with any more confidence. Quinn nodded slowly, as if he were poring over a menu and couldn't decide between the fish and the chicken. "All righty," he said at last. "That seems clear enough." He gave Owen Bennett a guileless smile and said, "I assume our work here is done?"

"You know the way out."

Presumably he meant out of the library, but Quinn wouldn't have been surprised to find two bouncers on the other side of the door, waiting to lift him by the elbows and chuck him all the way to upper Main.

He turned the key and let himself out, relieved to find the roped-off hall clear except for the security guard at the far end. Nevertheless, he made his way back to the party weighed down by feelings of dread.

I'll make your life hell.

It wouldn't be the first time. If Owen Bennett had rallied to his gardener's defense all those years ago instead of tossing him out on the street without having seen a scintilla of real evidence, then Francis Leary wouldn't have panicked and run, and God only knows how all of their lives would have turned out.

I'll make your life hell. So big deal. There was nothing new in that.

More to the point, though, would he make his daughter's life hell also? If Bennett was as prone to cutting people from his will as Olivia said he was, then . . . Shit. Quinn's Catholic upbringing would never let him handle that kind of guilt. He could sooner mug an old lady than be the direct cause of Olivia's disinheritance. On the other hand, Olivia seemed to be pretty good at getting herself disinherited, so maybe he was worrying about nothing.

There was another aspect that bothered Quinn more than all the rest: He had a strong sense that Owen Bennett was protecting someone. Who it was and why he was doing it— that, Quinn couldn't say. Considering that he was estranged from his brother, Rupert, Owen Bennett seemed pretty damned solicitous of the guy's feelings. Why was he bothering?

That's what Quinn had to find out.

He went back to the table he'd been sharing with Olivia, but she was no longer there. The party had reached critical mass, and the buffet area was filled to overflowing with swarming, hungry guests. There wasn't room to swing a masked cat. The din was horrific. Suddenly Quinn had a headache the size of Rhode Island. It couldn't have been from the champagne, which was anything but cheap; he just wasn't used to this kind of crush. The scene was too contrived and stagy for his laid-back, outdoor tastes. He wanted to get away, to have a moment to puzzle out the nuances of the interview in relative peace and quiet.

Where the hell was Olivia?

He turned and found himself staring into the masked face of a blond aristocrat whom he had once idolized and then overthrown. Rand Bennett—he'd know him anywhere. When they bumped into one another in town the day after Quinn's arrival, Rand had looked both startled and contemptuous. Not tonight. The brilliant blue eyes that gazed through the black mask at Quinn were still contemptuous, but this time they were overlaid with suspicion.

"Evenin', old man," said Quinn in a dead-on imitation of some pompous geezer he'd overheard earlier.

Rand ripped off his mask. Underneath it his fair-skinned face was flushed, not with anger, but from the cold—another fashionably late arrival, apparently.

"What's the deal?" he said in a sneer. "Has my sister got you so whipped that you're letting her use you to get at my dad?"

In a reflex of anger, Quinn started for Rand's throat, then thought better of it.

"I guess I am," he answered with a lazy smile. "Does it show?"

"You—!"

Rand's own lunge ended abruptly when someone pulled him back.

"Are you crazy, Rand? You'll screw up everything!"

Quinn wouldn't have known the man's face behind the big Phantom of the Opera mask, but his booming voice was a dead giveaway: Police Chief Vickers.

Rand twisted his shoulder from the chief's grip and muttered, "Just keep him out of my way, then!"

He stormed off without a backward glance, leaving Quinn to wonder exactly what it was that he was in danger of screwing up.

"Just keep pushing it, Leary," said the chief, and then he, too, walked off—toward the roped-off wing, Quinn noticed with interest.

Quinn watched him swing one leg, then the other, over the velvet rope and then head for the far end of the hall. Reporting for duty? It wouldn't surprise him if the little white envelope ended up finding a home that night, after all.

It was a depressing, disturbing pattern: Everyone around Quinn seemed to be in on something that he was not. He felt a little the way he had back in fifth grade, when Rand and his friends built a tree house on the estate and pulled up the ladder the one time Quinn had ventured to come near.

Rebuffed and embarrassed, he had kept his distance after that. But he didn't embarrass as easily nowadays, not after what he and his father had gone through.

"Oh, Quinn! Oh good, you're alive!"

He turned to see Olivia with a half-ironic, half-sorrowful look on her unmasked face. "I'm sorry, I'm sorry," she said, pressing her hands together in prayerful apology. "Will you ever forgive me?"

He was so happy to see her that he thought, *Forgive you? Oh, yes, and walk to the end of the earth for you besides.*

"Hey," he said in laconic dismissal of the fuss she was making. "No big deal. What do you say we blow off this shindig? I think they're out of party hats, anyway."

"God, yes, let's go."

As they made their way through the guests to retrieve their coats, he found himself wondering why he assumed that Olivia wasn't in on what he now regarded as a conspiracy. Why was it that he suspected everyone of harboring secrets but her?

Because look at her face, you moron. Look at her face.

He did, and what he saw was the face of an angel. Maybe not the best-behaved angel in the universe, but certainly one of the best intentioned. Quinn didn't often trust his instincts, but in this instance, they were far too powerful to ignore. And besides, he was falling for her, and he could never fall for someone he didn't trust.

He handed the hatcheck girl his ticket and they waited as she went off in search of their coats. Olivia explained that her mother had tracked her down and had taken her upstairs not to read her the riot act, but to say how sorry she was that it was never going to work out between Quinn and Olivia.

"She said that?" Quinn said, surprised.

Olivia nodded. "You have to understand, my mother's biological clock is ticking."

"Your *mother's* clock. Uhhh, I don't get that."

"She loves—and I mean, *loves*—babies," Olivia said

with a shrug. "She wants them around while she's young enough to enjoy them."

"Now that's something I never would have considered," he said, trying to seem thoughtful and wise. Holy shit. Considering that he and Olivia hadn't even been to bed yet—were all mothers so Machiavellian? Having been raised without one, Quinn really didn't have a clue.

Olivia smiled and said, "Don't panic. I'm only telling you this so that you know where my mother is coming from."

"Uh-*huh*. Sooo . . . what did you say?"

"What could I say? I told her that clock or no clock, with you or without you, I wasn't ready to—excuse me. Miss?" she said as the hatcheck girl handed them a single wool topcoat. "I had a long black velvet cape?"

The girl, young and bored and no doubt grieving that she had to work on New Year's Eve, shook her head. "Nope. This was it."

Quinn said with a smile, "You can't really miss it. It has a red lining. Why don't you try again?"

Big sigh. Back she went. They waited. She returned. "Nope."

"Do you mind if I look?" Quinn offered.

She had no objection, and he went through every coat on every wheeled rack in the room. He came back out just in time to hear the hatcheck girl say to Olivia, "Now that I think about it, there *was* a guy in here earlier, poking around. I assumed that he came back to put away his gloves or something. Do you think he stole your cape? Why would he steal it?"

"You know," said Quinn, gritting his teeth, "the whole point of a hatcheck girl is to check on the hats."

"I know that, sir," she said with sullen courtesy.

"Oh, never mind, Quinn. It'll show up somewhere. I'll be warm in your car," she said, but she was shivering already as the nearby doors opened and closed.

Something felt very wrong. The cloakroom was filled

with furs, and any thief worth his salt should have gone for one of them, not some funky cape.

"Can you describe the man you saw?" he asked the sulking help.

"No. I only saw him from the back. I couldn't even say if he was wearing a mask, but he was definitely wearing a tux."

"How did he get out of the room without you seeing him?"

"Is this an inquisition?" she huffed.

"Quinn, let it go," Olivia said, clearly anxious to leave.

Fed up himself, Quinn took his coat and wrapped it around Olivia and said, "I'll bring the car around myself."

When he pulled up, Olivia was waiting outside, looking waiflike and lost in his big black coat. Her face brightened when he pulled up, and he felt a surge of odd, unexpected triumph. She was throwing her lot in with him. Olivia Bennett, Princess of Keepsake, was about to take up with Quinn Leary, the gardener's son. Him!

How could he not feel triumphant?

Fourteen

As they drove away from the estate, he could see Olivia's spirits begin to rise noticeably. She didn't ask Quinn about the meeting with her father, and he didn't offer to fill her in. Maybe she knew that Owen Bennett tended to be free and easy with his checkbook whenever things got sticky. If she didn't, then someone else was going to have to tell her. It sure wasn't going to be Quinn.

In any case, by the time the Mercedes began the steep climb up the hill to her townhouse, Olivia seemed to have shaken off her jittery mood and had become, once again, the warm and alluring woman who'd had him going around in circles of lust and longing for the past few hours.

In the hall she dumped his coat over a tall-backed chair and slipped off her shoes, then said, "Turn around."

Puzzled, Quinn did as he was told. When he turned back to her, he saw a pair of gray pantyhose lying on top of his coat. Good news: There wasn't a whole lot of clothing left on her body. Bad news: Why had she made him turn around?

Glancing at a small brass clock on the mantel, Olivia said, "Not long to midnight. I'll make tea."

More bad news. He'd been thinking wine.

"Fine with me," he lied, and he followed her into the kitchen. He watched her put on a kettle, taking satisfaction from the sight of her moving, unbound, in that silvery, clingy dress. She was as fluid as liquid mercury, and probably as tricky to hold.

"Too bad I never got the chance to meet Eileen," he said, trying hard to keep his hands off those hips as she glided barefoot past him. "She sounds like someone I'd like to know."

"Eileen would never come with Zack having a temperature," Olivia said as she took out two mugs. "Frankly, I was surprised to see Rand there; he worries about the kids as much as she does. They're incredibly dear to him."

She added, "I suppose he felt obliged to put in at least a token appearance. New Year's Eve means a lot to my mother. My father proposed on New Year's Eve."

"A time for new beginnings," Quinn agreed, hoping fervently that this was one of them.

She brushed his sleeve as she reached for the tea canister. He turned and brought his arm around her, flattening his hands on the counter on either side of her. Penned in like that, she might have turned skittish, or even hostile.

No siree. "Hey, aren't you cramped in that monkey suit?" she asked, reaching up to his bow tie. With ease she undid the knot, then tossed the strip of black cloth on the counter—and furthermore, went on to undo the top three studs of his shirt.

Good news.

"All better," she said lightly.

"Much better," he said, lowering his mouth to hers.

Their lips met, their tongues touched. Her arms came up around his neck and he found himself sliding his hands along them, simply to savor the soft, smooth surface of her skin. He was used to working with stone—hard, rough, resistant—and she was everything that his work was not.

Liquid mercury she may have been, but she was turning him into a puddle of molten iron as he deepened the kiss, pinning her in his arms, all the while listening to the shriek of his blood roaring through his veins.

"B-boiling," she stammered.

"Oh God . . . you bet," he said in a groan.

"I mean—" She pointed limply toward the stove. The chrome kettle, spouting steam, was doing it with a vengeful screech.

He let her go, reluctantly, and she filled the poppy-red mugs. After that she set them with symmetrical precision on a small wood tray. She put a cobalt blue plate between the mugs. She laid two spoons, like a pair of oars, one on each side of the tray. And then, very carefully, she began carrying the tray out of the room.

"Should we think about tea bags?" he asked at last.

"Oh! Those. Right," she said, frowning into the mugs of boiled water. She looked up at Quinn and the frown remained. "*You.* Into the living room and stay there until I bring the tea."

Quinn smiled and took himself out of her sight, convinced that he was about to experience the best New Year's Eve he'd ever had. He tossed off his jacket—the place was nicely warm—and rolled up his shirtsleeves. Free from the distraction that was Olivia, Quinn was able to focus on the efficient majesty of her townhouse. It wasn't large, but all the glass sure as hell made it look spacious. During the day it probably seemed twice as big, because the floor-to-ceiling windows would bring much of the outside in.

He was standing at one of those bare, oversized windows, looking out into an unnervingly black landscape, when Olivia came in with the tray and set it on a bronze-legged table in front of a sinfully soft-looking couch.

Quinn stayed where he was, thinking now about that blackness and about the missing cape. Who took it, and where was it now? More important, where was *he* now?

"I found some cookies that are hardly soggy at all. Come sit. We don't have much time until they drop the ball," she said, flipping through the networks with her remote.

He walked back to the sofa and sank into a cloud-soft cushion beside her. The TV was broadcasting merriment from Times Square, but his mind was in computer mode now.

Why steal it? Did someone know it was hers? How? Either he had seen her arrive in it, or he had watched the two of them leave the townhouse together earlier. Of course, someone could have known from the get-go that the cape was Olivia's. A friend or a relative. Quinn decided to put that possibility aside for the moment. It didn't make sense, and he didn't want it to make sense.

"Quinn! Really! Where did I lose you?" Olivia asked, waving her hand in front of his face as if she were a hypnotist whose act had gone wrong.

"Hmm? Sorry," he said. "My mind was somewhere else."

"So I see," she said, standing back up. With a look of pure, devilish mischief she hiked her silver slip of a dress to mid-thigh and brought one knee down on each side of him, straddling him. She began working the lower buttons of his shirt.

"Now you're trying to shock me," he said mildly.

"Am I succeeding?"

"Real well." He had a hard-on that felt the size of his forearm. What was it that a great historian had once said? God gave man a brain and a penis, with only enough blood to run one at a time?

Right now, Quinn knew just where all the blood was pooled.

He looked up into Olivia's eyes, dark and dancing and inviting, and he decided, what the heck, first things first. "You're a witch, you know that?" he murmured, slipping his hand behind her dress. He gave a tug at the zipper and listened to the satisfying sound of its effortless slide as the fabric loosed what little hold it had on her body.

He had the sense that he was testing her and she was testing him, but no one flinched. She smiled, and Quinn realized that the smile had been seventeen years in coming.

"Sweet Olivia," he whispered, sliding the thin sparkly strap off her shoulder. He watched with pleasure as her eyes fluttered lower and her lips parted in a sigh. Greedy for her flesh, he nuzzled, then nipped her shoulder, marveling that it was like no other, and peeled her dress lower still, exposing bare breast. With his tongue he tasted its rosy tip, making her moan.

His craving for her was wide and deep, and it left him shaky. "Liv . . . ah, Liv," he said, unable now to utter more than the essence of her. He peeled away the silver fabric like a wrapper from a candy bar, exposing her other breast, sending his own hunger to a new level of anticipation, a boy with a KitKat bar all for his own.

Make it last, he thought, but he couldn't get at her fast enough. He began to devour her, dragging his mouth from one breast to the other, thrilling to the sound of her breaths coming fast, always in fear that, like a candy bar, she would somehow vanish in no time flat.

Her moans became shudders; her shudders, a series of whimpering pants, until she caught his face between her splayed fingers and kissed him hard. Her tongue was everywhere at once, reckless and wanting. He met and circled it with his own, in a dance as predestined as any in the animal kingdom. *Come to me, come to me* was the song on both their lips.

In one easy motion he twisted her up from his lap and onto her back, her left side lost in the seafoam-colored pillows that lined the sofa and tumbled over her like surf. Her face was flushed, her lips puffy and wet; he could not imagine a more desirable countenance.

"Let me love you," he said in a besotted voice.

"Quinn, yes . . . oh yes," she answered, lifting her arms to him. The gesture was so completely without guile that it pierced his heart with its devastating directness. Quinn found himself sitting up and sucking in a lungful of air, simply to get past the blow.

And that was his undoing.

Because as he did it, the beam of a car's lights cut across them like the sweep from a lighthouse. He couldn't believe it. Out there, somewhere below them, was a curving drive where cars were free to roam. Olivia's house was on a knoll and the windows were low enough that the combination provided ringside viewing for the curious as well as the calculating.

"Jesus!" he said. "We're on stage!"

"No, we're not. No one can see us. No one cares," she argued breathlessly, tugging at his sleeve.

An incredulous laugh escaped him. "Olivia—a car just went by. I practically saw the whites of the driver's eyes." He pulled her dress back up, as if he'd been caught doing something wrong, and felt a sudden surge of irritation at his guilty response. Damn it! It was the last feeling he wanted.

He stood up, determined to get past the welter of bad emotions stuck in his craw like lousy pizza. "Hey, kiddo," he said softly, "unless we tape newspapers over those windows, this is not going to happen. Not here, not on this couch."

Her smile was edgy; she was taking it personally. "No problem," she said, sitting up and pulling the sparkly spaghetti straps over her shoulders again.

It was absolutely the wrong time to ask the question, but it came flying out: "Have you ever worn that cape before?"

Obviously the blood had returned to his brain.

She stared at him. "Why are you asking me *that*?"

"Just . . . have you?"

"Yes," she said, clearly annoyed at the shift in his mood. "Once. To the Met, five years ago. Why?" she repeated.

He knew he shouldn't continue to obsess over the cape, but the blood was where it was. "If no one knew that you owned that cape—if it wasn't your trademark, say, during the holidays—then someone must have seen you in it for the first time tonight."

"Your point being?"

"My point being, it couldn't have been stolen for its value, not with all those furs around. Someone wanted it because it was *your* cape, Olivia."

She snorted and said, "I think you're confusing me with Elvis Presley. No one would want a cape because it's mine."

But Quinn was on a mission now, determined to put

some healthy fear in her. She was just too blasé for a beautiful woman living alone and fraternizing with the enemy.

He said, "Indulge me here, please. How could someone have known it was your cape? He could have seen you as we entered the great hall tonight. I admit, that's the likeliest scenario."

He hooked a thumb at the blackness pressing against the bank of windows. "Or he could have seen you as we left here. Which means he could be out there again. If that's the case, I'd just as soon that he didn't see any more of you than he has already," he said dryly.

Her response to that was incredulous laughter. "There's no one out there, Quinn." She stood up and, egging him on with a defiant smile, took hold of the straps of her dress. Apparently she planned to flash the darkness to make her point.

"Oh, for—humor me, would you, goddammit?" he said, reaching her in two long strides. He scooped her up in his arms before she could irritate him any more than she already had and hushed her objections with a hard kiss. Then he began carrying her up the stairs, he didn't know why. To prove how powerless she could be in some man's arms?

She seemed to have mixed emotions about his impulsive act. "Hey! What're you doing?" she cried. "Quinn! Put me down!" But she didn't struggle, and he was grateful for that. He was tired of playing games.

At the top of the stairs, he said, "Which bedroom?" and before she could answer, he toed the right door open and walked through it with her still in his arms.

"Drapes—good," was all he said. She laughed. He laid her on the bed and kissed her again, a wet and hungry promise, and then he began to unbutton his shirt.

Bemused, she said, "I feel like Scarlett O'Hara."

"I never read the book," he said, tossing his shirt on a chair.

"We'll have to rent the video."

He peeled off his undershirt and sent it sailing over to the long-sleeved shirt, then kicked off his shoes and unzipped his trousers. He looked up with a wry smile. "Next thing I know, you'll be wanting to rent *Titanic*."

"No, I've—"

Off went the trousers, off went the Jockey underwear, and whatever it was that she was going to say about *Titanic*, it never got formed into speech. ·

That's it, thought Olivia. Spoiled forever. That grin . . . on that body . . . Quinn Leary was the answer to a woman's fantasies. She felt a sudden moment of panic, a stab of inadequacy. He could be in a Calvin Klein ad. She couldn't.

"Almost forgot," he said, reaching into the hip pocket of his pants. He came up with two foil packets and slapped them down on the painted nightstand. "For starters. Now. Where were we?"

He looked and sounded so cocky. If any other man had approached her with such confidence . . . but this was Quinn, the mighty Quinn, and he was definitely entitled.

He sat on the side of the bed and said with a burning look, "Now you."

"Now me," she whispered.

He reached for the sparkly straps with hands that were shaky, and with infinite tenderness he slid the straps from her shoulders. And from that single, tender gesture, she knew: she was in love with him.

"You *have* seen *Gone with the Wind*," she said in a flash of illumination. "And *Titanic*, too." She knew it, because at that moment she could see straight into his soul. He was a romantic.

But he would never admit it. He gave her a wonderfully wry look and said, "Prove it," then peeled her dress down and down and down.

She felt cool air alight on her bare breasts, her fluttering stomach, her thighs in their high-cut panties. Nearly free.

He knelt on the bed, straddling her lower legs, and slid his hands up the sides of her body, letting them come to rest on her breasts. He kissed and teased and suckled until her nipples ached and she begged for mercy, whimpering *don't, don't*, when she wasn't murmuring *more, more*. Again and again he came back to her mouth, the way a thirsty man goes to the well, and every time, he told her how much he wanted her.

When he had her clawing at his back in frustration, he began a long, slow slide downward with his tongue, building her up, heating her up, making her frantic for release. Her underpants went the way of the rest, and she opened herself to him, welcoming him, and felt his hands, huge, cup her under her buttocks and lift her arching hips to his kisses.

No mercy for her; he kindled her until she was up, up, and nearly over the edge. She was holding back, trying to hold on, when she felt herself slip and begin to fall.

"Not that way, Quinn," she said in a gasp. "In me . . . oh, please . . ."

With a low laugh he said, "For you, anything."

He shifted his position to be even with her and kissed her harder than she'd ever been kissed before. It was new, wanton, rough, and she loved it, loved him. He had complete control over her responses, but she didn't care because she loved him, and if he told her to take a flying leap off a cliff just then, she would do it because he had asked.

She heard a tear of foil and then endured the damnable reassurance of him slipping a condom on himself, and then he slid in easily in one sharp thrust, taking her breath from her, exactly what she wanted, to be left dazed and filled and every nerve ending quivering, and then she cried, *"Wait!"*

"Wait?"

"Yes . . . for me to save up again."

He chuckled, then buried his face in the curve of her neck and said, "Sure," driving her right back up to the edge in no time at all, which amazed her, because she wasn't the type to come quickly or often.

She thought.

And meanwhile, always, always, she was aware of him in her, separated by that barrier, and she thought, what a waste, what a waste to hold back that seed. But the thought went away and she was left with only a mindless drive to comple-

tion, a primitive need to drive more deeply into her own pleasure. Wild, she was wild to have him. She sought and found
his hands and gripped them in her own on each side of her,
pinning herself down with him. Lifting her haunches in a rush
to take him all the way in, she matched him thrust for thrust
and groan for groan, his equal in everything except her terrifying, deep-seated need to submit, the only way to true equal-
ity. It was a profound, completely erotic thought, and it
whipped her into a blissful plunge right over that cliff, a free-
fall into space that must have been very like death, except for
the fact that she knew that Quinn was falling with her.

Olivia thought that maybe they'd died, after all.

She had no idea how long they lay in their own dampness
on top of the coverlet, wrapped in one another's arms. A
minute? An hour? She tried to move, but she didn't have
the strength. They could have been lying broken-boned at
the bottom of a canyon, the way she felt.

It was Quinn who stirred first. With a groan, he rolled
off her and lay flat on his back, shielding his eyes from the
light with the back of his forearm. "Tell me the earth moved
for you," he said at last. "Because I've just been to Mars
and back."

"I think it moved and fell on top of me," she said, staring immobilized at the ceiling.

"This feels like silk," Quinn muttered, sliding his hand
over the surface of the bed. "Is it?"

"Uh-huh."

"The condom dripped. Did I just wreck it?"

"Uh-huh."

"Oh, well. In that case . . ."

He trailed the back of his fingers lazily over her knee
and up her thigh.

"Oh, Quinn, really, I can't," she said, scandalized at the
thought of it. "Honestly. You don't know me. Really. I can't."

His hand slid from the top of her thigh to her warm, wet,
still-throbbing cleft.

Amazingly, it turned out that she could.

Fifteen

They lay curled in sleep, Olivia nestled in the curve of Quinn's body, as a sullen drizzle became ugly and turned to icy rain. A nagging northeast wind drove the sleet into the windowpanes, tap-tap-tapping at Quinn's subconscious.

He dreamed fear. It was all around him, a pervasive sense that someone was going to get killed. In his dream he was rushing from house to house, from river to woods, always a frustrating two steps behind a mysterious presence in a black cape. Death? Dracula? He wanted desperately to find out before it was too late.

At the same time, he was afraid. He was convinced that sooner or later he would catch up with the lurking evil, and he wasn't sure that he'd survive the encounter. But he continued to run from hill to hollow anyway, exhausting himself, his breath coming faster and faster until at last he was within reach of the presence. He grabbed at the cape, the way he'd been grabbed by the jersey a thousand different times on the football field, and the presence turned on him, rising up monumentally large and black and powerful and horrifying Quinn.

Quinn started from the nightmare, lifting himself up on one arm, his heart hammering wildly, his eyes wide open to see . . . nothing. Nothing more than the sweet curve of a woman, sleeping peacefully with long, slow breaths, her soul in a happier place than his had been.

He stayed braced on one elbow, waiting for his heartbeat

to calm down, and gazed at the sleeping form next to him. She was so innocent, so vulnerable. He had to protect her— and Mrs. Dewsbury, too—but he couldn't be everywhere at once. Was he deluded? *Were* they at risk? And how could he protect them, when he himself was the reason they were at risk, if they were at risk? Insane paradox!

Olivia . . . sweet Liv. He snuggled into the softness of her pillow, breathing her scent, restoring his baffled and battered spirit with the simple nearness of her. Oh, to wake up every day next to her . . . no man could ask for more. He slid his arm around her waist and snuggled her to him. Olivia sighed in her sleep and burrowed her hips into his crotch; and in the space of that single movement, his desire to protect her became transformed into a hunger to have her. Earlier that night he had wanted her desperately. Now he needed her, just as desperately.

He lifted his arm and brought it back to her buttocks, then slipped his hand between her thighs from behind. He had one goal in mind: to arouse her. If only he could make her want him . . . if only she would deign to receive him . . . he would consider it an honor of the highest magnitude. He had no rubies for her, no pearls. He had only his ability to give her pleasure.

Please let it be enough.

He began a slow, gentle caress, separating her soft, warm flesh, and then with feathery strokes he began to coax her back from her dreamworld and into the waking one where he lay alone and bereft.

She stirred, and then she stirred a little more. Her sigh, half moan, told him what he needed to know. He was coming to her, hat in hand, and she was willing to hear him out.

He quickened the pace of his strokes, focusing on the hard nub he found there, marveling that a thing so small could contain power so vast. Her moans were no longer sighs. She was inhaling deep, long draughts of air, letting them out on the sound of his name: "Quinn . . . oh, Quinn . . . oh, Quinn . . ."

She rolled over on her stomach and brought herself partially up on her knees, inviting him in, unmistakably. In a waking dream he swung his knee over her calves and brought himself in an easy slide deep inside of her. He was reaching into her, reaching out to her. She was the one, the only one, who could make his life whole again. His movements became a pumping scramble for oneness with her, a defiant stand against caped villainy and murdered dreams.

With one hand he gripped a spoke of the headboard, with the other he braced himself on the bed as he plunged over and over into her, hanging on for dear life, waiting for he didn't know what. And then she cried out, and he knew at once what it was: her. He was waiting for her. Had been waiting, for seventeen indistinct years. He felt an explosive, tremendous release into her, and his body collapsed on hers, but by then he was somewhere else altogether—on some other plane, in some other realm.

But with her.

Olivia Bennett, so-called morning person, opened one eye and was amazed to see that it was eight-thirty. She never slept past six.

She was alone in her bed. With a stab of disappointment she rolled over, and then she saw Quinn, dressed in shorts and T-shirt and sitting in the tub chair, watching her. His face was a study in serenity. He looked exactly like what he was: a man who acted with purpose and a sense of commitment. It gave her a rush to know that he couldn't be involved with her just for the thrill of it.

Through the window behind him, she saw scudding clouds being bumped out of view by brilliant sunshine. As with everything else in her life just then, it promised a new beginning.

"Happy New Year," she said to him softly. She stretched luxuriously and sighed, then jabbed an index finger playfully into the rumpled covers beside her. "How come you're over there instead of over here?"

"I wouldn't have been able to let you sleep if I were lying awake next to you," he said simply. He stood up and elbowed his shoulders back as if he'd been sitting in one position for too long, then slapped his flat stomach. "And— I was afraid you'd hear my stomach growling and think a wild boar had got into the room."

Smiling, she said, "Breakfast sounds great. Where should we go?"

"On New Year's Day? Unless you have a thing for Egg McMuffins, I think we should stay right here and scrounge up something," he said, walking over to the bed and sitting on it beside her.

"Here? Hmm. You know, I might be a little low on supplies. I didn't have a chance to go food shopping this week."

Or last. Or the one before that.

"No problem. I'll rustle up some pancakes," he said, taking her hand in his. "You have mix?"

"I . . . had to throw it out last summer. Moths," she said, feeling desperately ashamed.

"Got any eggs?"

"Egg Beaters. I think. No, wait. I defrosted the carton for a cat I was watching. That was dumb. She hardly went near it. I should've refrozen it."

"Bread?"

"A couple of ends. They might be a teeny bit green," she admitted.

He cocked his head and said, "You're not one of those anorexic types, are you?"

"*No*! Bring me one of your pies and see for yourself," Olivia said with spirit. She sat up but—intensely aware of the wantonness of their middle-of-the-night coupling—she was feeling suddenly shy, so she kept the sheet tucked demurely around her breasts and under her arms.

He noticed it, of course. "You shower first," he said, chastely kissing the top of her head. "I'll see what's down there. I can always run out to a Store 24."

"In your tuxedo?"

"Oh, hell—right. Boy. Those McMuffins are sounding better and better," he muttered on his way out of the room.

It rankled. "Hey!" she shouted after him. "If I wanted to, I could be a *great* cook. As it is, I'm a ... perfectly respectable one. Perfectly!"

She had to do it—she just had to tell that lie.

He backed into the room. "Oh, yeah? Pop quiz: how do you make crêpes?"

"Crêpes? What's the big deal? Some flour and ... and eggs and you mix it up," she said, waving her arms in a wild stirring gesture, "and you bake it and you're done."

He poked his tongue in his cheek and nodded. "Uh-huh," he said with a lazy, knowing smile.

It was only after he was gone that Olivia realized that the sheet had fallen down to her lap and that he had been, in fact, enjoying the view. With anyone else, anytime else, she would have been half annoyed, half embarrassed, but now she felt brazenly flattered.

You shameless little hussy, she told herself, smiling as she threw back the covers. She headed for the shower in a blissful, sated mood and turned on the water. How long had it been since she'd felt this good?

Get real. You've never felt this good.

And now that she had discovered this new and sexy self of hers, was her life about to become richer and fuller at last?

Not without Quinn, dimwit. Not without Quinn.

It was a scary thought: She was never going to be All That She Could Be without Quinn around to make it happen. It had always been true on an intellectual level, and now it was true on the physical. She was doomed, unless she could come up with a plan to keep Quinn in Keepsake. Her mind wandered through a dozen scenarios, all of them equally stupid, before coming back to the only one that made any sense to her.

We have to get married. Obviously. I'm just going to have to propose.

Olivia Bennett was a type A, independent, take-charge kind of woman; but even she could see that Quinn Leary might think she was possibly jumping the gun by proposing. Still, if the time and place were right . . .

She was wrapping a towel around herself, relieved to have a plan—no matter how whimsical—when Quinn walked in.

Right time? Right place?

"Chief Vickers is walking up your front steps."

"What?"

As if on cue, the doorbell rang. "Don't answer it!" she cried.

"The man isn't blind, Liv. He looked straight at the Mercedes as he walked past it."

"That could be anyone's. We don't have to open the door—I've seen the cop shows—not unless he has a warrant."

"If that's what you want to do."

Olivia could see that Quinn was convinced she was afraid to be caught with him. Could anything be further from the truth? "On second thought, we have nothing to apologize for," she said, tossing aside the towel and pulling the sweatshirt over her head. She jabbed her foot into one of the legs of her sweatpants. "We're consenting adults. Let's hear what the man has to say."

If this is Dad's doing, I swear I'll kill him.

"Fine with me," Quinn said with a shrug. "I'll put on my trousers and meet you downstairs."

Olivia dashed down the stairs and swung the door open to the dour-faced chief.

"Got a minute, Livvy?" he asked her.

"It's not the best time, Chief," she said loftily. "I assume it's important?"

"You tell me," he answered, and marched past her. In the sunlit entry hall he looked more official and misplaced than ever. He glanced pointedly up the stairs, then said, "You're missing a black velvet cape?"

"Oh, good. Someone turned it in. But you didn't have to make a special trip."

Unless you're looking for an excuse to spy on me and report to my father, that is.

The chief dumped the duffel he was carrying onto the varnished hall table, making Olivia wince. He unzipped the bag, reached in, and pulled out her sodden cape.

Dismayed, she cried, "Someone threw it in a ditch!"

"Not exactly," he said, holding the cape by the shoulders and letting it drip onto the slate floor of the hall. "Someone hoisted it up the flagpole on Town Hill. It stayed there most of the night until—wouldn't you know it?—poor Father Tom saw it early this morning. But here's the interesting thing," he remarked, spreading the front panels outward for her to see.

The satin lining had been slashed to shreds. Long, frayed ribbons of red hung like thirsty tongues from someone's private hell. Instinctively Olivia stepped back, trying to distance herself from the display of violence she saw there.

Quinn was now behind her. He said quietly to the chief, "I guess we don't have to ask if Father Tom saw anybody hoisting this. Might he have *heard* someone doing it, somewhere in the back of his mind? The wind was blowing like stink from the northeast, which means that the flag halyard would have been slapping hard against the flagpole all night. But that would have changed over to silence as the cape was hoisted and a load put on the halyard. It would give us a time of occurrence. Father Tom might even have seen a car go by sometime around then—if he could remember when it became quiet."

The chief snorted and said, "What're you, a junior detective now?"

Quinn didn't rise to the bait. Olivia wasn't even sure he heard the crack, so focused was he on the discovery. He took the cape from the police chief with a "May I?" and laid it out on the slate floor.

"It would be good if you could come up with a list of early departures from the gala," he told the chief as he crouched beside the cape, studying the gashes in its scarlet lining. "Or anyone who left and then came back. But I don't have to tell *you* that."

Apparently he did. Vickers aimed a scowl at the top of

Quinn's head and said, "You're implying it was one of Mr. Bennett's guests?"

Quinn didn't bother to look up. "I'm not implying. I'm saying."

Olivia, feeling queasy, stuck in her two cents. "My father doesn't know anybody who hates me that much."

"Not you, Liv," said Quinn. This time he did look up. His brow was raked over with concern and in his eyes she saw something she'd never seen before: fear. For her. Because of him.

She shivered. The chief saw it and said, "Your hair is all wet. You'll catch cold, Livvy."

She tried to be flippant and brave. "Probably someone just walked over my grave, that's all," she said with a tight smile at Quinn.

"Cut it out!" Quinn said.

"Oh, all right," she answered, deflated by the sharp tone of his voice. "But really—I mean, how can a guy in a *tuxedo*, no less, stroll in dress shoes through mud and snow and dog poop to the top of Town Hill, then hook up a cape to a halyard and hoist it to the highest point in town, without ever being seen? How?"

"We don't know that he wasn't seen," said the chief. "It's early days yet."

"He might not have been wearing a tuxedo," Quinn pointed out. "Not everyone at the gala came in black tie."

Olivia chewed on her thumbnail. "That's true." She turned to Quinn and said, "Was Coach Bronsky wearing a tux? I can't remember."

The chief exploded. "What the hell are you asking about *him* for?"

"I . . . I don't know," Olivia said, faltering before his wrath. "I suppose because he gave us such an evil look."

"I doubt he was the only one."

"*I* didn't notice anyone else. Did you?" she asked Quinn.

Quinn was about to say something but stopped himself.

"I suspect the chief is right," he said calmly. "We tended only to notice the good guys."

"Don't go characterizing people around here as good or bad, Quinn. You don't know shit about who's either."

"I guess we'll find out, won't we?" Quinn said as he got to his feet again.

The two men were the same height and standing eye to eye. All that separated them were twenty years and a beer belly. During all of those years and all of those beers, Chief Vickers had nourished a keen grudge; Olivia couldn't remember him ever saying a positive thing about either Quinn or his father, and she could see why. He blamed Francis Leary for getting away, and Quinn for the fact that his own son had never done much with his life.

It was hard to say which of the men standing there resented the other one more just then, but Olivia had no intention of finding out. "Does my father know about this yet?" she asked, tossing out the question like a biscuit between two growling dogs.

Chief Vickers turned and snapped it up first. "Mr. Bennett had a long night; I didn't want to barge in on him too early. And I wanted to make sure this was yours. I thought I saw you arrive in it last night," he said, crouching down to roll up the cape. "If you don't mind, I'll keep it for a little while."

"By all means," Olivia said, glad to see it go.

He stuffed the rolled cape back into the green-and-white duffel bag—a Keepsake Cougars team bag—and then he gave the visor of his hat a yank.

"Enjoy your day," he said with one last glance at Quinn. It was meant to be insinuating, and Olivia took it that way.

She closed the door after he left and leaned against it, mostly for support and partly to keep the man from coming back in. "Well, that was exciting," she said. "And I thought last night couldn't be topped."

Quinn shook his head. "It's not a joke, Liv. These attacks are too choreographed. Whoever is doing it is nuts and he's fearless; it can't get more dangerous than that."

Olivia used the sleeve of her sweatshirt to blot a small puddle on the glossy surface of the hall table. "Do you really think so?" she asked, angling her head to see that she'd got all the water. "I don't. I mean, they're pranks, that's all. Vicious, maybe, but they're still pranks."

"The effigy was a prank. Slashing the lining, that was an act of terror."

She looked up from her task at him. "I wish you wouldn't look like that, Quinn," she said softly. "You're scaring me."

"I want you to be scared, dammit! We don't have a clue what we're dealing with here. You may be the Princess of Keepsake, but trust me, that's just a figure of speech. You saw the cape. That could've been—"

The unfinished thought hung in the air between them like a half-spun web.

Quinn let out a sigh of exasperation and took her in his arms. He held her tight. "This thing is so damned frustrating—I can't think straight."

"Because you're hungry," she said in a muffled voice as she buried her head in his shoulder. "C'mon, let's go to McDonald's. They have a drive-through."

Olivia pulled a hooded sweatshirt over her head while Quinn donned his topcoat; they made a comically incongruous pair.

"All set?" he asked, holding the door for her.

"Starving," Olivia said. She stepped around the wet image on the floor as if it were a chalked-in body at a crime scene, and let Quinn lead the way to his car.

Sixteen

Ray Buffitt was the same amiable slob he'd always been, only now he was able to convert his bad habits into a social asset: The rented house in which he dwelled was considered a paradise by every one of his wife-fearing pals.

Quinn was given a quick tour of the place before the six men who were gathered there hunkered down for their marathon of football viewing. Since Quinn had never had the chance to go away to college, what he saw was an eye-opener.

Half-full beer cans, empty Doritos bags, crumpled Ding Dongs wrappers, and dried-out bean dip floated throughout the house like water lilies on a pond. There were exotic waterfalls, two of them: one from the leaking sink in the kitchen, and one from the sink in the downstairs (no one in his right mind would call it a guest) bathroom. There was white sand from a litterbox tucked in a corner of the kitchen, its gritty contents half kicked out and grinding underfoot. There were tropical fish (four guppies swimming in a tank) and tropical snakes (a boa constrictor in another tank, waiting perhaps to be fed the fish). All in all, it was a paradise, a fantasy.

A pigpen, just as Mike Redding had said.

As for the media equipment, it was all state of the art and thoughtfully arranged. The big-screen TV was hooked up through the stereo and jammed against a window to block the sun from washing out one's viewing pleasure. The CDs, many hundreds of them, were arranged on the eye-level shelves of two bookcases for easy selection (the *Sports Illustrated*s, except for the dog-eared swimsuit issues, were confined to the lower shelves and were harder to peruse, but it couldn't be helped). A pair of speakers as tall as Quinn were situated for excellent sound separation on each side of the non-working fireplace, which itself was being used to house part of Ray's vast and valuable collection of beer bottles.

"He had 'em appraised once," Mike explained to Quinn as they slugged down their Coors before the first game. "They're worth a fortune. Take that Blow Hole from Wyoming, Rhode Island," he said, pointing to an unopened bottle with a pristine label. "That one alone is worth two hundred bucks—extremely limited edition," Mike said in a voice of envy.

"I'd love to have an awesome hobby like that," Mike added with a sigh. "But Mitzi says beer caps only, no bottles." He shrugged and dropped his empty Coors can into a bamboo magazine rack. "What're you gonna do?"

Quinn made sympathetic noises, but the whole scene was beyond him. He had been raised by his father to be both methodical and thorough, and acts of domestic defiance left him unimpressed. Besides, seventeen years of exile had made him something of a loner; it was unlikely that he could ever feel like one of the guys the way he once did.

And yet they had welcomed him into their haven easily enough. Mike, Ray, Neal, Cutter, Todd—all of them were friendly and accepting in an offhand way. As far as they were concerned, Quinn was just another fist pumping in the air after a kick-ass play.

Quinn settled into a plaid easy chair whose arms had been shredded by the cat he now knew was called Digger, and began munching his way through a bag of Ruffles as Tennessee kicked off against Nebraska in the Cotton Bowl. His interest in the game was minimal; he was there strictly to keep his eyes and ears open for useful scuttlebutt.

In fact, he hadn't wanted to come at all, not after the

cape episode. But Olivia had refused to let him stay behind just to stand guard over her. She was bound for the outlet malls with Eileen, she had told him, while Rand stayed home with the kids. Eileen would have her head if Olivia begged out of their annual foraging expedition.

In any case, Olivia was far too independent to be watched over. It was both her great strength and her maddening flaw.

"Bronsky said the guy couldn't run—hah! Look at 'im go!" crowed Neal. "Bronsky don't know from squat!"

They watched the replay and then Cutter turned to Ray and said, "You ever gonna let Coach back in your house, Buffitt-man?"

"No way," Ray said. "Not after that."

Quinn's ears pricked up. "What'd he do?"

Ray said, "Ah, the asshole got drunk and smashed up some of my beer bottles. I like a drinker as well as the next guy, but I hate a mean drunk. If he—way to go, Dejuan! How many yards was Dejuan good for this year, Todd?"

Whenever anyone needed to know something, he asked Todd. An accountant by trade, Todd had an encyclopedic memory. Not to mention, he'd once won a pair of tickets to the Superbowl in a bar-sponsored trivia contest.

The game was pretty good. After a scoreless first quarter, the lead moved back and forth between the two archrivals. Quinn made sure that he hooted and hollered with the rest of them, but his mind was fixed firmly on the torn-up cape that Chief Vickers had recovered early that morning.

While the others gnawed on beef jerky, Quinn chewed on the ongoing mystery. Was he the only one who believed that each of the "pranks" was more ominous than the one before it? The goal was obvious—to get Quinn out of Keepsake—but how far was some creep willing to go to achieve it?

By halftime, the score was tied and everyone in the room was beered up and pumped. They switched to another game, but it was laughably uneven. Ray Buffitt, ever the perfect host, had anticipated the dread possibility and had programmed the best of two dozen CDs into a nonstop blitz of rock and roll.

"Don't wanna lose momentum, right?" was his explanation as he cranked up the volume.

Between the music and the two or three conversations being shouted back and forth over one another as the game played on the giant screen, there was a real danger of sensory meltdown. Quinn, used to the serenity of the outdoors, was going nuts. It was probably quieter in the commodities pit the day after Oprah told her audience that hamburgers scared her.

Quinn was about to rip the CD player out of its perch in the bookcase and throw it into the fireplace when Cutter shouted to him, "Hey, I forgot! Guess who asked me about you the other day?"

Quinn shrugged and shouted, "You got me. Who?"

"Alison's old man, that's who! I guess he recognized me from the old days when he used to bring in his truck for a tune-up; I don't know where he takes it now. Anyway, we were at the same self-serve island at the Shell—near the IHOP? I haven't seen him in years. Man, the old bastard is as ornery as ever. I don't know how Alison ever put up with him."

"She didn't," Neal said, flattening a beer can with his shoe. "She got herself her very own knight in shining armor."

"Oh, yeah—Sir Lancelot," Cutter said with a snort. "A lotta help *he* was."

"What did you expect? What did Randy Lancelot ever end up doing for any of us?"

"Not take us all the way, that's for sure. Sixth place, that he could do. Whoopee."

They laughed contemptuously and turned to other talk, leaving Quinn sitting there stunned. The exchange had come and gone in the crunch of a potato chip, but it left no doubt in Quinn's mind that Rand Bennett had been deeply involved with his cousin Alison. The question was, what kind of involvement? Quinn had never seen any evidence that the two had been close. Did that itself point to a secret involvement of a sexual nature? Or had Rand simply and quietly been acting like the big brother that Alison never had?

Quinn felt as if he'd been staring into a kaleidoscope and someone had given it a giant turn.

"Hey, Cutter!" he said, trying to get the talk back on track. "You never told me what Alison's old man said."

"Oh, yeah. He said, 'Is that punk still hangin' around town?' And I said, 'Which punk would that be, Rupert?' And he goes, 'It's Mr. Bennett to you, you little punk.' And I go, 'Not if your truck ain't in my boss's garage.' "

"Good one, Cutter," said Neal. "What'd he say then?"

Cutter popped a tab on another can and said, "His exact words were 'Tell Quinn I know where he lives.' That was it. Then he went inside to pay for his gas and leer at this chick behind the counter who was young enough to be his daughter, naturally."

"He's had plenty of practice at *that*," said Todd, sneering into his beer.

"Todd, put a lid on it, would you?" Mike Redding snapped. "It's ancient history. Ray, turn that damn thing down! The game's starting, for chrissake." He glanced at Quinn apologetically, as if he could no longer be responsible for the juvenile behavior of their old teammates now that they were grown.

It was another wild turn on that kaleidoscope. Quinn sat back in his plaid chair, mesmerized by all the new pieces he saw. A mere ten percent of his brain was needed for following the game and keeping up with the score; the rest was focused on the shocking innuendo that had been run past him in the last few minutes.

Rand. Alison. Rupert. It was a triangle of involvement that Quinn couldn't have imagined in his wildest dreams. Immediately his mind, like a computer, began mulling the possible combinations. The more he mulled, the queasier he got. He pushed away the half-eaten jerky; he couldn't stand even to look at it.

Someone impregnated Alison, and someone killed her.

Those were facts. Alison hating her father, Rand becoming her knight, Rupert leering at girls—that was all gossip. Quinn knew all about the downside of gossip. It wrecked dreams and it ruined lives.

But assuming that there was some kernel of truth in the guys' drunken remarks—what then? Quinn couldn't think about Rupert without picturing his niece. He couldn't think about Rand without picturing his twin sister. And he couldn't think about Alison without picturing her cousin. Olivia was everywhere in his thoughts, slinky in silver, soft in wool sweaters. Olivia—idealistic . . . loving . . . defiantly loyal to family and friends, including outcasts like him.

Oh, damn. Oh, hell. Please . . . let it have been someone with no connection to her. A bum. A teacher. The mayor of Keepsake.

By the end of the first game, Quinn resolved to corner Mike Redding in the next couple of days and find out what he knew. If Mike wouldn't talk, Quinn would go to Cutter, then to Neal, and on down the line. Someone had to be willing to pass on the full dirt—which was all Quinn believed it was. If there had been anything truthful to it, Mrs. Dewsbury or Father Tom would have heard about it over the years.

Yes. Idle gossip between horny teammates who'd lusted after the mysterious Alison themselves. Quinn remembered well their locker-room talk about the girl. Everyone wanted her; none of them had had her.

The Cotton Bowl ended in overtime. Quinn groaned inwardly as he cheered outwardly. Eventually Tennessee beat Nebraska and they all moved on to the Sugar Bowl. From the first pass, run all the way in for the touchdown, the Sugar Bowl was a blowout—boring, interminable, and embarrassing, at least to Quinn. The rest of the guys loved it, of course. As with sex, they didn't care who scored, as long as it was often.

By halftime Quinn had had all he could take. Over everyone's protests, he stood up to leave. His excuse was lame—

he told them he'd promised to bring back a prescription for Mrs. Dewsbury. It was the best he could do.

"Y'know—you may as well be married," said Neal with more than a hint of condescension.

Quinn laughed it off, but Mike was feeling his beer. "You should talk, Neal," he said with a burp. "You're gonna have to install a freaking dishwasher for having today off."

"Oh, like you're here free and clear? Who's in charge of the sleepover at your house next Friday? Huh? Who?"

"You guys are pathetic," said their bachelor host. "Tell you what. I'll give you eight bucks an hour if you come and clean this dump on your next day off," he teased. "I'll even supply all the rags."

"Hey, here's a thought," said Cutter, also single. "You can call yourselves the Merry Mates. Get it? Merry *Mates*?"

"*Haw-haw-haw.*"

Their pissing contest was still in full swing when Quinn waved them all a genial good-bye and took off.

Somewhere during the second quarter of the Cotton Bowl, he'd had a premonition. He didn't like to think of it that way; he was more comfortable calling it a hunch. Either way, he wanted to act on it.

Before heading back to Mrs. Dewsbury's house, he drove downtown, parked his car on one of the deserted streets there, and strolled around the corner to check out Miracourt. He was relieved to see that it looked the same: sophisticated and warm and inviting, and all in one piece. He strolled up to the window and peered inside, checking out the interior to make sure that everything was okay. Several glass-shaded lamps threw a soft glow over the fabrics and bric-a-brac scattered around the shop. It all reminded him of Olivia. He liked that.

Reassured, Quinn turned and headed back for his truck. And then, because he was brought up to be thorough and because he wanted to clear his head and because he could not shake his hunch of a premonition, he detoured and walked around to the alley that ran behind the shops.

The alley was narrow, deserted, and dark, with bleary lights standing guard over dark brown Dumpsters and cardboard boxes flattened for recycling. Patches of cobblestones peeking through asphalt echoed under his footsteps as he tried to figure out which back exit belonged to Miracourt. A stack of wooden crates, obviously from citrus fruits, told him that he'd reached the juicerie next to Olivia's shop.

He wasn't surprised to see that Miracourt's backside looked as trim and neat as its front. The metal door, painted a deep shade of green, was decorated with a handpainted wreath of twigs and flowers; the light that shone down on it looked like an old ship's lantern, another anticommercial touch. Quinn smiled. Leave it to Olivia to bring charm and whimsy to the most workaday site.

The door was closed, but Quinn tried the doorknob anyway. He winced as he did it, fearing that he would set something off, and was surprised when the knob turned easily. *Shit.*

He stepped cautiously inside a stockroom filled with boxes and bolts of fabric. The room itself was unlit, but a rectangle of amber told him that the shop lay directly ahead. He was in the cutout of light with no place to hide, so he stood and just listened. It was eerily quiet. Whoever had been in the shop had come and gone, of that he felt sure.

He walked into the warm glow of the shop itself and went immediately up the stairs to the second-floor loft. That's where Olivia's desk was, and her personal effects. Quinn decided that if anyone had gone amuck, he would do it upstairs, out of the view of window-shoppers.

And he was right. At the top of the stairs he saw her desk, a big wooden antique in great shape and set squarely in the middle of the loft. He could see that papers were strewn across the desk and all over the planked floor around it. As he got closer, he discovered something else: a humongous rat, bloody and eviscerated, lying sprawled across a stack of invoices and packing receipts on the desk.

Quinn stared with disgust at the mauled rodent. It was déjà vu all over again, except that this latest punch to the gut—maybe combined with all that beef jerky—was a little more strident, a little more vicious. The thought that Olivia was intended to stumble sleepy-eyed onto this scene the next morning was chilling.

As for the rat, Quinn actually found himself feeling sorry for it. There it had been, sniffing around for crumbs and minding its own business, when . . . *whack.* How exactly had the critter been dispatched? Surely not with a knife. Quinn turned the three-way lamp up to its brightest light and, flopping the carcass over with a pencil and a ruler, gave it a closer look.

As he suspected: a bullet hole, right through the middle. So the rat was a country rat and the prankster, an expert marksman. Surprise, surprise. Hunters were common in Keepsake: Some hunted for food, most for sport. It didn't much matter to Quinn why the guy had acquired the skill. The important thing was that he possessed it.

Automatically he reached for the phone to call Chief Vickers, then thought better of it. Olivia would want to be in on the loop. She might be home. Clutching a nearby sample of fabric, he used it to pick up the phone, then punched in Olivia's number with a pencil point.

She answered on the first ring. She sounded relaxed and happy. It made him sick to have to be the one to tell her what had happened, but there were no better options. The first words out of his mouth were, "Does Miracourt have an alarm?"

"Of course. My insurance requires it. Why?"

Shit—an expert marksman who was bright enough to cut the right wire. "The alarm's been disabled," he said. In a few terse sentences he explained where he was and what he'd found.

"I'll be right over," she said in a wobbly voice, and she slammed down the phone before he could ask about Vickers.

While Quinn waited, he looked around more carefully. Nothing seemed to have been stolen. There was only the rat and the papers strewn like flower petals in a path to the carnage. At the last minute Quinn thought, to hell with Vickers and proper procedure, and he rolled the rat up in a Miracourt bag like a gourmet cheese head, then tied it around for good measure with twine. He didn't want fearless Olivia taking a peek; he really didn't.

Olivia had no intention of looking in the bag.

"Take it out to the Dumpster—please!" she said, trying not to picture its contents. "If Chief Vickers needs the rat for an autopsy, he's welcome to retrieve it."

She forced herself to become all business. Snapping open a shopping bag, she said to Quinn, "Would you hand me the pinking shears?"

"The—?"

"Those scissors with the zigzag blades," she explained. Quinn gave them to her on his way out to the Dumpster, and she began to pick through the wreckage of her paperwork, using the scissors like tongs to retrieve the invoices and dispose of the packing slips.

Her hands were shaking as she did it. She told herself that it was with indignation, but that didn't account for her sky-high jump when Quinn came back into the loft and started to say something behind her. "I'm sorry," she said, as if she'd done something to be ashamed of. "I'm just—"

She threw down the shears and said, "Scared. Quinn, I'm a little scared now. This is two in a row. Why is he suddenly targeting me?"

Quinn took her into his arms and immediately she felt safe. If she could only stay that way, she'd be ready to take on the world. Once upon a time, she thought she *could* take on the world. Not anymore. This was not a world she either knew or understood.

Quinn held her close, caressing the back of her hair. "He's figured out how much I . . . I care for you," he said softly, "and he's sending me messages—"

"*Is* he a he?" she asked, hoping somehow he was not.

"I'm pretty sure of it," Quinn said. "Although, none of these stunts took exceptional strength—just a strong stomach."

"Which I don't happen to have," she said, shuddering.

Quinn sighed and said, "Anyway, the text of the messages seems to be, 'Go away and I'll leave her alone.'"

"I know," she admitted in a faltering voice. "I've read them that way, too. But . . . you're not going away. I don't want you to go away, so what will we do?"

He said nothing. For much too long, he said nothing. Olivia felt her heart plunge like a cannonball into her admittedly weak stomach. "Quinn?" she said, looking up at him. "Say something?"

She knew him well enough to know when he was picking and choosing his words with care. This was one of those times. She laid her head back on his shoulder and waited.

"Olivia," he said softly, "we have to wonder whether whoever is doing these things got your cousin pregnant, or murdered her, or both."

He was telling her that he thought the prankster was the killer. But that couldn't be. Not after all these years. It would mean that the killer had lived among them all these years.

"No. I don't see it," she said, shaking her head. "Killing a woman is different from killing a rat. *This*," she said, waving her hand at the bloody mess, "was disgusting and mean, but that's all. People kill rats all the time. They hire hit men; we call them exterminators. Or they use them for target practice—you remember how kids in school did that with their BB guns."

"I understand that, but—"

"No," she said, cutting him off. "I really do not see it. You're overreacting." She preferred her version of events to his, so much.

"I wish I could agree with you, Liv."

Olivia glanced at the papers that remained to be cleaned up. She wanted to wave a wand over them and make them go away. But no one else knew which things to keep and what to toss, not even Quinn. It was up to her.

She picked up the pinking shears and went back to work. "After this, I want cocoa. A Hershey bar won't do. We have to find cocoa. And marshmallows, too. We'll make a nice fire in my fireplace, and I'll make the cocoa extra rich and sweet—''

"Olivia, do you have a gun?" he asked, interrupting her ramble.

She stopped and stared, more distressed now than before and more determined not to let him know it. In a weird way, it was flattering. He thought she could handle a gun.

"No. I don't."

"Does anyone in your family? Does Rand?"

"Well, yes, I'm sure he does. For skeet shooting. You remember that he was always pretty good, don't you?"

Quinn shrugged. "I suppose. Sometimes you move on. But you're saying he's . . . kept up with it?"

"There's a range not far from here. It's what some men do in the country. Why are you asking? Do you think I'd actually tell Rand that I need his guns to protect myself? My God, he'd have my mother in hysterics."

"Yeah, you're right," Quinn said abruptly. "Forget I mentioned it."

"Now that I think about it," Olivia added, "I'd rather not have Chief Vickers know about this disgusting episode."

She raised her hand over Quinn's objections and said, "Wait, wait, hear me out. Vickers hasn't been able to do a thing so far about these pranks. And you know what? I don't think he wants to. We both know he'd rather you just went away. So what will we accomplish by telling him? He'll go straight to my father, upsetting him needlessly and making things even harder between you and me."

"That's not a good idea, Liv."

"Well . . . that's how I feel. It's bad enough that my father knows about the cape."

"Are you sure that he does?"

"Yes. He told Rand about it—in strictest confidence. Naturally Rand immediately told Eileen, also in confidence; she called me as soon as she heard. My mother, as usual, hasn't been told anything. Eventually she'll find out and then she'll be angry at all of us. But that's the way my family operates. I can't even keep track of all our confidences anymore; after a while, they begin to blur.'' She plucked the last bloody paper with the pinking shears and dumped it in the wastebasket.

Quinn pulled out the plastic liner. ''I always thought honesty was the best policy,'' he said, glancing up at her as he knotted the bag tight.

''Nobody lies,'' she said with a shrug. ''Just . . . nobody tells.''

Quinn smiled wryly at the distinction, then said, ''Are you missing anything from your desk—a knife, a letter opener, a pair of scissors?''

Olivia glanced at a small ceramic vase that she kept filled with pens and pencils, rulers and openers. ''Yes. I keep an X-Acto Knife right there. Why? Is it the murder weapon?''

''Not exactly. The rat was shot. The knife was used to draw and quarter it.''

Olivia took a deep, slow breath, then let it out just as deliberately. With a lift of her eyebrows, she said, ''Well! I hope he has the courtesy to replace the blade before he brings it back.''

She was dismayed to see that Quinn neither laughed nor smiled.

A little later on, they found the bloodied knife after all, lying on a bolt of winter-white silk.

Seventeen

The only night that Mike Redding was home and available for buttonholing by Quinn happened to be Mitzi's Bunco night.

Mike had to baby-sit, so Quinn found himself in Mike's basement workshop, trying to carry on a conversation with his old friend as he alternated between sawing wood for a new set of kitchen cabinets and yelling up the stairs at his three kids, who sounded bound and determined to tear the house down as fast as Mike could build it up again.

"God, I hate January," Mike growled. "At least in the summer they're outside."

He marked off a dimension with a carpenter's pencil on a sheet of lumbercore and carried it over to the table saw. "Hold that end up while I rip this, would you? Thanks."

The sound of bodies rolling and thumping on the floor above them made Quinn glance involuntarily at the ceiling to see if it was coming down.

Mike sighed. "I hate January," he repeated. "I hate Bunco. But most of all I hate being responsible for breakage when Mitzi's out for the night. You're a lucky sonofabitch you never married, Quinn."

"Yeah, well, the right one just never—"

The rest of Quinn's sentence got drowned out by the whine of the saw as Mike split the sheet into halves, then quarters. It was fairly obvious that Mike didn't care nearly as much about Quinn's love life as he did about woodworking. Mike was a hard-driving, extremely successful businessman, the owner of his own import-export firm, but his real passion in life was wood. Right now he looked overjoyed to be traipsing around in piles of sawdust, despite all the macho griping about being forced to baby-sit.

A bloodcurdling scream followed by a horrific *thunk* sent Mike back to the foot of the basement stairs. "Hey! Guys! You sound like a herd of elephants up there! I'm not gonna tell you again!"

He returned to his cabinetry and to Quinn. "So what's on your mind?" he asked as he took a sip of tea from a World's Greatest Dad mug.

Quinn put down his own mug and said, "When we were at Ray's, some of the guys were throwing rumors around about Alison. You tried to shut 'em up, and I appreciate the spirit in which you did it—but I'd like to hear what you know that I don't."

Mike looked suddenly uncomfortable. He shrugged and said, "Hey, it's nothing we *know*, exactly. It's just what we heard."

"I understand that they're just rumors," Quinn reassured him. "But I'd like to hear them anyway."

After a long pause, Mike said, "All right, I guess it's only fair. But it's pretty sleazy stuff. Don't ever tell Mitzi I told you. She's too much of a parent to believe it can happen."

Quinn nodded his agreement and waited.

"Look, it's just talk, but . . . after you and your dad left Keepsake, Myra Lupidnick got drunk one night with Monty Johnson and got a little blabby. She told MoJo that Alison once confided that her father used to like to feel her up. Later Myra took it all back. She said it wasn't Alison's father at all who used to cop the feels, but the owner of the dress shop where Alison worked after school."

"What, that shop on Main?"

"Yeah, it's not there anymore. Casual Shop? Something like that. The owner had already died of a stroke by the time

Myra ran off at the mouth to MoJo, so, you know, that was that.''

"Did anyone ever tell Vickers this?"

Mike picked up a sanding block. "You'd have to ask him," he said, gently hitting the raw edges of the sawn wood. "Anyway, no one really believed Myra. You know how she was. Hell, she went around bragging to anyone who'd listen that she took your cherry."

"Huh?"

"Did she?"

"No."

"See? She was a lotta talk. I'll say this for her, though. She gave pretty good—" Mike glanced upstairs and lowered his voice. "You know."

He chuckled in fond reminiscence and said, "You remember the time she sneaked into our locker room and—oh, no, wait, you were gone by then. Well, anyway, back then we figured Myra was just trying to puff herself up by spouting so-called inside knowledge. She was always trying to be somebody. That's the thing about going to a really good public high. The parking lot is filled with Jeeps and Corvettes, and the kids who take the bus have to walk right past them on their way to class. One way or another Myra managed to hitch a ride, every once in a while."

"Where does Rand fit in all of this?"

"That's a good question," Mike said. He pondered a vague spot in the air as he formed his answer.

Suddenly he moaned, "Oh, geez, I forgot to close the lid on the washing machine," and hustled over to the appliance. "Mitzi is gonna have a fit," he muttered, blowing sawdust off the agitator cap and out of the bleach dispenser. He dropped the lid and wiped off the top of the machine with the sleeve of his flannel shirt, then came back to the workbench where Quinn was waiting with arms folded casually across his chest.

For the rest of his life, Quinn remembered exactly what the scene looked and sounded and smelled like at that moment: the fine mist of sawdust swirling under the long fluorescent light, itself swaying lightly on its chains as the boys tore through the house; the pungent bite of newly cut wood tickling his nostrils; the giggly bickering of the kids somewhere distant. Everything seemed so right, so ordinary, so utterly benign.

Until Mike spoke. "Look, it's obvious that you and Livvy have something going, so I don't even know why I'm telling you this. I need your word that you'll forget that I'm the one who said it."

"You have it."

"Okay. Here's the deal: Rand Bennett apparently had a heavy-duty thing for his cousin Alison. Again, the source for all this was MoJo, and he's dead as a doornail after wrapping himself around that tree in the Alps, so believe as much of it as you want."

Quinn was listening so intently that he could hear the rasp of Mike's beard as he rubbed the palm of his hand along his jawline.

"You know what a hound MoJo was," Mike went on. "Before he settled for easy sex with Myra, he made a big move on Alison. She rebuffed him and must have told Rand, because Rand confronted him about it and beat the crap out of him. Now, the way MoJo told it to us, all he did was make an everyday, garden-variety pass. So why did Rand react like MoJo tried to rape Alison or something? That's what you naturally wonder."

Quinn was thinking that Alison's father had sexually abused her; that she had run to Rand for comfort; and that Rand had overreacted by taking it out on somebody else. That's all that Quinn was thinking.

"There's more," Mike said quietly.

Quinn didn't want to hear it. He did not want to hear it.

"MoJo said that when Rand had him pinned to the ground with his hands around his throat, Rand said to him, 'No one touches her but one man. Got it? One man. And you're not that man.' "

It was as bad as Quinn had feared.

"So MoJo somehow gets the courage to croak, 'Oh,

yeah? I suppose you are?' And Rand says 'That's for me to know and you to find out.' ''

Quinn's relief came out in a snort of laughter. '' 'For me to know and you to find out'? Come on, Mike, get real. MoJo made that up. No adult talks that way.''

"We were barely seventeen," Mike pointed out. "And it was a—slightly—more innocent age."

"It's still not conclusive."

"There's more."

"Christ. *What*?" Quinn snapped, annoyed at Mike for parceling out the revelation.

"The next day, when MoJo showed up in school with a black eye and a busted nose—remember? He told us he got in a fight with some biker?—Alison supposedly said to him, 'I'm glad you wouldn't take no for an answer. Because of you I just got engaged.' 'To who?' says MoJo. She answers, 'To someone I'm not supposed to marry, according to the Church.' ''

Quinn let out a long, low whistle. "Ho-ly shit."

"Exactly. I never was as smart as you," Mike said without irony, "but it doesn't take Scholar of the Year to figure out that marriage between first cousins is forbidden in the Catholic Church."

"So is a marriage to someone divorced," Quinn shot back.

Mike gave him a skeptical look. "Put it all together, man. She was talking about Rand. I don't know who got her pregnant, her father or Rand, but the promise to marry her—that had to be Rand."

"It looks that way," Quinn conceded, but all the while he was shaking his head in denial.

Mike added, "You remember how Ray and a couple of the guys got real quiet when the talk turned to Alison over at his house on New Year's Day? They're still scared shitless that someday this will all get back to Rand, and their asses will end up in a sling. The Bennetts own this town—you know that. Rand could pull some strings and have them fired from their jobs in the blink of an eye—and probably me as well if I were still working at the mill, never mind that I was their top-grossing salesman. As it is, Owen Bennett and his son have to make nice-nice to *me*. They know I'd rather buy Polartec from Malden Mills than Artica from him for my shop in the Philippines.''

Mike Redding was a bear of a man with a thick head of hair that was graying way too fast. Maybe it was the three boys; maybe it was his concern for his old teammates; maybe it was the time he was spending in the air between Keepsake and the Philippines, away from his family and table saw. Whatever it was that was stressing him out, Quinn did not want to add to his burden.

''Understood,'' he said simply. ''I won't drag your names into anything. Tell me one thing, though. When did MoJo tell you all this?''

''It was during our first New Year's Day reunion, four or five years after you and your dad split. We all got good and ripped and vowed to meet faithfully every year, wives and girlfriends be damned. Someone mentioned that we should've invited Rand, but you know how it is. We blamed him for that lousy season even more than we blamed you,'' he said with a wry smile. ''Anyway, that's when MoJo told us the stuff about Alison.''

''Was Coach at that first reunion?''

''Yeah. Why do you ask?''

''Just wondering.''

There was more thumping upstairs—this time, followed by a loud crash of something heavy onto the floor.

Mike cocked his ear. ''I didn't hear actual breakage, did you? Sounds like they just knocked over a bookcase or something.'' He went back to the foot of the stairs.

''Hey, up there!'' he bellowed. He listened for a response and got silence. ''Ah, the hell with it,'' he said, and went back to his tea.

There was stoic acceptance in Quinn's voice as he said, ''I appreciate this, Mike.''

''Hey, c'mon,'' Mike said, waving away Quinn's gratitude. ''We go way back. I owe you for all kinds of stuff, including the time you stepped in between me and the coach; he could have had me up for assault. Besides, I always thought your dad really got screwed. The way they jumped on him was criminal.''

Quinn left Mike to his sawing and hammering and headed back to Mrs. Dewsbury's to check on her before going on to Olivia's. He mulled over Mike's revelations, looking for an interpretation that he could live with, but he came up empty. The Bennetts—one or more of them—seemed to be up to their ears in the tragedy that was Alison.

The thought absolutely paralyzed Quinn.

He kept veering away from his suspicions, preferring to focus on his old coach. How did Bronsky fit in? He had been present when MoJo blabbed to everyone about Alison, and he had done nothing.

Quinn could understand why his old teammates had been too intimidated to expose the Bennett family to an investigation, but he couldn't understand how the coach, a close friend of Chief Vickers, could keep such incriminating information from him. Vickers had been a sergeant back then. You would think a pal would want to give a low-ranking officer his big break.

On the other hand, maybe Coach Bronsky was being bought off; maybe that's how he was managing to hold on to his job despite his drinking problem. Ironic that it was Olivia who'd suggested the coach might have friends in high places.

For that matter, maybe Chief Vickers had been bought off as well. He *was* the chief of police, after all. Maybe all of Keepsake was in on a conspiracy of silence. At the very least, it looked as if a lot of people had been turning a blind eye to the whole affair. It pissed Quinn off more than he could say.

Money and sex: They were powerful motives, and completely entwined in this case. Olivia believed that the rift between her father and her Uncle Rupert was over money— how they had handled their inheritances. What if it were over Rupert Bennett's sexual abuse of Alison instead? That would account for the genteel break between Owen and Rupert; Olivia's father didn't seem like the type to turn in his brother for being a child molester, no matter how appalling the crime.

Say that Alison *had* become pregnant by her father. In that case, it was possible that Rand had acted out of chivalry and had offered to marry his cousin simply to get her away from her abusive father. But would Alison keep a baby conceived in those heartbreaking conditions, and would Rand take over the fathering of it? It was hard for Quinn, knowing Rand, to believe that.

On the other hand, if Rand *was* the father, maybe he decided to step up to the plate and take responsibility for the baby. It was easy to picture Rand in love with his cousin: She was good-looking and personable—just like him. He was the Montague to her Capulet. The idea of love between first cousins of a feuding family would have appealed to Rand's emotional, tragic side.

There was a third possibility. Maybe Rand got Alison pregnant and regretted it. Maybe he wanted her to get an abortion and she refused. Maybe she began living some fantasy, hearing a proposal where none had been made.

And maybe Rand decided to murder her.

Quinn slammed his hand in frustration on the wheel of his truck. The two top suspects in his investigation so far were Rupert Bennett and his nephew Rand. Somehow Quinn had got himself in the bizarre position of actually *hoping* that it was Alison's father who had made her pregnant and then murdered her. It was the less horrifying of two horrific scenarios.

Quinn's mood was utterly black as he let himself in through the front door of Mrs. Dewsbury's big white house on Elm. He found his old mentor at a makeshift desk in the dining room, seated in front of her brand-new toy: a twenty-inch closed-circuit TV that magnified printed material a huge amount and made it possible for her to read again with ease.

Mrs. Dewsbury looked up from the screen at him and her face creased into a county roadmap of wrinkled joy. "Quinn, I *love* this CCTV thing," she said in a young girl's voice. "I had just about stopped reading, and look at me now!"

She motioned him over. She had placed a list of recent books acquired by the Keepsake Library under the camera, and the list was being magnified twenty times on the screen.

"See all the books I've checked off on this list? I'm going to reserve every one of them, from the biographies to the sexy historicals. This is—*truly*—a miracle! Thank you so much for buying it on the spot when you came across it. Two hundred dollars seems awfully reasonable for something so sophisticated."

It had cost Quinn two thousand dollars, but she never would have accepted a gift like that from him, so he had made up a story about finding the vision aid in the Granny's Attic shop of his uncle's retirement home in Old Saybrook. Even at that, she had insisted on reimbursing him for it.

"All it is is a camera and a TV box," he explained to defend the apparently low price. "The concept is actually very simple."

"It doesn't look that way to me," she said. She added, "How do I know it isn't stolen?"

He pretended to be scandalized. "Mrs. D.! What do you take me for?"

"Well . . . all right. Just be sure to cash my check, you hear? I don't want you carrying it around in your wallet for a month the way you do. It throws off my bank balance."

"Yes, ma'am," he said, delighted to see her so pleased.

She cocked her head at him. "I see you're not taking off your jacket. I assume this means that you won't be back tonight?"

"Nope. I just stopped by to activate the alarm, because the chances are good that you will not."

"Yes I will. But not right away. Helen next door is coming over to see this thing. Her mother has macular."

"But you'll set it after she leaves?"

"Mm-hmm," the schoolteacher said absently. It was clear that her mind was on something else, and it wasn't the library list.

Out of the blue, she said, "May I ask you what your intentions are toward Olivia Bennett?"

His intentions. Now there was the sixty-four-thousand-dollar question. He wanted to say, "Entirely honorable." But it was hard to reconcile that answer with his ongoing campaign to investigate Olivia's family.

"We're enjoying one another's company," he settled for saying.

"So are you and I. That doesn't mean that we'll be marrying anytime soon."

He laughed, then raised one eyebrow and said, "Just because I haven't asked you yet . . ."

"Quinn, I'm serious. Sleeping over is what teenagers do at slumber parties. You are thirty-four years old. You should be a father by now. If the attraction between you and Olivia is that deep . . . that irresistible . . . well, don't you think you ought to be backing it up with a commitment of some sort?"

Feeling cornered, he said, "I'd give her a fraternity pin, but you know how it is—I'd have to go to college first."

"Don't be flip. Besides, you're only a few night courses away from a degree, so stop trying to sound underprivileged. It will not work with me."

He shifted tactics and went on the offensive. "The 'attraction,' as you term it, has only been going on for a couple of weeks or so."

"The attraction has been going on all of your lives! Why do you suppose neither of you has ever married? Can't you see that you've been waiting for one another? My goodness—I thought *I* was blind."

"It's not as simple as that," he said, looking away. How could he possibly explain that his love for Olivia was now at odds with his love for his father?

Mrs. Dewsbury picked up on the torment he thought he was concealing. "*Quinn.* Look at you! What's going on?"

Now he did feel cornered. "The pranks," he said, hedging the truth. "They're demoralizing."

"Oh, those. Of course they are. But sooner or later, this man is going to do something stupid. He'll be caught in the act and made to feel ashamed. Or else he'll see that you're determined to stay in Keepsake, and he'll simply give up. That's what I predict. He'll simply give up and fade away."

It wasn't *what* Mrs. Dewsbury said, exactly; it was more the way she said it. Here she was, an eighty-something woman with limited means and failing eyesight, and she was bucking *him* up.

Quinn smiled and said, "I bow to your indomitable spirit, Mrs. D. You are one in a million." He bent down to kiss the top of her head and said on his way out, "Don't forget the alarm."

"The alarm . . . right," she said, off in a world of her own.

Quinn made love to Olivia with exquisite tenderness, even sadness, after he returned from seeing Mike Redding and Mrs. Dewsbury. Olivia was surprised by his melancholy, which seemed to run deep.

Afterward, they lay in bed under the covers. Olivia was propped on an elbow with her leg thrown over Quinn's as she twisted the hairs on his chest idly around her finger.

"Take me with you," she said.

He stared at the ceiling. "Not on your life."

"Quinn, why not? They won't open the door if you show up alone. Believe me about that. My uncle is eccentric, a recluse. If I'm with you, at least you'll get inside the house."

Quinn rolled his head in her direction and smiled wearily. "You never give up, do you?"

"I've never learned how to."

Nor had she ever learned how to stick out her lower lip and pout prettily to get what she wanted. Or how to use tears. Or, God forbid, the silent treatment. Olivia's basic philosophy in life was that if you had logic on your side—

especially if you were talking to a man—then you would prevail.

So why wouldn't Quinn let her prevail? That's what had her so stumped.

"Come on, work with me here," she said lightly, taking a tiny yank on his chest hairs.

"Ouch. Stop. No. You're not coming with me."

"Qui-inn," she wailed, trying to win by whining after all. "You're being irrational, and it isn't like you. I think I've made my case. I've come around completely to your side. I believe that you *should* propose the DNA testing to my aunt and uncle. I know that you'll be delicate about it, and I know how much it means to you to vindicate your father. I know how much you loved him. Much more," she confessed, "than I love my own father, ashamed as I am to admit it."

Quinn looked startled by the remark, and very interested. Oddly, she would have called his look hopeful. "You don't love your father?" he asked.

"Of course I do. But there's love . . . and there's love. And let's face it: I've never forgiven my dad for not offering me a job in the mill and generally for favoring Rand over me."

She sighed and said, "My feelings for my dad are based more on respect and—I wouldn't go so far as to call it a sense of obligation; more a sense of rightness. It's *right* that you should love your family. It's really sad if you don't, or can't. I'm not saying that people don't have valid reasons for being estranged from members of their families," she added thoughtfully. "I'm just saying that you lose some of who you are when that happens, and it's too bad."

Quinn said, "Do you feel that way about your mother?"

"Mom? Oh, no. I love her unconditionally. It's so easy."

"What about your brother?" he said softly. "What about Rand?"

"Ah—that one's more complicated. As you know, Rand gets under my skin a lot. And there are things about him that—I have to admit—I don't admire. He's hot-tempered.

He's egotistical. He sulks. He has no ambition. But deep down he's . . . all right. And more than that, he's my *twin*. There's a bond there that I can't explain. You really have to be a twin to understand.''

"Whereas I don't even have siblings.''

"Which is really too bad, because I'm doing a lousy job of explaining this, aren't I?'' Olivia said, laughing softly and flopping over on her back. "I think I'm more visual than I am verbal.''

Quinn took advantage of the remark to murmur, "You're a sight for sore eyes, I agree.'' Bracing himself on his elbow, he lowered his head to hers for a kiss.

"Wait, wait,'' she said, slipping her fingers between his lips and hers.

He sighed. "Who says you're not verbal?''

"Before you wipe out my short-term memory with a kiss, I really, really would like to get this business of my aunt and uncle resolved.''

He didn't look melancholy anymore. He didn't even look surprised. He looked annoyed.

"It *is* resolved. I go. You don't.''

"That's a bad decision. I must urge you to reconsider, sir,'' she said, trying to keep her tone charming.

"No! And you know what? You can be a real pain in the butt.'' Scowling, he opened his mouth to say something more, then thought better of it and rolled away from her.

It stung. She had never seen him so tense, so dark. It was disheartening. They'd grown up together and she thought she knew him inside out. True, he could be fierce and competitive. But this—she didn't know what to call it: Hostility? Bitterness?—this was new.

She was completely convinced that she was right and he was wrong. How could he not see that if she went with him to her Aunt Betty and Uncle Rupert, his job would be easier? All she could do was hope that he'd come to his senses and change his mind before lunchtime tomorrow, which was when he implied that he was going to try seeing her aunt and uncle again.

Olivia sighed, loud and mournfully. When she got no response, she switched off the brass lamp on her nightstand and curled up, facing away from him. The second sigh that escaped her was much more private and much more painful than the one she'd let out for his benefit. The second sigh hurt. She lay curled alone for a long time, with that sigh stuck in her throat, before dropping off to sleep.

Mrs. Dewsbury was upstairs, tired and happy and soaking her dentures, when a thundering crash sent her jumping through her woolen bathrobe.

The mirror! was her single, dismayed thought. *I knew it was too heavy to hang on that hook. He should have listened to me.*

Convinced that the heavy gilded frame had fallen on her Portuguese soup tureen and had left a hideous dent in her mahogany sideboard, she left her teeth fizzing in their glass and made her way down the stairs by the light of the bathroom to assess the damage.

He seemed so sure about hanging it that way. Why didn't the boy listen to me?

At the foot of the stairs she turned on the light, expecting the worst. She was surprised to see the mirror still hanging peacefully above the sideboard, just where Quinn had hung it.

That's odd. That's very odd. What else could it have been?

Instinctively she swung her gaze toward the next breakable object in the room. Her wonderful high-tech miracle, the bright new window into her old world of books, had been smashed to atoms. She stared in shock at the gaping hole that used to be a closed-circuit television. The pain was as sharp as if someone had driven a stake through her own eye.

And then came a sudden pain at the back of her head, and it was far more sharp and far more real than anything she could ever have imagined. After that, her sensations were neither sharp nor real. She felt nothing. Nothing at all.

Eighteen

The jangle of the phone ripped Olivia from her troubled dreams. She groped for the light, then for the receiver. It was nearly midnight.

A faint moan on the other end seemed to be some kid's version of fun. It was creaky, trembly, a pale specter of real speech—a little prankster's idea of a ghost.

"I'm sorry, you have the wrong number," Olivia said, irritated that her heart had been sent careening for nothing. She was in the process of hanging up when she heard, or thought she heard, the name "Quinn."

She brought the receiver back to her ear. "Who is this?" she asked sharply.

"Miz . . . Dewsbuh . . . Qui . . ."

"Mrs. Dewsbury? What's wrong?"

Quinn tore the phone from Olivia's grip. "I'll be right there," he said after listening for a scant second or two. He hung up and dialed 911 and in a few terse phrases directed an ambulance to the widow's house on Elm.

By the time he got off the phone, Olivia was dressed. "I'll start your truck and bring it around," she said, grabbing his keys from the dresser.

She was through the bedroom door before he could object. Outside, she brought the truck to a screeching halt alongside him and slid over to the passenger side as he climbed in, pushed the seat back and took off.

You should belt, she wanted to insist, because now she

was thinking thoughts of death. Instead she forced herself to say calmly, "What happened?"

"Someone hit her from behind. God, I'm going to get you all killed," Quinn muttered through clenched teeth.

Was that a promise? He was driving like a fiend. Bracing herself with a furtive grip on the door, Olivia said, "Why did Mrs. Dewsbury call me instead of 911?"

"I programmed your number on her speed dial. All she had to do was hit the number one."

That was the entire conversation en route to Mrs. Dewsbury's house.

By the time they reached Elm Street, the ambulance had arrived and the paramedics were trying the front and back doors. Olivia ran instinctively to the side of the house that she saw was sheltered from its neighbors by a row of towering hedges. Yes—an open window.

She climbed through the narrow window, one of the side openings of a walk-out bay, and found herself standing in the dining room across from Mrs. Dewsbury, who was sitting in a chair by the phone with her head drooped forward over her chest. Quinn had apparently let in the paramedics with his key. One of the them was tending to the widow while the other was laying out the stretcher.

Olivia was dismayed to see that the old woman didn't seem able to speak. Dazed and shaking her head, she kept waving the three men away. Her gaze was glassy-eyed—until she saw Olivia standing across from her. Then she seemed to snap into focus.

Weakly, she beckoned Olivia to her side as the paramedics continued to hover over her, trying to take her vital signs. She clutched feebly at Olivia's jacket and pulled her closer.

Olivia rested her hand lightly on the stricken woman's back as she bent down to hear. "Yes, Mrs. Dewsbury?"

"My teesh," said the widow. She pointed a finger straight up.

"Your—? Ah. I'll get them and bring them to the hospital," said Olivia, divining the widow's concern.

Mrs. Dewsbury gave her a trembling smile that started

tears rolling down her withered, pale cheeks. Olivia left her to Quinn and the paramedics and ran up the stairs and into the bathroom. She grabbed the glass with the dentures in it, intending to turn it upside down to drain.

That's when she saw that her hand was smeared with blood.

They were keeping Mrs. Dewsbury, despite her objections, overnight for observation. The staff physician at Eastwood Community Hospital seemed more impressed with the widow's iron skull than with her iron will.

"I doubt that there's a concussion, but I want to be sure; she seems a little disoriented," Dr. Tann told Quinn. "I don't know whether that's in character or not."

"It's not," said Quinn.

"She's not very happy about staying here, which isn't unusual with the elderly," the physician explained. "They like to be in familiar surroundings."

"Who doesn't?" Quinn snapped. He was incredibly tense. "What about all the blood?"

"It looked worse than it was; she didn't even need stitches. Any idea what was used for the blow?"

"Yes," said Olivia. "A dictionary. We found it on the floor at the foot of the stairs. Mrs. Dewsbury is a retired English teacher; she'll be amused."

The physician smiled wryly and said, "I doubt it. She's too upset about some television that got smashed."

"Can we see her?"

"No. Tomorrow's soon enough. I understand that she has a son in New Hampshire—but he's on vacation in Curacao with his family?"

"That's right," said Quinn. "He's due back at the end of the week. Should I try to get in touch with him now?"

"She's already said that she'd rather call him in the morning, which is reasonable. However, assuming there are no complications and she gets discharged, I'd still prefer that someone keep an eye on her for a while. When her family returns, maybe she can stay with her son, since his wife is available during the day. It's too bad," he added, "that Mrs. Dewsbury lives alone. She's at an age—"

"When her independence means everything to her," Quinn finished up. "She needs to hold on to the house; she was born in it."

"Be that as it may, she's eighty-one years old. She's in reasonable health but her vision is poor," Dr. Tann said, shaking his head. "Her days of living alone are winding down."

"We'll see," Quinn said coolly.

Olivia was touched by Quinn's fierce loyalty to his old teacher. For someone who'd had virtually no family of his own—but maybe that was why.

Quinn seemed more tight-lipped than ever as he said, "When exactly will she be released?"

"If her signs are stable she can go home tomorrow mid-morning."

"I'll be here."

The physician left Quinn and Olivia alone in the tiny visitors' room, a dreary cubicle with a small TV mounted on a wall above a bistro table that held an assortment of ragged, outdated magazines.

Suddenly the long night caught up with Olivia: the midnight dash through deserted streets, the shock of seeing an elderly woman assaulted in her own dining room, the lingering tension between Quinn and Olivia over something as trivial as whether or not she should go with him to her Uncle Rupert's house.

"Quinn," she said, humbled by circumstances, "I'm so sorry."

"For what?" he said bitterly. "*You* didn't knock her down."

The barely repressed rage in his voice didn't surprise Olivia. "You think it's the same man," she said, aware of the new burden of guilt he was feeling.

"Gee. I wonder why," Quinn answered. He walked up to the double window that looked out at a parking lot. His hands were jammed in the back of his jeans as he stared, not at the boring view, but at the windowsill, working through his wretchedness.

"We'll *get* this creep," she said. "This isn't about torn capes and dead rats anymore. Chief Vickers will take the case seriously, now that someone's been hurt. I wish I hadn't come in through the window, though," she added, aware that she'd trampled over the crime scene in her zeal to reach Mrs. Dewsbury.

There was no response. After a pause, Olivia began to get frustrated. "You act so paralyzed. You act as if everything's hopeless," she said, trying to get a rise out of him.

His response was surprisingly subdued, and that alarmed her even more than it frustrated her. "You don't have the whole picture," he said without turning around.

"What parts of it don't I have, Quinn?"

He shook his head.

Weary of his continued refusal to confide in her, she glared at his broad back and said, "Sooner or later I'm going to figure it all out for myself, you know."

"God help us, then," he said softly.

"*Damn* it, Quinn!" She said it so sharply that a passing nurse stuck her head in the room and shushed her.

Embarrassed that she had had to be reprimanded, Olivia said in a well-mannered hiss, "This is all your fault. You're acting as covert as a double agent."

"I'm sorry."

"Well, what do we do now? Sit here reading *Time* and *People* till morning? I already know who won the last election."

He turned. She was shocked to see his face. There was agony there, and guilt, but also a sense of menace. He was ready to annihilate someone.

"I'll take you home," he said, scooping up his jacket.

She folded her arms across her sweatshirt. "Absolutely not. I'm going back with you to Mrs. Dewsbury's house. I want to be there when you call the police."

"That's nuts. It's the middle of the night."

"I'm a witness—and maybe even an accessory," she

said, digging in. "I stepped all over any footprints under the bay window when I climbed inside the house. It's better that they get my statement now than have to chase me down later."

He sighed and said, "Fine. At least I'll be able to keep my eye on you. Let's go."

She grabbed her parka and fell in step beside him as he headed for the elevator. "And then tomorrow we'll tackle the other problem," she announced as they passed the nurses' station. "Our visit to my aunt and uncle."

"*No*, Olivia! Jesus! How many times do I have to tell you!"

"*Shhhh!*"

The good news was that Mrs. Dewsbury did not seem intimidated by the attack of the night before, despite a morning interrogation by Chief Vickers. The bad news was, she had developed a distressing tendency to lose her train of thought somewhere in the middle of a sentence.

"They're keeping me in this blessed place another whole day," said Mrs. Dewsbury, and Dr. Tann was right: She wasn't very happy about it.

"Did they say why?" asked Olivia. They knew of the delay, of course, which explained the small travel bag that Olivia was unpacking.

"Oh, I don't know. Something about my blood press— is it cold in here?"

Quinn, who was already half prostrate from the heat in the room, said, "I'll have a nurse turn up the thermostat." He ducked outside and when he returned, Olivia was helping Mrs. Dewsbury into a chenille bedjacket that she had found on the bedpost in the widow's bedroom. Olivia had grabbed other things, too, odd little luxuries: a brush, soft tissues, lotions, a bag of lozenges from the nightstand, and—for the doctor to see—medication for high blood pressure. Quinn was afraid that Mrs. Dewsbury would take offense at Olivia's liberties.

Not in the least.

"You're such a dear . . . so thoughtful . . . this is exactly what I needed."

Olivia threw Quinn a superior look and said, "Men simply don't understand that these things matter."

"What was I doing with this?" the widow said, staring at the brush in her hand as if it were a garden rake.

"You wanted me to run it through your hair for you," Olivia answered without missing a beat.

She took the brush and combed Mrs. Dewsbury's white hair, which looked to Quinn just about the same afterward as it did when they walked in, but the women seemed to think it was an improvement. After that, Olivia freshened the water in the drinking pitcher and moved Quinn's flowers to a more prominent spot.

Finally, when Mrs. Dewsbury looked reasonably comfortable and at ease with them, Quinn got down to business.

"How did your son take the news of all this?" was the first thing on his mind.

"I . . . haven't called him," Mrs. Dewsbury admitted sheepishly.

"The nurse didn't give you the number of the Windward Hotel? I called it in."

"She gave it to me."

"And you're having trouble getting an international call through the hospital's phone system? It can be confusing. Why don't I—?"

"It's silly to ruin Gerald's vacation," she said, fussing nervously with the sheet laid over her lap. "He gets so little time away. I don't want to be a bother."

They went round and round on that for a while, but Mrs. Dewsbury was adamant. Quinn didn't want to upset her, so he dropped the matter for the moment. That brought him to the delicate business of asking her what she remembered about the attack. He knew Vickers wouldn't tell him squat, so any information was going to have to come from the victim herself, and she was old and fragile and traumatized.

"Mrs. Dewsbury—guess what?" said Olivia before Quinn got the chance to bring up the subject. "When we were poking around under your bay window, we found a navy blue watch cap!"

Oh, perfect. *"Olivia—"*

"It's not Quinn's and I'm willing to bet hard cash it's not yours. We think it belonged to the guy who broke in."

The widow got a blank look on her face, as if she'd just remembered that she'd left the oven on.

"I never set the alarm!" she said, apparently realizing it for the first time. "I heard this tremendous crash and I came downstairs. And right before I was hit, I think I caught a whiff of bourbon. I know, because my Larry was partial to bourbon for his nightcap."

"Bourbon, huh?" said Olivia, obviously intrigued by the information. "Did you tell Chief Vickers that?"

"No. When he was here I wasn't quite . . . I wasn't . . . what was I saying?"

"We were coming up with a profile of the jerk who did this to you," said Olivia, and even Quinn had to admit that she made the discussion seem matter-of-fact. How did she do it?

Mrs. Dewsbury suddenly winced, and immediately Olivia was all solicitousness. She jumped up and said, "What hurts? Tell me."

Mrs. Dewsbury touched the back of her head gingerly and gave her a tremulous smile. "It doesn't hurt, exactly. I think I was reliving the blow just then."

"He hit you with your dictionary, you know," said Olivia with a wonderfully sympathetic smile.

"He did *not*," said the widow, bristling.

"But . . . we found the book on the floor by the stairs."

"Because I knocked it over when I was trying to reach a chair. Oh, no. It wasn't a dictionary, my dear. It was something hard and I think metal."

"A candlestick, maybe?" said Quinn. "That's what he used for smashing in the television."

"Yes, it could have been a candlestick," Mrs. Dewsbury decided.

Quinn said, "Chief Vickers will check the one lying in

the television for prints, but he didn't sound hopeful. In any case, the intruder wouldn't have smashed in the screen, then walked over to the stairs and . . . and . . ."

"Bopped me on the head."

"Bopped you on the head," said Quinn with a wry smile, "and then returned the candlestick to the TV screen."

"Was the other one on the table? I kept them placed on each side of the bowl of wax fruit that's on the table runner."

"I don't recall," said Quinn, but Olivia did. She said that the mate was on the table, just where it was supposed to be. Hell.

He mentally ran though a list of possible weapons: lamp, poker, knickknacks . . . Suddenly a light bulb turned on in the closet of his mind and he had a pretty good hunch about what the intruder *did* use for a weapon.

He turned back to Mrs. Dewsbury to say something and was dismayed to see a tear rolling down over her quivering lip.

"I could understand how someone would want to rob me," she said, sucking in her breath in a shuddering effort to gain control over her emotions, "but why did he have to smash in the monitor? I was so excited to have it. Ask anyone."

So that's why the son of a bitch sadist did it, thought Quinn. *Because you shouted your joy from the rooftops.*

The blow to the head, that was more difficult to account for. The act seemed motivated not as much by cruelty or sadism as by simple panic. Then again, Alison had been murdered by a blow to the back of the head. Was it mere coincidence, or a pattern?

There was nothing more to be learned. Mrs. Dewsbury was too weary to be cheered by Quinn's reassurance that he would find her another monitor. When they walked out of the hospital, it was with a fair amount of trepidation.

"I'm going to call her son," Quinn said as he and Olivia got out their car keys. "Obviously he has to know about this."

"I agree. Well, I guess I'll see you . . . ?"

"Tonight. Should we meet here?" he suggested.

"Yes. She needs to have visitors often, but in brief spurts. All right . . . well . . . bye," Olivia murmured, gazing at him with those fathomless dark eyes. Her look cut him up like a chainsaw, leaving a jagged streak of pain in its wake.

She turned to leave, but he caught her by the arm. "Olivia," he said, "I know I've been a shit. I'm, uh, having a real hard time with something right now. I hope . . . I hope that . . ."

What he was hoping was that she would understand. Blindly, without questioning, that she would somehow smile and say, *It's all right. Go wherever the path of justice leads you. I don't mind. Indict my uncle. Arrest my brother. Lock my dad in a small room and beat him until he howls. Break my mother's heart completely. Do whatever you have to, as long as you find out the truth. That's what counts.*

But her smile was sad and baffled, and worse, the spark that he loved seeing in her eyes was fading fast. She wanted him to share what he knew, and he couldn't. Not yet, and maybe not ever.

"I hope that we can work this through," he said at last in a voice wrung dry of emotion.

It wasn't much, but she seemed to take comfort from it. "I know we can, Quinn," she said earnestly. "We have so much going when we're together—as long as we *are* together, we can work anything through."

They kissed, a tender, hurried kiss that felt almost painful to him, and then they got in their cars and drove off in opposite directions—Quinn, with murder on his mind.

Olivia ducked into Miracourt just long enough to ask the help to hold down the fort until mid-afternoon, and then she got back in her car and headed for her parents' grand house at the end of upper Main. Her father would be at the mill, of course, which was fine with her. It was her mother she wanted to see.

The morning was gray but mild. Winter was easing its

grip on Keepsake, at least for the moment: It was the January thaw, right on time. Olivia rolled her window part of the way down, sniffing the gentleness in the air. What would it be like, she mused, if every day were as kind as this?

She daydreamed, again, about moving to California but decided, again, that she'd make a crummy Californian. How could she stand all that fine weather? When you lived in New England, moments like these—when Mother Nature stopped screaming at you long enough to give you a hug—seemed to make life all the more worthwhile.

How pathetic, she realized. *I'm thinking like an abused child.*

She was right about the weather, though: At the head of the drive she saw her mother wearing no coat, only her camel-hair blazer.

She tooted twice on her horn in reply to her mother's surprised wave, then pulled under the portico and left her minivan there. She'd dressed with special care and had left her coat unbuttoned so that her mother could see the olive-green silk dress she wore. With its autumnal scarf cinched by a pin, the outfit was a little on the fancy side for Olivia, but Teresa Bennett loved to see her little girl all decked out.

"Don't you look nice, honey," her mother commented predictably as Olivia bussed her cheek. "I've always liked that dress."

"Hi, Mr. Thurber," said Olivia to the gardener, who took himself off to the side to peruse his notes. "Mom, we have to talk."

"I'm afraid not now, Olivia," her mother said in mild reproach. "You can see that I'm busy with Mr. Thurber."

"But it's important. It's got to do with Quinn."

Anyone would think that Olivia had just let out a string of four-letter words. Her mother silenced her with a scandalized look and said, "Put on some coffee, then; I'll meet you inside when I'm done here."

"Mom, I don't have much time—"

"Olivia," her mother warned with a dangerous smile. "You'll have to wait your *turn.*"

Chastised, Olivia said, "Okay, I'll wait, but I don't really want coffee. This'll only take sixty seconds."

She paced the length of the redone kitchen for twenty minutes as she waited for her mother to finish her business with the gardener. It was dumb to have tried cutting ahead of Mr. Thurber. Teresa Bennett had always treated the help with at least as much civility as she treated her friends and relations; it was the reason people liked to do business with her.

Olivia sighed and put on the pot of coffee after all.

Eventually her mother came inside, and Olivia meekly set a steaming cup in its saucer on the granite-topped island where her mother liked to sit and read her morning paper.

"I'm sorry I interrupted you and Mr. Thurber," said Olivia before being handed an official reprimand. "By now I should know better. And I was indiscreet. About Quinn, I mean."

"I *know* what you mean," said her mother. "What's this all about? You come flying up the drive like a sparrow two steps ahead of a hawk, and you start flapping on about Quinn. What's wrong with you, Olivia? Do you understand the word discretion at *all*?"

"Not by this family's definition, that's for sure," Olivia shot back. She slipped onto the high stool opposite her mother's. "But listen to me, Mom. Something's happened. Mrs. Dewsbury was attacked in her house last night. She's in the hospital now."

Olivia related the few details she knew to her shocked mother, then said, "In a way, the attack just shows that Quinn is right. He has to prove his father's innocence—otherwise, whoever is doing these things will just keep on upping the ante. *I* could be next," she threw out, trying to alarm her mother into endorsing the logic of the plan she was about to announce.

So much for psychology. Her mother went directly past logic into a state of high anxiety. "Quinn has got to leave Keepsake!" she said, slapping the dark granite with the palm of her hand. "He's putting everyone around him in peril. Everyone!"

"Don't you think he knows that? That's why he's going out to see Uncle Rupert this afternoon."

"What . . . do you mean?" asked her mother. Her face had turned a deathly shade of pale.

"Well . . . *you* know. He's going to ask them about agreeing to have Alison's body exhumed for DNA testing. If she wasn't pregnant by Mr. Leary, then there would have been no real reason for him to have murdered her. That's pretty obvious."

Her mother simply stared. "But I thought that was all done with. I thought the district attorney refused to do anything about Alison. Why *would* he? Francis Leary is dead. I thought . . . that was all done with," she repeated numbly.

"I know it's upsetting to think about, but we have to be rational about this. Eliminating his father as a suspect is the only way that Quinn can stay in town without having to worry constantly that people he . . . he cares about are in danger. I mean, let's face it," Olivia said lightly, "he can't go installing a burglar alarm in the house of everyone whose hand he shakes. As soon as the test results become known—"

"They can't become known!" her mother cried. "That's nobody's business!"

Olivia stood up. "Of course it is, if there's a crime involved. That's why I'm going over to Uncle Rupert's now," she said, slipping into her long wool coat. "To help Quinn talk them into cooperating."

"What! Are you *insane*?"

"Why does everyone keep asking me that?" Olivia said with a laugh, determined to seem unconcerned. If she showed the least bit of empathy at her mother's distress, she'd never make it out the front door.

"Olivia, you cannot go there!"

"Of course I can, Mom," she said. She kissed her mother's cheek in farewell. "I know it's painful, dragging the whole thing up after all these years. But people have Alison on their minds anyway, with all these horrible acts going on. The whole town's on edge—except for Mrs. Dewsbury, of course. You can't believe how unflappable she is."

She glanced at her watch. "Shoot! Look at the time!" Snatching up her butter-soft bag from the back of the chair, she hooked it over her shoulder and said, "I still have to stop at the bakery for something sweet to bring Aunt Betty. Gotta run. If Quinn beats me there, he won't have a prayer of getting inside the house, though he'd be the last to admit it."

"Don't go!" her mother said in a sharp cry of agony, grabbing her arm. "Olivia, I'm begging you—don't!"

"I have to," Olivia said, unsettled by the depth of her mother's distress. "I'm only telling you beforehand because I don't want to do anything behind your back. Please, Mom," she said, freeing her mother's hand from her sleeve. "I've thought this all out. Aunt Betty was always fond of me. I used to stay over when I was a kid; she won't have forgotten that. She'll listen to me, even if she won't listen to Quinn. I promise I'll let you know how it goes. I'll even offer to tell Dad, if you don't want to."

Her mother grabbed her by the shoulders. Swaths of emotion were splashed across the tawny skin of her cheeks. Above her burning cheekbones, her dark eyebrows, heavier than was strictly fashionable, were pulled down in pain. Her look was as tortured, and as fierce, as the grip she had on her daughter.

"If you go," she said in a choked and agonized voice, "then don't bother coming back to tell me. *Ever!*"

Olivia blinked. "You don't mean that, Mom," she said, amazed and almost annoyed by her mother's melodramatic tone. "You're just saying that."

"I do mean it!" Teresa Bennett cried, and she burst into sobs. Tears rolled over her cheeks as she said over and over between hiccups of pain, "Don't, honey . . . don't . . . please don't . . ."

Now it was Olivia's turn to stare. Her mother had always been emotional—but this! She had always been kind to poor Aunt Betty—but this!

"Mom, it's no big deal," Olivia said, engulfing her mother as if she were a five-year-old with a scraped knee.

"You're getting way too upset for Aunt Betty's sake, honestly."

Her mother would not be consoled. Finally, in wonder and exasperation at her hysterics, Olivia stepped back and blurted out, "I have to do this, Mom! I love him!"

"You don't love him!" her mother shrieked, slapping Olivia's shoulder in her frustration. "You only think you do! You just want to fly in the face of your father! This is all about getting back at your father, Olivia, and nothing else!"

"But I do love Quinn!" Olivia cried, stunned by her mother's response. "My God—how can you say I don't love him? How can you possibly know how I feel?"

"You've never had time to love any man! They're annoyances to you, distractions from your career. Why would you suddenly think you love this one, unless it were to hurt us all?"

Olivia's purse had slid down to her wrist. Frustrated and infuriated, she looped the strap around her hand and slammed the bag in a vicious arc onto a counter. "Damn it! No matter what I do, it's not good enough for you! Dad wouldn't let me work at the mill. Now you won't let me love Quinn. What does it take around here? *You're* the one who always told me to follow my heart. *You're* the one who always told me to make my own dreams happen. Well, that's what I'm doing! I love him, Mother! *I love Quinn.*"

Three little words. They silenced as efficiently as a sword plunged directly through the heart.

Teresa Bennett became very still. Without another word, she moved away from her daughter and slipped back onto the woven seat of the wrought-iron chair at her new granite-topped island. Without another word, she moved her cup and saucer carefully to one side, then folded her arms in front of her on the dark green stone. Without another word, she bowed her head and pressed her brow against the soft ivory cashmere cocooning her arms.

Olivia stared at her mother for a long moment. And then she left, without another word.

Nineteen

Quinn went directly from the hospital to the police station and told Vickers where he could find the weapon that was used on Mrs. Dewsbury.

The chief laughed in his face. "You're completely paranoid, you know that? Too many years brooding in exile, if you ask me."

"Get a warrant," Quinn said. "Go to his house. Hell, stop by for a beer. You're a pal of his. Check the place out for yourself."

"I *am* a pal, Leary," he growled, "which isn't the only reason I'm telling you to get the hell out of my office. You've given me no cause to search the man's home. A dirty look on New Year's Eve and some psychological claptrap about—what?—sour grapes or something? That don't qualify as cause. Stop wasting my time. I'm late for a meeting already."

And that was that.

Seething, Quinn decided to retrieve the weapon himself. Maybe Vickers would call and warn his old friend, but maybe he wouldn't have the chance. It was worth a shot.

Quinn left his truck parked at the end of the block and headed for the bland little bungalow where Coach Bronsky had lived alone all of his life. He found it at the middle of a tree-lined street, looking—like its owner—saggier, baggier, somehow more mean.

A beat-up truck sat parked next to the house. As Quinn

suspected, Bronsky was home. It was the lunch period at Keepsake High. It didn't take a rocket scientist to figure out where a boozing coach who lived nearby would spend the free time.

The house itself presented a surly facade. The shades of the four windows that faced the street were pulled completely down, just the way they used to be. One of them had a big rip near the roller. For all Quinn knew, it was the same torn shade that had hung there two decades ago.

Even then, Coach Bronsky used to scare the kids. Not scare, exactly; more like thrill them. He was tough and mean and called them unspeakably insulting names, and underneath all their terror, they loved it. He was a role model for them, mostly because no one had a father with a repertoire of insults as vast as his. But the allure wore thin by sophomore year, and by their senior year, most of the guys despised him.

The coach was a bully and a browbeater, a grown-up version of the kind of boy who pulled wings off insects in the name of science. He had a meanness of spirit, a pettiness of emotion. He blamed everyone for everything. Quinn could not remember a single instance when Coach Bronsky admitted to a mistake or said he was sorry. He intimidated the younger kids with his size and the older ones with his authority. Single women shunned him. Mothers resented him. Fathers felt guilty that he had charge of their sons.

He was a thug.

A BEWARE OF DOG sign, rusted and hanging from only one of its holes, was wired to the chest-high chain-link fence. Quinn opened the gate without bewaring. The dog was dead, Quinn had no doubt—he knew where the bones were.

Quinn walked up the five cracked concrete steps. Ignoring the bell, which was missing its button, he knocked and then waited. Three rectangles of glass in the door, stepping down from upper left to lower right, had been shaded with blue-lined pages of looseleaf paper, and one of the sheets had been pried from its tape to make a peephole. At six-foot-three, Quinn was able to see through the hole into the house.

The view inside was dismal: an end table piled high with

magazines and dirty dishes and topped with a chartreuse ceramic lamp whose shade was akilter. A dirt-colored couch with lumpy, torn cushions. A carpet that was matted and gray and littered with bits of food and scraps of paper. And over everything, a pall of grime and grease, rage and despair.

Quinn stepped out of view through the pulled-away sheet in the window. Eventually the door swung open a few inches. The smell of whiskey—bourbon, Quinn assumed— added one more layer of sourness in the air between Bronsky and him.

"What do *you* want?"

"A word," said Quinn, slamming the door clear of the coach's grip. It hit the wall with a bounce as Quinn pushed his way inside and grabbed the coach by the throat with one hand, pinning him against the stairwell as he kicked the door shut behind them.

The warm, flabby flesh of the coach's neck felt irresistible to Quinn. He got a death grip on the man's windpipe, then loosened his hold just enough for the coach's head to slump back into position on his shoulders. Before the coach could catch his breath, Quinn tightened his grip and slammed him back into the wall again. This time he squeezed harder.

Bronsky's round face turned florid; his eyes were no more than slits above puffy bags and a foul-smelling mouthhole gaping for air. Just before the coach passed out, Quinn relaxed his hold on his throat, then tightened it and slammed him up against the wall another time.

Bronsky couldn't speak, and Quinn didn't want him to. Not yet. Quinn positively needed these dribs and drabs of release; the alternative would have been to kill his old coach with a single blow. He eased his grip just enough for a trickle of air to flow down Bronsky's throat. The gurgling sound he made, so like a death rattle, was deeply satisfying to Quinn's ears.

"Listen to me, you sorry sonofabitch," Quinn said, his face within inches of the loathsome one he knew so well. "You want to knock out little old ladies, you ask me first.

You want to terrorize single women, you ask me first. You want to panic a bunch of churchgoers, you ask me first. Got that?''

The coach was in no position either to shake or to nod his head. He squawked what sounded like a denial. It infuriated Quinn. He slammed the man's head against the wall again. This time the answer he got was more to his liking.

''Ayight . . . ayight.''

Quinn let him go. ''Where's the trophy you stole from the box in Mrs. Dewsbury's front room?''

Coughing and sucking in air as he massaged his throat, the coach croaked, ''I don't . . . have any trophy.''

''The hell you don't,'' said Quinn, sending the coach stumbling before him with a shove to his back. He scanned the living room, then said, ''Where's your bedroom?''

Since Coach looked like a man who didn't climb steps if he didn't have to, Quinn looked for and found a sleeping hovel on the first floor. It was at the end of the hall, next to the kitchen. He shoved Bronsky into the room and flipped on a light. The tiny bedroom smelled rank, a stale mix of booze and b.o. Quinn glanced around and saw the stolen trophy—a brass-plated football mounted on a wood base—sitting on a dresser whose drawers were hanging half out. He pulled a hanky from his hip pocket and used it to pick up the football by its stem. If the weapon still had fingerprints, it would have forensic traces of Mrs. Dewsbury as well.

The coach glared at him. He looked almost indignant. ''You're going to jail for this.''

Quinn snorted. ''I don't think so. Not unless I follow through on the yen I have to bash in your head with this thing. And even there, I'm pretty sure the town would thank me.''

He walked past the coach out of the room, but then turned back for one last warning. ''If I ever hear of another attempt by you to frighten someone—if you so much as whisper an unsettling word in anyone's ear—then I'll hunt you down and kill you. You know me well, Coach. You know I will. Are you sober enough to understand me?''

The coach's glare of defiance quickly turned sullen. He

let his gaze slither away from Quinn and hide in some laundry lying on the floor.

"Yeah, I get it."

Quinn muttered, "You asshole."

As he walked out of the foul-smelling house with his recovered trophy, Quinn glanced through the broken blinds of a filthy window that looked out on a small, overgrown yard. It didn't surprise him to see a mound of soil piled next to a dug-up hole in the ground.

Poor dog. His mortal remains were now in a plastic bag lying somewhere in the town dump. God only knows what kind of life and death the animal had suffered as the pet of this brute.

All things considered, Quinn figured the dog was better off in the landfill.

It was a fact that Coach Bronsky had an alibi for the time of Alison's murder—it was an unacceptable fact, but an undeniable one. Quinn would gladly have given all the money he possessed to prove that Coach had done the deed, but everyone knew that he and then-Sergeant Vickers had played poker with two other buddies all night long.

Besides, Bronsky had never been linked, even as tenuously as Quinn's father had, to Alison Bennett. No gossip, no anecdotes, *nada*. Quinn's old coach might have been a scumbag, but apparently he wasn't a murdering scumbag— although he'd just come damned close with Mrs. Dewsbury.

In the meantime, Quinn was approaching the house of Olivia's uncle with dread. His mind had locked onto three scenarios, all of them involving Bennetts. In one of them, Rupert Bennett impregnated his daughter and later murdered her. In another, Rand got her pregnant and Rupert murdered her. In the third, Rand did both. It was like juggling three hand grenades with the pins pulled out.

The house where Rupert Bennett lived, like his brother Owen's, was not visible from the road, but that was all that the two houses had in common. Rupert lived in a simple saltbox Colonial that dated from maybe the early 1800s. It had a classic, uncluttered look to it that appealed to Quinn; if he were to settle down in the east, such a house would be his choice.

It was built on a clearing in the middle of a second-growth forest. Someone had once farmed the land, but not for a generation or two. It wasn't hard to see the writing on the wall. The land around the house would be sold off, if it hadn't been already, for a shot of income. Evidence of poverty—more likely, of a money-sucking habit—was staring Quinn in the face. Rupert's house was as shabby as his brother's mansion was pristine.

Simply put, the Colonial structure was falling down in place. The roof was sagging, shingles were missing, the leaky wood gutters were doing much more harm than good. The windows needed glazing, the foundation needed tucking, and as for the sills . . . Quinn could almost hear the powder-post beetles munching away as he drove up. The craftsman in Quinn wanted to buy out the Bennetts then and there and save the house, but that was not why he had come.

The winding, rutted drive continued on behind the house, but Quinn took the spur and parked his truck directly astride the front door, which apparently was little used. He stepped out of the truck and—because the weather was mild—right into mud. He should have known better than to approach through the formal entrance, but he didn't want the Bennetts to feel that he had presumed by driving around to the back.

Would Rupert be in? Quinn almost hoped not. Betty Bennett didn't sound like the type of woman to say boo without her husband's permission. On the other hand, it was Rupert whose measure Quinn wanted to take. If he seemed nervous or panicky or anything other than predictably hostile, then that would be significant.

Quinn cleaned the mud from his workboots on a metal bootscraper set into a chunk of concrete, then gave a rusted hand-cranked doorbell a turn or two. Its loud, shrill ring was enough to wake up the dead. In a sense, it was what Quinn had come to do.

Eventually the door was opened by a churchmouse. Betty

Bennett was a hundred pounds of fearful impulse bundled in gray sweats. Under a wisp of graying hair, her eyes, washed by too many tears to the color of faded jeans, seemed incapable of returning his direct gaze. A quick, scared glance was all he got from her. He felt like Godzilla trying to sell Girl Scout cookies.

"Mrs. Bennett?" he said gently as he took off his baseball cap. "You probably don't remember me—I'm Quinn Leary. I wonder if I might have just a moment of your time."

To his amazement, she said, "Yes, all right," and opened the door wide.

Well, hell, that was easy enough, Quinn thought, stepping over the threshold. He followed her across wide-planked floors through a neat, cozily furnished parlor and then through a fireplaced keeping room, all the while wondering whether she wasn't leading him straight into an ambush. It didn't help his morale that a rifle seemed to be missing from an otherwise well-stocked gun case that they passed along the way.

The expected ambush took place in the kitchen: Olivia Bennett, wearing olive silk and a fancy bandanna and looking wildly sophisticated in the austere pilgrim setting, was sitting demurely at a big pine table by a massive hearth with a cup of tea and a giant muffin set in front of her.

Son of a bitch. Now what? Son of a bitch.

He looked at the niece. He looked at the aunt. He looked at the niece again.

"Now why am I surprised by this?"

"I can't imagine," Olivia said, forcing herself to seem offhand. "Didn't I mention that I might be stopping by my aunt's? I thought I had."

Quinn had arrived before Olivia had had a chance to prepare her aunt for his request. She'd barely got out the heads-up that Quinn Leary was going to be stopping by when they heard the crank on the bell. Her aunt, predictably, wanted to run and hide under the couch; Olivia had to reassure her that she would stay by her side and give her moral support. And meanwhile, Olivia's Uncle Rupert was due back from town at any moment.

Betty Bennett didn't know what to do with Quinn, that was plain to see, so Olivia took over as hostess. "Can I get your . . . something?" she asked, stumbling over the sentence. God, he had a look. Even she was nervous.

"I'm all right," he said in a perfectly even tone.

Ah, that tone. It spoke volumes.

He turned to Olivia's aunt and said in a much more gentle way, "I know it's distressing for you to see me after all these years, Mrs. Bennett. You suffered a terrible tragedy, and I'm a reminder of that time. I know that. I wish I could be someone else right now. I wish I could be someone you knew and trusted—but there's no one else who can make this request of you except me."

He added softly, "I'm here because no one else cares enough about my father to prove that he had nothing to do with your loss of Alison."

Once he put it that way, Olivia understood things much more clearly. He was right. She had no business being there. This was between him and Alison's parents. He *was* right. And so was her mother. What on earth had she been thinking?

Something about Quinn's soft, sympathetic tone made her Aunt Betty murmur, "Please. Sit down."

She pulled out a chair for herself so meekly, it broke Olivia's heart to watch her. Here was a woman as fragile as the butterflies she had raised in her greenhouse before a storm knocked it down. It seemed cruel that sweet Aunt Betty had had to suffer the loss even of a single butterfly. But to have her only *child* murdered, and then to have no one with whom to share her grief except a brooding, remote husband—that was unbearably cruel.

Quinn hooked his jacket over the back of the ladderback chair and sat down. For a big man with solid biceps and a tough-looking haircut, he seemed amazingly unthreatening. Olivia knew how tender he could be in bed; that had a lot to do with her impression. But there was more to it than that. Women responded to Quinn because he empathized with them. Because he was gentle and tough and kind and interesting and curious and chivalrous and, okay, super-confident, not to mention because he made pies. You could trust such a man. All you had to do was look into his eyes and listen to his voice.

And her aunt was doing just that. Perched almost primly on the rush-seated chair, Betty Bennett folded her hands in her lap and listened intently to Quinn as he presented the reasons that his father had fled in the night so very long ago.

"My father was a shy man, and gentle," Quinn said, without making it sound like a character flaw. "He was appalled at the thought of having to fight to defend himself. He was even more appalled at the threat of being locked in prison, away from his gardens. All my father ever wanted to do was to nurture growing things. He lived very simply. He didn't want money; he didn't need fame. But he needed—truly needed—to be taking care of things."

Quinn might have been describing the woman who was listening to him so raptly. Olivia watched as her aunt nodded sympathetically at one statement after another that Quinn was laying out before her. It occurred to Olivia, really for the first time, that Quinn's father and Betty Bennett would have been a match made in heaven.

How sad, she thought. What a waste of love. She let her gaze wander around the well-kept kitchen. From the gleaming finish of the pine table to the homey, hand-braided rug that her aunt had made from fabric scraps, everything around them spoke of nurturing impulses that had nowhere to go.

How truly sad.

"I'm not sure how familiar you are with forensic science, Mrs. Bennett," Quinn said, easing into his painful request, "but nowadays there are methods to prove someone's innocence that weren't around seventeen years ago."

"What kind of methods?"

"Well . . . have you heard of DNA testing?" he asked her softly.

"I do have some idea, yes, from watching news about the O. J. Simpson trial. But I didn't watch the trial itself," she added with a troubled shake of her head. "It was too awful to see."

"You were better off," Quinn agreed with a sympathetic smile.

Olivia began a major project of rearranging crumbs into a circle around the edge of her plate and didn't look up during the painful pause that followed.

"A DNA test means that they would take just a few cells of tissue to determine the genetic makeup of the . . . unborn child," Quinn explained while Olivia held her breath. "And they would compare them to a DNA profile which they would get from analyzing strands of my father's hair. The two won't match, you see, and that will clear my—"

"Oh! Your father wants to return to Keepsake, then?"

Her aunt did not want to understand the implications of what Quinn was saying; Olivia was sure of it. She was rerouting her attention from her dead daughter and unborn grandchild to Quinn's father and where he should live. That, she could handle.

Quinn said softly, "My father died just before Thanksgiving."

"Oh, I'm . . . sorry."

Olivia glanced at Quinn and then at her aunt. They were sharing a moment of hurt, an awareness of loss, that drove home how wrong it was for her to be sitting at the table with them. She'd give anything to be able to leave them alone. But she couldn't just stand up and go; she'd be trampling all over their fragile connection. She went back to arranging her crumbs with renewed intensity, as though the fate of the free world depended on having a perfect crumb wreath on the rim of her cake plate.

"The thing is, Mrs. Bennett, he was a really good man and he deserves to have his good name back. I've never known anyone more steadfast . . . more loyal . . . more heroic.''

"Heroic?"

Olivia was curious about that, too. It was the second time that Quinn had referred to his father that way. She saw color rise on Quinn's neck as he said, "After he left Keepsake, my father did some good things."

"So you want to do this DNA test and clear his name," Betty said. "I can't blame you, Mr. Leary, but . . . well . . . I'm not sure. I think it would be very''—she took a deep breath and blew it out—"hard."

Catching a lock of hair at the back of her neck, she tugged at it nervously as she stared at the clean-swept hearth. "Hard on my husband, you see. People would—they'd start talking again. Rumors . . . they can be *so* hurtful.''

She returned her hands to her lap and forced herself to look Quinn in the eye. It didn't last long. She dropped her gaze and studied the butter crock on the table instead. She said apologetically, "I think maybe we should just leave things be. I don't think my husband will agree to this at all.''

Olivia looked from her aunt to Quinn. She expected to see his jaw set the way it did when he was opposed. Instead he said softly, "Those rumors have already surfaced, ma'am. There's only one way to lay them to rest now."

Olivia blinked. What rumors? They weren't talking about Francis Leary any longer. What rumors?

Her aunt had turned as pale as the whitewashed walls of her kitchen. She stood up and seemed to shake herself free of Quinn's spell, like a child who's lingered too long in the park and knows she's going to catch hell at home. "You really should go now. My husband could be back anytime. I'm sorry we can't help you. I'm sorry," she said with something like urgency. "Your father sounds like a nice man."

But she was too late. They all heard the door to the mud shed slam loudly, and they all turned at the same time to behold Olivia's Uncle Rupert letting himself through it to the kitchen. Olivia hadn't seen him in over half a year. When she stopped by for her Aunt Betty's birthday in August he'd been asleep, and when she dropped off her Christmas presents in December he hadn't been home.

He looked much the same: lean and leathery and dour.

He sneered at Quinn and said, "Well, well, well. Look what the cat dragged in." He didn't seem surprised, and Olivia wanted to know why. Would he really know Quinn's truck?

Earlier Olivia had wanted to be invisible. Apparently she'd got her wish; her uncle didn't seem to be aware of her at all. "Hello, Uncle Rupert," she said rather loudly, as if he were not only blind but hard of hearing. "I haven't seen you for a while. How are you?"

He was watching Quinn the way a tom regards a stray who's wandered through his territory. Without taking his eyes away from him, he said to Olivia, "Since when do you care?"

He was right, of course. Olivia had never cared for him, not for as long as she could remember.

When she was a little girl and he was still part-owner of the mill and their families were closer, Olivia used to sleep over occasionally. He always came into Alison's bedroom to kiss them both good night, and Olivia had never liked it. His mouth was too wet, and he often smelled of old beer. After a while, she began to insist that Alison come over to *her* house for sleepovers. But her uncle had nixed the idea, and that was that. She and Alison stopped having sleepovers.

But now, what had seemed like an irrational childish aversion to a grown-up suddenly took on another meaning altogether. Something deep inside of Olivia seemed to shift and move, like ice over a pond in the January thaw. She felt her cheeks turn hot and her heart take off on a sickening run.

Quinn, still seated, broke the brutal silence. "I don't pretend to be here out of anything beyond self-interest," he said in a much more steely voice than he had used so far. "I've come back to Keepsake for one reason only: to prove my father's innocence."

"If you want my blessing, you're in the wrong place," her uncle growled. "Go see Father Tom."

"No," Quinn said coolly as he leaned into his forearms on the table. "It's the district attorney whose blessing I'll need. I'm here to say that the only way to clear my father's name—and yours—is for us to throw in our forces together."

"What are you talking about?"

"I think you know."

"Suppose you tell me."

Olivia saw Quinn glance at Betty Bennett, who looked ready to burst into tears. She realized in a blinding flash that her uncle was banking on Quinn's natural reluctance to inflict pain on downtrodden women. It was a game of psychological poker, and Uncle Rupert was calling Quinn's bluff.

The men remained locked in a standoff for a brutal moment, and then Quinn shrugged and said, "Okay. Since you want it spelled out."

Olivia held her breath. Her aunt gasped.

"There are rumors around Keepsake that your relationship with your daughter was—"

"No more than it should have been, goddammit!" Rupert said, refusing to look at the cards that Quinn was about to lay out. He turned to his wife and said, "Leave us! This isn't for a woman to hear."

Apparently Olivia didn't fall into the woman category. Either that, or she truly was invisible, because her uncle completely disregarded her as he waited for his wife to scurry up the stairs and out of earshot.

Olivia watched him with a feeling of dismay that was rapidly imploding into one of disgust. Was it possible? Those vague and uncomfortable feelings that she'd had as a child . . . the squirmy reluctance to be left, with Alison, in her uncle's care . . . the sinking feeling when he walked into a room, any room, where she and Alison happened to be.

Was it *possible*?

She stared fiercely at his face, willing her memory to dredge up some clues, any clues, as to what kind of man he was behind that domineering sneer. But as hard as she tried, all she could see was a truly awful version of her father. A taller, lazier, more irresponsible version of her father, a man who preferred to wear plaid instead of pinstripes. The same instinct to control was present in both brothers, but her Uncle Rupert was lording it over a much smaller empire: one shy woman, to be exact.

No. He might have been domineering and he might have been awkward—even repulsive—in social situations. But he was not the father of his unborn grandchild. Olivia was absolutely convinced of it.

He had been leaning his weight on one leg, one shoulder higher than the other as he watched his wife leave the room. Now he swung around fully to face Quinn. It was the posture of confrontation. Olivia had a sudden urge to duck under the table.

"I never touched her, not in that way," he said with a burning look. "She was my *daughter*, for God's sake."

His face, so like her father's and yet so utterly unlike it, was contorted with emotions that Olivia couldn't begin to understand. Rage? Grief? Horror? Frustration? They went so far beyond Olivia's limited palette of experience that she found herself groping for terms to describe them. The one thing she recognized, the one thing she knew, was that he was telling the truth.

She turned to Quinn to gauge his reaction. She was sure he'd look relieved; that he'd believe her uncle. But what she saw on Quinn's face was a look of surprise and, oddly, dismay. It left her completely bewildered.

"Agree to the DNA testing, then," Quinn said, ignoring her as thoroughly as her uncle was doing. "I'll pay for the attorneys, I'll pay for the test. The results won't tell anyone who the father is. But at least they'll tell everyone who he isn't."

Her uncle bent his head and squeezed his temples with the fingers of one hand as he tried to come up with a response to that. When he looked up, his eyes were glazed over with tears. Olivia gaped at him, astonished at the display of emotion.

His answer was choked, halting. "I went to the D.A. . . . I wanted them to do something. I wanted them to go after your father, go after someone. I got *nothing*. A cup of coffee, a pat on the back. They seemed perfectly happy to have your father on the loose and the murder unsolved. Christ, where was the justice? Where was the law? I hired a P.I. He didn't do shit."

He dropped his chin to his chest. "Ah, damn it to hell. The rumors won't end . . . they'll never end. Keepsake is obsessed with them. My God. My great-grandfather built this town up from a general store and a post office. Keepsake wouldn't *exist* if it weren't for the mill, if it weren't for the Bennetts."

He shook his head and sighed heavily. He looked resigned, even defeated, as he said, "Go ahead. Do whatever you have to do. Tell me what I need to sign. But leave me alone until then, do you hear? Both of you."

He turned away from them and left the room, his own private demons nipping at his heels with every step.

Olivia stood respectful and silent until she knew that he was well up the stairs, then turned to Quinn and murmured, "I think we're on our own as far as finding the door."

Quinn's face had a stony expression that left her feeling desperately uneasy. It didn't make sense; he should be happy that they were finally on the way to clearing the air. He *couldn't* be angry that she'd shown up despite his warning not to. It would be far too small-minded a response for someone like him.

"All's well that ends well—right?" she ventured with a tentative smile as they left the kitchen together.

His look stayed grim. "It's barely begun."

Twenty

"All Wools, Forty Percent Off."

Olivia placed the small sign, done in a calligrapher's exquisite hand, on a pretty brass stand and positioned it in a puddle of blue worsted spilling from its bolt in the window of Miracourt. Advertising a winter sale in her York Street shop didn't take much more than that. Her clientele was strictly local, and they knew that come January, all wools would be forty percent off.

The customers who flocked to her mill outlet from all over the region, however, were another matter. Olivia was targeting her Run of the Mill audience with a big, flashy flyer about to be included in a weekly newspaper that served the whole county.

> *GIANT WINTER SALE! OVER ONE MILLION YARDS OF FABRIC! DESIGNER WOOLS AT FIFTY PERCENT OFF LIST AND MORE! CLEARANCE ON ALL CORDS, WOOLS, AND VELVETS! SHEERS, LACES, LININGS, HOLIDAY PRINTS AND TRIMMINGS, SEVENTY-FIVE PERCENT OFF! SUPPLIES LIMITED! HURRY FOR BEST SELECTION! DOORS OPEN 6 AM! FREE 9 FT. GARLAND TO FIRST 100 CUSTOMERS!*

The asterisk warned in small print that the designer wools were seconds, that the sale could not be combined with any other offer, that all sales were final, that previous markdowns were not applicable, and that the sale ended February tenth.

Olivia proofread the ad with a certain amount of distaste. She hated having to grab people's attention by shouting at their eyes. But her father was right—this was how it was done in the outlet trade. Still, she found the flyer embarrassing. The thing was not only tacky, but sounded paranoid. How much nicer it was to know her customers personally, and to take back the fabric if they changed their minds, and to ask them how their kids were doing at hockey this season.

I'm a village shopkeeper, not an outlet entrepreneur; that's all there is to it.

It was an ongoing revelation to her, this softer, gentler side of herself. Was it because she had fallen in love? And if that was true, then why wasn't the same thing happening to Quinn? She wanted to believe that he had fallen as hard for her as she had for him, and yet every time they were together lately, he seemed a little more edgy, a little more . . . remote.

That was it: remote. She didn't like even to *think* the word, and yet there was no other way to describe the look that she now saw routinely on his face. He would be with her, talking and listening, and yet . . . somehow . . . not with her at all.

And I can pinpoint exactly when and where he began to act that way: New Year's Day, after Ray Buffitt's football bash.

Obviously that was where he had heard the rumor about Rupert Bennett being the father of his daughter's child. Armed with that knowledge, Quinn had taken a huge gamble with Olivia's uncle, and it had paid off. With Rupert Bennett's cooperation, Quinn would now be able to clear his father's name and—something Olivia hadn't even known was necessary—clear her uncle's in the bargain.

Hooray. Three cheers. Shouldn't they be drinking champagne?

"Beth, I'm going out," Olivia said to her assistant as she faxed her approval of the sale flyer. "I should be back in an hour. If I'm not, just close up here, would you?"

"Sure thing."

"Thanks. You're a doll."

Olivia grabbed her coat and blew Beth a kiss on her way out of the shop, then got back in her car to head back up the hill to her parents' house, aware that she had got absolutely nothing done all day.

This couldn't go on. Being in love and walking around with your head in a cloud was one thing, but this wasn't that kind of cloud. This one was filled with rain and fog and, worse, the occasional thunderbolt. All things considered, Olivia preferred to do her strolling in rose-tinted sunglasses.

She drove in deepening twilight through deserted streets toward her parents' estate, clinging psychologically to the thin streak of orange that slashed the cloud bank above the dropping sun. A cold front was pushing through, which meant that tomorrow would be bright and sunny. But the day would still be cold and short; so who cared, really, whether the sun came out or not?

I do, she decided. Anything to banish the sense of gloom that was plaguing her lately.

At that hour, she expected to find her father home from the mill, but finding Rand at her parents' house was an unexpected bonus. He was sitting in his Lexus parked under the portico. Was he coming or going? Going, apparently. He waved a hello–good-bye to her and started to drive off, but Olivia flagged him down. She wanted him to stay. For one thing, her mother was much more likely to let go of her anger at Olivia if he were around. And with Rand there, Olivia would be able to grill all of them at the same time about the appalling rumors concerning her Uncle Rupert. That way, they wouldn't have a chance to coordinate their stories.

By now Olivia was reasonably sure that she had been the only one among them who had lived so happily clueless for seventeen years. It pained her to think that her family had conspired to keep her in the dark like some rainforest flower that would wilt and die if put out in the sun. Damn it! Why was *she* always the odd one out in the family?

Rand buzzed his window down and said, ''Run while you can. She's in one hell of a mood.'' He gave Olivia his trademark bemused smile, the one that always left women's hearts aflutter, and said, ''That's the last time *I* offer to drop off Eileen's leftover borscht.''

''Did Mom say what was bothering her?''

''Nope. She just took one look at me and burst into tears. I said, 'What'd I do now?' and she shook her head and moaned, 'Not you, not you.' That was good enough for me. As soon as I could, I cut and ran.''

Still angry! ''Uh-oh.''

Rand gave her a sharp look and said, ''So you're the 'you' she was talking about? Oh, great. Is this about Quinn?''

''It's more complicated than that, Rand.''

She hurried around to the passenger side of the Lexus and dropped into the leather bucket seat, then brought her brother quickly up to date on the hair-raising showdown earlier in the day between Quinn and their Uncle Rupert.

Her brother's reaction was concise. ''Oh, shit.''

''You knew all along, didn't you, Rand? You knew that people suspected Uncle Rupert,'' she said, convinced of it now. ''Why didn't you ever tell me?''

''Why bother?'' he asked, staring straight ahead. ''There's no truth to it.''

''Still! It concerns us all.''

He turned and challenged her in a sneering voice. ''What would you have done if you did know?''

''Well . . . for one thing, I wouldn't have fought the idea of DNA testing when Quinn first suggested it. On the contrary, I would have pushed for it. I don't know why Uncle Rupert didn't do that himself when the rumors first surfaced.''

''The test wasn't invented, for one thing.''

''Oh. Right. Well, then Uncle Rupert should have just . . . I don't know, issued a statement of some kind.''

"Oh, *there's* a plan. Send a letter to the local editor saying, 'Just so you know, I'm not the one who knocked up my daughter.' Olivia, do you have *any* idea how rumors work? Don't you see how counterproductive it is even to bring them up? You're the Shakespeare expert. Do the words 'Methinks he doth protest too much' mean anything to you?"

"That's not the actual quote," Olivia couldn't help saying. "The actual quote is, 'The lady doth pro—' "

"Stuff it!" Rand said, out of patience with her. "The point is, after seventeen years, people's minds are set. The best thing is to let those opinions stay sunk in the mire where they belong. Why dredge everything back up? Why foul the air?"

"The point is to *clear* the air, Rand, once and for all. Maybe you can't do that without making a stink first."

"How easy for you to say."

"But it would be so much better if this were all resolved," she said, pleading with him to rally around to her view. "The truth is always better. Always. I agree with Quinn completely on that one. And I'm not just promoting that agenda for my sake."

Her brother let out a short, bitter laugh, but his voice turned almost wistful as he said, "You honestly believe that, Livvy? That you don't have an agenda in all this?"

"Well . . . yes."

When they were young, Rand had a little thing he did when he wanted to make a point: He would give her earlobe a gentle yank and say, "Listen up, little sister."

With a sad, sweet smile, he gave her left ear that gentle yank. But he didn't have to tell her to listen now; she was rapt with attention.

"Olivia, walk inside that house. Take a good, long look at our mother right now. Then come back out," he said softly, "and tell me that you believe this is all for the best."

Olivia shook her head. "That's not fair, Rand. Mom has always been an extremely emotional woman. She overreacts to everything."

"You say that about most women."

"Maybe most women overreact."

He sighed. "You're the brains of the family, Olivia. As by now we all know. But I wonder if you have the emotional smarts to back up all that theorizing."

This was new. "Meaning what?" she said testily.

"Meaning sometimes you have to hide the truth from someone you love *because* you love them."

"But then your whole relationship is based on a lie. No, I can't buy into that, Rand," she said, shaking her head emphatically. "I've never done that in a relationship, and I never will."

He shrugged and said, "You don't have relationships."

The point was offhandedly made, and yet it practically blasted Olivia out of the seat of his car. *You don't have relationships.* Is that how her family viewed her? As an uninvolved, ambitious, hard-driving witch?

"I do have relationships," she said, devastated by his remark.

"None that matter, Liv."

"I have Quinn Leary," she insisted, near tears now.

"Quinn? How do you figure you have Quinn? Are you married? The mother of his child? How do you have him? Where's the commitment?"

She bowed her head. "Quinn matters to me," was all she could say.

"Assume that he does," Rand allowed. "Would you lie to spare him pain?"

"Never!" she said with a fierce look at her brother. "Quinn wouldn't want that. And neither would I. And he knows it," she insisted. "We tell each other everything!"

But even as she said it, she could hear the Bard whispering in her ear. *The lady doth protest too much, methinks.*

Letting his head fall back on the headrest, Rand stared at the folded-up visor before him. "Yeah, well, you two have an unusual relationship. To say the least."

"It's true," she murmured, leaning back and staring in the mirror of her own visor, which had been flipped down;

but she looked and sounded as if she was trying to convince herself now. Quinn was so obviously *not* being truthful with her. The only question was, was he simply holding something back, or was he out-and-out lying to her?

Sighing heavily, Olivia rolled her head in Rand's direction and said, "I assume Mom and Dad are both aware that some people think Uncle Rupert had an incestuous relationship with Alison?"

She watched him close his eyes and mutter an oath. "We haven't chatted about it specifically," he said without opening his eyes. "But, yes, you can assume they've heard the worst."

"Then why did Mom get so upset after I told her that I was going to help Quinn persuade Uncle Rupert to agree to an exhumation? You would think she'd be happy to have the scandal cleared up."

She saw her brother's brow furrow, as if he'd been hit with a sudden, blinding headache. For a moment he was silent. Then, "Resolving the issue of paternity doesn't do much about the rumor that Uncle Rupert murdered Alison."

"Oh, but it does!" Olivia said. She sat up straight and turned to her brother. She was bursting with theories, some of them years old, some of them hours old.

"It's more than likely that whoever got Alison pregnant was the one who murdered her," she speculated. "Maybe to keep her from exposing him, because—who knows? It could be that he was married. Or in love with someone else. He could have been an older man. Someone prominent— the mayor, the coach, her doctor, anyone. And Alison was a minor, don't forget. It would have destroyed the career of anyone of any importance."

Rand sighed and said, "You've worked it all out, have you, Sherlock? Take some advice. Don't run all your brilliant theories past Mom just now. I doubt that she'll be as impressed as you are with them. If I were you, I wouldn't bring up Uncle Rupert at all."

"See, that's another thing I don't understand. Why is she so concerned for the sake of Uncle Rupert? Or even Aunt

Betty, if that's who she's worried about. It's not as if they're still close. Or do you think it's just the Bennett name in general that's concerning her? That makes sense, although I still say she overreacted this morning. Did she tell you about our confrontation? I mean, she really freaked. She—''

"I gotta go," Rand said, cutting her off.

"Well—all right. If you're in *that* much of a hurry," Olivia said, hurt, as she swung her door open.

She had one foot on the macadam drive when he said her name with that apologetic, melancholy smile that somehow always made things okay again between them.

"Look," he told her, "maybe it's just that time of year. You know how intense Mom gets about the holidays. Afterward, she invariably feels let down. Statistically, this is when people are most depressed and anxious, you know—when they're most likely to kill themselves or, if they're sick, just give up and die. Did you ever think that maybe Mom just has a case of the January blues?''

"Oh, come on, Rand," said Olivia. "You're not blind. Has she ever looked at you and burst into tears before in January?''

"I gotta go," he said doggedly.

They were twins. Olivia may not have possessed her brother's emotional acumen, but she knew when he was being less than candid. He was refusing to look her in the eye; obviously he was far more upset than he was letting on.

"Bye," she said, puzzled by his response. "Tell Eileen I'll call her tonight."

He drove off. Olivia decided, after all, that she did not want to face her mother just then. She told herself that she wasn't being cowardly, exactly, but that she and her mother needed a little time away from one another to calm down. Fortunately her parents lived in the back rooms of the house except when they entertained. They wouldn't even know that she had come and gone.

A cold blast of wind cut through her, making her decision

suddenly easier. Better to be with Quinn, snuggled in front of a fire.

She glanced at the main-floor windows in the front of the house before she turned to go back to her car. As she did so, a figure retreated behind the drapes and out of her view, but not quite far enough to be undetected by her.

In the soft light of the reception room, the same room that had been converted to a cloakroom for the New Year's Eve gala, Olivia recognized her father. He had been watching as she sat in the car with Rand. She was sure of it.

Quinn Leary felt like a man being sawn down the middle as he sat alone at a table at Vincent's, a small and nearly deserted Italian restaurant three miles outside of Keepsake. He nursed his beer, despite the waitress's efforts to replace it with a new one, as he watched twilight deepen into night. Myra Lupidnick Lancaster was late.

He was about to blow out the sputtering candle in the chianti bottle when she came in, looking different than she had at the tree lighting on Town Hill. Was it the big hair? She looped her coat on a peg near the register and turned to him with a self-conscious smile.

Holy cats, she was decked out for a prom: the dress, red and shiny and drifting somewhere above her ankles, was not exactly business as usual. On the other hand, spaghetti sauce wouldn't show on it, so maybe that was why she wore it. Quinn stood up with a hapless smile and pulled out a chair for her. The woman was married and the mother of four children; he hoped she remembered that.

"I'm really glad you agreed to meet me, Quinn," she said as she let him angle her chair for her. "I've been in such agony ever since I saw you on Town Hill."

Quinn didn't like the sound of that at all. He took in her red, red lips and black, black mascara, and then he motioned for a waitress just so he'd have somewhere else to look. "What'll you have?" he asked.

"Oh, a beer is fine." Myra looked up at the approaching waitress and ordered it herself: Miller draft, if they had it.

She turned back to Quinn and said, "When I called and you said that you had been thinking of calling *me*, that's when I knew. I told myself, this is definitely an act of God."

She made a small, quick sign of the cross which was so completely at odds with her getup that Quinn sat back in his chair, partly relieved but completely confused. "It must have been hard for you to get away," he said. "You have a big family."

Remind her, remind her.

"You're right about that," she said, rolling her eyes at him. "But George is home. Actually, he's been home all week on vacation. Well, not vacation, actually. Not in the regular sense. He's helping me and the kids pack. We're moving to Albuquerque. On Monday."

"Ah." Okay, so Quinn was a jerk who couldn't read women. He relaxed his guard and said more congenially, "It'll be a big change from New England."

"We're hoping. Two of our kids have asthma. And the living is so much cheaper there. George's people are out there—his father is a plumber, too, and George is taking over the business. Another good thing is that we'll have help with the kids when I go back to work."

"Oh?" He shouldn't ask, but he did anyway. "And what is it that you do?"

She said, "You'll laugh. I'm a nail stylist."

"Why is that funny?"

She wiggled her slender, pretty hands in front his face. The nails, once red, were broken and peeled. "I've been packing frantically all week, and seeing you was definitely a last-minute decision, so I didn't have time to—"

"Oh, that's all right," he said, aghast at the possibility that she'd primp any more for him than she had already. "I won't tell if you won't."

Something in what he said sent the gaiety in her face plunging into a free fall. "That's why I called you, Quinn," she said. "That's exactly why."

Trying not to act mystified, he nodded and said, "I see. Because—?"

"I can't take the responsibility any more. It's just too much. And now that we're leaving, I was going to just throw them out or give them to I don't know who. But then you came—really, it *was* an act of God, your showing up in Keepsake and then George's father getting that heart attack out in Albuquerque. An incredible coincidence, don't you think?"

"I don't know what else you can call it," he deadpanned.

She plunged one hand into the sack of a purse she had on her lap and fished something out. "Well—here," she said, holding a fist toward Quinn. He extended his hand and she opened hers, dropping a heavy class ring into his outstretched palm. "Look at the initials."

O.R.B. All that was missing was the *Jr.*, which Rand had always despised. Heart hammering, Quinn tried to seem sage. "Yep. The senior ring," he said, turning its faceted burgundy stone this way and that to catch the candle's light. Quinn had thrown his own ring away in disgust many years ago. "Probably only two men in town have those initials, and I guess the date tells us which of them lost this."

"Lost it!" She snorted and said, "Rand gave it to Alison just before she was murdered. It was instead of an engagement ring. She told me so herself."

They were first cousins. Not second, not third. First. The ring was a token of his promise to take care of her, no more than that.

But that wasn't what Quinn said to Myra. "I'd heard rumors around town about the two of them," he admitted, feeling a sick obligation to let her run. "How did you come by this, anyway?"

Quinn tried not to sound accusing; the last thing he wanted was to imply that he thought she was a thief.

"Well, *obviously* she couldn't wear his ring out in the open," said Myra, a little testily, "so she wore it on a chain around her neck, under her sweaters and things. She was afraid if she took it off and left it in her purse, her father might go rummaging around and find it. He didn't want her seeing boys; he was always looking for evidence of it. You remember that, don't you, Quinn? How Alison never got to date?''

He remembered it all too well. It had only added to Alison's allure, as far as the guys were concerned. "Something like that," he said, trying to ward off the sinking feeling in his gut. If Myra was making all of this up, she was as good a storyteller as Ulysses.

The waitress came with Myra's beer and she took a sip before resuming her tale. "Sometimes I think that's why Alison liked me," she mused. "Because I dated so much. I knew about, you know, psychology and stuff between guys and girls," she said, lowering those big, black lashes and batting them once or twice. She was Myra Lupidnick, after all; she truly could not help herself.

"Did she talk about Rand much?"

"Oh, not at all, at first. He was always 'this guy I like.' But I couldn't figure out where she'd get the chance even to meet a guy, much less develop some kind of relationship. I started watching her in school, I saw her talking to Rand in the hall once, and from the way she looked at him—from their body language—I knew.''

She shrugged and took a good long swallow of beer this time. "So I confronted her about it, and after a few times of denying it, she said, yeah, it was Rand. And then she opened up. I think, because she'd bottled it up so long and she had absolutely no one to talk to, and really, she was in love with him. It was . . . she really loved him. You know?''

Myra's face got a thoughtful, faraway look; she was back in her parents' split-level, advising the most beautiful and mysterious girl in town in matters of the heart.

"It was the real thing," she murmured at last, shaking her head. "I felt so bad after they found her."

"And yet you didn't say anything."

"No. I didn't," Myra acknowledged.

"Did the police ever question you?"

"Hardly at all."

She folded one hand meekly over the other and lifted the fingertips back a little, staring at her messed-up nails. She sighed, then looked up and said, "I was scared, Quinn. Don't forget, my dad was a foreman at the mill. He would have lost his job for sure. And after a while, when they didn't arrest anyone and the whole thing seemed to fade away, well, it didn't really make any difference anymore, did it?"

It was all he could do not to pop her over the head with the chianti bottle. *Idiot! You could have done the right thing and come forward and my entire life would have been different!*

But he knew better than to go down that road. He'd been down it so many times before, and it always ended smack in the same brick wall. He reminded himself for the thousandth time that a dozen lives had been saved because a crime, this crime, had gone unsolved. It was enough. In the grand, chaotic scheme of things, it was enough.

A thought occurred to him. "Does your husband—does George—know about any of this?"

"Oh, no. I could *never*. That's just what I mean. That's why it's been eating a hole through me all these years. Right here," she said, pointing a chipped red fingernail at her heart. "And I'm just . . . ready to start over. I really want to start over," she repeated, this time with a trembling lip.

A big tear rolled out and sat on her thickly caked lower lashes, unable to break through and run. Quinn waited, mesmerized, for the tear to fall, but she blinked and it flattened into a saline line in the rim above her lashes.

"I'm sorry," she said, dabbing at her eye with the back of her wrist and leaving a smudge on the skin there. "I didn't think I'd cry."

Considering the amount of mascara she wore, that was Quinn's assumption, too. Her sincerity and good intentions touched him—much more at that moment than they ever had in high school. Somewhere under all that makeup was the still-pretty face of an ordinary girl who had always wanted simply to please.

He reached across the table and squeezed her hand. "Hey, now, Myra . . . you've carried this ring around for a long time. You didn't have to do that. You could have just chucked it and forgotten about the whole thing, but you didn't. I think Alison would appreciate that you stayed loyal to her memory.''

"Really?" she asked, doing more dabbing, this time with a napkin.

"Absolutely."

He picked up Rand's ring and circled his thumb absently over the chiseled surface of its stone, sobered by the awareness that Alison Bennett had once slipped it over her finger and dreamed of setting up house with its owner.

But had she really? The ring wasn't proof of anything. Thank God, it wasn't proof—even of paternity, much less of a murder. Quinn could rationalize that much. He could live with the responsibility that Myra was handing over to him. For entirely different reasons, he would do exactly what Myra had done: nothing. And if the ongoing silence ended up boring a tiny hole in his heart, so be it—because this time, finally, it was his turn for happiness.

The waitress came over and asked to take their order, but neither of them was hungry, so they settled for splitting a side order of calamari. Quinn realized that he did not have even an appetizer's worth of small talk left in him, but he needn't have worried.

Myra, looking more relieved and brighter by the minute, suddenly said in a much perkier voice, "I almost forgot!"

She fished around in her purse again, and this time she came up with something more lethal. "The letter!"

Twenty-one

"What letter?"

"From Rand. Oh. I guess I haven't filled you in. Do you want me to start from the beginning?"

"Please."

Quinn accepted the letter from Myra, not daring to glance at it until he got his emotions under control. *A letter from Rand.* What next? A notarized confession? This was turning into the probe from hell.

Myra took a deep breath and said, "Okay, this is what I know firsthand. Alison and Rand had been . . . uh, well, doing it, since July in the summer after our junior year. Their first time was in the backseat of his—you remember the red Pontiac? God, I loved that car. It happened after he took her home early from a wake at his parent's house. Alison made up a story about how she thought she was coming down with something; that's how she got out of going home with her parents. Even Rand believed her. But I guess she knew what she wanted.

"After that, it was whenever and wherever they could. I remember she said they did it once in the gardener's cottage when you and your father were off buying some fancy trees for Mrs. Bennett. I'll bet you never knew that," Myra said, smiling behind her next sip of beer.

"How right you would be," Quinn said faintly.

Myra put down her glass with a grin; she was relaxed

and in her element now. "Anyway, that's pretty much how the summer went," she said. "Alison was happy, all things considered, and no one was the wiser."

"Except you?"

"Not me! I didn't know any of this at the time; those two were amazing at keeping it secret. And besides, Alison and I didn't really become close until after we went back to school for senior year. I remember I told her how pretty her hair was, but that it would look fantastic if it was highlighted. I've always had a professional interest in hair, you know. She said she couldn't afford highlighting, so I offered to do it for her. They have kits. Anyway, that was in early September. I didn't learn about Rand until late September, and by October I knew she was pregnant."

"She told you she was?"

"Not in so many words. She said, 'I think maybe we were careless a few times.' Well, what else could that mean? Later, of course, I knew. Eventually, so did everyone."

He nodded. "How did she seem about it?"

"Not depressed or scared, if that's what you're thinking. I remember she just looked . . . well, you know what they say about a pregnant woman's glow."

Quinn didn't have all that much experience with glowing pregnant women—none, to be exact—so he settled for a vague nod of recognition. "She had that glow?"

"Oh, yes. She was radiant. No morning sickness, nothing. And don't forget, she had Rand's ring. She had his promise that they'd get married as soon as they got their parents' permission. *Plus*, she also had his word in writing."

She pointed to the pale blue sheet that lay on the table in front of Quinn. It was his cue. He picked up the letter and began dutifully unfolding it.

Myra rested her cheek on her fist and said dreamily, "He bought that stationery special, you know. He told Alison that he wanted something permanent that wouldn't fade or tear. He wanted her to know how serious he was. I remember thinking, that was so sweet."

Dearest Alison,
I need you to know that their will never be another
girl in my life. You are the best thing that has ever
happened to me. I can't stop thinking of you, no mat-
ter where I am. In study hall, on the field, and driving
around. I drive around a lot, thinking of you. I wish
we could be together more. Nothing really matters to
me except you. You know, I'm glad you're pregnant.
Maybe I shouldn't be but I am. It's a sign that our
love was meant to be. And also, since your pregnant
our parents can't say no. I know my mother would
never want you to have an abortion no matter what.
And your mother wouldn't either. So I think we're o.k.
on that. Know this, Alison—I love you. I love you. I
love you.

> *Yours,*
> *Rand*

Misspellings and bobbled punctuation aside, the letter
was still powerful in its naive sincerity. Quinn felt like a
voyeur reading it, and yet he couldn't help himself. It was
like staring at a videotape of his past.

At least one mystery was now solved: Rand's embarrassing collapse as an athlete in the fall of their senior year.
It wasn't a poor recovery from his injury that had taken him
out of the competition with Quinn to be quarterback; it was
his obsession with Alison.

Quinn refolded the letter and laid it gently beside the
class ring—two such ordinary items, and yet so resonant
with power. He stared at them while the candle's flame sput-
tered and fretted in the chianti bottle, dropping bits of light
in a random pattern over the poignant still life.

Stilled life, he realized. Alison was dead. What did these
keepsakes matter now? Tokens of love, proof of malfea-
sance—what did they matter?

Quinn said wearily, "His feelings do seem straightforward."

"Guys always are," said Myra, still with her cheek on her fist.

She was watching Quinn for his reaction, and he was determined not to give her one. He said without emotion, "He wanted to marry her."

."At first,." said Myra.

She made herself sit up straight again, like a witness at a trial. "But then suddenly he asked for the letter back. He said she could keep the ring, but she had to give him the letter back. They had a *huge* argument over it. It was on a Sunday afternoon, late. Alison and I were working on the homecoming float that Coach and a couple of teachers had rolled onto the athletic field behind the goalposts temporarily.

"Alison's father was supposed to be picking her up any minute when suddenly Rand showed up on the field, I don't know from where. I saw him before Alison did. He looked grim. He didn't say boo to me, just marched right up to Alison and said, 'We have to talk.'

"They walked way over to the far end of the field. You couldn't possibly hear them, try as I might. It was getting dark, but I could see she was upset. She folded her hands across her jacket—body language, right?—while she watched him walk back and forth, back and forth, throwing his hands up every once in a while. He was more upset than she was, I think. Then Alison's father showed up and whistled her back and Rand cut across the field and disappeared. Her father was really pissed. He said, 'What did I tell you?' and gave her a kind of a shove on her shoulder. Not a *shove* shove, exactly, but a little less than a shove."

Quinn listened intently to her precise recounting of the event. No question, Myra was the perfect witness, not calculating enough to put undue spin on events, just an alert, keen observer. Shit. Quinn didn't like where this was going at all.

"I assume that Alison talked about it afterward with you?" he asked, hoping against hope that she had not.

"Oh, yes. She didn't say very much, but I could see that

something was going on inside her head. All she told me was, 'He wants the letter back . . . How *could* he? . . . I'm not giving it to him . . . The only way he's going to get it is over my dead body. Or yours.' Then she laughed—but she wasn't really amused, you know the kind of laugh I mean? She was hurt and angry. That's when she handed me the ring and the letter for safekeeping. I was supposed to hold on to them just until homecoming. She was going to tell both their parents about her and Rand that weekend— when they came to school for the big game. She didn't want the meeting to be in anyone's house. I thought that was really good thinking. It made a lot of sense, when you came right down to it."

Quinn, still stunned, had absolutely no response to that.

"That's the last thing Alison ever said to me; I never saw her again," Myra said, gliding to a halt on a glaze of new tears. "And that's all I know. I don't know who killed Alison. I hope it wasn't Rand. But I know who was the father of that baby." She sighed deeply; her long ordeal of silence was over.

Just in time for the calamari. The waitress laid an oval platter between them with a careful-it's-hot warning, and then a smaller plate in front of each of them. Quinn stared at the deep-fried loops with revulsion. He might as well have been looking at his own intestines, breaded and served to him piping hot.

Myra, meanwhile, was calling the waitress back with the apologetic courtesy that everyone in the service industry uses with everyone else in the service industry. "Miss? If it's not too much of a bother, could I possibly have some ketchup, please? Thank you."

Olivia paced the living room of her townhouse in a state of wretched anxiety. It was now clear to her that everyone in her family—everyone in Keepsake!—knew more about Alison's death than she did.

Maybe if she hadn't been so busy with school and then with her career . . . maybe if she had taken the time to actually listen to gossip, instead of always nipping it in the bud . . . if she had just sat back silently once in a while and watched, instead of always trying to run the show . . .

But she hadn't done that, and probably never would. Her brother was right. Her emotional IQ was down in the single digits. Could you raise your own IQ? Could you learn from your mistakes? She wasn't sure it was possible, but from now on, she was going to try.

And meanwhile, no Quinn. She glanced at the brass carriage clock that sat on the mantel mocking the time she was wasting just . . . pacing. She should be doing something! She had a million yards of fabric at Run of the Mill to mark down; she couldn't expect her young assistant, no matter how willing and enthusiastic, to make those decisions herself.

Oh—right. The stickers.

Before she forgot, she went straight to the closet in the second bedroom and fished out two rolls of bright orange circles from among her extra supplies, then tossed them in her leather carryall. There. Something accomplished. As soon as Quinn got in—if he ever got in—she'd grab a bite to eat with him and then race down to the outlet. It was going to be a long, long night there.

Couldn't the man have the simple decency to carry a cell phone? It was making her crazy not to be able to contact him. They might just as well be living in the Stone Age. Smoke signals, Morse code, carrier pigeons—*anything* was better than this. Inconsiderate man! She should just leave him a memo the way any business person would do. Yes. A curt note, damn it. If he wasn't going to call her, then that's all that he deserved.

She began scribbling an explanation to leave under her door knocker, but almost at once she tore it up. Quinn would have called if he could. Surely he would have called. Something must have happened to him. Oh, God, surely something awful. The ratslayer, the bonelayer, the twisted, evil sicko that had nearly killed Mrs. Dewsbury, had now come after Quinn. Of course he had! For whatever reason, it was

Quinn that he wanted, not anyone else. Everyone else was incidental.

Olivia felt a surge of fear for Quinn. What if he were lying in a ditch somewhere, stabbed or shot and bleeding to death? What if he'd been in an accident? He could have been in an accident. The roads were dark, winding, the intersections unmarked in a lot of places. What if he were dead? How could she go on living without him?

Don't let him be dead. Please, please don't let him be dead.

She felt hot tears spring up; her body began to shake. What could she do? There must be something. Call the hospital. She ran to the phone book to look up the number and then realized that because of Mrs. Dewsbury, she'd already punched it into her electronic notepad. Altering course, she ran for her carryall instead to retrieve the notepad. The entire time, she was aware that she wasn't being rational, that Quinn wasn't dead and he wasn't injured. What were the odds, after all?

I'm going out of my mind. This aimless, free-floating anxiety is taking its toll . . . I'm losing my grip . . .

She heard a truck pull up and ran to the window, her heart lifting to the sound of the engine she knew by now. *Yes!* Yes, yes, yes! Alive and well and all in one piece and she was going to kill the man the minute he walked through the door. She ran to open it before he had a chance to ring the bell; she wanted him to know how worried she was before she actually went and strangled him.

She opened the door to see Quinn dragging himself up the six steps that led straight to her. He was acting like a man climbing a gallows. It was a shock to her to hear the strain in his voice as he glanced up and forced out a greeting.

She stepped aside to let him in; he walked past without meeting her baffled gaze. Uppermost in her mind was her fierce resolve to be the new, the improved, the emotionally intelligent Olivia Deborah Bennett.

"Where the *hell* have you been?" she blurted out. "I've been worried sick."

"Yeah."

"*Yeah*? That's your explanation? I thought we agreed to meet at the hospital," she said, closing the door after him.

She watched him stop in his tracks as his head dropped back in realization. "Jesus," he muttered. "I forgot all about it. How is she doing?" he asked without turning around.

He took out a wood hanger from the hall closet and hung his jacket over it with care, squaring the shoulders before he looped the hanger back on the rod. Olivia took the gesture to be symbolic. She had the sense that he was stalling—again, as if he'd rather be facing some hangman than her.

A queasiness rolled over her, but she shrugged it off and said, "Mrs. D. is fine. As antsy as can be, of course; she wants to go home. The nurses are all threatening to roll her out into the parking lot and let her go anywhere she wants. You won't forget about her again, will you?" she added in an acid tone. "Or would you rather that *I* drove her home tomorrow?"

"No, of course not," he murmured, turning around at last. He held out his arms to her and whispered in an agonized voice, "I'm so sorry, Livvy. Oh, God . . . I'm so sorry."

Surprised, she let herself be drawn into his embrace. With a smile of confusion, she said, "You don't have to be *that* sorry, Quinn. I forgive you." She snuggled as close as she could to him and sighed deeply. "I was in a panic about you, though," she confessed. "It came on me in such a rush. I began to be terrified that I might be psychic or something awful like that. And I realized—you know what I realized?"

She pulled a little away from him so that she could look up at his face. "I realized how much I love you," she said simply. "I had been imagining all kinds of horrible ends—if you only knew!—and I'm just so happy . . . so *happy* . . . that you're here, and safe, and with your arms around me," she said, fitting herself almost shyly back in his arms. "I love you."

Olivia had been planning to make that confession for a while now, but she was probably more surprised than he was that she had chosen that exact moment in which to do it.

So! Wouldn't it be nice if Quinn felt the same urge?

If he did, he was suppressing it. She waited in his arms with her cheek against his shirt for as long as she reasonably could and then, disappointed, said, "I was going to order a pizza for us. Are you in the mood for one?"

"I'm not hungry," he murmured.

"Actually," she said, sniffing his shirt, "you already smell like a pizza. Or something. That's definitely garlic." She looked up at him again, this time with eyes slanted in comical suspicion. "Hey, you're not cheating on me, are you?"

He let out an incredulous snort, then held her so tightly it took her breath away. "Livvy, Livvy," he said suddenly, "let's make love. Now. Please . . . right now."

He caught her chin in the cup of his hand and brought his mouth down on hers in a fierce, deep kiss that sent her nerve ends humming, her brain cells spinning, and her knees and ankles crumbling beneath her. The suddenness of his desire rocked her; but she righted quickly, matching his kiss and meeting his hunger.

"Quinn, Quinn, let's agree never . . . ever . . . to argue," she said between kisses. "Over *anything* . . . ever . . ."

"Don't talk, don't talk . . ."

Still locked in their embrace, they bumped against the wall as they fumbled and tore at buttons and zippers. She was wearing tights under her wool skirt—the warehouse was drafty, she had to dress warmly—and he muttered an oath as he struggled to find the waistband. He yanked one legging part of the way down; she stepped out of the rest of it, trailing it like a kite tail behind her as they half groped, half stumbled their way to the wrought-iron bed.

They tumbled onto the down comforter—no more silk

for them—with Olivia underneath him, overwhelmed and unresisting.

He brought his hand up under her skirt, fanning his fingers, stroking her flesh, bringing down wetness. Electric, that's how it felt, electric to the point of pain. "Too much, too much," she cried, clamping her legs together. He hooked his hand on the inside of her thigh and pulled it away from her other one, exposing her again to his rough caress.

She was hungry, but not like this. There was a desperation, an urgency in him that intimidated. "Quinn . . . we have all night," she said, gasping.

"You're right . . . I know . . . all night . . . yes . . ."

He stopped and raised himself by his arms, staring down at her with a look she could only describe as demented.

"What's wrong? Why are you looking at me that way? All I meant was for you to be more gentle," she said in confusion.

He said nothing, only stared at her, his face twisted in contours of agony. "Why are you *acting* like this?" she cried.

"I don't know, I don't know, oh, God, I don't know." With a tormented look, he pushed her back down on the bed and said, "I hate this. I *hate* this!"

It left her flabbergasted. "Then why did you start—?"

He squelched the rest of her sentence with a kiss that was so brutal it hurt. She tried to push him away, a pointless exercise; he was so much more powerful than she. He caught her wrists. Her protests were muffled by his mouth bearing down on hers, drowned out by the anguished sounds coming from his throat. He sounded tormented, a beast in pain, and he was frightening her.

She broke away from his hold and dug her nails into his ribs, using all of her strength as she tried to push him away. It seemed to snap him out of it. With a cry of frustration he rolled off and away from her in one fluid motion, ending up sitting on the side of the bed with his back to her.

Olivia scrambled out of the bed and began tucking herself back in her bra and untwisting her skirt.

"I have to go to work," she said, in a seething rage. "I have . . . *stickers* to stick!"

Quinn propped his elbows on his thighs and dropped his forehead to the palms of his hands.

"Oh, God,"_ he mumbled in misery. "Oh, God." He was a portrait of remorse.

Olivia stared at him the way she would at a drunk coming off a bender. And then she turned on her heel and walked out.

She spent the next two hours in a state of shock, stickering any bolt or remnant that displeased her. And they all displeased her. Suddenly the colors seemed too dull, too bright, too busy, too plain, too irrelevant to possibly matter. She stickered them all, a compulsive personality gone amuck, until her assistant came up timidly and said, "Is it all right if I go home now?"

Olivia pulled out of her daze long enough to stare at her watch: ten o'clock. It was half an hour past closing time at Run of the Mill. She looked around and blinked, trying to clear the cotton from her head, trying to focus on the reality of her night so far.

She was able to remember it perfectly well. After the debacle in her bedroom, she had actually got into her van and driven the two and a half miles to the row of shabby old warehouses, some of them empty, that lined the banks of the Connecticut River. She had marched into the outlet, greeted the help, taken out her stickers, and got to work. She was here, wasn't she? All in one piece? With her stickers mostly stuck? Obviously she was fine. Obviously time had passed.

The fact that she couldn't remember the two hours that she had spent in this dreary hole—that, she could attribute to the numbing monotony of marking down merchandise. She scanned the cavernous room. Yes, there it was, all around her: merchandise. Mountains of it. More bolts and remnants than she could possibly sell, more than her customers could possibly sew, in a lifetime. In ten lifetimes.

As for the customers themselves, she was fairly certain that there had been quite a few of them rummaging through the piles, but now they were nowhere to be seen.

"You closed up?"

"Um . . . you told me to?"

"I did, didn't I. Okay. Thank you, Sharon. And I'm sorry for keeping you late," she added in a dull voice. "I guess I just got carried away."

Energetic Sharon, Olivia's most valuable asset by far, giggled and said, "Oh, that's all right. My friends don't get off work until one-thirty. This way, I'll have one less drink to nurse while I wait for them."

They left together, Olivia, reluctantly. Her world seemed to be collapsing around her; she was afraid to go out in it anymore.

All the way home, anxiety gnawed at the pit of her stomach, making her sick. As she careened down the road under bright stars flung across a clear black sky, wave after wave of nausea washed over her. More than once she was tempted to pull over, open her door, and throw up. She was deathly ill, deathly tired.

And unprepared for the sight of Quinn sitting on the bottom step in front of her townhouse.

Twenty-two

It was eleven at night and twenty degrees out; what was he doing there?

Olivia had the obvious option of driving right past him and entering her house through the garage that was built into the berm on the side. But he was Quinn, and he was there, and she couldn't quite make herself reach up to press the garage door opener on her visor. Instead, she parked alongside his truck. Better to get it over with.

Quinn got to his feet as she approached; she could see that he was stiff from waiting in the cold. "Still here?" she asked unnecessarily. For once, she didn't know what to say.

"I left," he said. "I drove around. I came back."

His hands were in his pockets, his cap pulled down low, his collar flipped up against the sharp wind that hacked at them both. Huddled into himself, he said, "I have nowhere to go, Olivia; nowhere to be, except with you."

Haloed in the haze of their frozen breath, they faced off for the second time that night. Olivia's mohair muffler lifted and fell in the wind, marking time as she searched his face, looking for answers to all of her questions. What did she know about him, really? Seventeen years apart: It was half a lifetime.

"All right," she said at last, too exhausted and cold to stand there. "Come inside."

She led the way, aware that he had a key to her place

but had declined to use it. Why? Was it mere courtesy—or was there something deeper at play?

"We have to talk," she said tiredly as she slipped out of her coat and draped it across the nearest chair. "Whatever is going on with you, it's scaring me, Quinn. We have to—"

"I know . . . I know," he said. He sounded deep in melancholy.

He threw his jacket over hers and surprised her by taking her into his arms.

She was too tired to resist, too tired to respond, too tired to do anything but repeat dully, "We have to talk."

"Shh," he said, holding her close and kissing her hair. "Shh. Just . . . let me hold you."

His body felt cold against hers. She wanted to bundle him, warm him, make him hot tea; she wanted to slap his face.

And yet there she was, too tired to do any of them. All she could do was negotiate. "Quinn, I want some answers. Before anything else can happen, I want you to expla—"

"Shh. Let me make it up to you . . . for before. Shh. I won't insult you by saying I'm sorry. The words aren't adequate for what I've done."

He let out an odd little laugh, as if he were indulging in his own private joke. And then he said in an aching voice, "I love you, Olivia. I love you so much . . . so much . . . you're everything to me." Holding her close, he caressed the back of her hair and whispered, "I love you more with each breath I take. Please believe that. No matter what happens, please believe that."

She nearly broke down in tears. *Now* he had to tell her? Now, when she felt as drained as a pool in January? She had been waiting to hear those words from him for seventeen years. Perhaps not consciously—but somewhere buried deep in her psyche, there had always been an awareness that other men were a waste of time. Only one was a match, more than a match, for her. And now she knew, beyond a doubt, that Quinn Leary loved her.

So why wasn't she jumping with joy?

She didn't know what to say to him—he seemed to want her to say nothing—so she snuggled against him and murmured innocently, "Are you hungry for that pizza yet?"

"Nope," he said, lifting her face to his. "You?"

She wasn't queasy anymore, but: "No pizza for me."

"I've got a better idea," he said, lifting her effortlessly in his arms.

"What? Lasagna?" she asked with a tired smile.

"Not exactly," he said, headed for the stairs.

"Fisherman's Platter?"

"Keep babbling, woman; it'll make the climb easier."

"Quinn, *no*," she said, laughing despite her exhaustion. "You can't keep doing this! I'm too heavy!"

"Granite is heavy. You're a basket of laundry."

"You say that now, at the bottom of the stairs; what happens when we both go tumbling ass over teakettle from the top?"

"Then we'll die in one another's arms."

"You say that now, at the bottom of the stairs."

"Shh."

He carried her up and no one fell, and then he carried her into her bedroom, just as he had their first time, and laid her on the bed, just as he had their first time. On New Year's Eve they had been wild and hungry and just a little bit drunk. Tonight they were tired and sorry and just a little too sober. But what they lacked in fire, they made up for in tenderness. Quinn loved her, and she loved him, and every touch, every kiss, every caress as they made love was wrapped in that declaration, one for the other.

I love you, Quinn. I love you. When Rand wouldn't let me in his treehouse and you built me my own, I loved you for that.

I did it because I loved you, although at the time I thought it was just to spit in your brother's eye.

And when you left those bright red roses in the Maxwell House can on the table in my treehouse? I loved you for that.

You knew it was me?

Who else? Not my brother!

That time you fell out of the treehouse, my heart stopped.

My mother told me you were a hero, carrying me home. I was always too embarrassed to thank you. Thank you. I love you.

And I was always too embarrassed to thank you for defending me when Old Man Ryckhart accused me of stealing his power saw.

One of Rand's friends framed you, but I have no proof. Rand defended you, too, Quinn. You probably don't know that.

Shh. What's past is past. I love you. I love you.

They fell asleep in one another's arms, two lovers who agreed, if only for the night, to spend it in that treehouse of theirs.

Olivia awoke before Quinn did. It was early, but she knew that he'd be spending the morning getting Mrs. Dewsbury settled in from the hospital, and she wanted to do something lovely and domestic for him first: make breakfast. After the mortifying empty-cupboard episode on New Year's Day, Olivia had made a point of stockpiling every breakfast item she could think of. She wasn't in such great shape for throwing together a lunch, and God forbid she should have to make dinner—but she could do breakfast in style now.

She eased the comforter back, leaving an exhausted-looking Quinn quietly snoring on his side of the bed, and went downstairs to take sausages and a can of OJ out of her freezer. After starting the meat defrosting in the microwave, she made up a pitcher of the juice, which she left on the counter to breathe. After that she got the coffee going. She was thinking omelettes. How hard could they be? For some reason she was truly enjoying puttering about in her kitchen.

The reason was sleeping upstairs in her bed.

It was chilly in the house; she needed her robe. Back up the stairs she went. The robe was in her bedroom, hanging on a funky clothes tree that she'd found while cruising the

Brimfield flea market with Eileen one fine day in May. In the glow of the hall light, she tiptoed across the room and was in the process of wrapping herself in floral flannel when the timer on the microwave sounded.

Beep, beep, beep, beep. Not especially loud—but Quinn shot up in bed as if four different cannons had blasted. He looked disoriented, even spooked. Olivia knew the look from the day before; she had hoped never to see it again. But then he spotted her standing near the bed, and his demeanor relaxed.

It felt so very good to see that happen. She grinned and whispered, ''Good morning, pizza man.''

''It can't be morning,'' he said with a moan as he dropped back on his pillow. ''I feel as if I've been shoveling snow all night.''

''Then go back to sleep.'' She pulled the covers over him and kissed his brow. ''I'll let you know when breakfast is ready.''

''Mmm.'' He yawned heavily and said, ''Who's cooking it?''

''Hey! *I* am,'' she said, sending an accent pillow sailing over his head.

He chuckled; it was sweet music to her ears. She was on her way out to the kitchen to cook up her first storm ever when she spied something shiny on the white carpet beneath the chair over which Quinn had folded his pants.

''Huh.'' Like a trout after a bright, shiny lure, she swooped down on it. ''Quinn? Look what I found on the floor. Is this a class ring?''

His head came up. Propping himself on his elbows, he said in a surprisingly tense voice, ''Yes. It's . . . mine.''

''But you told me you'd thrown your ring off a bridge,'' she said, moving toward a lamp in the hall.

''I—that was a figure of speech, that's all,'' he said. He threw back the covers and got out of bed.

''This isn't your ring. It couldn't possibly fit your finger—now *or* then.'' She stuck it under the light for a closer look.

"Jesus Christ, Liv! Do you have any concept of personal property?" he said, coming after her.

"It's from our year," she said, reading the date on the side of the stone. She began rotating the band, looking for initials. Quinn snatched the ring angrily away from her, but not before she had a chance to read them.

"*O.R.B.* Owen Randall Bennett," she said with a puzzled look at Quinn.

"Oscar Reginald Baxter. Orville Raymond Bonaparte. Obadiah Rufus Blackw—"

"Very funny," she said, trying to snatch it back without success. "There were no Oscars, Orvilles, or Obadiahs in our class. This is Rand's ring. But Rand told everyone he lost it swimming at the quarry. How did *you* end up with it? Quinn?"

Her voice had been edging higher with each succeeding sentence. By the time she got to Quinn's name it sounded shrill, even to her.

He looked so determined not to tell her anything. His eyebrows were drawn together, his mouth was clamped shut, his breathing was labored. His eyes glared at her through a curtain of suspicion. Prisoners of war must look that way all the time. The rising panic she felt was balanced by rising anger, and both were overwhelmed by plunging hopes. What kind of relationship could they possibly have if he regarded her as his number-one enemy?

"*Damn* you, Quinn!" she cried, hurling the words at him like dinner plates. "How can you treat me this way? It's offensive. It's insulting. It's—you said that you loved me!" she cried, because for her, it all came down to that. "I would never do this to you! I would never shut you out from something that was eating at me!"

He stood there, shirtless and in his drawstring pajama bottoms, looking more than ever like someone in shackles. Oh, how she dreaded that look, that posture.

"Quinn, Quinn, we can't go on this way," she said, shivering despite the robe she wore. She wrapped her arms around herself, trying to steady her nerves. "Please—if you love me, tell me: *Where did you get that ring?*"

Quinn tightened his fist around the ring and wondered why the floor didn't just open up and let him drop straight into hell. Apparently it was someone's plan that he should writhe on earth for a while first. He stared at the face of the only woman he would ever love, stared at her dark mop of curls and her blazing look of hurt and the way she bit her lip, trying not to cry, and he thought, this is the way to make me burn alive: force me to watch her suffer.

"I can't tell you," he said at last, in excruciating agony himself. "Please, Liv, don't ask."

Her sigh was quick and frustrated. "*You* would want to know!" she cried. "You would demand an answer!" She turned away, unable to look at him anymore. He saw her clamp her hand over her mouth and bow her head, as if she were going to be sick.

The worst of it was, she was right. He *would* want to know. He *would* demand an answer. Did she deserve anything less than he himself would expect? He had grown up with her; he had watched her struggle every day to be accepted as the equal of the males around her. The town princess she might have been, but he had never known either girl or woman who wanted less to be sheltered, less to be coddled. *Just give it to me straight.* It was her credo in life.

But still he couldn't tell her. Some instinct in him that ran deeper than logic told him it was better not to disillusion her.

He saw her shoulders lift with the huge, deep breath she took before hauling out the last big weapon in her armory: the ultimatum.

She turned slowly around to face him. Her chin was high, her gaze steady and true as she said, "This all has to do with Alison. Tell me where you got the ring, Quinn," she said gravely. "Tell me, or it has to be over between us. You *know* that it has to be."

It was over between them whether he told her or not; that

was the agony of it. The only question was, should he let her continue living in blissful ignorance? If—when—she found out about her brother someday, would she hate Quinn still more for not having told her?

It was a measure of how much Quinn respected her that he thought she would.

"Myra gave it to me," he said at last.

It took her aback, but not for long. "Myra! Then she stole it!"

"Alison gave it to her."

"Alison! Then Alison stole it!"

"Your brother gave it to Alison."

Her head was spinning now. "*What*? That doesn't make sense. Why would Rand give his ring to my cousin?"

"He loved her."

"Of course he did. We all did. But not to give her his class ring."

"He loved her. He loved her the way a man loves a woman. The way I love you."

The emotional body slam sent Olivia staggering. Her mouth fell open in shock and anger; she clutched at her lapels in a huddle of denial. "How can you *dare* say that?"

"Ask Myra."

"Myra lies! Everyone knows that! You can't believe Myra. She lies! Look what she said about being the one to take your . . . take your—she'll say anything to be the center of attention. You said so yourself!"

"I believe her," he made himself admit. "She knew too many details."

"You're naive, Quinn! She made them all up!"

"*I'm* naive?" he said with gentle anguish.

"All right, fine!" Olivia conceded. "I'm naive! At least I'm aware of it. But *you*! You'll believe any—" She stopped and sucked in her breath, stunned by yet another thought. "When did she tell you this?"

"Last evening."

More shock, new fury. "And you went from hearing that vile slander straight to my *bed*? How *could* you?" she cried.

"When you knew what this would do to you and me . . . to me and my family. My God . . . I can't *believe* this! You go dragging your feet through a muck of lies and then you march right in and make *love* to me?"

In his black despair, Quinn saw black humor. "That's not quite true. I didn't have any luck the first time I tried, remember?"

He was all too aware that he had felt miserably unable to make anything happen then. He had tried to bully himself into potency, which was absurd; he couldn't have made love to her in that frame of mind in a million years.

And meanwhile, Olivia was staring at him with a look that transcended shock: It burned with loathing and contempt. Maybe it was better that way. If he was forced to back away from her, bowing and scraping and with cap in hand, at least he'd have an excuse to resent her. It wasn't much, hanging that old princess label on her again, but it would have to do.

"Get out," she said in a shaking voice. "Just please get dressed and get out."

It was time to do just that. He had overestimated her. He shouldn't have been surprised by that, and yet he was. Surprised—and bitter. She should have respected *him* enough to know that he wouldn't tell her something so appalling without knowing it was true. As it was, Rand's letter was burning a hole in his pocket. He had no idea what he was going to do with it.

Olivia tailed after him into the bedroom and stood there as Quinn pulled on his trousers right over his PJs. He was in a hurry. He wanted to sail out of there on a wave of resentment; he knew it would be easier that way.

But Olivia had never been one to make things easy.

"You have no proof, you know," she said, practically taunting him about it. "Only one woman's word, and a ring that could have come from anywhere. Maybe Rand just *thought* he lost it. It could have fallen off his finger onto the blanket before he went swimming at the senior picnic. How would he know? He's a guy; they're always losing things. Then *she* picked it up and worked out a whole fantasy for herself. Myra had a thing for Rand; everyone knew that. She probably resented that he hardly looked at her, and she made up the story. Made it all up! It's the obvious, logical interpretation of events.''

In self-imposed silence, Quinn pulled on his undershirt and shot one arm, then the other, into the blue sand-washed shirt that Olivia had liked so well on him.

She circled him the way a country lawyer would, pointing out his flaws for an imaginary jury. ''You know I'm right, Quinn. If this were about anyone else, you'd use your formidable powers of logic to figure out the most likely, the most logical scenario. You'd reach the same conclusions I just did.''

He tucked his shirt into his pants and tightened his belt, all without looking at her.

''But no-oo. You're determined to clear your father's name at any cost. What's wrong? You couldn't wait for the exhumation? You had to jump at this outrageous, sordid version of events? It doesn't bother you that you're being irrational?''

Wallet? Pen? Comb? He patted his pockets.

''How unlike you, Quinn, to be irrational. You, the finest thinker at Keepsake High.''

He looked around the room. Anything left? Nope. He traveled light. The razor, the toothbrush, the roll-on—to hell with 'em.

She stopped her pacing and pointed an accusing finger at him. ''You know what I think? I think you're looking to sabotage my family in any way you can. It bothers you— doesn't it?—that they're well regarded around here. You think that by tearing them down, you can somehow build your father back up. It doesn't work that way, Quinn. I hate to keep harping, but again—illogical.''

Should he say good-bye? Interrupt her harangue? Probably not. She wouldn't hear him, anyway. He glanced at the door, ready to make his break.

''Myra's a liar,'' she said, faltering a little. ''If not a liar, then ... then at least an exaggerator of the first order. You probably just misunderstood her, Quinn,'' she said with an anguished look. "Men don't speak the same language as women. Haven't you read Deborah Tannen?''

Tannen. As if.

He sighed.

For whatever reason, that got Olivia going again. "At least admit you could be wrong!'' she cried. "Is that so much to ask? You're being so *irrational*, Quinn. Think about it! Someone would have picked up on the two of them. Some old biddy would have got wind of it and gone straight to my mother—or my aunt. You can't keep a love affair secret—not around here. Look at us! The whole town knows!''

He allowed himself to respond, not to what she said, but to the pleading tone in her voice as she said it. "You could have had enough faith in me to believe me, Liv,'' he murmured.

One little opening. That's all he gave her. One tiny opening. It ended up being the perfect place to drive the last nail into the coffin of their relationship.

"Believe you? Why should I? Myra's a known liar. The story's incredible. And there is no proof! *You. Have. No. Proof.* Show me the damned *proof*!'' she shrieked, rushing at him with a shove of frustration as her rage came crashing through her veneer of reason.

Caught off guard by her ferocity, he staggered back. Something in him snapped, a seventeen-year-old rubber band wound a little too tight. "You want your proof so goddamned much? *Here*,'' he said, reaching into his back pocket. He pulled out the folded blue sheet and flung it at her. "Here's your goddamned proof!''

He walked away. She could read it or she could flush it, he didn't care. In the hall, he stopped long enough to slap Rand's ring down on the table. Let her deep-six it in the quarry if she wanted to. Anything to bring this sorry adventure to an end.

He was outside, five steps from his truck, when he heard

a window above him being thrown open. Despite himself, he looked up at it.

"You couldn't let well enough alone!" she screamed, obviously ready to break down altogether. "You couldn't just prove someone's innocence. Not you! Not the mighty Quinn! You had to take it one step further! You had to prove someone else was guilty! I hope you're happy now! Damn you, Quinn! I hope you're happy!"

He felt as if he'd been shot between the eyes. His last words to her were: "I didn't call Myra, so help me God. She called me."

But Olivia couldn't hear him, not above her own heart-rending wails.

Twenty-three

It wasn't definite that Rand killed Alison. There was no proof.

After a morning of emotional devastation, that single uncertainty was all that Olivia had left to cling to. So many other horrors were certain now. It was certain that Rand was the father of Alison's baby. That Olivia's relationship with her family was changed forever. That she and Quinn were through.

She spent hours of heart-wrenching tears and unbearable agony holed up in her townhouse before being thrown into a sudden, violent panic.

The ring... the letter. They're evidence that could be used to indict Rand.

It was the most obvious danger in the world, and it had taken her most of the day to see it.

She scooped up the letter and the ring from her bed and began rushing around her townhouse looking for a hiding place. A closet? A vase? A bag of A & P coffee? Her jewelry box! Yes, somewhere obvious like that; the police would never look there. Of course they would! Somewhere else. The box of Kleenex on her nightstand? No one would ever look there. No, too risky! What if she threw the box in the recycle bin by mistake when the Kleenex were gone?

What if she did? That would be the best thing—to get rid of the evidence. She didn't even know if the letter was real. She was assuming it had come from Myra, along with the ring. Maybe Myra had forged it!

She studied the letter through swollen eyes. It was Rand's handwriting, all right, as distinctive as a thumbprint. She ran to the cupboard and grabbed a box of matches, then lit one and held a corner of the letter in the flame. It caught.

What was she doing? She couldn't do that! It was destroying evidence, against the law! She smacked the letter on the countertop and, even more panicky now, put out the smoldering flame with the sleeve of her robe. The last *I love you* was scorched, but not Rand's signature. So deep was Olivia's despair that she didn't know whether she should feel happy or tragic about it.

She burst into tears again, amazing herself. She wanted to be done with all that. She wanted to be completely adult about the whole affair. Her basic problem in life was that she had never been touched by tragedy, that was her basic problem in life. Alison, yes, her death *was* a tragedy; but other than that, Olivia's life had gone smoothly. Very smoothly. Too smoothly. That was the basic problem. One little setback like this, and—

Who was she kidding? An old gas oven that poofs and singes your eyebrows, that was a setback. One that blows up your house with you in it, that was a tragedy.

And I don't know how . . . I don't know how . . . I'm ever going to crawl out from under the rubble, she told herself, bowing her head in tears.

The doorbell rang, sending shock waves anew through her. She yanked the silverware drawer open and threw the scorched letter and the ring into it, then ran to see who it was. She peeped through the keyhole. *Shit.* Eileen.

Olivia stood without breathing, waiting for her sister-in-law to leave.

Not Eileen.

"Livvy? Livvy, are you in there? Olivia!" Eileen began knocking, then banging, on the door. She peeked through the sidelights while Olivia flattened herself from view.

The phone had been ringing on and off all morning and

Olivia had ignored it. Big mistake. And she had left her car parked outside for all the world to see, for God's sake. What a stellar fugitive she'd make.

Desperate to ward off a call to the paramedics by Eileen on her cell phone, Olivia took a deep breath, wiped her eyes, and opened the door. Smiling wanly, she tried to look ill.

She was a grand success. Eileen took one look at her and crumbled into motherly sympathy. "Oh, Livvy—you've come down with something," she cried, rushing inside to embrace Olivia.

"No, no . . . you'd better not," said Olivia, keeping her distance. "You're bound to catch it."

"Don't be silly; I never get sick. You poor thing . . . all alone here . . . you didn't hear the phone? The girls at Miracourt have been calling all morning, they told me."

"I just didn't feel like answering the phone," Olivia mumbled, which was true enough.

"I stopped by the shop, and when they told me they couldn't reach you, I made excuses for you—but I was worried, Liv. With all these things that have been going on . . . Well, forget about that now. Have you taken your temperature?" she asked, putting her hand to Olivia's brow. "You feel all right. Have you been *crying*?" she asked, scrutinizing Olivia up close.

Olivia drifted out of the sunlight and into the shadows of the living room. "No. Why would I be crying? I . . . was petting the neighbor's cat. My eyes got itchy. You know how allergic I am."

"Then why let the cat in your house, for pity's sake? Especially when you're not feeling well."

"I was looking for sympathy, I guess," said Olivia, managing a wry smile.

"But what about Quinn? He doesn't have to be anywhere."

"Oh, but he does. Mrs. Dewsbury gets out of the hospital this morning," Olivia explained, grateful to have something true to say. She had to get Eileen out of there!

But Eileen, in maternal overdrive now, was heading for

the kitchen. "You just go right upstairs to bed and I'll make you some lemon tea."

In the kitchen she glanced around and said, "You must have been right in the middle of making breakfast when you got hit with this thing."

"Sort of, yes."

"Poor baby. I'll straighten up," she said, heading for the eggs and juice and opened loaf of bread.

"No! No, that's all right," said Olivia. "I just need to lie down, that's all."

"Yes, do that, Livvy," said Eileen, clearly concerned now. "You look a little green."

"I think I'm going to throw up," Olivia blurted out, and this time she was telling the truth.

"Go, go," said Eileen.

Olivia turned and made a sprint for the guest bath, while behind her she heard Eileen call out, "My God, what happened to your sleeve? It has a big hole burned in it."

Olivia threw up in what was probably record time, rinsed out quickly, and raced back to the kitchen. "It passed," she said grimly.

Eileen had put away the eggs and bread and juice and was sponging off the ashes of Rand's letter from the Corian counter.

Olivia became faint with fear simply from the sight of it.

"How on earth did you manage to set your robe on fire? And this Corian is going to need repair," her sister-in-law said, scooping the ashes into her free hand. "You're in no state to be playing with matches."

"So . . . true," said Olivia.

"I'm going to heat myself a cup of this coffee. You have a whole pot of it untouched," said Eileen, opening the microwave door.

She discovered the half-nuked sausages and took them out, holding them toward Olivia for her inspection. "I think we'd better toss these, don't you?"

The meaty smell of the gray, greasy links sent a new surge of nausea through Olivia. "Haftathrup," she gasped.

Off she went, back she came, more terrified than before that Eileen had found Rand's letter. But Eileen was opening lower cupboards, not the drawers, looking for the garbage can in which to dump the sausages.

"Don't . . . don't, Eileen. Please. Go home," said Olivia, taking her by the hand and coaxing her toward the door. Weaker by the minute, Olivia felt as if she was dragging a bolt of corduroy behind her.

Eileen protested, but faced with the opened door, she had no choice but to go through it. "Well . . . all right. But please—answer your phone. When will Quinn be back?"

"Oh . . . not today."

"Oh, right—Mrs. Dewsbury. In that case, I'll stop by tonight. Flu is nothing to fool with, Livvy. You could become dehydrated and end up in a hospital. You never pay enough attention to your health. You don't exercise, you don't eat right . . . you think you're so invincible."

"Please, Eileen—not now."

"Okay, okay, no more lectures," she said, kissing Olivia quickly on her cheek. "I love you and I worry about you, that's all. See you tonight. Now go back to bed, and drink plenty of fluids."

Smiling dutifully, Olivia closed the door after her sister-in-law and sank exhausted to the floor. More tears, an endless supply of them; where were they coming from?

Eileen, her oldest friend . . . oh, God, and the *children* . . . Kristin and Zack would never recover from this. Look at Quinn, the scars he bore—and *his* father was innocent. And Olivia's mother and father—what would they say, what would they do, if they knew about their son? Her mind veered away from the thought; it was too appalling.

Gradually, inevitably, the tears stopped. And in place of the crushing sorrow that Olivia felt, something new came creeping in, as stealthy as a cat on the hunt: suspicion.

Did her parents already know? Bits and pieces of odd recollections flashed briefly across Olivia's mind like the Pleiades across a winter sky: her mother, a little too hysterical at the thought of testing the DNA of Alison's unborn baby . . . her father, taking Quinn aside on New Year's Eve . . . her brother, warning her that she didn't have all the facts . . . her father again, hiding behind those curtains.

Myra knew. Quinn knew. Was it such a stretch, after all, to assume that her parents knew? And if they knew that Rand was the baby's father, did they know even more about him besides? The thought was far more appalling than any that had preceded it.

Why couldn't it have been some stranger who did it? Or the coach . . . Francis Leary . . . even, horrific as the situation would have been, her Uncle Rupert. Anyone but her brother.

Her need to keep her immediate family intact was primal, desperate—and a revelation. Up until this day she had not known how much they mattered to her. Now she did—and it was too late.

She sat on the floor for a dreary eternity, unable for once to get up and go. The tears kept rolling down. Poor Eileen . . . Poor Kristin . . . poor Zack . . . poor everyone.

God help them all.

Quinn had ordered a new monitor for Mrs. Dewsbury to be delivered via air freight; it arrived half an hour after he brought the widow home from the hospital. She was furious at him for his extravagance, ecstatic at the speedy replacement. She did love her CCTV.

That evening, when they were sipping tea in the parlor after one of Quinn's pot roast dinners—like most bachelors, he was on intimate terms with aluminum foil and onion soup mix—Mrs. Dewsbury kicked back in her La-Z-Boy and said out of the blue, "I was thinking, maybe we should invite Olivia here for dinner one night."

The chocolate chip cookie that Quinn was eating turned into mulch. He swallowed hard, then said quietly, "Sure. Maybe when you get back from your stay with Gerald."

"I do like that girl," the widow said with obvious fondness. "I had no idea that she could be so warm and charming, so really delightful."

She nibbled at her fancy bakery cookie and said, "I remember her as being very different in high school. *You* remember her then: She was always so very—hmm, how can I put this nicely?—determined."

"She still is," Quinn said with a grim smile. He was thinking of Olivia as she hung out the second-floor window that morning, willing and able to pull out his hair.

"Yes, but I see a softer side to her now. She's grown as a person. You know what I think? I think she's very much in love with you. You've done her a world of good. I'm assuming, by the way, that you feel the same about her," Mrs. Dewsbury added with a gently probing smile.

For a hundred-pound octogenarian, she was flattening Quinn as well as any steamroller could do. He found it impossible to peel himself off the floor and skip around like a man in love. He mustered all the strength that he had left to say, "There will never be anyone else."

Two cookies later, Quinn excused himself and went to bed. It was seven-thirty. Mrs. Dewsbury laughed at him. Even hundred-pound octogenarians stayed up later than that.

Four days later, a package arrived at the big white house on Elm.

Quinn had been working feverishly to complete his long list of projects before climbing into his truck and driving off into the sunset. He was intensely aware that he had done massive damage to one woman's life. Somehow he hoped to make up for it by doing extensive repairs to another woman's life. It didn't make much sense, but in his present state of meltdown, it was all that his brain could manage.

"Wash your hands and sit down," the widow said, flipping two grilled cheese sandwiches. "The soup is getting cold. I don't see why you have to obsess over that work list, Quinn. Surely the flashing can wait until you get back from California; the weather will only get nicer."

True enough, but he wouldn't be around to enjoy it.

"Now that I know where the leak is coming from, it would drive me nuts to leave it the way it is," he said, more or less telling the truth. "I can't believe a smart lady like you let some con artists rip you off with those replacement windows," he added. "They're garbage."

"Well, at least I had enough sense to contract only for one side. Once I saw how flimsy they were—anyway, you needn't be so snippy about it," she said, obviously hurt by his tone. "What's the matter with you, anyway? You've been this way for days."

"Sorry." He didn't even try to come up with an excuse. Nothing short of terminal disease would explain a mood as foul as his had been—another good reason for having thrown himself into his chores.

"What was in the package?"

"I don't know; I haven't opened it yet."

"How can you not open a package?"

When it has Olivia's handwriting on it, he thought, but aloud he said, "Haven't had a chance, I guess."

"I'll get it for you," said Mrs. Dewsbury, a catalogue shopper from back in the days of the Wells Fargo wagon. "You eat."

He dumped half a box of oyster crackers into his Campbell's tomato soup, just to convince her that his appetite was normal and his mood jim-dandy. And meanwhile he wanted to tear at his clothes and howl at the moon with rage and frustration.

Four days without holding Olivia, hearing her voice, inhaling the scent of her hair. So this was what it would be like. Four days. Four lifetimes.

Olivia, he thought, shutting his eyes from the vision of her. Oh, God, please . . . Olivia.

He was having a hard time breathing, much less eating, but he plowed away at his soup and crackers, wondering how he could have considered it a treat when he was a boy, and why he had ever made the mistake of admitting that to his hostess.

He was rescuing the grilled cheese sandwiches from their

overlong stay on the griddle when Mrs. Dewsbury shuffled into the kitchen. She was managing to get around without her walker nowadays; it was one of the few bright spots in the black void that Quinn was currently calling a life.

"I'll do that, I'll do that," she said, waving the package at him. "Here. Open it. I'm so curious. There's no return address, did you notice?"

"Yeah." He took out his Swiss Army knife and sliced through the wide clear tape that sealed every edge shut— Olivia was nothing if not thorough.

He found it hard to believe that she was returning the ring and the letter to him, but if she was, he had an explanation ready for the curious old lady who was hovering near: the ring was his, the letter, an old note from his dad. Mrs. D. couldn't possibly read Rand's handwriting, much less recognize it.

That was the general theory, anyway.

He opened the flaps of the shallow box and stared at the contents. Olivia was not re-burdening him with the care and protection of the critical—and possibly criminal—evidence. She was merely returning, in order of importance, his pajama tops, Mennen deodorant, Bic razor, and Oral-B toothbrush.

"Well, that's odd," said Mrs. Dewsbury. "What are *those* all about?"

Quinn went blank. He was clean out of lies, excuses, and stories to tell. "Um," he said.

"Olivia sent these, didn't she?" asked the savvy widow. Without waiting for an answer, she said, "You two have had a fight. Well, that explains your mood, and why you've been hanging around the house and fixing everything in sight."

In silence, Quinn went back to the grilled cheese sandwiches, cutting each of them diagonally and allocating three halves for him, one for the widow.

"For heaven's sake, Quinn—how long are you going to let this go on? Whatever you do, don't turn it into a competition between you. Just say you're sorry and get on with your lives. It's so much simpler in the long run.''

"It runs a little deeper than that," he said quietly.

"How deep?"

"Too deep."

"You mean you two have broken it off?"

"It looks that way."

"That's ridiculous! Pardon the cliché, but you two *are* meant for each other."

"Thanks," he said tersely, taking his seat again. "That makes me feel better."

"Don't play the sullen teenager with *me*, young man," she said, tapping the table with the tip of her forefinger. "I want you to march right down to that little shop of hers and take her out to lunch and make things up with her."

Quinn was completely at a loss over how to deal with his old teacher. He'd never been mothered before, and he could feel his impatience waiting to spring.

He tried disarming her with humor. "What? And walk out in the middle of this fine repast?"

"Oh, please. I'm sick of tomato soup and grilled cheese sandwiches; you must be, too," she said, snatching away his plate and sliding the meal into the garbage can.

"Mrs. D.—!"

"Right now. You don't want to be going off to California for two weeks and leaving her so upset. Life is too short to waste time in anger. Quinn, believe me. No one ever listens to the old, but we know better than anyone: Life is *short*."

"Don't you think I'm aware of that?" he said through gritted teeth.

"Obviously you're not, or you wouldn't be doing this. Not only that, but you don't seem to understand how hard it will be to reconcile by telephone."

"Oh, for chrissake! There's not going to *be* a reconciliation!" he said, standing up so abruptly that he knocked his chair over. "And I'm not going off for two weeks!"

Right now, all he wanted was to get away from the widow's well-intentioned kindness. He'd made it just fine so far without a mother and without a wife. Obviously nothing was going to change.

The old woman searched his face and must have found the answer she was looking for in the misery that was etched there. "Oh, no. Oh, Quinn, no. You're not going to run *again*?"

"I didn't run," he said with an utterly grim smile. "I accompanied my father."

"Whatever! This time it's running!"

"This time, I don't care," he said, and he left to go off to McDonald's.

Twenty-four

A crooked heart. How fitting.

Olivia caressed the smooth surface of the red glass paperweight, a quirky Elsa Peretti design that so enchanted her when she came across it in a Tiffany catalogue that she had ordered six of them for the Valentine's Day window of Miracourt.

But that was a month ago, when the world made sense and her own heart was still in good shape. Now she rued the extravagance.

Still, Keepsake's shoppers looked forward to Olivia's window displays, and she did not want to disappoint them. Against a backdrop of discreet gray, she began to arrange tiers of classic French ribbons that she had painstakingly rewrapped around antique wooden spools—exquisite ribbons of velvet and organdy, passementerie and jacquard, in silk and cotton and wool.

Except for a single spool of red grosgrain, the colors were rich, muted, and subtle: earthy greens and old-world mustards, royal burgundies and not-quite-blues, and a shade of rose that hinted of the spring that must surely come, easing the pain of winter.

Olivia laid the glass hearts among the spools, refocused the halogen spotlights, and then stepped outside onto a deserted sidewalk to gauge the effect. She was unhappy with it. The left side seemed more harmonious than the right. Now what? Rearrange the whole thing?

She looked at her watch. It was nearly seven. Eileen and Rand were having a dinner party to celebrate their twelfth anniversary. Olivia had promised the children that she'd come over early to play with them; she hadn't seen them in weeks. Obviously that wasn't going to happen. If she hurried, she could just catch the end of the cocktail hour before having to sit through a meal she couldn't taste while smiling at chitchat she didn't want to hear.

The window would have to do.

February 5

Dear Mrs. D.,

So far, so good. Made it to Philadelphia, but then detoured to Harrisburg, PA on a whim (went that route out west with Dad the first time, and wanted to see if I could touch base with old ghosts there. I could. Made me feel better, somehow.) Anyway, heading south again. Hope you can read this tiny print on your CCTV.

Love, Quinn

On February 15, Olivia removed the Elsa Peretti hearts, but she left the spools of ribbon in place. She had no real inspiration for a new display. Anyway, why bother? The spools looked all right.

March 1

Dear Mrs. D.,

Forgot to put a stamp on my last postcard to you. Did you get the one from Cape Hatteras? Don't know where my mind has gone. I stayed there longer than planned. Liked the wild, windy beaches. Did a lot of

*walking. Hope all is well with you. Is the new window
flashing doing the trick?*

Love, Quinn

On March 3, Olivia bought three paper shamrocks from
the Hallmark shop on Main and tossed them on the spools
of ribbon. Green was green.

March 18

Dear Mrs. D.,

*Good talking to you last week. Glad to hear that
things are quiet up your way. Spent yesterday at a bar
in Lubbock called O'Toole's. Meant to grab a sand-
wich and ended up staying till last call. I'd forgotten
what it means to be Irish. Yesterday I was reminded.
Hope the squirrels are leaving your crocuses alone.*

Love, Quinn

On March 18, Olivia sat on the edge of her bed staring
at a little stick that she held in her shaking hand. She was
fighting back not only nausea but terror as she watched the
pink color move across the top.

After weeks of on-and-off vomiting, Olivia had decided
that simple stress could not be the cause. And since as far
as she knew there was no such thing as two-month flu, she
had bought a guide to medical symptoms and looked up
potential causes. Tumors, gallbladder problems, ulcers—all
were possibilities. Bulimia was not. That left morning sickness associated with pregnancy.

It couldn't be that, she knew. She and Quinn had always
used condoms. Besides, she was getting sick at all different
times of the day. They didn't call it afternoon sickness, after
all, or nighttime sickness. She had been looking up ulcers,
thinking that they were to blame, when suddenly it had
dawned on her: She couldn't remember her last period.

With a pounding heart she had tried to clear her brain of every other thought but her monthly flow. December, yes, December was easy to remember. It came before Christmas. She had been wearing a pale knit dress and the onset was sudden and heavy; she had had to go home to change the stained dress.

Okay, January. January, January. She couldn't remember most of the damned month. When would she have been due? Sometime in the middle. The middle was the wrenching breakup with Quinn. No, definitely: no period. But was that so surprising? She had skipped periods before in times of stress, and it didn't get more stressed than the middle of January.

February. When had it come in February? Obviously not at all. February was the darkest, the dreariest, the most depressing month she'd ever known. Much of her body and all of her mind—everything that wasn't absolutely essential to life—had shut down during the month of February. That explained the lack of a period in February. Surely that explained it.

But it was heading for the end of March; something should be flowing by now. Olivia hadn't the excuse of being frantic, as she had been in January, or desperately depressed, as she had been in February. Nowadays she wasn't happy, wasn't sad, wasn't anything at all. She was numb. Which was fine with her. Numb let her get on with her day and sleep through the night and get through the occasional visit with her family.

Her life was normal—almost abnormally normal. Her family, relieved that Quinn was gone, was being excruciatingly kind to her. Her mother seemed to have forgotten their blowup, her father had gone back to being preoccupied with getting his tax break from town, and her brother had begun again to exhale. On the professional front, both the shop and the outlet were making money.

So where was the blood?

She watched in horror as two lines showed up in the little window. *Two!* Her cheeks turned hot, her pulse knocked around violently in her head. *Pregnant. Pregnant?* Impossible! They had been so—

Oh, my God. New Year's Eve. In the middle of the night on New Year's Eve. She and Quinn had engaged in sex that was uncalculated, uninhibited, unbelievable—and unprotected. Would that have been her fertile time?

Fool! Idiot! Of course it had been her fertile time. That's what created the drive that made the babies! And yet the next day neither of them had alluded to the possibility of her getting pregnant. Not even a simple "Gee, we should be more careful next time." Their lovemaking had been somehow more sacred than that; she remembered well her reluctance even to bring it up the next morning.

Pregnant. For a long time, Olivia sat on the edge of her bed holding the stick. From there she could see the box from the testing kit, still half nestled in its bag from a Wal-Mart far away, sitting on the bathroom sink.

Of all the half-formed thoughts that took turns fighting for stage center of her brain, only one kept coming back: Thank God she hadn't gone to the drugstore on Main.

Punchy from his long drive, Quinn dropped his duffel bag next to the door and headed straight for the cordless.

The feeling of impending doom that hit him after he sent off the postcard from Lubbock was so strong that he had chucked his plans to knock around southern Arizona and had driven straight home instead. He arrived to find that his house hadn't burned down (though the plants had all died) and his business hadn't gone bankrupt (though it might be on the way), so his premonition must have had something to do with out east.

His first thought was for Mrs. Dewsbury, he told himself. She was old, she was frail, anything could have happened to her. But the darker thought, the more hidden thought, was that something had befallen Olivia.

It was ten in the morning out there, a good time to call. He waited impatiently through at least half a dozen rings, opening windows as he wandered through his rambling, one-story house on his way to the bedroom. As soon as he threw open the patio doors, he got hit with the scent of roses. Damn, if he didn't prefer this to March in New England.

"*Hel*-lo," came the cheerful, upbeat voice.

Immediately Quinn knew that nothing was wrong. "Hey,

Mrs. D.," he said, relieved. "Just thought I'd call and let you know that I made it back safe and sound."

"For goodness' sakes! What happened to panning for gold in Arizona?"

"I bought a few lottery tickets instead. How's your weather?"

"Oh, don't ask. It's been raining ever since you last called. I might as well be living in Oregon. Every joint in my body is killing me, including my two new fake ones. I'm not sure I can manage these stairs much longer."

"Baloney. You're just looking for an excuse to move in with your son."

She laughed out loud at that; she had told Quinn a hundred times how much she wanted to die in her own home. "Oh, I do miss you, dear. Every time Gerald and Kathy come over, they treat me like a helpless, doddering thing—or worse, a child. I really do not like being condescended to. You've spoiled me that way, treating me as a friend the way you do."

"Well . . . that's because you are," said Quinn, swallowing down a ridiculous surge of self-consciousness. No, damn it! He was done with emotional commitments of any kind. Been there, done that, got burned good.

"And Olivia stopped by," she added, giving the knife a little twist.

"How nice." His tone was dangerously polite.

Accepting the rebuff, she turned quickly to another subject. "I'm working to clear up a little mystery about you, by the way."

"Oh?" He didn't like the sound of that. "What mystery would that be?"

"I'm not saying. In case I'm wrong, I don't want to look like an old fool. But I'm willing to bet my Social Security check that I'm right. I'll know more tomorrow, after Judy Damian drops by."

"Ah, Miss Damian the librarian. Is she driving the library van nowadays?"

"She's doing a little research as a personal favor to me. We're in cahoots. How do you like *that*, Mr. Leary?"

He laughed politely, puzzled by her smug tone. He was in the kitchen now, holding open the fridge door and staring at its lone contents, a six-pack of Coors. His idle mind was computing that it had cost him about five bucks a bottle to keep them cold for the past three months.

"So . . . I take it that all's quiet on the eastern front?" he asked, knowing she'd understand what he meant.

"Oh, yes. No tricks, no pranks, no random acts of violence. The town has been absolutely quiet since—"

"I left," he said, helping her over her embarrassment.

"It *was* Coach Bronsky behind it all, wasn't it?" she said. "He's the one who bashed in my monitor."

Quinn sighed. He had bought a forensics kit and dusted the trophy weapon for fingerprints himself; it had been wiped clean. "It's nothing we'll ever be able to prove, I'm afraid."

The widow snorted and said, "I'd like to bash *him* one. But never mind, I've had my vengeance: Coach Bronsky has been fired. He showed up drunk once too many times for the school committee's taste. Of course he's filed a grievance, but I'm not worried. He's finished at Keepsake High, and good riddance to him."

"Well, well."

Immediately Quinn began to work out the ramifications. All in all, he'd rather have the coach staggering drunk around the field than sitting home drunk with time to brood. "Look, I want you to make absolutely sure that you—"

"Yes, yes, I know. Keep the alarm set at all times, even when I'm pruning roses ten feet from my door."

"Even then." They chatted another minute or two before Quinn, dog-tired and still nursing a headache from his St. Paddy's Day hangover, hung up with promises to keep in touch.

Now what? Threaten the coach again for good measure? It would be so much simpler if the man would just drink himself into a stupor every day. But Bronsky wasn't a worst-case wino, and it made him all the more dangerous. Hell!

Consumed by guilt with no hope of absolution, Quinn headed for the medicine cabinet in search of aspirin. His stomach let out a sullen, hungry growl, like some beast in a cage who could care less if his handler wasn't up to speed. *Feed me.* Quinn popped the aspirin and, rubbing his stomach, went foraging through the cupboards. He hoped the beast liked Dinty Moore.

Rubbing her belly surreptitiously under her coat, Olivia stood in line at the Book Bay, the biggest, most anonymous bookstore in the area, clutching a Dorothy Sayers mystery and a Fodor's Guide to Bermuda with a copy of *Pregnancy and You* sandwiched discreetly between them.

Don't get sick, don't get sick, this is a bad time; don't get sick. Think about something else.

But the book on babies might just as well have been a real live toddler bouncing on her arm. She could think of nothing *but* the baby she apparently was carrying—at least, if the three pregnancy kits were to be believed. She had made an appointment with a gynecologist (in the next county) to make the results official, but in the meantime, she wanted to learn all she could before deciding what to do.

She knew virtually nothing about pregnancy. Because it had little to do with running a business, Olivia hadn't paid much attention whenever her friends—even Eileen—became pregnant. The women all got bigger and bigger, and then they went into a hospital and when they came out, they were smaller and had a baby in their arms. Olivia was only slightly more knowledgeable about the whole process than the child who's been handed a bill of goods about the stork.

A tap on her shoulder sent her jumping. She whirled around.

"Mrs. Hyart! What a surprise! Well, how do you like that! Gosh. Shouldn't you be in your quilting class?"

The sixty-ish woman smiled and shook her head. "Tonight's my reading group. I'm here to pick up our copies of *Rebecca* so that I can pass them out for next week's discussion. We're doing three months of classics."

"Ah! What an interesting life you lead!" said Olivia with revolting cheerfulness. She sounded unhinged; truly, she was scaring herself.

"What about you?" asked Mrs. Hyart, tilting her head

to read the spines. Before Olivia could react, the appallingly curious woman said archly, "*Pregnancy and You*?"

"It's a shower present."

"Oh, trust me, then; she probably has it."

"Bridal shower! I'm moving along."

"Do you think that's—? Well, all right," said the woman, straightening back up with an apologetic smile. She acted as if she'd just stepped on Olivia's newly planted pansies.

Olivia whipped out her Visa, paid for the books, and got out of the Book Bay as fast as she could. She was thinking about the doctor she'd signed up to see; obviously she should have chosen one in the next state, not merely the next county. Damn all small towns! Suddenly the charm of them eluded her completely.

She drove home and read until midnight, trying to devour every fact, every nuance, every clinical detail of what it meant to be pregnant. By the time she closed the book and went to bed, Olivia understood many things, including her craving for cheese and her aversion to fish, but she didn't know the answer to her most burning question: What should she do about this incredibly unexpected development?

Her dreams that night were muddled and terrifying. Old college chums with sophisticated attitudes about unwanted pregnancies drifted in and out of them, and her cousin Alison was screaming at them all, and Quinn was racing to catch Alison before she dropped into the quarry and drowned. Only Alison wasn't drowning, she was hanging by her neck, and Olivia was crying and trying to cut down the rope and pull her cousin to safety. But Alison was too heavy; Olivia needed Quinn.

In her last dream, Olivia had the horrifying sense that she was going to fail; that Alison wasn't going to make it and it was going to be Olivia's fault. Just before it happened, she woke herself up. And after that she kept herself up, propped in a sitting position against two pillows, one of them Quinn's, until the first glimmer of light appeared and a robin began its absurdly cheerful refrain from a branch of a maple outside Olivia's bedroom window.

It was the first day of spring.

Twenty-five

Judy Damian was all aflutter.

"You were right, Mrs. Dewsbury! It *had* to have been Quinn and his father. The timing was right, the place was right—and you have the postcard to corroborate it all!" The librarian collapsed her umbrella and untied her rain bonnet, then unbuckled her trench coat as Mrs. Dewsbury tried to rush her along.

"What a wonderful memory you have! How many people can recall news from seventeen years ago? Certainly not me. Oh, this is *so* exciting! I'm so happy for Quinn, really I am! I always knew he was special. And now look—I was right!" she said, pulling a couple of Xeroxed sheets out of her carrier and waving them in front of the widow's failing eyes.

"Judy, please calm down; you're going to have a heart attack," said Mrs. Dewsbury. She herself was far more tense than giddy. "Give it to me, would you? I'd like to read it for myself."

She laid the first sheet of the seventeen-year-old newspaper article on the moveable platform under the camera of her CCTV and adjusted the focus, then selected the white-on-black exposure to make the print jump-out clear for herself.

She caught her breath at the date, magnified twenty-five times so that she wouldn't mistake it. "I knew it! October twenty-third—less than two days after they took off from

Keepsake. That's about how long it would take to travel on a bus as far as Harrisburg, don't you think?''

''Absolutely,'' said Miss Damian. Biting her lip and shaking her head with emotion, she added, ''Why didn't Quinn *say* something after he came back?''

''Quinn? He would never bring up something like this, not until later, after he'd proved his father's innocence.''

''And now he's gone again!''

''Shh! I'm trying to concentrate.''

Mrs. Dewsbury kept her focus locked on the monitor as she moved the platform where the news piece from the *Pittsburgh Courier* lay. Slowly and methodically, she read the information being flashed so large on the television screen before her.

HARRISBURG, OCT. 23—A BUS TRAVELING WEST ON INTERSTATE 76 BETWEEN NEW YORK AND PITTSBURGH AND CARRYING THIRTY-SIX PASSENGERS OVERTURNED AND CAUGHT FIRE ON AN EXIT RAMP NEAR HARRISBURG EARLY THIS MORNING. TWO UNIDENTIFIED MEN ABOARD THE BUS ARE CREDITED WITH SAVING THE LIVES OF AT LEAST A DOZEN PASSENGERS WHO WERE OVERCOME BY SMOKE. TWO OTHER PASSENGERS DIED IN THE IMPACT.

WITNESSES SAY THAT THE YOUNGER MAN, STRONGLY BUILT AND IN HIS EARLY TWENTIES, PULLED THE DAZED AND SOMETIMES UNCONSCIOUS PASSENGERS, MOST OF THEM ELDERLY OR WOMEN WITH CHILDREN, FROM THE CONFINES OF THE SMOKE-FILLED BUS. THE OLDER OF THE RESCUERS, A MIDDLE-AGED MAN, WAS SEEN TO CARRY TWO CHILDREN FROM THE BUS AND ADMINISTER CARDIOPULMONARY RESUSCITATION TO ONE OF THEM UNTIL THE FIRST OF A DOZEN EMERGENCY VEHICLES ARRIVED ON THE SCENE.

FIREFIGHTERS QUICKLY PUT OUT THE BLAZE, BUT THE EXIT RAMP REMAINS CLOSED UNTIL AN INVESTIGATION CAN BE COMPLETED. THE DRIVER HAS NOT BEEN CHARGED.

THE IDENTITIES OF THE RESCUERS ARE NOT KNOWN AT THIS TIME. RHYANNA WHITE, A PASSENGER ABOARD THE BUS, STATED TO POLICE THAT AFTER THE ARRIVAL OF THE

PARAMEDICS, THE TWO RESCUERS, WHO ARE BELIEVED TO
BE A FATHER AND HIS SON, FLAGGED DOWN A PASSING
VEHICLE AND LEFT IN IT. THE CAR WAS A TWO- OR THREE-
YEAR-OLD GOLD COUPE, POSSIBLY A CHEVROLET CAMARO,
WITH ONE OCCUPANT. ANYONE WITH INFORMATION IS
ASKED TO CONTACT EITHER STATE OR LOCAL POLICE.

"Oh, Quinn," murmured Mrs. Dewsbury after she finished. "Oh, Quinn."

"Quinn was seventeen at the time, but you know how
mature he looked. And he was a big guy, even then. He
could easily have passed for someone in his twenties."

"This is awful, this is tragic. This is so unfair."

"But . . . I thought you'd be happy," the librarian said.

"So did I."

After a moment the younger woman said hesitantly,
"What do we do now?"

"I wish I knew," said Mrs. Dewsbury, slumping in front
of her CCTV. "I wish I knew."

Quinn parked his truck in the cemetery lot and made his
way on foot to his father's grave, dreading the moment as
much as if his father were alive and anxiously awaiting news
of Quinn's adventure out east.

But he wasn't. Francis Leary was dead and buried, and
the grass growing over his grave was well established. A
patch of clover had sprouted near the middle of the mound.
It drew a mournful smile from Quinn. His dad loved to see
clover growing in grass he maintained; it was proof that the
soil was herbicide-free.

Quinn dropped down into a catcher's crouch, with his
hands dangling loose between his thighs. In his state of despair, it was the nearest position to prayer that he could
swing.

"I blew it, Dad," he murmured, "I blew it big time. I
went charging off to Connecticut like a stoned Crusader,
convinced that I could unmask the villain in the piece and
set your reputation right once and for all.

"Well, guess what? The villain in the piece turned out to be me. You got it—your number-one, overachieving, underwhelming, self-destructive, star-crossed son.

"I did manage to win one tiny little skirmish: at least three people are now convinced that you're innocent. The rest of the time I spent sacking and plundering an innocent woman's relationships with everyone she's ever loved. I was *real* thorough, Dad, even for me. By the time I left, there was nothing left standing, emotionally speaking, except her white-hot hatred for yours truly."

He plucked some of the strands of grass that had escaped the caretaker's weed whacker and were growing tall beside the new headstone. "So here's where we stand," he continued, convinced he had to say it aloud. "Olivia's brother— or even worse, her father—killed Alison to keep her quiet. You remember her brother Rand: nice guy, bit of a charmer, family man now, active volunteer in town events. And Owen Bennett—still a ballbuster, to be sure, but holding Keepsake together single-handedly by keeping the mill in operation there. As I say, I make a hell of a better villain than either of 'em.

"Did I mention that Rand has two great kids and a dynamite wife? She's Olivia's best friend. And Livvy adores the kids. Well, she used to be able to, anyway."

Quinn ran his hand tenderly over the patch of soft clover. "Think there's a four-leaf version in there for me?" he whispered. "I could use a little of that vaunted luck o' the Irish."

A puffy cloud scudded between the sun and the grave, subduing hope. The silence was overwhelming.

Quinn sighed and said, "So! Heard any good undertaker jokes lately?" He laughed softly at his own lame idiocy, then stood up.

"I'm sorry, Dad," he said, looking down at the grassy mound at his feet. "I'm sorry. I wanted to get this one thing—this one fucking thing—right. And I blew it. Oh, God, how I blew it."

He felt a hard lump in his throat, and then tears. He

closed his eyes, overwhelmed by the crushingly bleak life that lay ahead of him, and then suddenly he dropped to his knees and bent prostrate over the grave. His forearms prickled from the newly cut grass; he grabbed clumps of it in his fists and pulled, trying to open the door to eternity.

He wanted advice; he wanted love; he wanted, in this most despairing moment of his life, to connect again with humanity.

"Oh, Christ, Dad, I blew it," he said, his body riven with sobs. "I blew it . . . I blew it . . . I blew it . . ."

Olivia was sitting in front of her computer in the loft of Miracourt and grinding out numbers for her accountant when she heard sharp tapping on the storefront window below her. Determined not to lose her train of thought, she kept plugging away at her column of numbers. The shop was closed and tax day was looming. A sale wasn't worth it.

The rapping continued, more urgent than before. Olivia stood up and peeked out the Palladian window. No UPS truck was parked below, but it was pouring out, which she hadn't realized, so she went downstairs to answer the summons. Whoever was there must be desperate.

She was amazed to see Mrs. Dewsbury under the shop awning, peering through the door as she rapped on the window with the handle of her black umbrella.

Olivia rushed to unlock the shop and let the old woman in, chiding her for being out in such awful weather.

"I take my rides when I can get them," Mrs. Dewsbury said, using the umbrella as she would a cane. "Father Tom stopped by for tea, and he offered to give me a lift downtown. He's waiting in his car now, so I have to be brief." She glanced around her and said, "Where can I sit down?"

Olivia ran for an old armchair that she liked to update every once in a while in a new fabric and keep handy for the weary, and she settled her old teacher in it. True to her word, Mrs. Dewsbury got right to the point.

"I've agonized over this long enough. I know very well that Quinn wouldn't want me meddling between you two—

don't look at me that way, my dear; I'm older and wiser than both of you put together—and up until now I've respected what I know would be his wishes. How*ever*.''

She unzipped her black purse and took out two sheets of paper that were folded in half and handed them to Olivia. ''This is the man you're throwing away. If you read the article and can still do that, you're a lot less smart than I've always assumed. All right. I've spoken my piece,'' she said, using the armrests to push herself up with an effort from the chair. ''Do you remember what I told you on the day before you took your SATs?''

In a daze, Olivia stared at the silver-haired teacher in the porkpie rainhat. She shook her head.

''I said, 'Don't disappoint us.' I'm repeating it now, Olivia. This is the most important decision you'll ever make. All *this*,'' she added, waving a hand at the shop, ''is nothing. Not by comparison. Good night.''

She turned and began limping toward the door. Olivia rushed to hold it open.

''I don't know—thank you,'' she mumbled in confusion. She had no idea what she was supposed to be grateful for.

She waved at Father Tom as he emerged from his black sedan under another umbrella to get the door for Mrs. Dewsbury. The car drove off, puffing steamy exhaust into the wet, cold night, and Olivia locked up shop again. She sat in the tapestry-covered armchair and, with more dread than curiosity, she unfolded the pages.

Harrisburg, Oct. 23—A bus traveling west . . .

Olivia read the article through, and then she went right back to the dateline and read it through again. She remembered Quinn's words when he was reading her the riot act back on pie day: *a situation where my father could have—should have—been honored as a hero.*

This was that situation, without a doubt.

With a deep sigh, made even more profound by the hormonal swings she was daily enduring, Olivia folded the pages and laid them on her lap. It didn't seem possible that one man could be so good, so brave, and so wronged all in one lifetime. And to have lived his life in hiding . . . and then to die without having been vindicated—it was almost unbearably sad. No wonder Quinn had been so determined to clear his father's name.

No wonder.

After a long and mournful moment, Olivia stood up and drifted over to the storefront window. She had replaced the spools of ribbon—finally—with bolts of frothy spring fabrics: pink organdy, pale lime chiffon, and white netting bunched in makeshift tutus for all those sewing mothers whose little girls had dance recitals coming up.

It hit her: Francis Leary had never lived to see a granddaughter in a tutu.

She fingered an edge from the bolt of chiffon. It was such a delicate fabric. It would take a number-nine needle; anything bigger would leave holes. Her mother had sewn her a tutu once. Pink, of course; there was no other color for a six-year-old ballerina with dark curls, an attitude, and legs just a little too short ever to be called lithe.

Mom, that was a really nice thing you did. You weren't very good with a Singer. Even I remember the seams you had to tear apart and resew. It was a labor of love, I know that now. Thank you.

She sighed. Everyone around her seemed to labor from love. Even her father . . . why else did he drive himself so hard, if not for the mill workers? He would never admit it, of course, but he felt a tremendous responsibility to every one of them. He wasn't fighting for that tax break to enhance his own wealth; he could easily move the mill to Mexico and make a lot more money. *Keep it in Keepsake*: It was the creed he lived by.

And Eileen—Eileen had love to spare for everyone. She handed it out like candy. Rand? No father loved his children more than Rand did. That's what was so hard: to reconcile this Rand with . . . that Rand.

She couldn't destroy her family by turning Rand in. She couldn't. She was going to have to live in misery with the secret for the rest of her life.

Which brought her back to Quinn. Everything that he had done, he had done for love. Olivia knew that. It was the most heart-wrenching fact of all. But it didn't change the impossible situation that the two of them were in.

Oddly soothed by the steadily falling rain, she wandered back through the softly lit shop, looking at it with Mrs. Dewsbury's eyes. Did it have any worth? Any meaning at all? Olivia wasn't sure of the answer to that anymore. She paused at a bolt of Ultrasuede and slid her hand over the fabric: soft . . . smooth . . . like a baby's bottom.

Quinn's baby. Francis Leary's grandchild. She was carrying good and honorable and heroic instincts, passed to yet another generation. She couldn't have Quinn. But she *could* have the best of him to love and to care for.

Poor Mrs. Dewsbury. She had shown up with her black umbrella on Miracourt's doorstep like an elderly Mary Poppins, convinced that she could make things right between Quinn and Olivia. She hadn't done that; no one could.

But she had made Olivia feel so much better about having the baby alone.

After weeks of wet spring weather, the sun rushed in full of apologies and determined to make amends: The day was bright, benign, and deliciously warm, a perfect spring bouquet offered to sullen and sodden New England.

Sometime during Saturday's downpour, Olivia had learned that Rand would be home with the kids all day on Sunday. She had made up her mind to see him then—but her mission would have been so much more fitting in rain.

She drove with extra care to his house, which was built, like hers, high above the Connecticut River, upstream of the mill. That upstream view of the water was all that her house and his had in common, however. Olivia had opted for a place she could afford. Rand's reproduction Colonial was sited on a rolling lawn with mature trees, a guest house, a greenhouse, a chicken coop, a barn, a paddock in the making—and a mortgage that was mind-boggling.

But on a day like today, who cared? Certainly not

Olivia's brother. She found him running around with his children on the flat part of the lawn, engaged in a game of Frisbee made a little more tricky by the fact that Zack couldn't throw a Frisbee and Kristin couldn't catch one.

The real star of the show was Samantha, their golden retriever. Sam caught the plastic disk perfectly in her mouth every time—whether it was whizzed to her or not—and then she ran down to the river with it, and the kids ran after her, and invariably someone slipped and fell and got even more muddy, which apparently was the real point of the game.

It all looked a little too frisky for Olivia, who was still getting used to the idea of being pregnant, so she declined to play. Since she was wearing jeans, she dropped down on the damp ground and watched them go at it. Pretty soon Samantha ran up to her and knocked her over, and Olivia ended up just as muddy as everyone else.

"Sorry about that, sis," her brother said, laughing, as he stuck out a hand to pull her up. "Sammy can't believe you're not playing. Frankly, neither can I. How're you doing?" he asked her as they walked back to the house over the children's howls of protest. It was obvious that he thought Olivia was still brooding over her breakup with Quinn.

Right now, he couldn't have been further off the mark. "I'm fine, really," she said, rolling up her sleeves above the wet and muddy elbows of her white shirt.

"You *look* good," he said with a quick sideways glance. "I guess your appetite's back, anyway."

Automatically she sucked in her stomach. Not that it did any good.

Rand kicked off his muddy moccasins in the mudroom and proceeded barefoot to the fridge. "Beer?" he asked her.

"Oh, that sounds—"

Alcoholic. She declined and said she'd rather have water.

"Water? At least have a Coke."

Olivia shrugged and said, "I don't need the caffeine." For whatever reason, she threw up less when she avoided it. The baby knew more about nutrition than she did, it seemed. She poured herself a glass of water and sipped while her brother took a long, satisfying slug of beer and then washed up at the sink, keeping an eye out the window at his kids as they romped in the yard.

He was wiping his hands on a towel. His fair skin had great color from the sun and the exercise. He was smiling, relaxed, in a wonderful mood. He looked as happy as she'd seen him in half a year.

Could she do this?

"You know, it's no accident that I'm here today," she said, mustering every bit of her formidable resolve.

"I figured," he said, cocking his head at her. "Normally I don't rate. What's on your mind, Livvy?"

Most of the smile and all of the ease had gone out of his face. He knew, more than anyone else, when it was serious between them.

Olivia looked away, then made herself look into her brother's eyes. She had rehearsed her opening line so many times, and now she couldn't remember a word of it.

"I have some things of yours," she blurted out.

Twenty-six

Rand's laugh was tight as he said, "Oh? You finally gonna return my Abba tapes?"

She said, "These go back to almost as long."

Olivia had tucked the ring in the front pocket of her jeans, the folded letter in the back. She hadn't dared risk being knocked unconscious in a car accident and having some rescuer find them as he went through her handbag looking for names of next of kin.

Fishing the ring out first, she handed it to her brother.

He looked at it and nodded. There was no shock, no dismay, no panic: only the simple, eloquent nod of recognition. She remembered it for the rest of her life.

"You got this from—?"

"Quinn. Who got it from Myra."

"And you're wondering how Myra came to have it?" There was a glimmer almost of hope in her brother's eyes as he asked her. He so clearly wanted her answer to be yes.

Olivia dashed that hope when she reached into her hip pocket and brought out the pale blue sheet with its charred edge. With downcast eyes she handed it to him. "This too."

"Oh, Jesus."

There went her forgery theory. She thought he would read it, or maybe rush to his big Viking stove, turn on a burner, and set it afire. Instead he stuffed the letter in the front pocket of his grass-stained khakis. He looked ashamed and embarrassed, as if it were a note from the principal.

He didn't seem to know what to do about the ring. The ring was different. The ring was okay to have. He held it between his thumb and forefinger, thinking of—what? Alison? The big game? The path not taken? He surprised Olivia by slipping off his wedding band and slipping his class ring on that finger. Making a fist with his left hand, he rubbed the surface of the ring with the palm of his right.

All the while, he was in some other place, during some other time. Olivia had no idea how to get to where he was, so she waited.

After a while, he looked up and said, "Why give these to me?"

She shrugged and said, "Too law-abiding to destroy them myself, I guess."

"Why not give them to Vickers?"

She blinked. "You don't know? You honestly can't figure it out?"

"Zack? Kristin?"

"And Eileen. Mom. Dad. Why do you *think*, you idiot?" She could feel all the horror come rushing up like acid bile. There it was, that sudden urge to be sick. Convinced despite her doctor's assurances that she was harming the baby every time she threw up, she made an intense effort to control the nausea.

"I have to go," she said coldly, and she turned to leave.

"Livvy, wait!" Rand called. Now there was anguish in his voice.

She whirled around. "*What?* What can you possibly say in your defense?"

"I didn't kill her. You have to believe me, Liv. I loved her—I thought I loved her, anyway. I was seventeen, for God's sake!" he said, raking both hands through his hair.

Olivia studied him as closely as she ever had in her life. The stakes were high; his answer mattered.

"I don't know how it happened," he said. "One minute I was her cousin, someone for her to vent to, and the next, we were . . . But I didn't kill her, I'm telling you. I was all set to marry her, to raise the child—well, you saw the letter,'' he said with a smile that was bitterly wry. "I was just your average teenage doofus. God only knows how I thought I'd support us or where we'd live. Certainly not in Keepsake.''

Olivia had only one question: "Does either Mom or Dad know?''

He shook his head. "Eventually reality set in and I started having second thoughts. I wanted Alison to put the baby up for adoption. She got angry; we had a fight over it. But before anything got resolved, she disappeared. Then they found her hanged at the quarry. I was as shocked as anyone. Livvy, I'm telling you the truth,'' he said with a look of burning desperation. "I've never lied to you—not when it counted.''

Olivia had expected her brother to deny murdering Alison, but she hadn't expected to believe him. The emerging agony she felt was because she had absolutely no acceptable fallback scenario to him being the murderer.

Her next question came out in a whisper. "Who do you think killed her, then?''

Grimacing, Rand rubbed his brow with his middle finger and said, "Uncle Rupert? I've always assumed that she told him about us. You know how possessive he was—''

"No, no, it wasn't Uncle Rupert,'' Olivia said, feeling a new wave of nausea kick in. "When Quinn and I went over there, he told us that he had pushed hard for the investigation to go forward back then. With no results. Didn't I tell you that part?''

"No,'' he said with a blank stare.

"It wasn't Uncle Rupert. Someone else.'' Her heart was beginning to feel as cold and glassy as an Elsa Peretti paperweight.

Rand looked frightened now. "Oh, man . . .''

Their thoughts were locked on exactly the same plane. Neither spoke. The only sounds were of children screeching and a big dog barking.

And then the deep, resonant chime of the front doorbell.

"Oh, hell," Rand said. "I'm going to have to get that. Your car's out front, the kids are outside."

"I'm going, then," she said. "I've got to get out of here."

That didn't happen. The visitor was their father, and he was in a fury of indignation.

"Those sons of bitches on the council aren't going for the tax break," Owen Bennett said, waving his briefcase at both of his children.

Rand was stunned. "Dad, no way! The whole point of this last postponement was to get Murphy in line."

"Murphy! Murphy managed to turn everybody *else* around! You know what you can do with Murphy!"

"How'd he do that? It's impossible!"

"Is that so? Tell it to the mayor. I just had lunch with him. He gave me the heads-up: The plan will be shot down five to two at Tuesday's council meeting. All right, let's get to work," he said, heading for Rand's study. "I want to have dates, I want to have profit projections, I want to have numbers to rub in their smug, short-sighted faces. I want that mill shut down *mañana*!"

"Oh, Dad, not that," cried Olivia, following him into the small office. "You're not really going to move the mill to *Mexico*?"

"Oh no?" he said grimly. "Watch me. Three god-damned generations of Bennetts have busted their humps to keep this town afloat. I've watched my profit margin tighten like wool in a hot dryer. No more! Keepsake can go the way of every other mill town in New England. See if I give a damn."

Dismayed to see that he wasn't just posturing, Olivia said, "That's not even true! Look at Aaron Feuerstein at Malden Mills! Three generations in Lawrence have busted *their* humps, and Feuerstein is still committed enough to have rebuilt a burned-down mill from scratch!"

Owen Bennett leveled his daughter a look as calculated, as cold, as any she had ever seen. "We can't all be heroes,

Olivia; I'm sorry to disappoint you. Now run along. Rand and I have work to do.''

Brother and sister exchanged one quick glance, and then Olivia walked out in a state of shock.

It wasn't her uncle . . . it wasn't her brother.

Who was the adult that Alison would have gone to first? Of course. Who was the one who would have tried hardest to make her pregnancy go away? Of course. Who would have tried, first, to buy Alison's compliance, and failing that, taken more drastic measures? Who had the most to lose in reputation and prestige, and the money and the will to see that that didn't happen?

Who else?

Sickened still further by this latest turn of events, Olivia detoured to a clump of forsythia and threw up behind it, then rinsed with a bottle of soda water she carried everywhere now.

Suddenly she heard her niece cry, "Auntie Livvy, Auntie Livvy, I see you!"

Kristin was peering at her through the yellow shrubs, obviously assuming a game was afoot. "Now it's our turn! You count to a hundred, and Zack and me will hide. No fair peeking!"

"Oh, wait, sweetie, no, that isn't—"

Her niece, muddy from her Mary Janes to her nose, halted and turned for further instructions. Were there other, more special rules to be followed? She was ready! She was willing! Her eyes were huge with expectation, her mouth opened and ready to swallow everything that her beloved aunt was willing to tell her. Hop on one leg? Run away backward? Just say the word.

With a laugh that was half sob, Olivia dropped into a crouch and held her arms out wide. "Hug first. Then we'll play. And make it a *big* hug."

Kristin broke into a wide, gap-toothed grin and ran full speed into her aunt's arms, then squeezed as tightly as a five-year-old could. Anything for love.

Olivia breathed the child's innocence deep into her lungs

the way a firefighter would suck in air after escaping a smoke-filled building. It was all for the women and children now, her silence.

The men in her family were tainted.

Quinn Leary was in the last few days of building a stone wall for a well-heeled cosmetic surgeon in Santa Barbara. He enjoyed the work, enjoyed not having to make any decision more earth-shattering than which stones would lie flattest on top of which other stones. When his beeper sounded, his first impulse was not to respond. He had taken very few commissions since his return to California, and he liked it that way. For now, he was going to continue to pick and choose.

But that's not why he had the beeper. Thanks to the marvel of caller ID, he knew that it was Mrs. Dewsbury trying to get in touch with him. The widow was strictly A-list, so he grabbed a bottle of water from the cooler in his truck and found himself a shade tree.

He was concerned—Mrs. Dewsbury would never call before the rates changed unless it was important. Presumably it had nothing to do with her recent discovery about the burning bus. He never should have sent that provocative postcard about Harrisburg, not to a woman as shrewd and well-informed as she was.

He sighed. She looked like such a little old lady. Why the hell couldn't she *behave* like a little old lady?

He dialed her number. She answered at once.

After gliding through opening pleasantries, she said, "My dear, I have some very interesting news for you."

"Don't be coy, madame," he said, sitting back against the tree. "It's not your style."

He was slugging water from the bottle when she said, "All right, then. Olivia is pregnant."

Out came the water through his nose and down the wrong pipe, giving him a choking fit that ended in tears.

"How do you know this?" he managed to croak.

"Promise you'll keep it a secret until the day you die?"

"Yeah, yeah—*who*?"

"Father Tom. He did *not* hear it in the confessional," the widow hastened to say. "He heard it as gossip. There's a difference, you know. He's not bound—"

"I don't care, I don't *care*," said Quinn. "Just tell me how reliable the rumor is."

"On a scale of one to ten, I would say eight. Father Tom heard it from his housekeeper who heard it from her niece, who works in the billing department of an ob-gyn in Middletown. Apparently Olivia didn't want to put in a claim to her insurance and insisted on paying cash. Well! Even though she'd gone to a clinic outside of Keepsake, the girl in billing still recognized the name. I mean, really. Bennett Milled Goods. It's like being a Hershey in Pennsylvania. Olivia should have used an assumed name if she really wanted it kept secret. Of course, in that case I wouldn't be calling you now."

Quinn let her roll to a complete stop before his next question. "Who else knows about this?"

"I imagine it's just a matter of time before everyone does. Father Tom may have been one of the first; I doubt he'll be the last," Mrs. Dewsbury said dryly.

"When did Liv make that initial visit?"

"Early April, I believe."

"Has she gone since?"

"Oh, yes. More than once."

She was keeping the baby, then.

"And why did it take the blabbermouth so long to blab?"

"It's ironic. She was pregnant herself, and went out on maternity leave right after Olivia's initial visit. Father Tom's housekeeper eventually went to see her new grandniece, and that's when she got the scoop. Since then, of course, the housekeeper has made it a point to keep herself informed."

Just as well that Quinn was sitting down; he was reeling. He thought of asking, "Is Olivia seeing some other man?" but the question seemed absurd. He knew she wasn't. The conviction came from the same place deep down in his soul as the belief that the baby was his, conceived on New Year's

Eve. It had felt, on New Year's Eve, as if they were reaching for the stars. Now he knew that they'd managed to snatch one and bring it down to earth.

It was going to be a girl.

"I'll be on the next plane," he said.

"I knew you would. Hurry home, dear."

Olivia's mother had created charming hanging baskets of annuals for every shop on the cobblestoned court.

"At first I just made one for you—to hang from the lamp in front of Miracourt," Teresa Bennett said. "But then I thought, why stop there? Is it really so much of an effort to make up ten of them? I hope the other shopkeepers won't think I'm being presumptuous."

Olivia flattened her hands against the rear window of her mother's Explorer as it sat in the street with its engine running and its air conditioning on. The cargo area was filled with magic: green-glazed pots that would hang where they were told, tumbling over with bright pink ivy geraniums and silver-green lamium and exploding with compact daisies in the middle.

Olivia straightened up and gave her mother an enthusiastic squeeze. "They will *love* them. Do you want me to take them around to the shops for you, or would you rather do it yourself?"

"Oh, honey, would you? I'd feel a bit funny."

"I'll be glad to—but let's hang this one first."

She was standing on the second rung of her stepladder, reaching up to hang the pot from a cast-iron hook on the antique lamppost, when her mother smiled and said, "Speaking of pots . . . ," and patted Olivia's stomach.

"Mother!" Olivia said, shocked to the core. She scrambled down the ladder.

"Livvy, I was only teasing," her mother said, taken aback by her daughter's vehemence.

Olivia folded the stepladder with a smack and said primly, "It's *not* very polite."

"I'm *sorry*."

"Well . . . never mind. I'm just self-conscious about it, that's all."

To say the least. She was going to have to tell her mother, and soon. But, oh God, she didn't know how. One thing was apparent: The charm of the moment was gone. "I'll unload the car," Olivia said stiffly.

"I'll help you," offered her mother, much more subdued than before.

It was so awkward. Quinn was everywhere in those pauses between them, which seemed to come more frequently now. It was Olivia's fault, of course; she was the one who had pulled back from her whole family. But her mother obviously was assuming that it was because she had objected so violently to Quinn, and now that he was gone, she was always trying to bridge the gap between Olivia and her with little gestures of affection. With no more success than today.

For the past few months Olivia couldn't help wondering whether her mother had known about Rand and Alison's affair. Now she had begun to wonder whether her mother might not know even more than that. If Owen Bennett had acted true to form and had tried to clean up the scandalous mess that his son had got into, then how could his wife not know it?

All in all, better to stay estranged.

Olivia spent the next hour passing out hanging baskets to pleased and grateful shopkeepers. It was such a beautiful day, and she enjoyed wandering around the cobblestoned court. She came back to Miracourt with real reluctance, which surprised her; the shop had always been her first love and her paramount joy.

But today she was drawn to flowers. If she owned a garden, she'd be home in it. She watered the dusty miller and ruby-red impatiens that were just getting started in the long box beneath her shop window, and then she dragged out the stepladder again; she wanted to rehang her mother's pot so that the sun-loving daisies faced south. Small gestures, perhaps, but they appealed to her newly discovered nurturing instincts.

She was standing on the ladder, gazing with pleasure at the flower baskets that hung from every lamppost in the court, when something propelled her to look toward Main. Whether it was a car horn or loud music or just plain magnetism, she never afterward knew, but the first thing to pop into focus was Quinn Francis Leary, striding toward Miracourt as if he were late to pick her up for dinner.

She hadn't seen him since January 14: four months. Long enough for his hair to grow out and hers to be cut short. Long enough for him to lose weight and her to put it on. Long enough for her to forget how tall he was, how rugged, how head-turning handsome.

Long enough for her to have lost touch completely with deep, abiding joy.

Twenty-seven

"Hello," she said, gazing down at him.

"Should you be climbing ladders?"

He knew.

"I'm eighteen inches above the sidewalk, Quinn. I think I can handle it." *I love you, I missed you. How could you leave me?*

"It was a question, Liv; I didn't come back to tell you what to do."

"Good." *Why did you come back at all? Nothing has changed.*

"I understand that there's been a . . . development."

Oh. Right. That one thing. "You heard it from Mrs. Dewsbury, I take it?"

He smiled. It was such a sad and melancholy smile. "I'm not allowed to say."

"I don't know why people bothered inventing the Internet," Olivia said, climbing down the two rungs. "A few Mrs. D.'s strategically placed could do the job just as well for a lot less money."

He had been appraising her figure, Olivia knew, deciding for himself if the rumors were true. For one vindictive moment she wished she owned a muumuu.

She tried to close the ladder, but for some stupid reason the metal spreader wouldn't fold. "Here, I'll do that," Quinn said, moving in to help.

"No, really, I can do it myself. I—ow!"

He'd closed the spreader on the edge of her little finger, hardly a tragic event. But Olivia was feeling tragic, and her cry reflected the sharp pain in her heart more than the little pinch on her hand. Again Quinn apologized, this time profusely.

"It's nothing," she said, sucking the spot. She glanced at it and added; "A little blood blister, that's all."

With a shaky laugh he said, "Before I maim you for life, will you agree to see me somewhere? Livvy, my God, we *have* to talk."

How odd. Not so long ago, Olivia was begging him for the very same mercy.

She glanced around the court. There was Ella, spying on them over the checkered café curtains of her bakery. Burt was outside his antique shop next door, feeling a sudden need to resweep his sidewalk. Mark—no discretion there; he just stood in front of his music shop with his arms folded, watching the show. Any minute now someone was bound to pop out of the sewer with a manhole cover on his head and snap a photo of Quinn and her for the bulletin board at the foot of Town Hill.

She crossed her arms and hugged her sides, mostly to cover her stomach, and said, "Okay. I suppose I owe you that much. Where do you want to meet?"

"Your place?"

"Are you crazy? No!" she shouted. "You can't just waltz back into my life!"

She was overreacting; even she could see that. "Somewhere else," she said, lowering her voice, "but nowhere public. I don't want to be hashing this out in a restaurant or, for that matter, where we're standing. God, I'm *sick* of this town and its gossip," she added. She felt like taking all of the hanging baskets back.

She stared at the sidewalk while she chewed her lower lip. Finally she looked up and said, "I know where: the gardener's cottage. My father is in Mexico—yes, Mexico," she snapped when Quinn did a double take. "He won't be home until after midnight, and my mother always stays near a phone when he's away. We won't be bothered at the cottage.''

It was the perfect place: private, but too haunted by memories of Quinn's father for Quinn to try any funny business.

''Miracourt is open late tonight,'' she added. ''I won't be able to meet you there until ten. Park off the estate somewhere and then walk in.''

''All right, I'll see you then,'' Quinn said, searching her features for some sign of welcome.

He didn't find it.

By the time nine-thirty rolled around, Olivia had already made a quick trip home to change from her slacks—obviously too tight—to a denim jumper with an empire waist, which she slipped over a black top and tights. It was the kind of outfit she'd wear on a cool night in front of a fire with someone she loved.

The night was cool, anyway.

She drove to the cottage second-guessing herself the whole way. What if her mother had guests? What if she decided to drag them down after dinner to ooh and ahh over some new antique in her charming guest house? Olivia thought about it and decided that if that were the case, she would simply introduce Quinn to everyone as the father of her forthcoming baby, say good night, and the hell with them all.

I will not put this baby through any more stress. This baby comes first. It was such a new priority in Olivia's life, and it was all the more fierce for being new.

She drove through spitting rain to the entrance of the estate, then punched in the security code that activated the low iron gates, closing them again after she let herself in. The Hansel-and-Gretel cottage was enveloped in blackness; she had forgotten how dark that part of the estate could be. With neither flashlight nor umbrella, she had to pick her way carefully to the front door. Angry, tense, made more jumpy by the swaying moans of the trees around her, she rooted through her bag for her key, then fumbled for the lock on the darkened stoop. To the west, thunder rumbled behind flashes of light.

Getting closer.

In her hurry, she dropped her keys.

"Shit!"

"Liv—?"

"Yah!" She jumped half a foot before whirling around to face the looming shadow that was Quinn. "What're you *doing*, sneaking up on me like that?"

His voice was bran-muffin dry as he said, "Sorry. I was trying to be discreet. I guess I should have shouted your name from a hundred yards away."

"Oh, never mind. Let's just get inside."

She picked up the keys, plucked the cottage key from among them, and unlocked the door. Pushing it open, she let Quinn precede her; presumably he remembered his way around.

"Shall I turn on a light?" he asked from inside the dark hall.

"I'll do it."

Olivia stepped over the threshold in a state of high alert. That wasn't just some burglar or serial killer waiting for her; it was Quinn Leary. Her heart was pounding loud enough to be heard up at her parents' house. Olivia took a deep breath to calm herself, but all she accomplished was to inhale the scent of Quinn. It rocketed her back to dark and intimate times; she felt a spasm of hatred for him, hard on the heels of her lust.

How could he do that to her? How could he whip her around emotionally like that? Just . . . just standing there!

It's not him, it's the hormones, stupid. Try to remember that.

There was a fifteen-watt lamp on a semicircular hall table that stood under an oval mirror just inside the door. Olivia turned it on and Quinn stepped back from her with what she took to be exaggerated, ironic courtesy.

Immediately Olivia went around and closed the shutters, top and bottom, in the two sitting rooms that fed into the hall. She didn't bother turning on any other lights.

"We can talk in here," she said, beckoning him to have a seat in the parlor.

He declined her choice of a chair for him—too late, she remembered that it had been his father's favorite—and sat on the love seat instead. It was Olivia who took the easy chair, covered now in unmanly chintz.

The moment had the feel of a summit meeting between warring allies. If there was some way to ease the tension—a joke, a pleasantry—Olivia couldn't think of it. She was like a wader trying to get her footing in shifting sands and roiling surf. She didn't have energy for anything except to keep from getting knocked down and sucked out to sea.

"The baby is due September thirtieth," she announced, no doubt unnecessarily. "Everything looks fine so far. And by the way, I do not plan to find out its sex beforehand."

"It's a girl."

"Is that so?" she said. "Well, gee, now you've ruined the surprise for me."

"Sorry," he said. He drummed his fingertips on the rolled arm of the loveseat. "It's just that I know."

"September thirtieth," she repeated, looking around for the thread of her thought. "Naturally I don't expect you to contribute to his support. You know as well as anyone that I'm perfectly capable of earning all we'll need. And, of course, I have expectations."

"Do your parents know that you're pregnant?"

"They do not. Yet."

"Then I don't think you should be so quick to count on those expectations."

"And I don't think you should be so quick to judge my parents. They would never let their granddau—son starve, or go to any college that wasn't Yale."

"I'm sure you're right," he said, taking the hit. "But as I've seen firsthand how fickle life can be, I'd feel more comfortable if my daughter had a little something in the bank."

"Stop it, Quinn. Stop calling h . . . it . . . your daughter."

He looked at her with edgy surprise. "But the baby is mine. And the baby's a girl. I believe that makes her my daughter."

Another wave washed over Olivia, this one of resentment. How dare he stroll back to Keepsake and begin lording it over her? She had been brought up by an authoritarian. One in a lifetime was one more than she needed.

She stood up. "I know how tenacious you can be, Quinn, and frankly, I'm not prepared to fight you. I don't need any more stress. So, yes, you can set up a trust fund at the appropriate time. Our attorneys will be in touch. In the meantime, I would very much appreciate it if you'd leave Keepsake as quickly and quietly as you came," she said, turning away.

She was being ironic, of course; by now everyone in town knew Quinn had returned. As for leaving quickly, she had no hope at all that he would do it, but that didn't stop her from trying. With her arms folded across her chest and her back to him, she said to him for the second time in her life, "Please? Would you please just go?"

A mistake, to turn your back on an enemy that was once an ally.

She felt his hands touch her shoulders lightly as he said her name, and she reacted explosively, whirling out of his reach and shouting "No! *No!*" at him the way she'd been taught to do at an attacker.

After their formal, civilized exchange, her eruption seemed all the more shocking. Quinn looked stunned, then offended, by turns. He put his palms face out to her, reassuring her in a scathing way that he meant no harm.

"Listen to me," he said. "Just . . . listen. I came back because you and I, the two smartest kids in school—and, I'm sure we thought, on the planet—have managed, either accidentally or on purpose, to get you pregnant. That is a fact. You are carrying our child. I can see it in your face . . . in the way you carry yourself . . . in the way the wheels of your mind turn in a different way now.

"Which means that I am part of your life whether you

like it or not. I wish you liked it, Liv. God knows, I wish
you did,'' he said in a husky plea. ''Just . . . say the word
. . . one simple 'yes' . . .''

Her icy silence was far more final than any shouted ''No,
goddammit!'' could be.

''All right, all right. I understand. I do. But in the meantime, I am *here*. I'm not going to California before the baby
is born, and—truth?—not after. I'm here. I'm here for you,
and I'm here for her. This child is going to have a mother
and a father in her life. Not like me. I'm here, Olivia,'' he
said, watching her warily. ''Deal with it.''

Her plan for dealing with it was not to deal with it at all.
Compared to everything else that had rolled over her so far,
he was a tsunami. She didn't dare try standing up to him.
Her only chance—and it was slim—was to run.

Which was what she did. ''Do what you want,'' she told
him. ''But don't plan ever to see me again. Whatever you
have to say, it will have to be through an attorney.''

All of his composure, all of his confidence, suddenly dissolved. In a voice thick with emotion he said, ''Livvy . . .
Livvy, don't do this! You were entitled to cut out my heart
and hurl it to the winds, but this . . . Liv, it's a *baby*, for
God's sake . . . yours and mine, conceived in love . . . more
love than we'll ever have for anyone else but her . . . for
other babies of ours . . . Liv, can't you see that? Don't, don't
do this. Don't cut yourself off from me.''

''What do you expect me to do?'' she cried. ''You've
made my life completely unbearable. I'm going to have to
get through it as best as I can. The baby is my biggest
complication—and my only consolation. And if I—''

What was she doing? She wasn't fleeing anymore; like a
fool, she was trying to face him down. Run. *Run*.

''Go away, Quinn. *Please*? So that I can lock up here
and get on with my life?'' She was losing her footing, slipping in the shifting sands of her loyalties. Tears welled up.
She wiped away one that spilled over.

Quinn, who had not dared to touch her during his im-
passioned plea, took her hand and dropped a feathery kiss

on the wet spot, and then, even more tenderly, kissed the tiny red blister on the edge of her little finger.

Closing her eyes to hold back other tears, rivers of them, she let him have his way this one, this last, time. She could feel his warm breath on her fingers, hear his voice whisper, "I love you," as he relinquished her hand. But she didn't see him leave, because she couldn't bear to watch.

She kept her eyes closed until she heard the door of the cottage shut behind him, and then she collapsed on the love seat that he had vacated. In misery, she slid her hand over the soft brushed cotton of the upholstery, searching for his leftover warmth. But Quinn had been out of it too long; all traces of him were gone.

Olivia allowed him time to walk down the hill and off the estate, and then she went out into the hall where she took one last look around at the flowered walls, overstuffed chairs and well-worn antiques of the cozy cottage. She would not come here again.

A clap of thunder made her jump. She wanted to get home, to hide under the covers, to put this latest and most searing trauma behind her. She wanted to sing soothing songs to her baby and think happy thoughts of impending motherhood.

Instead she turned off the lamp, opened the door, and stepped over the threshold into the arms of a living nightmare.

Twenty-eight

"Inside, bitch!"

It was his voice more than his hold on her that terrified Olivia. It was crazed and singsong and out of touch. If only she didn't know it so well!

She tore loose from his grip, surprising him with her strength. Her mind shut down in denial as her body reacted on automatic: *No, this can't be happening. To the car, to the car.*

She made it to the car, made it to the door, made it to the handle on the door.

And then he had her again.

He yanked her by her arm hard enough to pull her off her feet. She stumbled, fell to the ground on one knee, felt something tear and heard something crack, and then she was being dragged back in agony to the cottage she had just disavowed. She got out a single cry for help before he slapped her with his free hand, slapped some stars into her, and then got a firmer grip around her, muffling her mouth and dragging her the rest of the way easily. She tried to bite. No good; he held her too tightly for that.

What, what—what could she do? Kicking, screaming, biting, all those tricks—useless! She cursed her small size . . . karate . . . why hadn't she learned? Her heart was thundering, her lungs laboring, as he kicked open the door and threw her inside.

He lunged after her, an easy prey: his eyes were adjusted,

his own strength intact. But she eluded him again and staggered from sofa to table to chair to table, overturning whatever she could in his path. Eventually he tripped, swore, reached out, grabbed her ankle and caused new and more wrenching pain as she went nose down on a musty oriental carpet. She should scream—but who had the time? She was too busy trying to claw out of his grip.

She pulled her ankle free of his hold but he caught her other one, and this time he had her. He mounted her from behind, crushing her under his weight and straddling her the way he would a horse. "Make a sound . . . and I'll break your neck," he said, even more out of breath than she was. He grabbed one of her hands, then the other, and twisted them behind her back. In two quick seconds she was handcuffed. Handcuffed!

He rolled her over, then dragged her by her armpits to the love seat and propped her up against the back of it. Dazed, bruised, and in wrenching pain, Olivia fought back waves of nausea as she waited in fearful silence for his next move. Think, think! she told herself. But she tasted blood in her mouth, surely an omen, and her mind kept shutting down in terror.

Nudged by a rising wind, Quinn walked against traffic, away from the cottage and toward the rental that he had dutifully parked far from the estate, two blocks away on Pine. Behind him the sky lit up repeatedly and rolled with thunder . . . but still no real rain. He was sick with heartache, and angry as well. He wanted the rain, would welcome a downpour. Anything to wash away the dread misgivings which clung to him like sweat on a clammy night.

Olivia watched him crawl around on all fours, searching for a turned-over lamp that still worked. In the dark he seemed bigger and more powerful than he had on the field: There, he had paled in size and strength next to the kids he tyrannized. Olivia had always been surprised that they could be afraid of him, this middle-aged man with a gut who often slurred his orders and paced the sidelines with an unsteady gait.

She wasn't surprised anymore.

Finally the coach found a lamp in working order which he righted on the floor. With a grunt he rolled onto his right hip, sitting across from Olivia.

Wide-eyed and still panting with fear, Olivia studied his cruel, weather-beaten face and tried to gauge the depth of his psychosis. Could she pierce through it with logic, with threats, with pleas for pity? Or was he too far gone to be reached?

His own breathing was deep but even now as he said, "You got a lotta fight for a girl. 'Course, I'm not as young as I used to be." He leaned back on his left elbow, stretched out his right leg and, with a grunt, reached into his front pocket.

The knife that he brought out and opened was enormous. Olivia could see that it wasn't new; the blade that gleamed under the lightbulb had been sharpened so many times that it had a hollow.

"Oh, Coach . . . why are you doing this?" she said in a low wail.

His laugh was no more than an explosion of phlegm. "Why-why-why. I remember that's how you were in school. Always with the why-why-why."

He ran the blade appraisingly across the flat of his thumb and said, "Believe it or not, this wasn't planned. Everything else, oh, yeah; but not this. This was—hmm, what's the word I want? You would know," he said, glancing slyly at her from under bushy brows. "Serendipity! That's it." He grinned, flashing a set of big yellow teeth that she found especially repulsive.

"Talk about luck. There I was, poking around the potting shed for a can of gasoline, when in you drive. I figure you're going up to see your mommy—lonely tonight with your dad in Meh-hee-ko, poor doll—so naturally I'm surprised when you pull in front of the gardener's house instead. And even more surprised when the fugitive quarterback comes strolling up behind you.''

He gave her leg a little nudge with his foot. Leering, he said, ''I figure you two are here for a little slap and tickle, hey? Quinn sneaks in on foot, you close all the shutters, and then you go at it. Because you like it a little on the dangerous side,'' he added, jiggling the knife in her face. ''Am I right?''

Gazing fixedly at the blade, she said, ''No, that . . . that's not how it was.''

''If you're talkin' about that dustup you two had in front of your shop this afternoon, I heard all about it. But weren't you here to kiss and make up?''

She bowed her head and he said, ''Oh, well, so I was wrong. Whatever. You know what I'm thinking? This might work out even better than Plan A, burning your mommy's house down. Tell me what you think. Pay attention now. I know you'll find any flaws in this scenario.

''You told Quinn to fu—excuse me—buzz off in front of half the town today. Okay, that much, everyone knows. After that, he follows you here. You fight again and he storms out, maybe after doing a little damage to you. Since he hates this house and all it stands for, he decides to do something about you *and* it. He has an inspiration. The potting shed is right next door. It has gas cans for all the mowers and tools stored there. He thinks to himself, 'Now here's a simple, straightforward solution to my problem.' Or rather, he doesn't think at all. He just acts. Call it a crime of passion. With a good enough lawyer, he might even get off.''

Scraping the blade against his chin stubble, the coach said musingly, ''It could fly.'' He remembered that Olivia was there. ''Think?''

Oh, God. She wracked her brain searching for a hole in that all-too-plausible scenario. ''Why would I risk meeting him under my mother's nose?'' she said, grasping at straws.

''Ooh, good one. Thank you. Why, indeed? Uhh-h-h . . . okay, how's this? You're here because you didn't want to make a scene at your place. You have neighbors. This house don't.'' He shrugged in apology. "I know it's a little dumb. I'm not as smart as you.''

Dumb it was, but it was true. Her heart sank.

"Quinn and I aren't together anymore, Coach,'' she pleaded in a last-ditch effort to reason with him. "If you're trying to get back at him by hurting me, it won't work . . . truly, it won't!''

"Sure it'll work. Besides, this gets back at everyone, not just Quinn. Oh, yeah. Plan B is lookin' better all the time. No kidding; talk about luck!'' He looked genuinely happy as he scrambled to his feet and began looking around the room.

While he was distracted, Olivia made a desperate attempt to stand and make a run for it. But the handcuffs hindered her and all she got for her trouble was a brutal kick in the thigh above her injured knee. She nearly passed out from the pain.

"I *said* . . . sit.'' He stood over her. "You're beginning to piss me off, you know that? I guess you're a Bennett after all. Your mother spurns me . . . your brother loses me the job of a lifetime at Notre Dame . . . your father gets me fired from this shitty one . . . and now you're being a real pain in the ass.''

All of it was news to Olivia, but one claim stood out more than the others. "Spurned you?''

"She never said? I tried to take her out. More than once. Thirty-seven years ago come June. She wouldn't have no part of me. I guess she'd set her sights higher than the likes of a high-school coach,'' he said in a sneer. "Her! A baker's daughter!''

His voice dropped into a sudden, savage growl. "The bitch—it all started with her! I could have been someone . . . done something with myself!''

"You killed Alison!'' Olivia said suddenly. "You killed her to try to frame my brother and hurt my mother. You knew Rand was boycotting the senior party that night and didn't have a decent alibi. But you didn't count on my father to line up doctors to testify that Rand wasn't strong enough yet to stage the crime. You hate us all,'' she cried, ''and you killed Alison!''

''Ah, what're you talkin' about? I didn't kill shit.''

Disappointed, Olivia seemed to collapse in place: she would not even have the small comfort of knowing he was the murderer.

She closed her eyes, blinking back tears of defeat, and then forced herself to engage him again. Anything to stall for time.

''So . . . so it's not Quinn that you've had the grudge against all this time?''

''Him, too, goddammit! Him more than your brother! Leaving me with my thumb up my ass just when scouts are swarming the field, when I've had my first interview, when we're *that* close to a championship. So *yeah*, Quinn, too! All of 'em! It's all their faults! Nobody's had the shitty breaks I've had! Nobody! My whole life . . . one after another—''

He stopped abruptly. ''Ah, what the hell. I'm wasting my time here.''

He grabbed the fringed silk shawl that Olivia's mother had draped so artfully over a chair, and he tied it tightly around Olivia's mouth. She shook her head and tried to mumble a protest as Bronsky walked away; the scarf was making her gag. In seconds he was back, this time with a tieback tassel from one of the drapes. He bound her feet with it.

''Okay, that should do it,'' he said, almost bemused as he looked down at her. ''Sorry we don't have a railroad track handy to tie you to. You stay here, now. I'll be right back.''

When the rain came, it came suddenly and horizontally, raking Quinn's back like shotgun spray and plastering his clothes to his shoulders and legs. He sprinted toward the rental that he'd parked on Pine, confused for a second by an empty space where a van had been. The white Camry— that was his, right? Grateful that he hadn't locked it, he made a dive for the front seat and slammed the door after him. He slicked back his hair and started his engine, then turned on the lights and glanced in the rearview mirror as he got ready to pull out.

His soul turned to ice.

The car parked on the other side of the empty space behind Quinn—surely he'd seen it before. A pickup with a headlight bashed in . . . surely he'd seen it. . . .

Parked in front of a chain-link fence that had a BEWARE OF DOG sign half hanging on it. *Jesus Christ. Oh, Jesus Christ.*

He swept every thought aside except one: Get to the cottage *now*. His mind, his hands, the feet that pushed the pedals, all were locked on a single, imperative goal: *Get to the cottage now!* He peeled out of the parking space and turned down Main, bound for the cottage that was a block away in the next galaxy.

Olivia shook her head at the coach so violently that she became dizzy. He misinterpreted her as he tipped the gas can and carefully trickled its foul-smelling contents on the rug, over the love seat, and across Olivia's black tights.

"I know what you're thinking," he said, "and you don't have to worry. I'll knock you out before I light the match. What do you take me for, an animal?"

But Olivia wasn't thinking as far ahead as the match. It was the smell she was focused on; the smell of gasoline made her sick, so sick that she always tried to breathe through her mouth when she filled up her car. And she didn't want to throw up—oh, God, not now, she couldn't. If she did, she would choke and die. *And the baby—oh, she is a girl, she is—and her name will be Jessica . . . Jessica would die with me . . . don't throw up, don't throw up, don't . . .*

"Oh. One other thing. I need your key. I'm going to have to lock you in, naturally, to slow people down." He went out into the hall where she had dropped her handbag in the initial scuffle.

In a profound state of disbelief, Olivia watched him fish

out the keys and try several different ones in the deadlock before finding the one that fit.

She continued to take shallow breaths. She was about to be immolated, and yet the number-one problem she faced was nausea. If she could beat the nausea, if she could just hold on . . .

As it turned out, she got a little help in that regard. Coach Bronsky came back into the parlor, stood over her, and said, "Have to leave this lamp on, I'm afraid. I don't want to risk a spark, turning it off. I'd blow myself up—and how much fun would that be? 'Course, you won't know if the light's on or not," he said.

And he was right. After the sharp blow to the back of her head, Olivia's world became all black, all white, all the time.

The iron gates were still locked. Quinn turned wide and gunned the Camry, crashing through them and setting off a pompous alarm. Forget the element of surprise. If Bronsky was around, Quinn wanted him scared and running. He roared up to the house that once had been home and slammed on the brakes in front of it.

The wind and most of the rain had eased off now, and he was able to make out the coach, standing outside in front of a single square of light—an open parlor window. Quinn jumped from the car and was instantly wrapped in the reek of gasoline, which solved the puzzle of why the coach was poised by the window.

Jesus.

Too late. Quinn saw the single, tiny flame erupt at the end of the matchstick . . . saw the match arc, in seeming slow motion, through the open window . . . and then the *whoomp* . . . and then the horror of flames everywhere, reaching out and clawing at the coach, who let out a howl of pain and began slapping wildly at himself, then dropped shrieking and rolling onto the wet grass.

Olivia! In the house or not? Quinn hardly had time to spare the coach a glance before lifting a huge pot of geraniums and smashing it through a second window in the back of the parlor, sending the inside shutters flying open. He climbed through the window, ignoring the shards stuck in the glazing, mentally thanking God that a lamp was lit in the room, making a search possible.

He found Olivia unconscious behind the love seat, a few feet away from approaching flames. Holding his breath, he scooped her up and ran, desperately aware that she had been turned into a human wick by the psycho outside. He carried her through the dark bedroom that used to be his, stumbling into furnishings set in unaccustomed places, his mind reeling from the horrific possibility that Olivia could burst into flames in his arms.

And then came heaven: The two big windows that used to look out at the grounds were now a pair of French doors. With one savage kick, Quinn sent them flying open and escaped with Olivia into the safe embrace of damp night air, far from the house. He laid her on the grass and undid her gag.

Breathing? He lifted her chin and tilted her head back, then turned his head with his ear over her mouth and listened for the sound of her breath and tried to feel the warmth of it on his cheek as he watched her chest for movement. *Please, please, breathe, Livvy.* Convinced that she had broken ribs, knowing that she was pregnant, he dreaded the thought of CPR.

Yes—breathing! She regained consciousness with a fit of coughing, and the sound was music to his ears. Reassuring her with motherly, mindless words, he cut through the cord around her ankles with his pocket knife and cursed the handcuffs; he hoped her captor suffered extra agony for those.

"Sweetheart . . . Liv . . . I've got to get you to a hospital," he said, lifting her in his arms. "Maybe I can get the key to the cuffs—"

She said hoarsely, "No . . . never mind . . . only the baby . . ."

Her head fell forward and her shoulders hunched in sudden pain, and he knew, despite never having seen it before, that she was in labor.

God in heaven—what more?

He carried her around to the front of the cottage, astonished to see that it was still in flames; that three police cars, lights flashing and radios chattering, crowded the area; and that a hook and ladder was heading up the drive through the chaos to fight the fire. He hadn't been aware of anything except the injured bundle of life that he held in his arms.

The first one to speak through the din was the police chief, and he had a gun drawn. Quinn looked around: they all had guns drawn. What were they, crazy?

"Hand over the girl, Quinn. Nice and easy, now."

"Don't be a fool, Vickers! We have to get her to the hospital. She's hurt!"

"Fine, we'll do that," he said, cautiously holstering his gun. "Just . . . hand her over. I'll take care of it."

"No, goddammit, let me through!" Quinn said, moving toward his car. "I'm not the one who did this—Coach is!"

"That's not what he said," Vickers answered. "We'll have to straighten this all out. But Olivia comes first. Hand her over to us, Quinn. You're wasting time!"

Even as Vickers negotiated, Quinn was aware of the sound of a siren fading down Main. The coach was being hauled off in an ambulance! The coach, getting care before Liv!

"Yes . . . all right," he said in a confusion of agony.

"No, Quinn," Olivia moaned, pressing her cheek close to his chest. "Stay with me!"

"Oh, sweetheart—" Quinn turned to the chief. "Which car, goddammit?" he said savagely.

"Give her to me, Quinn."

"No, Quinn, don't do it . . . stay with me!" She buckled inward with another contraction, unable because of the handcuffs even to satisfy the instinct to clutch her belly.

The scene bordered on the surreal. By the light of leaping, dancing flames, he scanned the faces of half a dozen hostile police officers and their chief, a lifelong friend of the psychotic villain who had been bent on destroying all that Quinn held dear.

"We're going to the hospital *now*," he growled. He turned and began carrying Olivia toward one of the squad cars, ignoring Vickers, ignoring the guns. "Someone get in that last car and drive; this woman is in labor," he shouted over his shoulder, throwing Olivia's ill-kept secret into the flames with everything else.

The standoff dissolved altogether when Olivia's mother suddenly burst from the shadows behind the police officers. "Oh, my baby, oh my God, Livvy!" she shrieked, throwing the scene into even more chaos.

After that, it became a blur. Everything happened in slow motion, or maybe it didn't happen at all; Quinn was never able to recall. Bits and pieces, those he remembered: someone freeing Olivia from the handcuffs; Olivia's urgent, anguished ramblings and Quinn's own fury at the unnerving noise of the sirens; her mother, a ghostly image in the rear window of the squad car riding ahead; a pair of latex gloves, but on whose hands? All of it was a jumble.

In the hospital they took Olivia away from him and treated him for his cuts. He gave a terse statement to Vickers, bitterly aware that it was only because of Olivia's intercession that he hadn't been hauled off to jail. After that he went to the visitors' room, and there he sat like one of the stones in one of his walls, in a state of total inertia.

Across the room, Olivia's mother waited with her head tipped back for support on the wall behind her, a trail of tears rolling out intermittently from under her closed eyelids.

So far she and Quinn had exchanged no conversation. What could he say to her? "By the way, the baby that Olivia is in danger of losing—that's mine"? The chances were good that Teresa Bennett had figured that out. She had probably also figured out that Quinn was responsible for Olivia's self-imposed estrangement from the rest of her family. And finally, although it paled by comparison, she was probably chalking up the loss of her beloved guest cottage to him as well.

All in all, it was hardly surprising that she was so quiet.

Rand's arrival changed all that. His mother jumped up from her chair and flew to embrace him, and Quinn became aware, as he never had been before, of how instinctively families circled their wagons in times of crisis. With Quinn it had only been his father and him. It was hard to make a circle with just two wagons.

He got up to leave, to make it easier for them to rail at him in his absence. He didn't care. He was too sick at heart to think of anything else but the woman who was fighting for their child's life in there.

He was on his way out of the room when Rand grabbed him roughly by the arm. "Where do you get off playing God? Coming back the first time to demand justice, then coming back again—for what? She doesn't want any part of you. The whole *town* heard her say that today!"

Quinn shook his head. "Cool it, Rand," he said, fighting an impulse to knock him down. "We're all wound up a little tight right now."

"Rand, you don't know everything—" his mother began.

"I know one thing: Livvy wouldn't be in there now if it wasn't for him." He swung back to face Quinn and said, "Do you deny that?"

Quinn got the word out through clenched teeth: "No."

"Rand, stop . . . I didn't tell you everything on the phone. I didn't—she's pregnant by him!"

"*What?*" Again he turned back to Quinn. His face was flushed with a complex of emotions; Quinn couldn't begin to guess which ones.

"Nice going, ace," Rand said in a voice tight with contempt. "Anything else that you'd like us to know?"

"I'm not the one with the secrets."

The cut drew blood, but not enough to bring Rand down.

"Why can't we get it through your thick head that you and you alone are responsible for everything that's happened so far? We were all fine before you showed up. There was no problem before you showed up!"

Quinn exploded. "Get real, Rand!" he said, fed up with his refusal to accept responsibility for himself. "Myra had your ring, your letter. She was moving to the other end of the country. She would have given them to someone else if I hadn't been around. Would you rather it were Vickers?"

"What ring? What letter?" Teresa wanted to know. Her voice was high and shrill, the voice of a mother who's out of the loop.

"Shut up, Quinn. Shut the hell up!" Rand growled.

But Quinn had been pushed over the edge one time too many. He was tired of hanging by his fingernails and having to claw his way back to their level.

"Listen to me, you fool," he said. "Some of what happened *was* because I came back, but not all of it. The coach has been planning bloody vengeance for years; Olivia told me that on the way over. It was your father's decision to move the plant to Mexico that pushed him over the edge; time was running out for him to make good on his paranoid delusions. He was after your mother tonight. Would that have been any better?"

"Bullshit! Why should we believe you?"

"Ask your sister. Jesus, you don't deserve her! Tonight she was dragged, beaten, doused with gas, and in premature labor, and still all she could think about was that Coach didn't kill Alison. She desperately wanted him to be the one who did. How does that make you feel, pal? Your sister's hanging by a thread and all she can worry about is you and whether you were the one who killed Alison to cover up your affair gone wrong."

"Rand—then it was true!" Teresa cried. "You *were* the father! Oh, God, how I hoped that you weren't. All these years, I hoped, I prayed, I wanted it to be—God forgive me, I wanted it to be Rupert. Oh, Rand, Rand . . . then it was *true*," she wailed.

Rand, battered from both sides, said in a daze, "I'm sorry, Mom. I am. No one regrets it more. But I didn't kill Alison, you have to believe me." He whirled around on Quinn and said, "Don't you dare try to tell me I did!"

Hotly, Quinn said, "If you didn't, who did? Your father? Your father, who's gone behind you your whole life long with a shovel and pan, cleaning up your messes?"

"The answer to that is, yes," came a voice from behind Quinn.

It was Owen Bennett, looking every one of his sixty-five years and carrying an overnighter in one hand. "So you can stop the shouting match right now. I was able to hear you all the way back at the nurses' station." He put down his bag and came over to his wife to embrace her. "How is she?" he asked Teresa softly.

"Livvy will be all right. They don't know yet about the . . . about the baby."

He held his wife close and rocked her in his arms. "Shh . . . everything's going to be fine, honey. Everything is going to be fine."

Quinn stared at them in disbelief. "You're all living a fantasy, you know that? Everything's *not* going to be fine. It hasn't *been* fine! Understand this: When Vickers comes back to grill me again as he's promised to do, I'm not holding anything back. Not a thing!"

"You don't *know* anything," Owen Bennett said calmly over his wife's head.

"Maybe not enough to satisfy Vickers; nothing I tell him ever does. But I'm damned if I'm going to continue to be part of this conspiracy of secrets and lies. Christ! How can you live with yourselves?"

Teresa Bennett broke away from her husband's embrace and made an imploring dash for Quinn. "You can't do that, Quinn. You can't! Think of Olivia! Think of that child!"

"That's exactly what I'm doing," he said coldly, disengaging himself from her grip. "Excuse me, will you?"

He turned and began walking away, desperate to be breathing clean, rain-washed air. But he wasn't out of the room before he heard Teresa Bennett's voice, clear and surprisingly calm, say, "My husband didn't do it, Quinn. And neither did my son."

Twenty-nine

Quinn stopped and turned to see husband and son with the same wary and baffled expression on their faces. As for the object of their stares, Teresa Bennett looked as convinced as they looked confused.

"Please don't tell me that you're the one who killed Alison and then strung her up beside the quarry," Quinn said wearily, unwilling to suffer through some heroic attempt by her to shield either of the men standing beside her. He'd seen enough Bennett-style loyalty to last him a lifetime.

Owen Bennett took a step closer to his wife. "Teresa, don't say another—"

"I did not kill Alison, Owen," she told him with remarkable dignity.

Owen looked relieved, but Quinn did a double take. It was hard to believe that this was the same woman who a minute ago had been an emotional wreck. "But you know who did?" he asked her, almost politely.

"No one killed Alison."

"Ah, we're back to the old suicide theory," Quinn said with a sigh.

"No. Alison died accidentally."

Quinn snorted and said, "I wonder why the police didn't think of that. She was just playing around with a rope, practicing how to tie her bowlines, when something went terribly wrong?"

"She fell," said Teresa, unimpressed by Quinn's dry wit.

"She came to the house in the afternoon; no one was home except me. She told me that . . . that Rand was in love with her," she explained, faltering for the first time. "And that she was pregnant. I was horrified, outraged; I went for her, I admit. I was going to, I guess, shove her or something. Maybe slap her. I don't know. She was quick, she jumped out of my reach. But she caught her foot on a table leg and fell backward. She hit her head on the marble hearth. I think she died instantly—certainly within seconds."

She paused. No one moved or spoke. Quinn felt instinctively that he was in the presence of a truth teller. Her gaze, dark and beautiful still, swept over each one of them, compelling them to continue with her on her melancholy journey into the past. Quinn understood what a powerful presence she had once been, would always be, among those of the opposite sex. The atmosphere in the small room was electric, rolling from one to the other and leaving the hairs on the back of Quinn's neck standing on end.

All of the men believed her, of that there was no doubt.

She wasn't looking at any of them now, but seemed to be peering into some dark and forgotten corner of her mind. Peering so hard that she squinted, as if there were no hope of getting any real light there, so she was just going to have to do the best that she could.

"I didn't know what to do. She had no pulse, she wasn't breathing. I ran to the phone to call an ambulance, but I knew she was dead. What could they do? They would ask questions. There would be an inquest, an autopsy perhaps. My mind went completely blank. I hung up."

She sighed and said, "And then I ran to the gardener's cottage."

It was a megawatt jolt to Quinn's system. His head snapped back and his knees went limp. It was all he could do to keep standing.

"I knew that Francis Leary had . . . feelings for me. I'm sorry, Quinn, this will be hard for you, but you wanted the truth. He had spoken of how he felt—obliquely, of course— one afternoon when we had been working a long day in the garden and I invited him in for iced tea. He was so sweet,'' she added with a smile that wasn't at all self-conscious. ''Another day, he reciprocated with tea in the cottage, and I could see that he had made an effort to lay out a pretty table. But he never hinted at those feelings again. I think . . . well, I think he understood that I loved my husband. But he wanted me to know, that's all.''

She seemed embarrassed by the recollection. Holding herself close, she walked away from them all and up to the window that overlooked the parking lot, the same window that Quinn had stared through as he and Olivia had waited for news about Mrs. Dewsbury.

''I knew, in any case, that I could trust him completely. So I ran straight to him and told him what had happened, why Alison had come to see me. I told him that she had said she was pregnant, but—and this is the truth—that I thought the baby might be Rupert's. Rupert was always so possessive about her . . . jealous, even. And Rand and Alison were always such good friends; Rand *would* do something silly and chivalrous like offer to marry her,'' she said, throwing a mournful smile over her shoulder at her son.

''And who could believe Alison? She was always such a hard girl to know. I would have confronted you about it, Rand, but I never got the chance.

''Anyway, I told Francis everything. I told him that the scandal would destroy our family. That it would make it impossible for us to stay in Keepsake and for Owen to keep the mill . . . everything that was in my heart, I told him.''

She turned around and said with a painful laugh, ''I wasn't so composed in the cottage as I am now. The truth was, I was hysterical. But Francis managed eventually to calm me down, and then he came up with a plan. He would stage it to look as if Alison had committed suicide. The blow to the back of her head, that would be from hitting the quarry wall when she threw herself over the edge with . . . with the rope around her neck. He—''

She turned slowly away from them again.

''He took care of everything.''

She sighed, and except for the vague hum of hospital machinery, there was no other sound. Three men, none of them shy, and there was no other sound.

Quinn was reeling. In a daze, he said, "My father? He took care of everything?"

Teresa Bennett turned back to face him. "He did it for me, Quinn. And when the police began to close in on him, he ran. Not because he was afraid for himself, but because he thought they might figure out what really happened. By running, he was drawing suspicion away from me, from my family. I'm sure that's why he did it."

"For you. For your family," Quinn repeated, trying to get it into his head. All he could think was: Once again, aced by the Bennetts. Two lives, shot to hell, all for the Bennetts.

Almost automatically, he reached back for his single best defense against self-pity: Twelve lives were saved because of his father's misbegotten chivalry. Children's lives and mothers' lives. In the great, twisted revolution of force and matter that made up the cosmos, everything had somehow worked out.

He had labored through that reasoning so often before, but now, with a creation of his own struggling to survive, he understood it in a profound and almost religious way. *It all works out. Somehow, some way, it all works out. Believe that.*

He bowed his head, humbled at last into acceptance.

After a long eternity Teresa Bennett said to her son, "Quinn is right, Rand. You will have to tell Eileen. She loves you so much. I think you'll be all right . . . but give her time."

To her husband she turned and said, "I'm sorry, dear. I know you were afraid that it was Rand who killed her, all these years. I should have told you, but I couldn't bear to see the look in your eyes that I'm seeing now," she whispered.

She reached up to touch his cheek where a tear had rolled down. "I'm sorry."

Last of all, she turned to Quinn. "Your father was the kindest man I've ever met, and the truest gentleman. I didn't know that men like him existed outside of women's imaginations. I can't ask you to forgive me," she said softly. "And it's too late to ask him."

She sighed and looked longingly at the door, contemplating flight herself, Quinn supposed. Or maybe she was simply willing someone to come through it and give her, just once, some good news.

In any case, that's what happened. Dr. Jack Whiteman, the physician in attendance, had a cautious smile on his face as he said, "The news is encouraging. There was no bleeding, the membranes are intact, the cervix hasn't dilated. She's stronger than she looks. We're going to keep her here for a bit, and after that, she'll need to limit her activities and get plenty of bed rest. If Miss Bennett is conscientious about restricting herself, then the chances are very good that she'll carry to term."

Teresa Bennett said calmly, "Thank you so much, Doctor," and burst into tears.

Her husband rushed to her side. She threw herself into his arms, and between heartrending, uncontrollable sobs, Quinn heard her say over and over, "Oh, thank you, thank you, God . . . oh, thank you, God."

Quinn had trouble speaking with the hard knot in his throat, but he said to the physician as he was about to leave, "Can I see her?"

"You're—?"

"The baby's father."

"Two minutes."

"You bet."

Pale and shaken, Rand said, "Mom . . . Dad . . . I'm going home. I, ah . . ." His sigh was a long, shuddering effort to get his own emotions under control. "I'm going home."

He and Quinn exchanged one brief glance, and then Rand walked quickly out of the visitors' room ahead of him, perhaps in a hurry to make up for lost time.

Quinn never could recall how he got himself from the

visitors' room to the side of Olivia's bed. Possibly with wings, maybe on a magic carpet—but there he was, still knocking back that lump in his throat and wishing he could will away the tubes and the black-and-blue marks and the cast on her leg.

Olivia gave him a trembly smile. "We made it . . . she and I made it, Quinn . . . thanks to you." Her smile firmed up as she said, "I'm glad you had experience saving people from fires."

She was so beautiful, an angel booted down to earth expressly to dazzle him through the remaining years he had to live there. Pray God they were many.

He brushed aside a curl that had flopped over a bandage on her forehead. "I love you," he said.

He was surprised to see a flush in her cheeks. "And I love you, but you'd never know it the way I acted today. Oh, Quinn, I'm sorry," she said in a soft wail. "This whole thing wouldn't have happened if I hadn't sent you away."

Quinn shook his head and said, "We're not going down that road—ever again. We're not going to look back anymore, Liv; too much wonder lies ahead."

But Olivia wasn't quite ready to turn around and face happiness square in the eye.

Plucking nervously at the sheet, she said, "I have to keep looking over my shoulder, Quinn. My family's past is like some big, horrible crow, flying low behind me and waiting to peck me to pieces if I trip and fall."

"Not anymore," he told her.

Perhaps it was her mother's place to explain—Quinn had no doubt that she would be doing that—but he wasn't willing to let this one, this great love of his life suffer a single new moment of anxiety over someone else's mistakes.

"It was an accident," he said, and he went on to explain how good people with good intentions had ended up doing a horrible deed.

When he was done, she murmured, "Will you ever forgive him, do you think?"

"I already have." He couldn't help adding, "What about you, Liv? Can you forgive your mother?"

"I don't . . . know." She frowned in confusion, and yawned, and then closed her eyes. "They've given me . . . just a little something . . . for the pain," she explained with a sigh. "I wonder . . . what my mother can take . . . for the . . ."

She was gone. Asleep, whether she wanted to be or not.

Quinn got up quietly and turned off the light above her bed. In the dim glow of the nightlight, he studied her bruised and scraped face, aching to make it all better.

Almost without an effort, he was able to picture her in the same bed with color in her cheeks and their daughter in her arms.

I wonder how she feels about the name Jessica.

Smiling, he stepped quietly from the room. He would ask her first thing in the morning.

Epilogue

"*No, no, no,* Jessie! No, no, sweetie. Come here. Sit by me. Sit by Mommy."

Olivia held out her arms over her impossibly bulging stomach, but Jessie had other ideas. Off she ran, charging out of the conference room and down the halls of Sayles & McCromber, fully prepared to be chased, caught, and swung in the air. Wasn't that Daddy's favorite game?

"Quinn—!"

"Say no more—I'm on the case," said her husband ahead of her. "That's a little lawyer humor, get it?" he said with a wink on his way out.

Eyeing the sticky handprints on his glass-doored bookcases, Albert Sayles sighed and said, "Children rarely manage to sit through real-estate closings."

He was kind enough not to mention that this one hadn't started yet.

"I'm so sorry, Mr. Sayles," Olivia said for the fourteenth time since their arrival fourteen minutes earlier. "The sitter didn't show, and I couldn't reach my sister-in-law. Maybe if *I* hold Jessie . . ."

She began the massive effort of lifting her unwieldy body out of the wooden-armed chair, but that sent the elderly bachelor into total panic. "Please, Olivia, it's no trouble," he hastened to say, gesturing her to keep her seat. "I'm sure Quinn has the tot in hand."

The joyful shrieks of the tot in question bounced loudly

down the hall and into the conference room, causing Mr. Sayles to suck much air through his nose.

"Oh, dear," said Olivia, trying to look dismayed. "I hope no one's reading a will just now."

"She seems a handful," he said on the exhale.

"My mother says she's just like me."

"I don't recall that they ever brought you into the offices."

Fifteenth time: "I'm so sorry."

"When are you expecting your—?" He nodded vaguely at her stomach.

"A week?" Olivia hazarded. "It's a surprisingly inexact science. It's been a wonderful pregnancy," she added, although he couldn't possibly care. "Whereas with Jessie . . . So I'm hoping that this child will be a little more laid back."

"That *would* be nice. For you, I mean. Naturally."

And there they left it until the arrival of the seller of the big white Victorian that Quinn and Olivia had contracted to buy. Mrs. Dewsbury, dressed in burgundy twill and walking with the help of her Sunday cane, came stepping in smartly ahead of Quinn and Jessie.

Relieved, Olivia greeted the widow with a big grin. "Ah, you're here—and don't you look nice, Mrs. D."

"My dear, *you* look *enormous*!"

"*Nur*-mus," said Jessie, holding on to her father's hair with lollipop hands. Her vocabulary was getting better every day, even if her hygiene wasn't.

The elderly woman took a seat, and Mr. Sayles popped out of the room to see how long it would be before her own attorney showed. Clearly he wanted to get the show on the road.

The widow was in a state. "I was up all night, fretting," she confessed to Quinn and Olivia. "I ought to have made up my mind sooner about selling you the house. I feel just terrible. How will you handle a move and a new baby, not to mention that one up there?" she asked, pointing to the dark-eyed monkey who seemed to be enjoying the view from atop Quinn's shoulders.

"Don't be silly. It's not as if we're moving right in," said Olivia, handing Quinn a wet wipe for Jessie. "We'll need to get the workmen into the kitchen and—"

"That's another thing. You're paying me far too much for the house; it's falling down."

Quinn laughed and said, "Are you kidding? We practically stole it out from under you. I just hope the AARP doesn't hear about this."

"Oh, you stop that," the widow said gaily.

"You stop that!" mocked Jessie as Quinn reached up over his head to clean her hands.

Olivia was glad to see that Mrs. Dewsbury was exhilarated at the prospect of moving into a retirement community and passing the house on to someone she loved. Quinn had been very careful about approaching her, checking first with her son and afterward insisting on three separate appraisals before he made an offer over and above the highest of them. Everyone was happy, Olivia, most of all. It was much too quiet outside of town, and besides, they were bursting their seams in the townhouse.

Mr. Sayles returned with Mrs. Dewsbury's attorney, a man even more bent and white-haired than he was, and they began the numbing process of handing over a venerable piece of Americana from one generation to another. Olivia signed wherever they pointed, but—her advisor at Harvard would have been ashamed of her—her mind wasn't focused on the numbers at all.

Her mind was where her heart was: in a big white house on a wide street in a nice neighborhood in the center of Keepsake, where an old porch swing had been left hanging on its chains especially for her. She planned to spend a lot of time there, nursing her newborn baby while Jessie ran around on the lawn. When the children were in school, maybe she would go back full time to Miracourt. But not now . . . not yet. Now was the time for porch swings.

She glanced sympathetically at her husband, stuck with the job of deciphering dust-dry legalese while he rubbed sleepy Jessie's back.

Poor Quinn. What a long list of projects she had lined up for him: a lamppost at the turn into the drive . . . a pergola in the backyard, leading to a small, stone-walled, and very secret garden . . . a fountain like the one he had carved from granite for her mother, with a tiered waterfall tumbling soothingly into a tiny hollowed pool . . .

All in his spare time, of course.

"What're you smiling at?" he murmured, echoing hers with one of his own.

"Oh . . . nothing. Just happy, I guess."

Poor, poor Quinn.

The Memorial Day dedication didn't begin until six. There had been plenty of time after the closing on their new house for Jessie to nap and Olivia to put up her feet and rest. Quinn, still traumatized from her difficult first pregnancy, hadn't wanted her to go to the dedication at all, but Olivia had insisted.

"Quinn! You volunteered to build the memorial wall, stone by stone and with your own hands. How could I not go to this?"

And so she put on a maternity dress of pale blue floral linen and dressed Jessie in buttercup yellow, and they picked up Mrs. Dewsbury and drove to Town Hill to wander the grounds before the official ceremony to honor Keepsake's fallen.

It was a wonderful afternoon, sunny and warm and mild. Mrs. Dewsbury went off to the penny sale tent in search of bargains, and Quinn and Olivia pushed Jessie in her stroller past the bake sale table, emerging at the other end with a gooey cupcake for Jessie and brownies for themselves.

Nibbling their treats, they stopped to buy a dozen tickets from Betty Bennett, who was manning the booth for the Sewing Club's charity raffle of a wedding quilt.

"My aunt seems happy, don't you think?" asked Olivia as they wandered out of earshot.

"Very. Sad to say, but the divorce is the best thing that could have happened to her."

"She didn't think so at the time."

"Even before it, she was happier than your Uncle Rupert will ever be. She has the capacity for joy. He doesn't."

As usual, Quinn's understanding of people Olivia had known all of her life was better than her own. She was too close to them, she had long ago decided; she couldn't see them as clearly as he could from the sidelines.

They were resting near the gazebo in chairs set up for the band concert when Rand came by in search of Mrs. Dewsbury.

"Try the penny sale tent," Olivia told her brother. "What's up?"

Rand sighed and said, "She left a message with my office that she wants to bring her old Kenmore stove to the new place when she moves in on Monday. I've explained to her that her stove is gas and that there's no gas available on that side of town yet. She says she'll wait."

"She will, too," Quinn said with a laugh.

"Is she your most difficult buyer?"

Rand shrugged. "Average. It's a retirement community; the elderly tend to know what they like." He leveraged himself out of his chair by pushing hard on his thighs. "Frankly, I admire that generation. Their credit is perfect and they understand the value of a dollar. But—I can't produce gas where there is no pipeline. Has Eileen showed up with the kids yet?"

"Haven't seen them."

"Tell her I'll be in the tent with Mrs. D."

He walked away, a man with a mission.

Smiling, Olivia said to Quinn, "Getting out of the mill— and from under my father's thumb—was the best thing that's ever happened to him. Look at him hustle. He really wants to succeed. It's an amazement to me."

"He's just a late bloomer, that's all. Some people are like that. Look at you," Quinn said, slipping his arm around her shoulder and sneaking a kiss. "Getting better every day."

"I feel like an elephant at a tea party," she grumped. "I want this baby born. *Now*."

"Yikes, watch what you're saying," said Quinn. He leaned over Olivia's stomach and said through cupped hands, "She didn't mean that. There's no hurry. Anytime after the weekend is fine."

"Oh, stop," said Olivia, laughing, as she batted him on the head. "Ah, there's Eileen. Over here!" she cried, but she needn't have. Kristin had spotted her cousin and was speeding like a cheetah toward the stroller.

Olivia got out her wet wipes and went to work, handing over a less sticky but still chocolate-covered little girl to her bigger-girl cousin. She watched with pleasure as the two of them went romping on the green, with Zack on the sidelines trying to look cool but itching to join the fun.

Yes. This is as it should be.

Eileen had the same thought. "Thank God we all toughed it out."

"I think of that every single day," Olivia said, turning in surprise to her sister-in-law. "Every single day."

Quinn could see girl talk coming; he excused himself and wandered off toward the book sale table.

"Is your father here yet?" asked Eileen.

"He will be. I don't think he's ever missed a Memorial Day ceremony. And this year there's Quinn's stone wall. He'll feel obligated."

"He does have a way of soldiering on. Who would have thought he'd keep the mill in Keepsake this long?"

"Oh, he won't relocate the mill anymore."

"Too old to do it?"

"My father, too old? Hardly. I think keeping it here is his way of compensating Keepsake for the . . . inconvenience . . . our family has caused people," Olivia said with a dry smile. "Even if he *is* going slowly broke doing it."

"Mm." Eileen sipped her Snapple through a straw and sat back with a thoughtful sigh. "Any chance that your mother will show?"

Olivia shook her head. "Once you become a recluse, it

becomes harder and harder to go anywhere. Mom has scarcely been out to buy a quart of milk in the past couple of years; I can't imagine she'd suddenly show up at a town event like this. In fact—''

A grating screech from the sound system being tested brought everyone to attention: The memorial was about to be dedicated. The two women gathered up their children and their men, and they joined Father Tom and Mrs. Dewsbury and Chief Vickers and the rest of the townspeople assembling in front of the low fieldstone wall that Quinn had built behind the flagpole on Town Hill—the same flagpole from which Olivia's velvet cape had hung in scarlet ribbons, one sleet-driven night.

But that was in another lifetime, as far as Olivia was concerned. Quinn had said it best: All's well that ends well. She slipped her arm through his, and they stood with Eileen and Rand and their children in the front of the crowd, on the left side of the memorial.

"I guess my dad's not coming," Olivia said, scanning the assembly. She was both surprised and disappointed.

Mayor Mike Macoun, newly re-elected and on his last term, began a long and heartfelt speech about patriotism. It was the Memorial Day weekend, after all, and the stone wall was being dedicated to men and women from Keepsake who had died in service to their country. Everyone stood respectfully, trying to reconcile thoughts of war with the wonderfully fine evening and friendly gathering.

They nodded when the mayor effused over Quinn's generous contribution of time and material in the creation of the fieldstone memorial that would grace Town Hill for centuries. The low V-shaped wall was beautifully made with no visible mortar and had been the talk of the town for weeks. Quinn had built it as a labor of love, but ironically, everyone who could afford one suddenly wanted one: He had been turning down commissions left and right.

After a round of grateful applause, the mayor cleared his throat and added, "We're here today to honor Keepsake's fallen heroes, but there are two of ours whose heroism has never been properly acknowledged, and now seems like the proper time to do it.

"Twenty years ago come October," he said, "Francis Leary and his son—the man who built this wall—were instrumental in saving the lives of a dozen women and children and elderly in a terrible bus accident near Harrisburg, Pennsylvania."

His words were electrifying. Olivia didn't dare look at Quinn. She didn't have to, to know the surge of emotion he was experiencing. She could feel it in the hand that was holding hers, hear it in his quickened breath.

"A lot of us have heard about the incident," the mayor continued, "but we haven't rightly figured out how to acknowledge it. Well, due to the hard work and generosity of a prominent citizen who wishes to remain anonymous, the Keepsake Memorial Commission has been able to locate and fly in several of the survivors from that terrible time. They're here with us today, and I would like to introduce them to you now. Here are: Rhyanna White Johnson, Martin Lindsey, and Christy Ptak."

The mayor motioned for the three to join him at the speaker's podium, and they came shyly forward. Then he turned to Quinn and said with a smile, "Quinn? I think these folks have something they'd like to say to you."

The mayor stepped back. For an awful second, Olivia was afraid that Quinn might refuse to step out from the crowd. But he was acting on behalf of his father now; he had no choice. Flushing deeply, he walked up to the podium.

Rhyanna White Johnson, a beautifully poised black woman in her thirties, recognized Quinn instantly. She let out a cry and opened her arms wide as he approached, engulfing him in a bear hug. Martin Lindsey, two generations older and obviously frail, hung back until it was safe, and then he took Quinn's hand in both of his and thanked him quietly and repeatedly.

Christy Ptak, who could not have been more than Jessie's age when Quinn and his father pulled her from the bus, was the last to come forward. She couldn't have understood in any profound way that she was standing there because of the heroism of a father and his son; possibly she was there because it was a free trip out east, a lark with meals and lodging thrown in. But she was the one of the three who seemed to have moved Quinn most deeply. His mouth compressed in a tight line of emotion as he nodded and accepted her tentative hug.

He's thinking like a father . . . he's thinking of Jessie . . . Oh, Quinn . . . how I love you.

Tears were running freely now; Olivia hardly heard the mayor's announcement that a memorial plaque would be installed at the base of the flagpole to honor Francis Leary. She lifted her hands to wipe her eyes, because she didn't want to miss any of it, not a look, not a smile.

But letting go of Jessie's hand had an inevitable result: The child, set free, took off at a gallop, heading not for her father at the podium, but for the opposite side of the semi-circled crowd.

"Oh, Jessie, wait—!"

And then Olivia saw where she was headed. Owen Bennett was standing soldier-straight in the space behind where the survivors had been waiting.

And next to him, his wife.

"Gammy, Gammy, Gammy!"

Teresa Bennett turned from the podium to the fat-legged child making a beeline for her. She dropped down low and held out her arms, and some of the old joy, and all of the old radiance, returned to her face as she hugged her granddaughter tight.

Survey

TELL US WHAT YOU THINK AND YOU COULD WIN

A YEAR OF ROMANCE!
(That's 12 books!)

Fill out the survey below, send it back to us, and you'll be eligible to win a year's worth of romance novels. That's one book a month for a year—from St. Martin's Paperbacks.

Name _____

Street Address _____

City, State, Zip Code _____

Email address _____

1. How many romance books have you bought in the last year?
   (Check one.)
   __0-3
   __4-7
   __8-12
   __13-20
   __20 or more

2. Where do you MOST often buy books? *(limit to two choices)*
   __Independent bookstore
   __Chain stores *(Please specify)*
       __Barnes and Noble
       __B. Dalton
       __Books-a-Million
       __Borders
       __Crown
       __Lauriat's
       __Media Play
       __Waldenbooks
   __Supermarket
   __Department store *(Please specify)*
       __Caldor
       __Target
       __Kmart
       __Walmart
   __Pharmacy/Drug store
   __Warehouse Club
   __Airport

3. Which of the following promotions would MOST influence your decision to purchase a ROMANCE paperback? *(Check one.)*
       __Discount coupon

    __Free preview of the first chapter
    __Second book at half price
    __Contribution to charity
    __Sweepstakes or contest

4. Which promotions would LEAST influence your decision to purchase a ROMANCE book? (Check one.)
    __Discount coupon
    __Free preview of the first chapter
    __Second book at half price
    __Contribution to charity
    __Sweepstakes or contest

5. When a new ROMANCE paperback is released, what is MOST influential in your finding out about the book and in helping you to decide to buy the book? (Check one.)
    __TV advertisement
    __Radio advertisement
    __Print advertising in newspaper or magazine
    __Book review in newspaper or magazine
    __Author interview in newspaper or magazine
    __Author interview on radio
    __Author appearance on TV
    __Personal appearance by author at bookstore
    __In-store publicity (poster, flyer, floor display, etc.)
    __Online promotion (author feature, banner advertising, giveaway)
    __Word of Mouth
    __Other (please specify)_____

6. Have you ever purchased a book online?
    __Yes
    __No

7. Have you visited our website?
    __Yes
    __No

8. Would you visit our website in the future to find out about new releases or author interviews?
    __Yes
    __No

9. What publication do you read most?
    __Newspapers *(check one)*
        __*USA Today*
        __*New York Times*
        __Your local newspaper
    __Magazines *(check one)*

__People_
__Entertainment Weekly_
__Women's magazine *(Please specify:_____)*
__Romantic Times_
__Romance newsletters

10. What type of TV program do you watch most? *(Check one.)*
    __Morning News Programs (ie. "Today Show")
     (Please specify:_____)
    __Afternoon Talk Shows (ie. "Oprah")
     (Please specify: _____)
    __All news (such as CNN)
    __Soap operas   *(Please specify: _____)*
    __Lifetime cable station
    __E! cable station
    __Evening magazine programs (ie. "Entertainment Tonight")
     (Please specify: _____)
    __Your local news

11. What radio stations do you listen to most? *(Check one.)*
    __Talk Radio
    __Easy Listening/Classical
    __Top 40
    __Country
    __Rock
    __Lite rock/Adult contemporary
    __CBS radio network
    __National Public Radio
    __WESTWOOD ONE radio network

12. What time of day do you listen to the radio MOST?
    __6am-10am
    __10am-noon
    __Noon-4pm
    __4pm-7pm
    __7pm-10pm
    __10pm-midnight
    __Midnight-6am

13. Would you like to receive email announcing new releases and special promotions?
    __Yes
    __No

14. Would you like to receive postcards announcing new releases and special promotions?
    __Yes
    __No

15. Who is your favorite romance author? _____

WIN A YEAR OF ROMANCE FROM SMP
(That's 12 Books!)
No Purchase Necessary

OFFICIAL RULES

1. To Enter: Complete the Official Entry Form and Survey and mail it to: Win a Year of Romance from SMP Sweepstakes, c/o St. Martin's Paperbacks, 175 Fifth Avenue, Suite 1615, New York, NY 10010-7848, Attention JP. For a copy of the Official Entry Form and Survey, send a self-addressed, stamped envelope to: Entry Form/Survey, c/o St. Martin's Paperbacks at the address stated above. Entries with the completed surveys must be received by February 1, 2000 (February 22, 2000 for entry forms requested by mail). Limit one entry per person. No mechanically reproduced or illegible entries accepted. Not responsible for lost, misdirected, mutilated or late entries.

2. Random Drawing. Winner will be determined in a random drawing to be held on or about March 1, 2000 from all eligible entries received. Odds of winning depend on the number of eligible entries received. Potential winner will be notified by mail on or about March 22, 2000 and will be asked to execute and return an Affidavit of Eligibility/Release/Prize Acceptance Form within fourteen (14) days of attempted notification. Non-compliance within this time may result in disqualification and the selection of an alternate winner. Return of any prize/prize notification as undeliverable will result in disqualification and an alternate winner will be selected.

3. Prize and approximate Retail Value: Winner will receive a copy of a different romance novel each month from April 2000 through March 2001. Approximate retail value $84.00 (U.S. dollars).

4. Eligibility. Open to U.S. and Canadian residents (excluding residents of the province of Quebec) who are 18 at the time of entry. Employees of St. Martin's and its parent, affiliates and subsidiaries, its and their directors, officers and agents, and their immediate families or those living in the same household, are ineligible to enter. Potential Canadian winners will be required to correctly answer a time-limited arithmetic skill question by mail. Void in Puerto Rico and wherever else prohibited by law.

5. General Conditions: Winner is responsible for all federal, state and local taxes. No substitution or cash redemption of prize permitted by winner. Prize is not transferable. Acceptance of prize constitutes permission to use the winner's name, photograph and likeness for purposes of advertising and promotion without additional compensation or permission, unless prohibited by law.

6. All entries become the property of sponsor, and will not be returned. By participating in this sweepstakes, entrants agree to be bound by these official rules and the decision of the judges, which are final in all respects.

7. For the name of the winner, available after March 22, 2000, send by May 1, 2000 a stamped, self-addressed envelope to Winner's List, Win a Year of Romance from SMP Sweepstakes, St. Martin's Paperbacks, 175 Fifth Avenue, Suite 1615, New York, NY 10010-7848, Attention JP.